THE WOMAN'S GUIDE TO MURDER

A twisty, darkly comic take on the classic
country house murder mystery

VICTORIA DOWD

Smart Woman's Mystery Book 1

Joffe Books, London
www.joffebooks.com

First published in Great Britain in 2020

This paperback edition was first published
in Great Britain in 2022

Cover art by Emma Rogers

ISBN: 978-1-80405-204-4

For Kev, Delilah, James and Sarah.

Rule 1: Never stay in an isolated country house with a disparate group of possible sociopaths . . . or a book club.

A BODY IN THE SNOW

It happened when the snow first fell, violet white, branding our eyes with its glare and covering our steps almost as soon as we had lifted our feet. The cold bit deep into our faces and when we opened our mouths to speak, snow singed our tongues. The wind laced round our legs as we leaned into the fierce air.

It was just as Mother shouted towards Aunt Charlotte, 'This is madness!' that we first caught sight of the body.

The woman was only half visible beneath the rotten trunk of a long-dead tree, the snow silently covering her. The tree had fallen long before this body appeared, parts of its withered trunk already eaten away. She had been shoved into its hollow along with her strange nest of gaudy scarves and silk shawls. Fully dressed, she was wedged face down in the dirt, her legs impolitely spread, a disrespectful pose for her final moment. I wanted to rush over, gently ease her legs together and cover her carefully with one of her thin scarves. It was strange that the preservation of her dignity could over-shadow the simple fact that someone had killed her.

The whip of the storm stung our raw faces. She would be completely lost under her blanket of snow soon. She must have lain here since last night, cold pearls of snow scattering across her back. Whoever had done this, whoever had handled her like so much meat, had stepped outside the boundaries of humanity.

I could feel the familiar panic rising like bile. There was a blank moment, the same as climbing into a scalding bath, before I understood the pain, before it settled and gathered itself. Then it dragged up through me.

I tipped my head back and stared into the battlefield sky. Two stinging tears were dislodged and traced down my cheeks, framing my face. The black twigs of the tree clawed at the sky, as if they too were trying to escape. We stood, three women, none of whom had ever known how to respond to death, staring at the crude tomb of a stranger. A bird watched me, its cold charcoal eyes saying, *I know you*. Suddenly, its wings splashed up, an ink stain against the sky.

None of us could have known, when we first climbed the steps of the house, just how much blood was going to flow in those next forty-eight hours. The Slaughter House, that's what the press would call it later.

* * *

Six women and a dog assembled in an isolated country house. There was one non-woman, as Mother refers to men, but he's one of the dead now too. We're all very Bechdel here. I don't think of murder as inherently masculine. Certainly not now. But I do think about murder a lot. Most of the women I know do. Maybe that's just the company I keep.

This had started out as some aspirational weekend retreat for my mother's book club; I was just the uninvited guest. They had a reading list as challenging as most middle-class toilets and, for reasons that will become obvious, I'd always known it as booze club. Some of us would go on to kill, some

2

would die. I survived. When our story finally emerged, it went as viral as the plague, but we women remained a collection of loosely drawn figures, our story nothing more than a vapour trail. We just became ill-formed spectres and the subject of many fabulous speculations. Until now.

I always come back to my motto — the truth cannot be libellous. And the truth is that when we entered that house, we were like everyone else, with all our dirty little secrets and festering resentments.

What is also true is that my mother was certainly not the sort of person anyone would want by their side on a life-threatening weekend. As we drove down the long gravel drive to the house, she made her position quite clear.

'Dearest Ursula.'

I held up my finger to interject.

'You are not even supposed to be on this trip,' Mother went on, 'so please do not at any point feel the need to utter your opinion on anything. Stay silent throughout.'

I dropped my finger.

'May I remind you, this is my one and only weekend away with my book club and you had to come and piss on it. You are here on my sufferance and if you hadn't had another one of your *incidents* . . .'

'Mother,' I said, 'I've not just wet myself. I'm sure I will cope.'

'And yet you so rarely do.'

'How hard can your book club be? You've read *Gone Girl* three times in a year.'

'That is not the point. We are a serious literary group.'

'Old detective novels and a few slightly titillating thrillers you relate to because the characters drink too much really doesn't constitute a serious literary group.'

She pursed her lips with her usual motherly contempt. 'If you hadn't been doing your girl-in-the-attic routine again, I would be winging my way here without my self-absorbed child.'

'I'm twenty-five!'

'And yet you act like a teenager and dress like a pensioner.'

I turned to look at the side of her face. 'Oh, so we're doing the analysis thing again, are we? Can you just stop trying to fix me like I'm a leaky tap or something?'

The Look.

Mother's side-line is trying to remake me in the way she might deal with an untidy bed, giving it hospital corners, clean fresh sheets every day and the fake sweet scent of lavender. My refusal of this sanitized treatment only angers her even more; my attempts to explain that there should be layers, stripes of life and sediment, are always met with her dismissal of the idea as just an excuse for dirt.

'And,' I added, '*you* did the "locking me in the attic" routine, as you so beautifully style it. Which is just shit parenting rather than Gothic fiction.'

'That was because of the *incidents* after . . . your father left.'

Her foot slowly ground down into the accelerator as if it were someone's throat. Whose is not important right now.

Mother and I have always had a very healthy relationship, full of banter and playful repartee. We have always been so close, ever since Dad's death.

Dad was God, in case you were wondering. Until he died, of course. And no, he wasn't murdered. Just a common or garden death.

I was thirteen when he died and Mother immediately sent me to boarding school. In fact, she ploughed much of the life insurance into my new school and spent most holidays at the bookshop working from dawn till dusk to keep me there. She owns an antiquarian bookshop in Kew and somehow resisted the temptation to call it Pandora's Box. She's Pandora and I'm Ursula, Ursula Smart. She never considered Ursula's Box, that's just not a thing. That, and the fact we're not really called Ursula and Pandora Smart. Those are the pseudonyms I chose for us. My real name is another misdemeanour I set firmly at my mother's door.

I looked out of the greasy car window. We'd arrived at Ambergris Towers. The vast carved facade of tombstone granite loomed down in disapproval. As with every journey I ever took with Mother, she had begun by telling me not to lean my filthy head against the glass. I'd started this one by posting #BoredWithMother comments on Twitter, and ended here, with my head resolutely against the car window, scrolling through various memes involving matricide.

'You can put the bloody phone down now,' Mother snapped. 'Like a bloody worry bead.' She opened the door and made one of her characteristic exiting-the-car final comments that don't allow for any answer before the door shuts. It's not the most charming of tactics, but it's effective. 'You'd think you'd have changed the screen by now.'

I didn't bother to tell her I kept it that way purposefully to avoid the upset of breaking a new screen. Mother wouldn't understand the value of keeping things broken so they can't be broken again. She'd say that kind of pretentious navel gazing is why everyone thinks I'm weird and dislikes me. She's got a way with words, my mother. By everyone, she means her and her mid-life-crisis friends who she keeps around to make her look *normal*. Their interpretation of being middle-aged is very similar to history's description of the Middle Ages: nasty, brutish and short, which as it happens is also a very neat description of Mother.

As I walked around the front of the car, she stopped and looked at me as if she was about to begin dissection. She spoke quietly, almost to herself, but we both knew better than that. 'Why you had to shit on my one weekend away in the entire year, I have no idea.'

'I thought you said I'd pissed on your one weekend away.'

'Selfish, just like your father.'

'He's dead,' I muttered. 'Or had you forgotten?'

Her face turned bleak. That's as much as she emotes really. She's tried all manner of prescriptive facials, massages, ointments and injections, yet they all just make her look infuriated and solidified. She is, however, what you would call 'well groomed' — although that does make her sound faintly horsey and she hates all animals. All living things, really. Her philosophy is that life is awful and we should just accept that. This was the stoic, no-nonsense attitude she adopted when my father passed away.

A spiked silence rolled over us as we stood by the car and the November wind circled. The smell of damp decay hung in the air, mingling with a faint trace of cinder smoke from distant bonfires.

The leaves murmured along the gravel path that led up to the dark oak door of Ambergris Towers. The blank eyes of its windows reflected mists silvering the fields. A shroud of fog sat on the shoulders of the distant hills. This was a cold, dank world we'd landed in, desolate, and the house stood ashen faced among it all.

I watched Mother walk towards the house, away from the car, away from me. I pictured her all those years ago, walking away from the car on that other dead November afternoon.

I almost savour the smell of it now, that strange, addictive perfume of the crematorium. It had the cloying, fake floral note used to cover death and the funeral parlour's preservative unguents. Mother's face was as set as a death mask then, too. But that was just a new round of Botox.

The day of the funeral had been neutral — not cold, not hot — and had begun with no promise. There was a distinct flavour of nonchalance, of nothing special happening. The used air circulated round us in the overly large car. There was no indulgence in emotion.

Tears blistered in my eyes and I remember trying not to blink so that not one bead of sadness would be dislodged. Her motionless hand lay on the perfect line of her dress. People had stared at us as we rolled by, trying to see the mourners' faces. Death is not just something to fear. It fascinates. Some people even crossed themselves. But God wasn't with us that day.

When we arrived, everything had the jaded air of being pre-ordained, the next in a whole stream of funerals. It didn't strike me as strange then that something so unexpected and sudden could be so easily and swiftly organized. I touched my mother's sleeve, but she walked away from the car. Maybe she hadn't felt my hand there.

Dad had been my childhood. When he died, I thought it must have been partly my fault — I'd stopped being a child, so it was time for him to leave. He'd collapsed in the flowerbeds, clutching his chest. When his heart slowed into its last beat, he took my last childish breath with him. I sat with his head in my lap and I bent over him. That's when I felt him exhale for the last time. I remember the must of him, the yeasty breath sweetly spiced, like marzipan on Christmas cake. I drew my next breath alone. And it was then that I tasted a new world: cold, sharp, flavourless. It was a more insipid world, one with fewer shades, fewer possibilities, less to beguile or charm — a flat disinterested world that is the real world, the world my mother keeps telling me I need to wake up to. But I've found no use for it yet.

It was strange to me that they said it was his heart. His heart had always been the greatest part of him. Perhaps it had loved enough. In the end, it gave way as easily as a weak knee, nothing more than tired flesh. I used to think his heart just had too much love and stopped with the weight of it all but Mother disillusioned me of that. 'Certainly not *too much* love! Anything else but that!' Yet he died with an expression on his face that I will never forget, an inexplicable look of . . . defeat. His face was rigid. I couldn't tell when his eyes stopped being able to see me. His cheeks were still so pink, ruddy as if life still played there, even though his body was already a lifeless rag.

I watched Mother now, walking away from me yet again. She had never known defeat in her life. Dad used to refer to her as a great work of modern art — highly intelligent, highly strung and utterly impenetrable. I smiled at the memory but, sadly, not enough to myself.

She turned, her feet crunching on the gravel.

'What are you grinning about now?'

'I was just thinking about Dad.'

'And you're smiling?'

I watched her fingers clench, the bright rings and baubles he gave her still adorning her hands in memoriam. Mother misses him so much that it can occasionally spill over into bitterness. That's what death does to you — it warps you, then it hardens you into the new shape you have become.

Rule 2: On location. Pay close attention to all the details of your new environment.

THE HOUSE

I was statically warm in my travelling clothes. Not that I have 'travelling clothes'. I find that jeans and all things black suffice for most occasions but when heated to a certain degree they do, admittedly, release a kind of mildewed fug.

'And you stink.' Mother sniffed as if to demonstrate the fact.

'What are you, twelve, Mother?'

'Air freshener is not a cologne,' she sang viciously, as she reached the steps to the house.

This was one of Mother's favourite little mottos, along with 'The floor is not a storage area', which I interpreted as meaning, if you've been doing something dirty or secretive, remember to tidy away the evidence. Cleanliness may not really be next to godliness, but it can certainly hide a multitude of sins. Living under the same roof as Mother requires the art of concealment, but we're more comfortable with the term *tidiness*.

Today, Mother had her usual veneer of calm with a hint of carefully applied scent that definitely wasn't Febreze. I, meanwhile, had found it slightly more challenging to maintain my sheen. My hair naturally sprang into tight bedsprings, while my clothes gathered in great creases round the tops of my thighs and gave off a sullen odour as if my flesh had been brewed in the fabric.

Mother only needed to do *The Look* to let me know it wasn't quite the right impression for Ambergris Towers. It was clear that a little piece of history was weeping as I climbed the sweep of extravagant steps.

The mansion had a suitably stern face. Vast stone carvings frowned over the shadowed windows. The ancient misery and despair reserved for the unspeakably rich bled from every stone. I must stress there was no actual blood. Not yet anyway. Nonetheless, there was a profound melodrama to the house that only the most ornate language could accommodate. We should have arrived in the chaos of a great thunderstorm, our hair dripping with rain, our eyes blurred until an acid-white flare engulfed the sky to illuminate the stone-faced house.

As it was, Aunt Mirabelle greeted us at the end of a rather morose day.

'Definite nip in the air today,' she said, shuddering. 'Let's get you in and sorted, Pandora.' She put her arm around Mother and gave me her usual vinegar smile.

Aunt Mirabelle is not my aunt but my mother's childhood friend and my godmother, although I'm sure God had nothing to do with it. She is not real family, as I remind her frequently.

'Say hello to Aunt Mirabelle,' Mother directed.

'Hello, Mirabelle.'

Mother did that thing with her lips that her facialist told her was counterproductive, as if she'd pulled in the drawstrings to stop anything escaping.

Mirabelle laughed. 'Still the precocious little child, I see.'

'Oh yes' — Mother can't remember my childhood — 'Gone *vegetarian* now.' She mouthed it like it was a urinary infection.

'She'll starve.'

'I know.'

I watched disinterestedly, as they played with me like two cats pawing a dying sparrow. It was clear that, for once, Mother might be right about one thing (if still remaining true to her extreme narrow-mindedness): this was not the time to have become a vegetarian. What seemed to pass for home décor here, were the heads of large, dead animals staring down from the walls of the entrance hall, caught in their moment of death, which someone had taken great pains to preserve.

Mother turned to me. 'You'll starve,' she nodded, with her usual hangman's compassion. Mother doesn't do maternal.

In her faux-country clothes, the polish of London still smeared all over them, Mirabelle looked every inch the wife of a banker. It would be too crude to put in print my shortening for 'wife of banker' but I'm sure you are with me. Why Mother had chosen to befriend such an inferior woman was a marvel to everyone. They didn't seem to like each other, even when they were together. But they had been friends for so long, they'd forgotten why.

As we entered the vast hall, our footsteps echoed on the dark stone. An elaborate staircase rose up, snaked round and drifted away into a cavernous roof. The long picture windows seemed to be impervious to light, with only a faded glimpse of day allowed to seep through the heavy stained glass. Grim colours spread a bruised light over everything. It cast a quiet, ecclesiastical shadow as if it had been designed by someone who had many things to hide.

Thick veils of dust sifted through the still air, as though the house was slowly disintegrating into powder. Aged wood panelling and heavy varnished frames slowly crumbled, leaving a lingering dry tinder scent that permeated everything. This house was the kind of monolith the rampantly wealthy Victorians created as a mausoleum to live in. It was an unnerving old house and it wasn't too much of a leap to imagine someone stuffing their mother and sitting them in the window. I looked over at Mother. It was a tempting thought.

'We've got the run of the place,' said Mirabelle.

On cue, footsteps fell methodically above our heads and a door slammed in one of the myriad vaults above.

'Oh, except for the ghost.' She laughed extravagantly.

We didn't.

'It's the housekeeper. Deathly old bat didn't know where the wine was.'

The house had been Mirabelle's idea but, of course, Mother had booked and paid for it. A secluded mansion, let for only a week every year by its owners, a sort of Airbnb Brigadoon. A chance to get away from it all and presumably do some serious book club work, whatever that might entail. She'd probably seen it advertised in the back of one of those snob-rags she liked to read, *Country Life* and the like, which bore utterly no resemblance to Mirabelle's life but suited her aspirational hunger.

Generally, their book club entailed arguing about which book to choose — hence *Gone Girl* three times. There would then follow a series of increasingly unpleasant emails about timings, venue and rather more personal matters: an elaborate meal at someone's house with secret outside caterers, the house selected generally being the most recent one to have had a new kitchen/basement/spiral wine cellar/dungeon installed. There would be a frail discussion of the book — which no one had finished/started/bought, unless it was *Gone Girl* — crescendoing in an onslaught of intrigue and opinions, focusing on various mutual acquaintances, all fuelled by copious amounts of Prosecco. If you're a member of a book club, I'm sure this will be painfully familiar but this house, with its lavish history of family misdemeanours and foul play, had yet to experience anything to measure up to the hysteria of a book club session at full throttle.

Mirabelle was a solid woman who had, ever since I was a child, been a remarkably accurate copy of the Trunchbull we'd seen in a production of *Matilda*. Mirabelle and Mother had momentarily lost me at the theatre that day. But I could see them from my hiding place. I'd watched them from a balcony. I'd watched how close they were. Mother always allowed Mirabelle to get much closer than I was allowed. *Personal space, Ursula. Personal space*, she'd always chime.

I watched her now, lingering on the edges of my mother as usual. She led us from dining room to reception as if introducing us to her country seat. Infuriating as it was, it did have a certain Cluedo-esque flavour, especially if I imagined Mirabelle as the stout, flush-faced cook, or possibly even the murder victim.

Each room was garlanded with momentous paintings — exotic battles, faded safaris, and the vast, billowing sails of romanticized ships. Family crests looked fallen. Faces loomed from dark varnished portraits, their unblinking eyes locked into the paint as if silenced for eternity but desperate to speak, to shout out, to warn. In places, dark outlines stood out starkly where missing portraits had once hung, as if they'd been scorched away by time. Perhaps family black sheep or bad apples, windfalls from the family tree left to rot elsewhere.

Every lacquered surface had ornately beautiful pieces immaculately placed. Mother always says that there is no requirement to suffocate every surface with clutter she has no time to clean. She likes to keep our home as clean as if we're living in some post-death house clearance. She won't even permit photographs in the house. 'Dust traps!' she cries, as if their dirty faces could lean out and clamp their jaws on passers-by. My photographs of Dad are locked safely in my dressing table, carefully preserved in the pages of *Jane Eyre*, somewhere I don't think will ever trouble Mother. God knows where Mother keeps her photographs of him — within the pages of *Gone Girl*, perhaps.

'To the library,' Mirabelle announced, which didn't seem important then. It may not seem like a familiar or essential room of a house, but it would become central to *this* house and *this* occasion. To anyone with even the flimsiest knowledge of murder mysteries, libraries are a prime murder location. Perhaps all those books relax people to the point where they can let fly their passions and either seduce someone or murder them.

The library at Ambergris Towers was a dream of solitary seclusion. Mirabelle said the housekeeper had explained the family made their fortune in the whaling industry and the sale of fat therein extracted — which is of course rather ironic, given that Mother and her book club have each paid out individual fortunes to have their fat extracted.

All manner of crannying nooks had been carefully provided to offer maximum privacy or disguise. Alongside each wall of extravagantly leather-bound books was an alcove with a finely crafted armchair. There was no abandonment of the past. On the contrary. Here, they had embraced it. A large old-fashioned radio remained, as if Chamberlain had just announced we were at war, its clock frozen in time with its hands stuck on twelve o'clock and, judging by the quantity of dust accumulated on its face, it had been twelve o'clock for many years. There was a dream-like silence, not even punctuated by the ticking of time.

It wasn't hard to imagine a whisper of wild and nefarious acts muffled within the confines of those books. But then Mother always says I have a dark and disobedient imagination. Mirabelle is, of course, even more acerbic, often telling Mother how I make things up. '*You shouldn't listen to a word she says. She's a little storyteller!*' She even accused me of lying when Dad's Bible went missing. It was mine to have and no one would have willingly given it to me. I find people like Mirabelle make it easier for me to justify my actions.

After Dad's death, she painted me even more as the shadowy spectre — 'Always with her head in a book,' she said dismissively, as if it was a gutter. But as with most people who only see a silent person holding a book, they never imagine the raging flames behind the still, quiet eyes. I quickly discovered reading books was a perfect disguise. Sometimes I even suspected Mother was on to me, accusing me of hiding in my books. She just didn't know what I was hiding.

At least I knew I could find solitude among the thousands of pages here — a safe harbour from the storms of Mother and her book club. They weren't the kind of book club who would be troubling the library. They'd already dismissed it and moved on. I, however, stayed. I had, after all, found the perfect place for seclusion away from their judgemental eyes. We should all have our hiding places. We should all have our secrets.

The family at Ambergris Towers were clearly of the same mind. Judging by the space allocated for perfect concealment, this was a family with a lot to hide — like most families, I suppose. They were so private they had strictly followed Mother's policy of no photographs. And yet, a thin atmosphere of lives lived and lost permeated every portrait, rug and candlestick. It was as if they had simply set down what they were doing and drifted into the past. They could all be here, watching us, waiting to see what would unfold. A remembrance of those lost lives seemed to cling to the fabric of every room, as if the brittle veil between the dead and the living had in some way been cracked, letting their spirits seep across the border.

Cough.

I swung round, suddenly very aware that I might not be on my own. My eyes flitted over the lost corners of the room. Shadows clustered in the remnants of light and seemed to make small movements as the draught caught at the curtain edges and fringed lamp shades.

'Hello?' My voice was dry.

Cough.

A faint movement in an alcove. My chest rippled.

'Ursula, what are you doing here?' Bridget Gutteridge, book club's number one fan. 'I thought this was for book club members only.'

'I'm with Mother.'

'Technically, the rules state—'

'Book club doesn't have any rules. You don't even have to read any books.'

'I'll have you know, young lady, that I have read *all* the titles we have studied.'

'What, *Gone Girl* — paperback edition, *Gone Girl* — hardback edition, *Gone Girl* — Kindle edition, and let's not forget the very special *Gone Girl* — audiobook?'

Bridget narrowed her eyes. She made no attempt to disguise the fact that she was judging me.

'You're not an *official* member,' her words were nettle sharp, 'so you shouldn't be here, and you definitely won't be allowed to discuss the book.' She gave a slight shuffle at the end, like a visual full-stop, and the slate-grey roof of her hair moved as one complete shell. She clasped her fastidious little fingers together as tight as if she were slowly strangling an imaginary person right in front of her. Perhaps she had someone in mind.

Yap.

There was a scuffling around her ankles.

'Oh, Mr Bojangles!' she trilled. 'Come on, little man. Did the bad lady scare you? Oh, Mr Bojangles.' She picked up the small dog, a shih tzu, she'd informed us proudly. She cradled him as though he were a child, rocking him slowly, as she murmured, 'Mr Bojangles, oh Mr Bojangles.'

'Well, Mr Bojangles isn't a member.'

She paused her cooing and swaying. She and the little dog watched me silently.

She shielded the dog's ears with one hand and, lowering her voice, said, 'Mr Bojangles is a dog.' She shot a quick look at him. 'He cannot read.'

'That's not been a bar to entry so far.'

She tutted and marched the dog out as if they were in the ring at Crufts.

I sat alone for a moment, watching the motes of dust fall through the sallow light. A thin hum of silence was occasionally broken by the creak of wood or the forlorn sigh of the wind. I glanced at the empty fireplace and in the gloom, I could see a sparse pile of little bones. A bird perhaps. Chalky grey droppings were splattered and dried around the remains.

It had taken some time to die alone in that grate. A few broken, black feathers lay beside it as though they were some sort of dark offering or remembrance. No one had seen it die. No one had cleaned it away. There was something familiar about this house and its cold sense of loss. A thread pulled in my thoughts. It was almost as if this place was in mourning.

A draught suddenly bristled around me as though a window had been opened and the outside world touched my skin. I felt something on my cheek, a damp air as if someone near me had breathed out. My chest clenched — the cold air caught between my ribs. I swung around and looked out of the window but only the grey world stared back, as still as a gravestone. A translucent sun was falling in the sky, casting only an insipid light. We were at the hinged point of the day when darkness was stirring and would soon turn over into dusk. The day was unravelling.

I looked at the sombre lines of books, a fine layer of dust in a settled path across their spines. Even though everyone had left, there still seemed to be the slight tremor of life, of something watching me. Its eyes lingered at the edges of the room. I knew this feeling well enough: I was unwelcome.

Time to go.

When I found the others, Mirabelle was still conducting her gauche tour. She showed us the gardens from the French windows with a dismissive 'Garden'. Illiterate crone, does she not know in a place of such elegance as this, it is always *gardens*, never a *garden*? Such small nuances mark out the uncultured from those who are worthy of the invitation. Mirabelle has never been worthy of anything except a swift blow to the head with a sharp instrument.

As we threaded our way aimlessly from room to room, Mirabelle wittered on blithely about irrelevancies, ignorant of the fragile beauty of her surroundings. Each room thrummed with the insinuation of past lives, remnants of their voices whispering through the walls.

A wood pigeon hooted rhythmically, lulling the house into a composed, comfortable familiarity. And this shambling, aged house did still breathe with a little life. There were distant echoes of joy here — the thwack of a cricket bat, laughter and music. But there was sourness now, a morose resentment. Had we brought it with us? Perhaps.

The house was teeming with bedrooms, corridors, staircases, locked doors and passageways that seemed to lead back to the same place. It would be far too easy to lose your way here and never be found again. Mottled, black mirrors peered from shadows, eager to capture new faces. So many faces remembered in their silvering surfaces, each lingering on that lost moment when someone looked deep into the watery depths, a tiny fragment of them caught there for ever.

I checked my phone for the nth time, but there was still no signal, of course, let alone Wi-Fi, and it occurred to me that on our tour I'd seen no telephones at all. Bedrooms had the usual chests of drawers, dressing tables, nightstands. The hallway had a liberal scattering of side tables and consoles. But there wasn't a phone in sight. This growing realization made it seem like we had stepped from a golden age back to a darker one. It was no longer seclusion but isolation.

'This is you,' as usual, Mirabelle looked me up and down before pronouncing my name, '*Ursula.*'

It was impossible to give me an ill-appointed room here. Mine was handsome in the oldest sense of the word. No clutter, no detritus, none of the vague items that can only find space in a spare bedroom. This was a perfect capsule of solid brown furnishings and faded florals. Everything was as I had expected, or at least, gave the impression of being so.

Again, as with downstairs, there were no personal items or photographs, so in that way it was just like home. But Mother never likes to provide a comfortable guest bedroom. '*Don't make them feel too welcome,*' Mother always says. '*Otherwise they'll stay for ever. Remember Doreen Dellamer!*' This was a lady who worked at the shop. She fascinated me with her fanciful tales of a childhood among duchesses and lords. All children love to imagine they are from a long-lost branch of royalty, an adopted princess waiting to be rediscovered.

'*We didn't adopt you*,' Mother would say. '*We tried to have you adopted.*' She'd laughed in that unnerving way she had of making me doubt it was just a joke.

Mother let Doreen go, as she did with so many staff, and when Doreen could no longer pay her rent, Dad moved her into our spare room, previously Mother's dressing room. Mother was livid and that quickly fermented into basic hatred. One of Mother's first petty acts after Dad's death was to evict Doreen. I suppose grief can sometimes make people act in strange, divisive ways.

'Right, Pandora, now for you.' Mirabelle grinned as if something was hurting her, which I've imagined many times. 'I've not put you and the inconvenience next door to each other. Is that OK?' She often referred to me as though I was a sort of broken toilet.

'Fine,' Mother said.

The faintest cobweb of a smile spun at the corners of Mirabelle's lips.

They didn't wait for my response and were already disappearing down the hall but I could hear their undisguised discussion of my faults.

'When is she going to stop dressing like that? Don't they outgrow the dying hippy look when they leave university?' asked Mirabelle. 'And so obsessed with murders. Head always in some grubby crime book.'

'Oh, they all go through a *dark* phase. She'll grow up soon,' Mother shrugged. 'When the money runs out.'

Their voices trailed away down the long, bleak corridor.

There were enough corridors, hallways and rooms at Ambergris Towers that I could escape or hide at any moment. What I didn't know then was how invaluable that would be for a killer, as well as for me.

Dad had always loved to escape too. In his case, off for a smoke, of course. We all knew it — the crafty Polos hid nothing. He just smelled of tobacco and manufactured sugary mint. But that was lovely: warm, an enticing smell of a life well-lived and conducted with some abandon that never hurt anyone but himself. It would, of course, kill him — indirectly, but still, a death is a death. So really, I suppose he did hurt someone — kill them, in fact. Himself. The one person I loved and who loved me in return. I should hate him for that but I don't. It just can't ever seem like it was his fault.

He kicked the habit ostensibly in 1994, but the dark mint scent of smoke still permeated his clothes, his breath, his hair for at least another ten years after he '*gave up*'. It's an odour you just can't lose, like death — like grief. The very distinct flavour of grief lingers so long you forget what life smelled like without it.

He tried them all, patches, e-cigs and even hypnosis. He went to acupuncturists, doctors and quacks. But the old analogue cigarettes still drew him in, closer to a rasping death. He always came back to them, like a sad history or a lost love that could be embraced one last time before saying goodbye. It was always one last time.

I would nestle into the arms of that old, wrinkled leather chair down in his shed that Mother had Farrow-and-Balled and I'd watch him at work on his experiments. Bubbling tubes and a rainbow of colourful flasks drew a vaguely Willy Wonka-like portrait of him for my childish eyes. Some dads homebrewed in their sheds, but mine was a chemist, a teacher by trade, and the smell of all those sharp and strange liquids and potions sometimes falls in a chemical wave of memories, washing me all the way back to that shed.

He told me not to tell Mother, which was completely unnecessary as I never told her anything. I can still smell the warmth of an afternoon mixing chemicals with Dad, fag firmly clenched in his tight lips as a dribble of smoke curled up. 'Wronding,' he'd call it with a wink — Wrong Bonding.

Mother had the shed demolished the week after the funeral.

My memories have become battered by time and sections have splintered off into the lost shadows of the past. I dream of him often in broken visions, snap shots of a half-invented past.

I've taken those fragile elements and stitched the remnants back together to make a new dialogue, one that makes sense to my adult mind. But I know it's a Frankenstein version of reality. That's why I never rely wholeheartedly on memory — particularly when it circles a death.

What's left is a patchwork quilt of a childhood. Perhaps nothing special, but it felt that way to me — or at least, I've reinvented it so that it does now.

In the end, he just died — like all of us will. It was a wasteful death. Meaningless. The faceless voices who held the knowledge simply said his massive coronary was induced by excessive smoking. It had spread its weedy tendrils through his lungs and twined deep into the heart of him—infecting, decaying and hardening. How strange that those small paper stubs he left behind had encased such a slow and painful death.

I still feel him with me now, the warm welcoming haze of the nicotine trailing in around me. I can conjure him out of anything or nothing, from simple memories and air. On a grey finish to an evening, as my sky marbles over with regret and time is calling everyone else back home, my mind clouds over with thoughts of him. I can sense him, feel him everywhere. I can look up and see him in a bird, as if freedom has thrown his spirit high on the wind. He is always with me. Except, and I always return to this one single thought, he's not.

I sat down with my tangled thoughts on the edge of the bed and opened the bedside drawer. Empty. I unzipped my bag and took out his old Bible. I quickly put it in the bedside drawer and closed it. I don't really read it, but it's sort of my lucky charm, a talisman if you like. It watches over me in the abandoned dark hours and keeps me safe from whatever might go bump in the night. It's nothing more than that though. God doesn't live in my bedside table.

Rule 3: Just like tinned fruit and cream, family and friends often curdle.

FAMILY AND FRIENDS

The bell sounded with a sharp crudeness, as if the house knew the nature of its guests by now.

My aunt had arrived — a real one this time and not so beloved of my mother due to the lack of her own choice in the matter. Aunt Charlotte had arrived on a raft of silk and velvet, fur and largesse. Her voice was an octave too low and her shoulders an inch too broad to be seemly. Occasionally, men had been known to fall in wonder at the sheer *Titanic* beauty of her well-worn face and untamed hair, but she had never succumbed to anyone's doubtful charms. She was the old-establishment version of wild and she smashed through any social boundaries with her hockey stick manner and antique furs. She was intrinsically everything my mother had attempted to extricate herself from — a life of old-school affluence that bred bad teeth, frazzled hair and an iron will. The make-do-and-mend rich that had always made Mother crave a disposable world where kitchens were replaced having never seen a meal prepared in them and bathrooms had a makeover after only a few quick years of use. The world celebrated change, but Aunt Charlotte only ever admired staying power. When she bought a kitchen table, it was bought to outlast her, to have the scars of life etched into its surface as deeply as her face. Everything had a history, a reason for being in her life. Her jewellery told a story, histories of bygone ladies, formidable dames whose artefacts could not be owned without grave and grandiose design. All this and the mingled scent of mothballs and Chanel served to repel my mother with a force so powerful it was impossible to disguise. This was the kind of revulsion only a sibling could truly provoke. Yet, there's a symbiotic element to their aversion. They both rely on it, expect it. They have sent each other a carefully wrapped dead plant for every birthday in living memory. Mother keeps hers on what she calls her Wall of Death, outside in the garden.

'Charlotte, darling, how are you? No one told me you'd arrived!' Mother has always been a dreadful liar. She received the usual coral red lipstick print on her cheek, suffering the kiss with obvious distaste.

'I'm surprised you didn't hear her,' Mirabelle said.

The more I see them together the more I'm convinced that relatives and friends were never meant to be in the same room. My only expectation when they are together, particularly now, is that there will be aggravation, irritation and even murderous thoughts.

I sometimes wonder if Mother forces everyone together in some sort of social experiment just to watch what happens and see how long they'll last.

It had always been accepted that Mirabelle harboured a particular loathing for Aunt Charlotte — no doubt exacerbated by the ogre Aunt Charlotte being a genuine sister to her beloved Pandora, instead of a fabricated relative like herself.

But Aunt Charlotte was no fool and despised Mirabelle with elegant disdain, as if the Queen were meeting a traitor at her Garden Party. There was the initial exaggerated surprise that someone such as her, an infiltrator, should even be present, followed by the maintenance of decency, propriety and an obvious loathing. Aunt Charlotte always presented the image of healthy mistrust of the enemy in a sort of Churchillian way that infuriated Mirabelle.

'Ursula, darling, look at you! You've grown!'

Aunt Charlotte's memory seemed to revert to me being eleven years old with each new meeting.

A gong sounded as if some sort of ritual was about to commence.

'Dinner is served!' called a sonorous voice — a gentleman with, we were soon to discover, enough aloofness to set him apart as the butler.

'Good Lord, Ursula. Whatever shall become of us?' Aunt Charlotte roared and held me at arm's length. 'Are we to be murdered in our beds this very night? Look at this place, it's like a tomb and now the dead are rising!' Aunt Charlotte has always had a taste for the dramatic. Mother puts it down to her being dropped on her head as a baby. Mother did the dropping, of course.

Dinner was predictably tedious. Mother and Mirabelle made disparaging remarks about the food and Aunt Charlotte. Aunt Charlotte suffered from her 'gastrics'. But then we all suffer from her gastrics. Every Christmas in living memory has smelled of her intestines. She calls it her 'nasty cough'.

Yap.

'She brought the bloody dog?' Aunt Charlotte adopted the look she reserves for customer service representatives.

'*She* has been accompanied by Mr Bojangles, if that's what you're driving at, Charlotte.'

'If I was driving at anything, Bridget, it would be you and your yappy hound.'

'Charlotte,' Mother sighed wearily, 'thinking and saying, two different things. Out loud. In loud. Remember?'

Aunt Charlotte cast a withering glance across the room.

'Are you the only staff?' Aunt Charlotte sniped as if she was more accustomed to a tide of employees rather than just

Margery Braithwaite who *does* on a Monday and Thursday for her.

'No, Madam,' The Butler drawled, 'there is a house-keeper, Mrs—'

'The creepy old bat I was telling you about, Pandora darling,' Mirabelle interjected.

'Mrs Angel,' he concluded, as he served the sole.

'And you? We can't go on calling you *the butler*, that would seem a little too impersonal even for this.' Mirabelle grimaced at the old man. I fear it may have been an attempt at a smile.

'Angel,' he pronounced coldly.

Mirabelle's smile melted. 'As in . . .'

'Yes, Madam. I am Angel. Mrs Angel is my wife.'

A dark cloud of silence rolled in.

'Why it needs three of them for us, I don't know,' Mother murmured in her usual shrill murmur.

'Two,' droned Angel.

'Two what?'

'Two, *Madam*.'

'No, no, no, man! Two of what?' Mother sighed in frustration.

'Two staff, Madam. Why it needs *two* of them, you do not know. Not three.' Angel continued to slop pieces of dead fish onto each plate, so slippery they might still swim.

'I paid for three.'

'I am not aware of such matters, Madam, but I'm sure you will certainly be repaid in full. As you suggested, Madam, it should not need three of us to take care of *your* needs.'

Mother was dumbfounded, which actually looked quite hostile on her face.

'Well, it's certainly pricey, however many Angels there are,' she muttered. Mother has always been fiscally aware. When Dad was alive, she would ritually berate him for the fact that his job did not always provide enough to satiate her needs. Teaching was a higher calling then and this grated with Mother. *I'd be richer if you were dead*, I vividly remember

25

her joking. They were close and Mother's dry comedy could easily have been misconstrued if the wrong person had been listening. Thankfully, it was just me with my ear to the other side of the door.

But on this occasion, she was perfectly correct. The insurance, the savings and investments Dad had shrewdly made over the years were far and away beyond her expectations, especially on his teacher's salary. Finally, he had provided her with the income she knew he was always worth. She never doubted him. She could finally afford to realize her dream of sending me to St Cuthbert's — which she'd always wanted for me. Mother put me first and foremost. It was a wrench to be sent away so swiftly after Dad's death but Mother had to be strong for both of us. That's what mothers sometimes have to do, and I admire her for that. At the time, obviously, I expressed my emotions in a rather different way, but my therapist explained that was counterproductive. I am learning new ways to Mother's heart. It is a long and sometimes arduous conflict to maintain equanimity within a family and that is why I like to maintain constant vigilance. Otherwise, it can easily derail and the perfect calm washes away. Despite our differences, I don't want to find myself truly at war with Mother.

Dinner was a solemn, awkward combination of warm wine and insults; the perfect atmosphere for book club. They'd decided to read *Strangers on a Train* by Patricia Highsmith after Bridget had mistaken it for *The Girl on the Train* and ordered all the wrong copies. Nobody cared or noticed. But Bridget seemed genuinely sad when she explained her error.

She cleared her throat, which is never a good sign with Bridget as it means she's readying herself to make one of her pronouncements. 'So, shall we talk about the book? After all, it is why we're here.' She laughed peevishly.

'Book?'

'Charlotte, *in loud* remember,' Mother reminded.

'I was simply saying, *Charlotte*, that this is a book club weekend, so shouldn't we really—'

'Later, Bridget, thank you.' Mirabelle, for all her many faults, was useful in silencing Bridget.

They never talked about the book much beyond the cover anyway. As with most book clubs, the first rule of book club was *you do not talk about the book*.

The taut silences at dinner, dismissive comments, and casual rudeness reminded me so much of home. Mother has no other way of dealing with family and friends. I consider myself fortunate to still be in Mother's favour, given that I am related to her.

'Sit up straight, for Christ's sake, Ursula.'

'Don't be such a motherfusser.'

'I beg your pardon, young lady?'

'I was just saying, pity there's no music for us.'

I had always admired Dad's way of lightening the mood at difficult family occasions. At fraught moments, he would simply get up and start playing the piano. Although Mother never welcomed his playing. I still remember the derision she set aside for his Clair de Lune. We all smiled and wept at its memory at the funeral. Afterwards, I overheard Mother mention something to Mirabelle about how 'haunting' she found it. At least that's what I thought she said, and I clung to that half-heard moment for many years.

The walnut dining table shone with the reflections of our faces drawn out into long distortions. There was a glitter of dark expectation among the silverware, china and vast array of glasses. The wine glowed liquorice dark through the sharp-cut crystal as if it was stained glass. As we drank, our lips were soon marked purple black and the usual sense of trouble was beginning to percolate slowly. It pervaded every book club get-together so it didn't seem strange this time but the warning signs were all there. I'm constantly vigilant with family and friends. The slightest change or nuance could be important — or perhaps even vital. It could even be a life saver.

Our brains were rattled again by the Hammer Horror doorbell. Old Angel — he wasn't that old, middle-aged perhaps, but Old Angel sounds better — began his slow journey to the door. Maybe it was his gliding phantom-like way of walking, his hunched silence or deathly pallor that created an impression of Old Angel.

His announcement of the arrival of 'Miss Cowdale' was greeted with a fairly toxic blend of disappointment and hatred. Obviously, Mother thought she was marvellous, but Aunt Charlotte and Mirabelle acted as if he'd just announced an hour-long session of colonic, or *precious me time* as Mother knows it. Bridget just continued to feed her dog little bits of food, saying quietly, 'One for Mr Bojangles. One for Mummy.'

'So Less made it,' I said, adopting a casual, almost offhand tone.

Mother shot *The Look*. 'I've told you before, less of that, thank you, Madam.'

'Less of Less, do you mean, Mother?' I smiled, but it was never a real smile when Less was involved.

Less was Joy Cowdale. She had a face like a scrunched-up paper bag and a mind just as empty. From a very young age, I remember her leeching on our Christmases, birthdays, everydays. She was always clinging to Mother with her fake brand of alternative lifestyle and stylish sly doublespeak. '*Life's a journey, so be prepared to walk many different terrains.*' It was so vacuous it almost seemed harmless.

Yet beneath it all was a singular lack of enthusiasm to celebrate life or, more specifically, anyone else's life. She just had the naked ambition to have the life she wanted and at any cost. She did not enjoy the pleasure or achievements of others. If the spotlight was not on her, she turned it there. Somehow her shadow fell long across our lives.

I began by calling her Joyless, which, of course, with time lost its Joy and became simply Less. Every time I said it, her look was as sharp as hate and as fresh as the first time, so in some ways she did bring unexpected joy to the world — my world, at least. But then, just when I'm enjoying her frustration, the sadness always sails back in on billowing sheets of memory.

Mother's birthday was always a sacred date to observe. Dad had taught me that much. He'd been dead for two years when Less had made her first vicious move. Even though it was just Mother and me now, and it had to fit around my school terms, we still had our *family meal*. In some ways, it was the only time we ever really came close to each other. I'd booked our usual place — quiet, local, none of Mother's rapacious, vile friends. Although to be fair, Less had phoned to ask if Mother would like a party and I explained that couldn't happen because of our little ritual, which she understood. Less was, after all, a very *understanding* person, what with all her chakras and meditation. She even asked if there was anything Mother wanted. I'd laughed, as Mother wanted everything. I told her I'd saved for a fancy-ish bag but beyond that, anything would do — smelly candles, scarves, make-up — she knew the score. She knew it very well.

I remember the first thing that struck me was just how many of them there were. It must have taken a Herculean effort on Less's part to assemble so many people for Mother's surprise birthday party and on the exact night I'd arranged for our meal together. Mother's friends were swarming our house and all made-up so terrifyingly that they looked like villainous clowns. Their clothes were expensive renditions of pantomime costumes — flounces, frills and buttons all unexpectedly placed to invite attention and comment. '*Soooo, what's this? Is it new?*' Oh, of course it is! Their clothes were always new, as if they needed to change their identity every time they went out, like people in a witness protection programme.

They drank as if nothing could quench their thirst; they were loud with rasping voices and eyes intently searching for prey; they were like caricatures of human beings, an alien species mimicking people but missing the subtleties of human existence.

At the peak of their raucous noise, a small chime of a glass caught the edge of the room. Heads slowly turned and the attention Less so craved washed over her in delicious waves. I saw her through the crowd, head tilted up as if basking in the light of devotion.

'Present time!' She spread her mouth into the image of a smile and for a second her gaze caught mine. The malice flashed over the dark pearls of her eyes. 'Pandora, *darling* birthday girl, lead on! Let's do it in the sitting room. Come on everyone. It's from *all* of us.'

Mother went first, then Less, with one last brutal smile aimed deep into me. And then everyone, the entire room, all filed past me in a single septic line, staring as they went by, until I was alone in the room holding the small gift I'd saved to buy.

They stayed in that room, laughing, for an age until finally one ventured out. 'Oh, Joy does feel so bad not including you, darling. She just feels dreadful, but she didn't know you'd be here and Pandora did so want that gorgeous handbag. She really will treasure it and it's from all of us — well, almost all of us.' She laughed before she left me alone again.

Less slid over later. 'Now, don't you go making me feel bad. Your mother never mentioned you were going to be around this weekend.'

I sat in the loo and stashed my present behind the toilet brush. The cleaner took it away with her after the party, but I kept my humiliation.

This is only one of the reasons Joy will always be Less to me — Less than human — and why I could cheerfully watch her die.

'Ursula, don't you dare be rude to Joy!' Mother's excited voice cut me from my reminiscing. 'She's been a fucking rock — a fucking rock. Do you hear me?'

'Yes, Mother. A fucking rock.'

'Joy, darling! I was just telling Ursula—'

'That you're a fucking . . .' I left a nice neat pause and took a slow drink of my wine.

They waited. Less balanced herself between the hall and the dining room, not daring to move. I took another sip of wine then smiled. 'Sorry, sorry. What was I saying? Do you know, I've totally lost my thread. Anyway, this wine is delicious.' I held up my glass and looked at her through the wine, her face appearing as glossy and red as a boiled sweet. 'Come and join us, Less. Such a pleasure to see you again. Do you know, I haven't seen you since you took my Mother to Paris for my birthday.'

Mother slowly rose and embraced Joy — not something I say often, so that was one thing to thank the woman for, I suppose.

'Come on in,' Mother gushed. 'Have some food. You, Angel man. Get the food.' She turned to Less. 'It's fucking awful but there's wine.'

Less settled her tight little frame into the seat opposite me and scanned the room. Angel began serving her some slippery fish but she held her hand over the plate. I don't think Angel had realized the meaning of the gesture as he carefully let the dead sole fall over her hand. Less made a strangled squeal like a snared piglet. She had not touched real food since 1983.

'Less, darling, you look famished!' Aunt Charlotte announced. Some relatives are not born tactful.

'So how are you, Less?' Mirabelle asked. She knew full well that Less's current husband had lost his job in the City and that this was the only thing that mattered to her. It would be an arduous few months of extricating herself from another victim of a life of Less. Then the meat grinder would have to crank up again and there would be an inordinate amount of attention focused on finding Less another husband — or sacrifice, as I know them. There is an old adage that you can choose your friends but you cannot choose your relatives. I take this just a little step further in that you cannot choose your mother's friends — or kill them. That doesn't exclude harbouring malevolent thoughts. No one can see those.

Keener psychologists would perhaps put this line of reasoning down to a child's jealousy, but you see in my case I had never had any of my mother's attention to start with. I just thought — and circumstantial evidence can attest to the fact — that Less was utterly and unashamedly foul.

'Struggling on, Mirabelle. Thank you for your concern.'

With her uncanny sensitivity to a room's atmosphere, Aunt Charlotte set off on some tale of her train journey and a bright young man who hadn't been able to take his eyes off her legs. Aunt Charlotte has always enjoyed the imagined attention of men. Whole meals have been spent in whispered conspiracy concerning a man at another table who is looking at Aunt Charlotte. '*Look at him! Just look! He's undressing me with his eyes. I'm naked! Naked, I tell you. The dirty bastard!*' Aunt Charlotte has never been a good whisperer.

Her voice rattled the air now with a long, drawn-out explanation of what the gentleman on the train had intended to do to her from behind his newspaper.

Less cleared her throat and everyone tried to ignore the irritating caustic squall of her voice. She was forced to resort to her usual tactic of blatant rudeness.

'Excuse me, but can I just have my light on for a tiny moment?' It's this kind of needy assertiveness squeezed through that pinched tight mouth that makes everyone she meets wish her catastrophic harm. Or perhaps that's just me.

'I suspect you're all aware that I have lost someone I had a special place for,' Less began, the facsimile of a smile imprinted on her lips.

Was this a heart beating for the departing husband?

'My wonderful housekeeper, Tia, has had to leave the country and I'm bereft.'

'Can we just get to talking about the book, please?' Bridget interrupted. 'It *is* why we're here,' she sang, with a pained grin.

'Later, Bridget,' Mother sighed.

The rest of the meal was odious.

* * *

Walking through the house to bed, it felt as if this entire world had fallen into a deathly sleep. Night sat heavily on these rooms, a tired darkness slumped across the corridors, exhausted with life. This house demanded a stately pace. There would be no rushing here to find shoes, to dress children, no shouting for dinner — no shouting at all. It had an undeniable elegance in its faded layers of velvet and silk wallpaper worn smooth by time. But like a fragile wedding dress stored for countless years among layers of delicate tissue papers, its bygone beauty was being slowly corroded by time.

The only time I ever saw Mother's wedding dress was on a mannequin in the charity shop window next to Dad's favourite suit after he died. It was like seeing a fun, headless version of them.

My bedroom at Ambergris Towers was dank and cold in that upper-class way. The slightly frosted, mildewed air spoke of the decades of privileged inhabitants, the austere custodians of such monoliths, struggling to maintain a dignified decay. There was a severity to the furnishings. The mattress was limp, the drawers heavy with ancient paper linings and the lingering scent of mothballs. The rugs still clung to their luxurious past but relentless footfalls had mown familiar pathways into their pile. A serene atmosphere lent the room a sense of peace and security. This would not last through the night.

The day was being slowly unpicked and a long ribbon of darkness wound through the house. There were none of the sounds I was used to in London — no distant cars, no planes or alarms, no boarding school tears or thumps in the night. Not even the occasional scream. This house and the land around stopped for those hours of darkness, like a child afraid to move an inch for fear of detection by whatever might be stalking the night world beyond her bed.

That was one of the worst things about my dad's death. No one came to me in the night anymore. No one unmonstered my sleep. I would lie there in petrified silence, unable to move or speak as the familiar phantoms rose up around my bed. It was as if they had been set free to roam where they wished without anyone to check them anymore. My champion had gone, and I was all alone with my fear. Mother said it was character building to deal with my concerns myself. She was right, but what kind of character it built remains to be seen.

In the overpowering hum of silence, I heard something. Music. My mind scrambled for clarity in the smothering darkness. A strange, unnerving melody carefully arrived. I looked at the clock: midnight. Of course.

It began with the slow, careful tap of each separate note. The ghost of a familiar tune I half remembered began to form and circle my room. I slowly sat up and felt the sudden pinch of cool air. The soft notes threaded between one another, weaving a slow song that rose and fell in delicate waves. I leaned and slowly clicked on the light. Was there a shadow that lingered too long, caught on the edge of my vision for a moment? So often, it's not the things we see plainly that scare us. I blinked and it was gone. But the music still curled through the room, much clearer and more inviting now the light was on. It was quite recognizably a piano and, though distant, unmistakeably the melancholy tones of Clair de Lune.

I rose quickly and didn't wait to put on slippers, dressing gown or any of the other things I'd forgotten to pack. As I opened the door, a great wave of music ran over me. It was elegant and accomplished — and just as Dad had always played it. I began walking hurriedly but soon broke into a jog, fearful it would end before I got to the piano.

The long leaded window at the top of the stairs cast a gaunt light. But as the clouds splintered open the moon appeared, opaque as a blind eye in the darkness. Its light bloomed out under the clouds and cast a strange gaslight blue all the way down the stairs and into the hall. There was no one there but the music continued.

I bolted down the staircase and swung round the end of the bannister. Still no one appeared. This house was iron cold with loneliness. And yet the music still played.

I paused with my hand on the sitting-room door. Fear gripped my breathing until it was so shallow I felt nauseous.

I could smell the sweet tang of his tobacco smoke. The clear memory of my father at the piano rose before me. I closed my eyes and pushed the door open.

The music stopped and in the darkness I could see that the piano lid was closed. The room was empty.

Rule 4: Always observe your fellow guests. Listen very carefully to what everyone says and be aware of all movements.

SUGGESTIONS FOR THE SUGGESTIBLE

I'm standing in the garden, Dad lying just in front of me. Smoke drifts in grey clouds between us and I can't see him properly. A flint-eyed rook sails in on the breeze and lands silently next to him. Dad's face is all crumpled with anguish. There the bird sits, watching. And then it begins with its busy pecking of his kind eyes.

Peck.

Peck.

Peck.

I open my mouth to scream but it is his voice I hear.

'Don't let them, Ursula. I can't see her. I can't see.'

Peck.

'I can't see her. I can't—'

And this is how I woke in the early hours of the morning, shouting. I couldn't breathe in those first seconds of limbo, the breath wedged in my throat as if a wet cloth had been stuffed down there. The thick darkness confused me and I had no recollection of where I was. The bed was shaking and it took me a moment to realize it was me shaking it. I touched my face and it was slick with sweat. The salt of it mixed freely with my tears, stinging my eyes, but I didn't try to close them. I never do in those moments, otherwise I sink straight back to the garden. Once or twice I have and all I've found is his body, with one black feather beside him that always blows silently away before I get to him.

I waited, like a child making sure there was nothing moving in the darkness, before I reached for the lamp and fumbled with the switch. The acid flare burned my eyes and I could hear the blood drumming around in my ears. My hands were clammy and my fingers trembled as I reached into the bedside drawer and brought out Dad's Bible. I placed it carefully on my lap and opened it. Inside was the familiar square shape he'd cut into the pages. Dad's little secret, now mine, a hip flask filled with brandy that he'd secreted inside the Bible. 'Spirit of the Lord,' he'd laugh and, with a wink, take a long sip. I don't know why he'd decided on Bible brandy, presumably because that was one place Mother would never look. I put it to my mouth, my hands still shaking, and felt the cold lip of it jitter against my skin. And I drank. I drank it like poison until it burned all the way down to the core of me, scalding every inch it travelled. Then I sat clutching it to me. The tears fell unchecked until exhaustion and the brandy took over.

I drifted in and out of dreams but there'd been just enough of a window of sleep for my old bed fellow, the Night Terror, to stalk back in and lie across the rest of the night. He squatted on my belly and then he stretched out his long, thin fingers until all his fear covered my face and sunk into my dreams.

I've tried keeping myself awake many times to avoid the tormenting little demon, but then it infects every waking moment. I once managed three nights of deprivation. It was bliss but sleep inevitably snared me and the beast just came back roaring. The only answer I have is that it's better to give in to it.

When I'd roused myself enough to dress, I hid myself in the sitting room, drifting on the noxious waves of stale brandy that still washed over me. It seemed like a good place to avoid breakfast. My head was heavy and my arms weak. I couldn't help staring at the undisturbed thin film of dust on the piano lid. My head was lousy from my near sleepless night.

I could hear Mother and Mirabelle as they came down the stairs, deep in suspicious mutterings about Aunt Charlotte, the house, the food and anything else they could hate.

'Breakfast. Now, Ursula,' Mother rasped, as she passed the door to the sitting room. She paused and frowned. 'You need to eat,' she said, pointedly. Somehow, she had an unnerving radar where I was concerned. She always knew exactly where I was and invariably what I'd been doing.

Breakfast was another sordid meal served in the stultifying splendour of the dining room. Aunt Charlotte in her usual boisterous voice and tweeds had some complaint about an English man serving his own breakfast. Most of Aunt Charlotte's etiquette comes from Julian Fellowes' movies so has a touch of the melodramatic and insane about it.

'And why is the bloody dog here again?' she barked.

Bridget stiffened. 'Mr Bojangles is entitled to eat too, isn't he?'

'Elsewhere.'

'Well, I paid extra for him to have bed and breakfast.' She fed the small animal another sausage. 'So he has every right to be here, don't you, my baby?'

Aunt Charlotte shook her head slowly.

'You people need to relax,' Less commented in her smooth judgemental voice.

She had cultivated a smug expression that she had mistaken for serene. She informed everyone that she had completed an hour of yogalates before any of us had even woken up, making me wish even more that I hadn't.

Angel entered with another basket of stale bread rolls and placed them on the dining table, much to the disgust of

Aunt Charlotte. Fellowes must have had a position on bread rolls at some point.

'What is this?' Mother demanded.

'Bread, Madam.'

'I realize that, but it's hardly the wholesome array of spectacular local food and foraged artisan produce we were promised.'

Angel stared with empty eyes that could easily have been misinterpreted as the look of a man who didn't care.

'Where are the sausages?' Aunt Charlotte frowned.

'Oh,' Bridget smiled, 'I think Mr Bojangles just had the last one.'

'Good Lord, Angel, what do you and Mrs Angel eat? Surely not stale loaves and slippery fish, unless you really are as devout as you appear.'

Angel closed his eyes slowly. 'Mrs Angel is partial to an omelette, Madam. I use fresh farm eggs, onions, plenty of wild mushrooms, cheese, a grind of black pepper and a good sprinkle of salt. Every morning. For thirty years.' There was a tarnished edge to his words.

We stared at our meagre basket of hardened rolls.

'If I'd wanted a recipe, I'd have asked for one, man,' Mother sighed. 'Look, I was promised artisanal, foraged food—'

'I used to forage with my sister's family in the woods in France,' Mirabelle reminisced. She often did this. I suspected it was lies. 'Just by the farmhouse they converted. Well, before it fell down. We went truffle hunting . . .'

'Like pigs?' I offered.

Mother issued *The Look*.

'You find the *real* food when you've foraged for it yourself,' Less began in her sanctimonious voice. 'My yoga instructor runs a retreat—'

'Is this the same sort of *retreat* as the weed farm you went to?' Aunt Charlotte laughed. 'Bunch of hippies getting stoned.'

'How dare you? That was a spiritual centre for enlightened mindfulness. Something you should think about!'

Angel coughed, was ignored, so coughed again, this time as if he had swallowed something and was choking.

'What is it?' Mother asked with her usual *joie de vivre*.

'Excuse the interruption, Madam, but Mrs Angel—'

'Where exactly is Mrs Angel, Angel?' Mother asked, irritably.

'Performing her duties, Madam.'

'Must you call me Madam? You make me sound at least fifty-five!'

Mother is fifty-six.

'I was just wondering if you and your party had decided upon any entertainment for your sojourn, Madam.' There was an unmistakable emphasis on the Madam this time.

Mother and Mirabelle stared vacantly at one another. I suspect the entertainment they'd had in mind was rather more bottle-shaped.

'Oh, Angel, is this appropriate at the breakfast table?' We all waited for the inevitable announcement that Angel had in some way looked at Aunt Charlotte rudely with devilish devices in mind. We stared at the sombre face of the old butler and even Aunt Charlotte seemed to shy away from any lewd suggestions.

Angel cleared his throat. 'Might I suggest an evening of confluence with the spirits?'

'We brought our own.'

'I'm sorry, Madam?'

'Gin.' Mother drummed her fingers in frustration.

Angel attempted a smile. It looked rather terrifying. 'No, Madam, you have misunderstood my meaning. A medium, that is to say a psychic, lives close by and some of our guests like to take advantage of the atmosphere here at Ambergris Towers.'

Mother did her puzzled-but-not-in-any-way-misunderstanding face.

'It's rather Gothic don't you think, Madam?' And he motioned upwards.

We looked up in unison.

'You'd have to ask my daughter about that sort of rubbish.'

'Hmmm . . .' Aunt Charlotte mused, 'there are a few gargoyles up there.'

'And down here,' I said quietly, but Mother still heard.

'Eavesdroppers, Madam.'

'I beg your pardon?'

'They are eavesdroppers, Madam. It is where the phrase originates, I believe, people listening, watching from up in the eaves.'

'How appropriate,' Mother said, rolling her eyes.

Angel continued as if he hadn't heard her. 'There is an elderly lady in the village, who specializes in the darker arts.'

'Darker arts, Angel?' Aunt Charlotte bellowed. 'What is this, Harry Potter?'

'Who?'

We looked at Angel in bewilderment.

He continued unperturbed. 'She does a little fortune telling, tarot reading, matters of that nature. Many of the guests adore it. I can inform Mrs Angel if you have a preference for this.'

'Well, I'd like to know when we're going to start discussing the book,' Bridget said sourly.

'Not now, Bridget,' Mother sighed.

'Oh, I think it would be wonderful to invite the spirits in!' Less held up her arms and the intricate system of bangles and charms stacked from her wrist to her elbow slid down, creating the very unflattering impression of a shower hose.

'Don't be ridiculous, Less.' Aunt Charlotte regularly said this to Less. It still didn't stop her being ridiculous.

Less widened her mineral black eyes before carefully and coldly adding, 'I'm a very *spiritual* person. I just can't help it. It's the way I am.'

'Shall I enquire if she is available for this evening, Madam?'

'Oh let's! Please, Pandora? Oh, say we can?' Less often adopted this annoying demeanour of a small Enid Blyton child — the kind that you hoped would fall down a well.

Mother sighed. 'Let's just let her have it.'

'I would if I had my twelve bore,' Aunt Charlotte muttered.

'Ha!'

'Shut up, Ursula.' Mother looked at me with withering eyes.

'Why me? It was her who said—'

'Very well, Angel,' Mother continued, 'let the old witch come and tell us our futures.'

'Yes, Madam.'

'But they'd better be bloody rosy. I'm not paying to be told that I face a life of misery and despair. I can see that for myself.'

I have never seen Mother genuinely miserable and certainly she never despairs. She has always been fully in control of her destiny.

'She has very reasonable rates I believe, Madam.'

'Cross my palm with silver and all that!' Aunt Charlotte snorted.

'I believe it's twenty pounds an hour, Madam. Payable in notes of any denomination. Silver will not be necessary. Should I go ahead with the booking for this evening, Madam? Might I suggest the library after supper?'

Mother watched him with the keen intent of a rat. 'You have a lot of suggestions for a butler, don't you, Angel?'

'Madam, I am here to be of the utmost assistance.'

'I can see that. And what about your charming wife, Angel? Are we to be graced with her presence at any point during our visit?'

'Yes, Madam. In fact, I believe she was intending to conduct a tour of the house and grounds this morning after breakfast.'

'Already done it, chum,' Mirabelle grunted.

Angel looked at her with finely honed contempt. 'Perhaps she may offer a few more of the House's treasures for your contemplation, *Madam*.' Each Madam was a new barb.

'So, when are we going to discuss the book?' Bridget said, with a slow insistence.

'Later, Bridget,' Mother snapped. 'We'll be there in a moment, thank you Angel.'

'Thank you, Madam.' He left with a slow, deliberate step that put one in mind of an animated corpse.

As he was leaving, a question escaped from me before I'd even looked for Mother's approval. 'Angel, were you playing the piano last night?'

Angel didn't turn to look at me, but very coolly answered, 'The piano has not been touched for some time to my knowledge, Miss. I shall speak to Mrs Angel about giving it a thorough dusting today.' It somehow felt like a rebuke.

'Perhaps while you're at it you could do something about the clock,' Mother said. She pointed with her knife. 'It can't always be ten past twelve. Tell me, Angel, does anything work in this ruin?'

All eyes were on the large old radio and the clock's dead hands.

I got up and moved to the door.

'Where do you think you're going?'

'The library, Mother.'

'*The library, Mother*,' she mimicked. 'Whatever for?' For a book club, books were remarkably low on their list of priorities.

'To listen to the news,' I said. 'I do it every morning.'

'What? I've never seen you do that.' Mother's irritation crackled like a well-stoked brazier. I resisted the temptation to say she never noticed anything I did. 'Another affectation you've adopted, Ursula?'

'Will that be all, Madam?' Angel said slowly.

'Yes, yes, go.' Mother flicked her wrist.

I couldn't tell if it was me being dismissed or Angel.

'So worrying for you, dear, like you say — all these *affectations*.' Mirabelle's voice was, as usual, smooth as poison pouring into my mother's ear. 'And where will it all end? She can't be a precocious child forever!'

'Why ever not, Mirabelle?' I said. 'You've certainly never stopped being a bully.'

It was almost imperceptible, but as I passed Angel I noticed a minute swelling at the base of his face. It was the only sign that he was clenching his jaw so tight it might shatter at any moment.

'May I assist you, Miss?' he asked, as the two of us walked into the hallway.

'No, no, thank you. I'm just going to the library.'

'Did I hear you saying you were going to listen to the radio, Miss?'

'Hmm? Oh, yes.'

'I'm afraid there's no radio in the library, Miss.' He paused. 'I can walk to the village later for a newspaper if that would suffice?'

'No, no,' I sighed. 'I'll be fine. I might even read a book, who knows?'

Rule 5: Control is very important. Be careful of those who hold the lead
too tight, they might just strangle you.

THE LADY WHO DOES

'Everyone must have a lady who does.' One of Mother's many
mantras. She has a mantra for every aspect of life that requires
hard work. For instance, 'You should dine out at least three
times a week.' The rest, of course, is always amply provided
for by ready meals. Mother's freezer is colour-coded based on
Farrow and Ball's colour chart — ranging from grey through
to beige and a kind of green-based slurry for 'healthy' days.

As far as the house is concerned, for as long as I can
remember, Mother has had a revolving door of cleaners and
various housekeepers, regularly fired for incompetence. No
one ever lasts more than a couple of months. It's as if she
doesn't want anyone getting to know us or our house too
well. We once had a whole gang who came tooled up with
Henrys, heavy-duty Marigolds and thick butcher's aprons
giving the impression to the neighbourhood that we were
either being fumigated or a murder had occurred in our
home, neither of which was pleasing to Mother given that
Dad had just passed away.

Mrs Angel, however, was a real housekeeper. Or at least, she certainly gave the impression of being utterly in control of every aspect of Ambergris Towers. Her soft hair was lined neatly across her head in silvery coils. There was a hint of powder, but for conformity rather than beauty. Her sturdy brown leather brogues and thick support tights told of a woman accustomed to standing. She had the unshakeable strength and poise of a monarch — hands clasped before her, body unswayed, mind in perfect harmony. There was no reaction to our presence other than a slow blink and a well-practised, 'Good morning, ladies.' It was as if a state dignitary had arrived — the Lady of the Manor. I suddenly had the urge to curtsey until Mother gently kicked me in the shin.

The housekeeper conducted the tour immaculately. But still, it was excruciating in its detail. No one listened to any of it, except for the gory bits where generations ago there had been civil war, murders and vile deaths in the beds we now occupied. The children she spoke of seemed to live unnaturally short and painstakingly dull lives — although this could have been more a feature of Mrs Angel's delivery which was unfailingly monotone. She seemed to glide through as if nothing could shake her. Dead master in his bed? Not a problem, she would just close the curtains as if closing her eyelids to the morning sun. A rattlesnake in the lavatory? Easily despatched with the household cane that, of course, disguised his Lordship's rapier.

'Bloody cold, though,' Mirabelle moaned.

Mrs Angel fixed her with a stare. 'Although the rooms might seem chilly to a member of the middle classes used to central heating and cheap prints, Madam, I'm sure you'll be completely familiar with the effect of overheating a house containing valuable oil paintings.'

Mirabelle stared open-mouthed. If she had a tail, she would have wedged it firmly between her legs and crawled away. In fact, I can't guarantee that Mirabelle doesn't have one somewhere in those ill-fitting slacks. I watched her grip Mother's arm in that overfamiliar way she has that somehow steps over the boundary of friendship into a darker impression that she might in some way be controlling her.

The tour culminated in the gardens (not garden) designed around a Capability Brown concept, with more follies than a wayward politician. This landscape had the superficial appearance of an elegant stately garden and yet it was all somewhat faded. A sallow air seemed to weave around it. Not far beyond the main house, the topiary was a little unkempt, the grass too long and unweeded. Diseased trees had been left to fall or hollow out, creating new colonies of fungi among the febrile rot. Nature was clawing at the edges of this vanishing kingdom. Where conformity had once ruled, messy life was breaking free. Soon the land would take this back and swallow all their worldly goods. Perhaps that's how it should be. All things must pass and return to the soil.

Less looked weak by the end of our journey and excused herself for her usual meditation/sleep/bath/self-absorption/joint. The sky aged and took on a new wilted, colourless quality. Each of us felt a cool shiver of wind cross our skin.

'Let's go in and have *luncheon*,' Mother said.

'And then we can start discussing the book.' Bridget trotted primly through the doors with her dog on the leash, both their noses held high.

Mrs Angel closed her eyes and nodded. She was as solemn as the pewter sky. She'd have made an excellent mourner — one of those paid ones or perhaps an extra in a film. Mourner Number One.

It was after *luncheon*, which didn't seem any different to lunch, that the first soft swirl of snow began. The feathery flakes landed in a silent warning not to come outside again.

We settled into the slightly less uncomfortable sofas in the sitting room. There'd been a feeble discussion of the book that quickly dissolved into various intrigues involving neighbours and soap opera characters, which dovetailed so neatly it was hard to tell who was real and who was fictional. But as the afternoon drew on, we gathered quietly round the fire and clutched our teacups with a new wariness.

This was no longer a pastiche of the winter country estate. The fierce fire was a necessity, not an adornment. The heavy velvet curtains murmured at the edges as the wind built.

Mrs Angel entered, holding her hands firmly together in front of her. 'You will be dining at eight.' She had a remarkably elegant way of issuing a question as though it was a command.

Mother was having none of it. 'That will be satisfactory,' she stated firmly. Before Mrs Angel could glide away, Mother took another loud breath. 'Will there be a menu for our *perusal*?'

I don't think I'd ever heard Mother use the word *perusal* before. Clearly she felt it added gravitas to the situation. Mother only ever feels the need to add gravitas when she thinks she's on the back foot. Dad used to laugh at her adopted grandeur. It infuriated her as only he could.

When Mother feels the need to over-vocabularize with a complete stranger, you know it's going to be tense. That's the thing with people unused to staff — they are suspicious of them. No one, except for Mother, could have been suspicious of Mrs Angel, but with her streak of petty snobbery, Mother felt that an old woman who was paid to clean should not be the captain of the ship. Generations of aristocracy emerged unscathed from handing over the real reins to Nanny, followed by housekeepers and butlers galore, but women like Mother would never bow to the Lady Who Does. Mother has just never learned to let go of the reins. My therapist says she's never learned to relinquish control. He says this from experience. He's Mother's therapist as well. He does a cheaper rate for two. It does make me wonder what he passes on about me to Mother. I often feed him useless information just to mess with Mother's head. Which seems only fair as I know she does the same with me and pays him extra when she wants him to persuade me something is a good idea.

'The menu has always been presented at five o'clock, Madam. As is customary.' Another silence. 'Unless, of course, Madam would prefer we break with the usual tradition and protocol.'

'Tradition? This place is like falling into a *Past Times* catalogue.'

'They went bust,' Mirabelle said, distractedly.

Aunt Charlotte gasped audibly.

'Well, I'm not sucked in by any of this,' Mother continued, 'I think we'll stick with the *protocol* of the customer always knows best. I'll need to see that menu before five o'clock. You'll bear in mind that during our stay here I am the mistress of this house and as such I set the *protocol*. Is that understood, Mrs Angel?'

Mrs Angel took every word stoically, a soldier in the trenches. I couldn't help feeling admiration for the staunch, old woman.

'Very well, Madam.' She left with some dignity, I thought. It would be hard to say she was chastened but there was a distinct smell of woman scorned in the air. Just which woman, it was hard to tell.

'And the book, when will we—'

'Not *now*, Bridget!' Mother hissed.

Rule 6: Never invite spiritualists, fortune tellers or anyone communing with the other side into your home. They may see more than you imagined.

THE ARRIVAL OF THE FORTUNE TELLER

In my experience, it's very important at family gatherings to lay on adequate entertainment, otherwise guests succumb to boredom, followed by excessive drunkenness, which inevitably leads to poor behaviour of varying degrees — from the basic insults level, to violence and possible fatalities.

I say this from bitter experience of our dreaded Christmas. It was stultifying enough when Mother's lot came — Aunt Charlotte and Mirabelle. But when Mother had to entertain Dad's relatives, it was an extinction-level event. Mother would wail for days about the huge workload and impossibility of accommodating 'the entire tribe', which was his mother and father. Dad had no other relatives he was aware of, although following his death, many raised their heads above the parapet to peek at the will.

Christmas was excruciating, the gift opening a bitter mess of disappointment. But nothing could rival the period of time after dinner, a real wasteland of recriminations and dark looks. Apart from the fact that they all hated one another, the trouble was, there was nothing to do.

Here at Ambergris Towers, the choice had been made for us — tarot reading and fortune telling. Although I can't say this particular activity would have sat well with my dad's parents. After his death, they were always airing their '*superstitions*' to the point where, finally, Mother was forced to sever all contact. When they died together in a car crash only a year later, that too was surrounded by *superstitions*, but nothing came of any of it. It took me many years to realize they had been saying 'suspicions', which just goes to show that little girls shouldn't listen at doors. Some habits are harder to break than others, though.

At Ambergris Towers, the entertainment was shrouded in actual superstition or 'nonsense hocus-pocus' as Mother called it.

'Well, I don't see what's wrong with properly discussing the book,' Bridget moaned. 'It's what we—'

'At least it's saved us from *that* eye-watering boredom,' I murmured.

'You're not a member of the club, so that's none of your concern.'

'Is the dog a member of the *club*?' I asked, widening my eyes at her. 'Did you pay extra for Mr Bojangles to discuss the relative merits of the book, as well as bed and breakfast?'

'I just don't understand what sort of woman comes to a house and does that sort of charlatan nonsense,' Mother grumbled, as if some form of sinful entertainment had been proposed.

Soft flakes of snow hurried across the dark light of the gardens. The granite sky occasionally let a blade of moonlight through and we could see the trees and fine sculptures encrusted with ice, the naked stone figures clothed in rimy white folds. It was no more than a mere powdering by then. Everything was sifted with a fine mist of snow as if it had been conjured from a Victorian Christmas card scene. We'd abandoned Christmas cards in our house on what Mother called 'environmental grounds'. We still displayed the ones we received, of course, as it wouldn't be entering into the spirit of Christmas if we didn't. I have yet to find the time to unpick this logic.

I never attempt to question my family's take on Christmas. I'm just there, *like the Ghost of Christmas*, as Mirabelle says. She wishes it was Christmas past, but I'm still around.

The snow added a dark luminosity to the gardens. Up-lit trees cut new shapes of light from the hard gloom and as the velvet snow gathered, it made the air around it seem even more brittle, light shivering over it as if it was broken glass. A new malevolence sat here, a stillness to the whole scene as though we'd stepped onto a stage set and, out there in the dark, our audience was watching us. It was as if the snow might stop mid-air and everything would be frozen into that fragile second, all of us suspended in this snow globe — and with one push, it could so easily be shattered.

A single black rook sailed in through the mist, stark against the grimy sky. It settled on a wind-twisted branch and my mind turned to another garden. As Dad lay dying, I had looked to the sky for help and there it sat on the fringes of a tree, that bird, that solitary rook watching my pain unfold.

The doorbell sounded, old and muted by rust, pulling me back from solemn thoughts. I didn't blink for fear my tears might dislodge and there'd be another frustrated cross-examination of my feelings. I watched the startled rook rear into flight, its black wings streaking the stone sky.

No one responded to the bell and it rattled again, like gaoler's keys, and with a new insistence. Someone else was stepping into our new strange world. There'd been no sound of a car, no crunch of gravelly footsteps. When we peered into that silvered world, we couldn't even see footsteps on the white drive. The silent snow had momentarily sedated us but now, an anxious flavour drifted in on the wind. The dark gardens glistened with shadows — it was clean, with a cruel-edged sharpness. A soundless, still world watched us through the windows, poised as if waiting to see the effect of this new visitor.

Angel entered, thin and wraith-like against the bone white backdrop. He spoke carefully. 'Would Madam require the presence of the spiritualist here in the sitting room or perhaps in the library? Most guests choose the library for the additional atmosphere.' Other families just don't seem to get asked these kind of questions on holiday. But then Mother never took us on holiday. We once went to Corfu with Dad — he booked it and 'surprised' Mother. I had been in absolute raptures diving under the waves with Dad by day and listening to him reciting Greek tales by night. He told the Sirens' tale with such appalled relish that I remember thinking he genuinely seemed to fear being dragged onto the rocks by them. But Mother swore heavily for a week. Apparently, it was middle-class and crass. Dad resisted the temptation to suggest that might suit her. It was blazing hot and Mother never let us forget that her skin was under threat and her hair would never recover.

After that, Mother satisfied her urge to pack expensive things in an expensive case by holidaying with Mirabelle in places that would never accept a child and probably wouldn't have accepted Dad either. This was my first holiday with Mother since the mythically awful trip to Greece.

Mrs Angel visibly steadied herself before she introduced Madam Zizi, who sounded more like a local bistro than a spiritual guide to another world. Rare volumes surrounded her as she sat behind a low card table at the far side of the room. The curtains were already drawn and she was lit solely by three candles, which sat precariously close to her elaborate costume. She was draped in an avalanche of cheap charity shop scarves, wrapped inexpertly about her shoulders and head. In fact, she had so many veils and accoutrements it was not beyond the realms of possibility that she would soon begin dancing and pulling away each veil before demanding one of our heads on a plate. Her bangles and chains jostled and bickered with one another. The smell of mothballs raised the possibility that she may well have fallen out of one of the many wardrobes and wandered down here still smothered in old clothes. The light was so dim and the wig so badly fitting and low slung across her face that only her squinting eyes were visible.

We lingered at the door, wary as schoolgirls outside the Head's office. The dog ground itself low into the floor, baring its teeth and growling as if it sensed something.

'No.' Bridget held up her hand, trying to calm the animal. 'No, I'm afraid this is not what Mr Bojangles and I were expecting.'

'It's a fortune telling. She's a fortune teller. What more was there to expect?' Aunt Charlotte asked incredulously.

'*This* is a book club so we were *expecting* discussions of books not this . . . this heathenism!'

'Just to be clear, Bridget,' I asked, 'when you say, "we were expecting", you mean you *and* the dog, don't you?'

'Mr Bojangles has expectations too!' She turned and began walking away, tugging on the dog's lead, its eyes sharp with fear. 'We will be spending the evening in our room reading.'

'It's a dog. It can't read,' I called, but she didn't respond.

'Please excuse her. How do you do, Mrs Zizi?' said Mother, loudly, as if she was speaking to a befuddled bag lady, which to be fair, seemed appropriate.

The woman nodded slowly, and the entire stack of scarves and jewellery lowered and trembled. We watched, anxious to see if she could pull the tangle back up or if the lot would fall off in a great bundle of washing. Finally, painstakingly, she righted herself and the mountain of clothing.

Mrs Angel coughed pointedly. 'Perhaps you ladies would prefer to visit Madam Zizi individually so as to preserve your *secrets*.' She smiled a long, slow grimace that looked as though she was suffering from a digestive disorder.

'We don't have any secrets,' Mother barked.

I laughed spontaneously.

Mother re-issued *The Look*.

'I'll go first.' Less seemed to be the only person actually inspired by this. 'I'm the most spiritual person here so

I'm the most likely to get something out of the experience. I've found my inner self.' Less had spent so long searching for herself, finding herself, losing herself again that it must have been positively bewildering for her. Unfortunately, she always seemed to find her way back to us.

Mother had known Less since university and since then Less had tried everything: Pilates, yoga, juice cleanses, charcoal cleanses, cardiac diets, blood-based diets, macro, baby food, vitamin injections, vegetarianism, veganism, Paleo. She'd been gluten-, alcohol-, caffeine- and lactose-free. In fact, she was so free of everything, it's a wonder she didn't just float off like an untethered balloon. I'd have been very happy to cut the rope to be honest. Most people would. Most people see through her eventually. Most people except Mother. Even when Less stole from us.

The only thing anybody really needs to know about Less is that she's a liar and a thief. She stole from my mother and father on numerous occasions but Mother turned a blind eye. Cash went missing every time she came to the house: a random ornament, a scarf, jewellery. Dad often challenged Mother about her pilfering friend, but Mother would not accept it. This woman somehow remained in Mother's blind spot and nothing anyone could do would lead to her being exposed. Finally, when large sums of money vanished along with some family heirloom cufflinks, he spoke up. On that occasion, Less had left her herbal tea untouched on the kitchen table, trails of steam still lingering above it, and didn't reappear for what seemed like years. It was as if, like a cheap trick, she'd just disappeared into smoke. Aunt Charlotte said it was *to* smoke — weed to be precise. Aunt Charlotte was always sticking the knife into Less.

'Less, you are *such* a trooper!' I said, with a deep smile. 'Don't you remember, Mother, how Dad would say so himself?' I paused as if I was remembering, but I was really imagining slowly pushing a pin into her Voodoo doll. 'Wait, was it "trooper" he said?'

Mother rolled her eyes.

'I don't know why you let *her* come!' Less blurted.

'What? What did I say wrong?' I said innocently.

'She's always—'

'Me? What about you with your—'

Mother held out her arms semi-messianically. She closed her eyes.

'Does Madam require assistance?' Angel enquired of Mother's awkward pose.

Mother opened one eye and slowly began to lower her arms.

'Let's just get on with it,' Aunt Charlotte said, with grim joviality.

Less did some of her loud ritual breathing exercises to centre herself and attract attention. When she did this, there was always the hope that one day she might stop breathing entirely.

She adopted her usual air of serenity and drifted into the library.

'Watch the silver, Angel,' I managed to cry before the door was closed on her seething little face. Not actually on her face, unfortunately.

I'd hoped there might have been a traditional body-in-the-library style scene at this point but unfortunately Less reappeared half an hour later with a great big supercilious grin that cried out to be slapped. She felt *spiritual*. I felt murderous. It is remarkable how many times these two reactions have gone hand in hand for me and Less.

'So, how was it?' Aunt Charlotte whispered.

Less closed her eyes momentarily. 'Enlightening!'

'Did she tell you anything about yourself that you didn't already know?'

'No, no, Less knows everything about herself.'

Mother stared at me intently.

'I felt like she definitely knew me, that there was a real *connection* there.' Less fixed her gaze on the middle distance, as spiritual people often do. We all followed her eyeline and looked at the spot on the wall. 'She knew all about me,' Less sighed in her hideous Zen-like manner. She turned and walked out, fluttering with incantations about chakras and karma.

Mother straightened and said, business-like, 'Right, who's next?'

A black hole of enthusiasm opened up. Finally, Aunt Charlotte relented. 'I suppose I'll give it a go.'

Angel had appeared at the door. He was the sort of man who had an unnerving ability to be in a room without seeming to have entered it at any point, as if he had been conjured from nothing but air.

'That won't be necessary, Madam.'

'I beg your pardon?' Aunt Charlotte puffed.

'What I mean to say, Madam, is I can see that enthusiasm is waning and since we have only our guests' enjoyment at the front of our minds, might I suggest some other form of entertainment? Trivial Pursuit perhaps or—'

'Out of the way man!' Aunt Charlotte blustered. She looked terrifyingly Brynhildr-esque.

'Madam, I simply . . .'

She fixed her gaze on him. 'You, sir, will not deny me my spiritual enlightenment. Now, move or I will move you.'

Angel bowed his head like a dog backing down. 'Let me escort you, Madam.'

'If you must, Lurch.'

We listened to Angel knocking hard on the door and shouting, 'Another guest wishes to hear the predictions of Madam Zizi.'

I choked back a laugh.

'She must be deaf,' Mother said quietly. 'Sounds like *he's* trying to raise the dead.'

There was another theatrical pause, before a small voice called, 'Who will question the powers of the spirits now?'

And then we heard Aunt Charlotte call back, 'It is I, Charlotte.'

A large door creaked in the distance as if the BBC sound department had taken up residence.

I turned to enjoy the moment of farce with Mother, but she was already whispering on the sofa with Mirabelle. The smile slid from my lips. This is one of the most hateful things people do to each other. They exclude. Don't get me wrong, I have always felt excluded, so it doesn't usually hurt, but sometimes, just sometimes, it nettles me.

Aunt Charlotte was gone for an inordinate period of time during which we had nothing to do. I watched Mother and Mirabelle whispering and giggling, and I felt the old familiar jealousy gnawing deeper and deeper. I ground my fingernails into the palms of my hands. Just once, I wanted her to hold me, like I saw other mothers hug their grown-up daughters. I wanted her to laugh with me and say easy words like '*We just love hanging out together. We've always been really close. We're best friends.*'

As with all fantasies, they only make reality seem worse. Mother hasn't even responded to my friendship request on Facebook and it had been her idea in the first place that I go on social media to try and find some friends.

Mother and Mirabelle gradually began to slip into vague intoxication, their conversation dissolved into the occasional observation about a mutual acquaintance followed by some noises in agreement. Mirabelle's head began to nod as she drifted in and out of sleep. Angel had disappeared again — he just seemed to evaporate without anyone noticing, presumably due to the constant stream of requests for drinks.

We sat in uncongenial silence, the fire gently highlighting Mother's brooding face. Just as she was about to launch into another catalogue of my failures, Aunt Charlotte returned, uncharacteristically quiet and pale.

'Charlotte?' Mother stood.

Aunt Charlotte perched on the edge of the frayed arm of the sofa — a perilous decision for such a broad woman. She rocked and stared into the fire. 'Interesting.'

'Charlotte, what on earth is the matter? You look like you've seen a ghost!'

'Aunt Charlotte?' I asked. 'What did the woman say?'

She flickered from her trance and managed a half-hearted smile, but corpses have looked better. 'Nothing much really,' her voice had an uneven quality to it. 'She wittered on about meeting a dark stranger. She did say something rather strange. Something about "Who will be your sister's keeper?" I'm afraid I didn't really understand and that was about it, really. I'm fine,' she waved a hand weakly, 'just a little tired. Certainly takes it out of you, all this spiritualism! No wonder Less looks so *drained* all the time.'

Mother still looked concerned. She began to tinkle the dreadful little bell to call Angel again. It had been used so much that evening that it began to sound like a crazed cat was loose in a room full of birds. 'You need a stiff drink, Charlotte. Brandy, that's what you need.'

'No, no. I think I'm just going to take myself off to bed. I'm tired and this place is as cold as a tomb.'

The fire was raging.

Without a sound, Angel was at my shoulder again. I couldn't even hear him breathing now.

'Ah, be an angel, Angel, and bring a brandy for Madam.' Mother smiled at her attempt at humour.

Angel did not. From the look on his face, I presumed Mother wasn't the first to hit upon the idea that his name might be a source of dry wit.

'No, really, Pandora. I'm going to take myself off to bed. I want to enjoy tomorrow.'

'Suit yourself. Might as well bring the bottle,' she called after Angel, before he disappeared again.

Aunt Charlotte slipped away quietly. Interest in the fortune teller's tales had dwindled to nothing on the basis that it was, in Mother's words, 'utter horse shit'. Mirabelle stirred and said she'd go and sort it out.

'I'll pay, darling.' Her hand lizard-like on my mother's arm. Mirabelle always mentioned when she was paying for something — twice to my recollection.

She left me to watch Mother polish off the brandy and fall into snoring beside the fire. The flames dwindled and a dense, burnt air settled in. Eventually, I left her there. When I've attempted to move her in the past, it has ended badly.

As I walked up the dimly lit staircase, I heard Angel whisper softly from below, 'Have a good night,' in such an ominous tone I imagined him adding, '*If you can!*' and laughing maniacally.

The house fell into a corrupted sleep that night, our heads thick with fire smoke and stale brandy. I half-heartedly fought sleep, knowing it would come for me, knowing what waited on the other side. I held the open Bible and shakily drank the brandy, trying hard to fix my mind on a day, just one day, when I hadn't felt anxious or scared, where the day hadn't ended with my lonely, wide eyes staring into a frightening world. The memory of those days grows loose, the details faint no matter how frequently I go over them, like lines in a play.

The darkness here was so complete, it blindfolded us. But with one of my senses completely dead, others were heightened. The smallest sounds were magnified and all I could do was listen as the windows chattered like old ladies' teeth. The soft insistent patter of the snow against the glass sounded like small fingers padding at the windows. The minutes were being tapped out for us.

Rule 7: Don't go out into the snow alone.

ISOLATION

We woke to a childhood world thick with snow. A layer of fine icing had encased the crumbling carved face of the house until it bore more than a passing resemblance to Miss Haversham's cake.

Our isolation had a perfection to it, a pureness that was almost beautiful. But isolation can often lead us on to dark thoughts.

When do we stop embracing the need to run out into the snow? Dad would take me sledging knee-deep in icy cotton-wool drifts. We'd wade to the top of the hill and catapult ourselves into oblivion. We'd pretend to be dragons breathing out smoke and we'd shoot straight through the white trails of our own breath. A snowbound world was not a silent one then. It was filled with shrieking voices, the slice of plastic on snow and the crunch of feet racing on to the next excitement.

When I abandoned childhood, snow brought stillness. It hindered movement. I couldn't get to college, the shop, anywhere. It wasn't something to speed through anymore. It was another enemy.

Snow holds everything in a freeze frame of silence. It preserves.

We all sat in solemn wonder at the breakfast table as the great windows glared back at us from a blinding white sea. It was a sheer light, icicle white and so luminous its ferocity burned our sleep-soaked eyes. Great pillows of snow had gently eased up against the glass at the bottom of the French doors. Nothing moved. It was quiet but not peaceful. The room was cut through with a sharp tension, an anxious pause, as if we were waiting.

Angel was there. Maybe he had been all along, but my sight only now adjusted to his silhouette. He was flustered, his usual composure slightly ruffled. As if to highlight this, in one step he stumbled and fell to his knees, dropping a plate. Shards of vintage china bloomed across the carpet along with bacon and great gobs of scrambled eggs.

Everyone sat rigid on sudden alert. Mirabelle glared from above her strategically placed reading glasses. Her black eyes swam like tadpoles behind the grey glass. She wasn't reading so there was no need to have them on. In fact, to my recollection, I'd never seen her reading which was surprising given that this was a book club. She had no real need of the reading glasses save to give herself a veneer of respectability.

'Aha, a fallen Angel,' Mirabelle observed sharply.

'Don't be so insensitive, Mirabelle.' Less was serenely irritating this morning. She sat immaculately as if scolding us for our poor postures. She took each mouthful of quinoa-infused air with a meticulous opening and closing of her mouth that made me want to force feed her.

Mother was locked in a filthy hangover, which she was disguising as food poisoning.

As Angel clambered to his feet unaided, he began scooping the shattered petals of the plate and the splattering of eggs into a small pile.

I pushed back my chair. 'Let me help you.'

'You will not,' Mother flared. 'We're paying a fortune for this!'

The dog bolted out from under the table and began gnawing at the bacon.

'Can't you control that thing?' Aunt Charlotte grumbled.

'He's only helping!' Bridget ran forward.

Mrs Angel appeared. People had a habit of just appearing here. She began solemnly sweeping away the mess. She glanced at her husband and then quickly looked away again. She saw me watching.

'Would Madam require anything further? Some fresh tea perhaps?' Her smile was crisp and methodical.

'I'm not paying for it, you know' — words that tripped from Mother's mouth with such regularity that it should be emblazoned on some sort of crest for her. It'll be carved on her headstone. Though my therapist says I shouldn't linger on that image too often.

Angel did not glance up from sweeping away the remains of the china, but the dog could not be dissuaded from the food.

'I hope this is all organic,' Bridget said, as she stood over the Angels. 'Mr Bojangles only eats organic.'

'I need to get a message to London,' Aunt Charlotte announced, as if she'd stepped out of a Victorian melodrama.

'I'm afraid that won't be possible, Madam.' Mrs Angel stood up, her smile broken-glass sharp.

'I can assure you that it is possible and you will sort—'

'Madam, we do not have a telephone here, as the literature clearly states. This is a retreat from the pressures of the outside world. And I'm afraid the driveway is blocked with snow as is the road into the village. It's impassable. When we went out—'

'We shall starve to death!' Bridget screamed. 'We have to get out. Now!'

Mrs Angel watched her with slow, patient eyes.

'We could eat the dog,' I suggested to lighten the atmosphere. It didn't.

Bridget looked shocked for everyone else's benefit and covered her dog's ears.

'I thought you were vegetarian,' Mirabelle sneered.

'Madam, there *is* sufficient food,' Mrs Angel began in a deliberate voice. 'We are no strangers to isolation here.'

'That's obvious,' Mother murmured from her fragile shell of pain. I could smell last night's brandy festering with a familiar foetid sweetness on her breath. No matter how exhausted or anxious I am, I never fail to brush my teeth before breakfast for this very reason. No one wants to smell the remains of someone's sorrow.

Aunt Charlotte rose and seemed to expand to fill the space around her. 'Young man.' Angel looked suitably mystified. 'I am not accustomed to isolation. I am a member of three bridge circles and the Women's Institute. I do not *do* isolation.' Her hands were firmly embedded on her hips. 'Who's got a mobile with them? Has anyone got a signal?'

It had been the first thing I'd checked when the long road of boredom that lay ahead became obvious.

'What?' Less looked aghast. 'No phones, no mobile, no internet, no transport? It's like a prison!'

'You'd know,' said Aunt Charlotte.

'We shall all die!' Less was beginning to sound genuinely alarmed, but it's hard to tell with her. 'We have to get out. I can't be kept in confined spaces.'

'Because of all that solitary?' Aunt Charlotte laughed.

'It's a mansion,' I offered.

'I have just as much right to speak as anyone else here,' Less said, defiantly. 'I am a human being and I deserve—'

'We could see it as a good opportunity to discuss the book.' Everyone ignored Bridget.

'Oh, for God's sake, Less, please spare us from your *rights*. Someone has got to take control here.' Aunt Charlotte looked ready to lead her troops — possibly to certain death but nonetheless, she was keen.

'Oh, and that should be you should it? Just because you're loud and stupid?'

'How very dare—'

'Stop it! Stop it right now! All of you.'

The room fell silent and we stared at Mother. Her eyes looked darker, more sunken than usual, her skin as gauze thin as a moth's wing. Suddenly she looked older, in an exhausted, resigned way. Her face seemed longer, drawn down by time. I had grown so used to her being self-assured and polished that the slightest gap in her armour, the slightest slip was magnified. I relied on her utter perfection but I knew she was flawed — just how flawed, I didn't know yet.

Mother spoke slowly, as if picking her way carefully through the words. 'We must work together. All this will pass. Besides, it's only a weekend. We can survive that, I'm sure. Now, Charlotte, if you desperately need to make contact with the outside world, can I suggest a small search party wraps up well and takes a walk to the end of the drive to assess the accessibility.'

'It was blocked when we—' Angel began.

'Oh, for goodness' sake,' Mirabelle said. 'Can't we just settle in here for the day and deal with this tomorrow?' This was uncharacteristically lazy of Mirabelle. I watched her shift awkwardly.

'We could discuss the book,' Bridget offered.

'I can't believe Charlotte has anything so pressing that we need to freeze to death in the wastelands so she can make a phone call.'

'How bloody dare you, Mirabelle? I will have you know that the WI has a meeting this Thursday and I am chairing. I need to secure my keynote speaker. I don't suppose that would mean anything to you as you've never organized a thing in your life — least of all your life!'

'And what is that supposed to mean?'

'You know very well.'

We stood around in a pack and watched Aunt Charlotte and Mirabelle.

'If you are referring—'

'You know exactly what I'm referring to. Your insistence on being my sister's personal limpet. On drowning her with your constant presence. If George were here today . . .'

A sharp tension seemed to vibrate in my ears with a thin, shrill note as if the room was suddenly filled with static. His name fell like darkness. Even the Angels, busy cleaning, seemed to understand the unspeakable that had been spoken and stopped. George. His name always seemed so alien to me. He was Dad — never George. His name seemed to jar whenever I saw it written down on documents or heard it spoken by officials, which there seems to be a storm of when your father is dead. There is never really room on the form to explain — Name of Mother — *Pandora*; Name of Father — I always hesitated, unsure whether to put *George (dead)* or nothing as if he didn't exist anymore. Speaking or writing his name made him a different person. It was as if he were a complete stranger with a whole other life I never knew. I suppose that is the same for many fathers and their small girls. We can't know the adult life they lead and still hold them in such complete perfection. Once the light goes out on their saintliness, they become human, real and imperfect. The man called George was imperfect in a way that Dad never was.

I closed my eyes and heard the rook's brittle laughter again. My dad's voice was there, as always. '*I can't see her . . .*'

I swayed and fell back into the chair.

'Ursula.' It was Mother's voice.

I opened my eyes quickly, but she wasn't looking concerned. She was irritated. She was only ever annoyed at my perceived weakness.

Less leaned over me. 'What a *display*.' She was looking at me, but her words were directed at the rest of the room. She let the smile leak out slowly over her face. 'Have you ever considered a career in amateur dramatics?' She laughed and looked around for approval.

'Perhaps a walk might clear everyone's heads.' Mother drew out her chair and rose with a contrived grace that she so rarely possessed. She left the room slowly, presumably so she didn't throw up. I waited for her to look back at me, check on me, but she didn't.

Mirabelle and Aunt Charlotte sat in perfect disgust with one another for a few more minutes, like children trying to out stare one another.

'Maybe we'll discuss the book later,' Bridget said quietly. I left them to their recriminations and tea.

As I stood in the hall and leaned my back against the wall, I waited for my anger to subside. I tried not to let Less get to me. But sometimes I can feel it building inside me and I can't stop it. I just can't seal up the cracks and stem the flow of all that bitterness I feel.

* * *

It was strange how much more isolated we felt when we went outside. The warm, almost cosy environment of the house had somehow served to cosset us from the extremes of the outside world. We hadn't really appreciated the enormity of our situation until we were firmly against it. Less had chosen to stay in the house, seeking solace and mindfulness in the bathroom for the rest of the morning instead. Mirabelle had decided hell would freeze over before she offered assistance to *that bitch Charlotte*, and Bridget had retired to read to Mr Bojangles. So it was just the three of us, Aunt Charlotte, Mother and I, who set off on our intrepid expedition.

Charlotte was wearing every item of thick, country clothing she owned, which gave the overall impression of an extra from *Last of the Summer Wine* being hunted on the moors. Mother was quiet, which is always disconcerting. She didn't seem to be engaged with our journey or its purpose. She was just there. I suspect sometimes she misses Dad enormously. Perhaps the mention of his name still took its toll. Even though she had found him annoying, unstylish and witless, she must have really missed him when he was gone — like old pyjamas. I'd always assumed she took an unseemly short amount of time to recover from his death but then maybe she never recovered at all. *We can't all be as melodramatic as you, Ursula*, she'd always say.

Outside, the statues and pots were fleeced with snow — nudes and gods draped in ice. By the door, a pair of goddesses stood petrified and semi-naked.

'She wouldn't make much of a hunter without any—'

'For Christ's sake, shut up, Charlotte,' Mother said, sharply.

Aunt Charlotte blustered on ahead, rambling on about her field sports group and stomping out each step, as if laying some sort of trail.

The fierce cold filled our faces. It was hard to open our eyes wide enough to let in any more than a slip of light. Stinging sharp gales buffeted us, our bodies curling over against the cold. It was a leaden sky that hung low as if it threatened to crush us. The wind shivered through to my core.

'This is madness!' Mother shouted.

Rule 8: Remember, there is a fragile line between life and death.
One wrong step and you will no longer exist.

THE FIRST BODY

That was when we saw the first body. The mess of garish scarves and matted hair against the drifts of snow was such a desolate, stark image. It was crudely obvious what we were looking at.

'The fortune teller!' Aunt Charlotte said in disbelief. She was rammed so deep beneath the fallen tree that the brutality of her death was clear. It only took a moment for that image of her poor, twisted body to scorch itself into our minds. We would never forget that scene.

No one forgets their first dead person. Mine, of course, had been Dad.

When I found him, what remained of his life seemed so precious, so delicate, that I handled him with the greatest care and sensitive touch. As the life eased out of his body, his head grew heavier in my lap, not lighter. But I still held him, even though it was futile, as if he were a glass shell of himself, more cherished than ever. Even when all that remained was a slack mask of the face he once wore, empty of every thought and emotion he'd ever had, I held him as I would a newborn who had all its life ahead. No such honour had been accorded this woman.

I wiped the tears away quickly and as I looked into that desolate makeshift grave, I felt sick. I should have felt ashamed for the way I viewed those pitiful remains, but I didn't. I just felt revulsion at what that poor old soul had been brought to through no fault of her own.

She lay at a crippled, unnatural angle, her head pushed face down and sideways, her legs flared out. Strands of black hair were drawn out mermaid-like across the snow. Without death's hands on it, the picture might have been somewhere near beautiful. But it was very far from that. We waded towards her through the thick drifts of snow, her faded chiffon scarves catching in the wind and rising up like hands against the iron sky. My mind snagged on random snapshots of my dad dying and laid those images over this abomination. With each step, I took slow, careful breaths and wiped away each tell-tale tear as it fell.

Humanity had abandoned this woman's killer and led them to this terrible deed. This was a perfectly merciless act.

The three of us stood round the body and the silent snow drifted down like feathers, as if there was some delicacy to this brutal scene. We didn't know what to do. There were no words. We looked to each other, but none of us could speak. The air froze in our mouths and we looked at the remains of a life that lay between us. We had stood like this once before and that image returned now, overwhelming everything. I watched the line of a tear course down my mother's cheek and Aunt Charlotte pulled us in towards her. She smelled of home and lost moments that would never return. So much loss can erase parts of you.

We spent a long time in that pose, as if this had to be atoned for. I like to think we settled the old woman's spirit in those moments and laid her to rest. If we could not bury her, then in those silent minutes I felt we committed her body to whatever world awaited her.

Then the real world collapsed in on us.

What could we do in the middle of a snowstorm with a dead body? For some reason, I took out my phone and photographed it as if it was the scene of a car accident for some petty insurance claim. There was so little we could do that doing anything at all seemed helpful. She'd been wedged deep underneath the tree. We all bent down and peered closer, looking for a sign of how she might have died. Her wig hung lifeless from the side of her head revealing the dark, congealed mess of her skull against the pure white snow. She had been bludgeoned to death with a huge degree of force and purpose. The intent was without question. The murderer, and that was the first time this frightening word had sprung into my mind with all the black force of it, had not deviated from their purpose of destroying this old woman as efficiently and convincingly as possible. It was a definitive, unswayable need to kill her, obliterate this woman's life completely, that had led the hand to take up some weapon and beat out this woman's brain until there was no possibility of life remaining. The weapon? We scoured the area as much as we could in the snowstorm, but there was no trace of it. This killer did not leave murder weapons to be discovered. This killer was far more efficient than that.

No one needed to ask the obvious. No one said, '*What do we do now?*' There was nothing we could do. The snowstorm was thickening by the minute, and her body was heavy with death. To touch her, to drag her out seemed wrong and against nature and every detective story we'd ever read. And yet, we couldn't just leave her. I reached forward to touch her neck.

'What are you doing, Ursula?' Mother grabbed my arm. 'What if she's still alive?'

Mother let out a steady sigh. 'Of course she's not alive. Look at her!'

I waited a moment with Mother's hand on my arm. 'I need to see her face,' I said decidedly, as if I was convincing myself.

We all paused. They knew what I meant. She had been so completely shrouded by scarves and shadows in the house that none of us had seen her properly. Now, our curiosity and our human need to see her face was overwhelming. She was not a real person until I'd seen her face. I had to give her that respect at least. I could not walk away and just leave her as a dead, faceless body.

'We have to,' Aunt Charlotte said solemnly and nodded. We looked at Mother. She waited and then she nodded too.

I lowered myself to my knees, the cold seeping through my jeans almost as soon as I touched the snow. My hand was shaking as I reached towards the mess of black fibres. The wig had a plastic, synthetic feel that had begun to freeze until it was crisp. I parted the black threads, trying to avoid the streaks of sticky blood. One of the silvery scarves rippled across my arm and touched me. I flinched and looked back at Mother and Aunt Charlotte. Both stood wide-eyed, staring at me in anticipation. My quick breath clouded the air. Mother nodded and I pulled back the curtain of hair.

I froze.

'Ursula?' Mother said softly. Aunt Charlotte and Mother leaned forward. Before both swiftly recoiled at what they saw.

'Doreen Dellamer,' Mother whispered.

Doreen Dellamer. The unceremoniously sacked book-shop assistant Dad moved into the spare room. The lodger Mother had moved out after Dad's death. She polluted our mourning until finally she had drifted on to leech somewhere else. What was she doing here?

She gazed up at us mutely, battered and abandoned in the snow. She had been nothing more than a woman going about her life. How or why she had ended up in these side-show clothes masquerading as a spiritualist, I didn't know. But her presence seemed far from a coincidence.

Whatever the reason, there was no option but to leave her alone in that frozen grave until some kind of help arrived, although it was hard to imagine what that could be right then.

'We can't just leave her here!' Aunt Charlotte protested. 'What about all the animals? They'll . . . they'll rip her to pieces. She'll be buried by the snow.' She was almost pleading with us, her face anguished as if we were in some way consigning this poor woman to a fate worse than her death.

'Charlotte,' Mother said, as close to compassionate as I have heard her, 'we have to leave her now.'

'What?'

'Listen to me carefully, Charlotte. You cannot help her now. There's nothing you can do. She's gone. We can't move her. Look at the snow. We shouldn't move her. The police will want her left how we found her.'

Aunt Charlotte began shaking her head. 'Then we have to get help. We have to *do* something.'

'How?' I was shouting at her now. 'We can't go on any further in this.'

'But we can't go back there! There's nothing back there. There's no phones, our mobiles don't work. We can't get any help. We can't call the police. We can't . . .' Aunt Charlotte was frantic. 'What if the killer's still out here?'

Our eyes flicked to the trees and back round the lawns. The snow was coming faster now, thicker.

'We have to get back,' I shouted at Aunt Charlotte. '*Please.*'

She looked at me and then back at the body.

'Charlotte, we have to go now,' Mother said, firmly, and began pulling her arm.

We started slowly walking away and I watched Aunt Charlotte look back sorrowfully, as though we were in some way forsaking this woman. But I looked towards the outline of the snow-covered house and the closer we got the more it began to feel like it was us who had been forsaken.

The snow had already begun to form thick callipers round our legs, making anything more than the merest shuffle impossible.

With each laboured step, the reality began to grow clearer in my mind. No one was coming, no matter how loudly we might scream at the sky. We were heading towards a house, which quite possibly harboured a killer — a killer who had brutally battered an old woman to death and without ceremony, shoved her lifeless body under a tree trunk to rot with the ageing wood. We had nowhere else to go. We were stuck with the murderer, isolated from the outside world, with no escape.

Rule 9: Nothing brings out a person's true character more than the fear of imminent death. Watch everyone very carefully.

FEAR

Death and extreme grief bring out a new liberated attitude to life. Nothing is worth anything anymore so why worry? My shoes had holes and Mother sent me to boarding school wearing them on a bleak day of rain — I couldn't even feel the soaking socks. I couldn't feel anything. I didn't feel sad to be sent away, or lonely or abandoned. I felt dead. I don't think I've felt much more in the decade or so since. I was the ghost, the mute that lay in the corner bunk, eyes open all night, barely living, my head emptied out to make room for all the grief.

Discovering a murdered woman and being trapped in a house with her killer was just one more thing happening to me. I know why it is called 'loss'. Not because that person has gone, abandoned you, but because you lose pieces of yourself. I've lost so much of myself and had to replace so many pieces that I don't even remember what the original me should look like. That person has been swept away on black dreams.

Mother always says the more emotions you show, the weaker you become. But here at the frightening peripheries of life and death it was hard to keep everything locked in. My fears, my horror, they were already starting to burn through me from the inside. I didn't know how long I could keep it all together.

The weather was beating us back remorselessly. The house still seemed so distant that I began to imagine it might be a mirage, nothing more than a trick of the frozen mist. Part of me wished that was true. As we drew closer, and the shape became clearer in the white air, it wasn't relief that we felt. My mouth was dry and every breath felt sharp. I tried to stay calm, tried not to let the tears betray me, as every step drew my legs deeper into the snow. Mother and Aunt Charlotte were slightly ahead and had no time for words of encouragement or a friendly arm.

Finally, the ground felt firmer beneath our snow-heavy boots. We emerged onto a more manicured section of the lawns. The fountain was caught mid-stream, a plume of ice reaching out its crooked fingers, as if the house was drawing us in. I looked up to the windows that watched our slow approach, the empty eyes of the house, watching our struggle. A shadow passed over one of the panes in the attic. Mrs Angel had said it was off-limits due to structural concerns. Such worries were irrelevant as we dragged ourselves through the thick snow binding our legs.

Mirabelle was at the door, her eyes pinched as she scanned the landscape for our return. We walked on through the clouds of our breath clinging to the cold air.

'There's a body out there,' Aunt Charlotte panted. The wind seemed to beat out the seconds. 'It's the fortune teller.'

'Doreen Dellamer,' I added, and watched Mirabelle's face crinkle with half-remembered confusion.

'We need to get help. Where are the Angels?' Aunt Charlotte fell easily into a practical mode, as if she had almost been waiting to take the rudder.

Mother stamped the snow from her dainty feet, her whole frame powdered white. She shook herself like a dog.

'Get to the fire,' she commanded me, and I had no will left to do anything other than obey. There was no space for disagreement. There was a business-like air among us, an angry excitement. Something had ignited in us. We were suddenly held in a common pursuit — survival.

Mirabelle trod carefully, lesser somehow for not having experienced the journey and our discovery. She was momentarily excluded from our circle. And it stung her. 'Let's get you warm,' she said — so sincerely — to Mother, wrapping that ever-present proprietorial arm around her shoulders.

'What's going on?' I heard Mirabelle say to Mother.

'I . . . I . . . don't know. There's a body. She's been hit over the head,' Mother turned to look at Mirabelle, frowning in confusion. 'She's dead.'

A quick thunder of feet above sounded like someone running. We stopped. Silent. A door slammed. We looked to each other in confusion. The Angels were not given to racing around the corridors. They conducted themselves with a steady languor.

Less suddenly leaned over the bannister. 'You guys made it!' It had never occurred to me that we wouldn't.

She broke into a trot down the stairs her feet flying over the steps. 'You must be frozen through,' her voice, as usual, out of tune.

'We found a body,' Mother said quietly as she walked past. The way she said that word — *body* — had a distracted tone to it that made it sound out of place, almost callous. I watched her fiddling with her gloves as if they were somehow more important.

'You . . .? A body?' Less didn't move. She looked to each of our faces. 'Of what? I . . .'

'You'd better come into the sitting room.'

We walked in a steady, silent line, as if we were somehow ashamed. Perhaps we were. Well, at least some of us, anyway.

As we opened the door to the sitting room, Bridget was standing right behind it. She looked surprised, as if she'd suddenly been caught. She had. She'd clearly been listening in.

'Bridget?' Mother said.

'I was just coming to see how you were getting on.'

We stood awkwardly at the door, all of us watching her.

The fire had been going for some time and the room had built up a charcoal-blue haze. It made the air heavy and, as I sat back into the old stuffed chair, I felt my eyelids already starting to fall.

'I don't understand,' Less sat precariously on the edge of a chair and I imagined her falling off. She tried to look relaxed in a clichéd version of louche but I could see how tight the sinews were gripping every bone in her body.

'What's not to understand, Less?' Aunt Charlotte bristled in that agitated manner she has when she doesn't know what to do with the river of anxiety building inside of her. When Dad died, Aunt Charlotte was so cross about ridiculous irrelevant things, that he was wearing a dirty sweater, that his hair was unkempt and his shoes not shined. 'What will they say? What will everyone say when they come to look at him, all dirty and unloved?' I hated her then for saying that. To my childish eyes, his cheeks still looked pinched pink and ruddy with life.

'There's a body out there, in the snow,' Aunt Charlotte continued, 'and it's being covered as we speak. We can't get to the village. That's not a possibility and this stupid house doesn't even have a telephone.' She shook her head. 'Why we have marooned ourselves here I do not know. This is the—'

'Stop,' Mother said quietly. 'That's not going to help anyone, Charlotte, least of all *Doreen Dellamer.*' The way she said the name was just how I always remembered it — mockingly, almost in a deprecating way. It was definitely not fondness.

'Wait,' Less said, 'Doreen? Who the hell is Doreen? How do you know her name?'

I thought for a moment. Then they all started talking at once, just as they always do. Words were spilling around the room — fractious, stressed words said before people had time to think through what they were saying. I tried to listen, to separate the voices out. Perhaps someone was saying something that could be important in calmer moments.

Mother sighed. 'She used to lodge with us. Years ago. It was only for a few weeks.'

I remembered it as being much longer, but I didn't say anything.

'You knew her?' Bridget asked, doubtfully.

'I don't believe this!'

'What's not to believe, Less? There is a body out there in the snow. A dead body and she used to live with Pandora before she was a dead body. That's it.' Aunt Charlotte stated it so matter-of-factly. I was not used to her being the cold, emotionless one. But then each of us deals with death in very different ways.

The fire cracked into the momentary silence, sending a sharp spark into the smoky air.

'You remember Doreen, don't you, Mirabelle?' Mother looked up at Mirabelle who stood by the fire, prodding at the stray ember. Mother's eyes were softer and needier now. 'Doreen Dellamer.'

'Yes, dear,' she said, 'you very kindly took her in.'

'After she'd sacked her,' Aunt Charlotte added.

'She was the fortune teller,' Mother said, staring into the fire. I rarely hear self-doubt in Mother's voice, so it seemed strange, unnatural. She suddenly looked at me and repeated it, this time in an insistent whisper as if urging me to explain. '*She was the fortune teller.*' Mother's hands were shaking. 'Why did she do it?' she whispered. 'Why did she come here after all this time? Why could she not just leave us alone?'

I stared at Mother. The edges of her seemed to agitate and flicker against the glow of the flames. In fairness, it could still have been the effects of the cold, so I rang the annoying little bell for Angel.

It may just have been our unease or our need for something, anything, to happen, but it seemed like an inordinate amount of time before Angel appeared. He opened the door and simply said, 'Madam.' He didn't comment on our

79

disarray, our shock or the distinctly unsettled atmosphere in the room. He didn't seem to notice.

'Some tea, please,' Mirabelle asked, without looking up.

'You'd better bring something stronger too,' Aunt Charlotte added, gravely. 'We've had a shock.'

'Very well, Madam.'

'Angel,' Aunt Charlotte said in her most tolerant voice, 'there seems to be a body in the snow. Would you know anything about that?'

'No, Madam.'

'I thought you said you'd been out there earlier.' Bridget fixed her eyes on him.

'Madam?'

'Well,' Aunt Charlotte burst in exasperation, 'didn't you see the body?'

'No, Madam.'

She raised her eyebrows. 'Well, perhaps you could assist in dealing with it in some way.'

'Yes, Madam.'

'For God's sake, man!'

Mother leaned forward and placed a firm hand on Aunt Charlotte's knee. Staring sharply into Aunt Charlotte's face, she said, 'What Madam meant to say was could you, in the circumstances, perhaps suggest something?' I felt as if there was a conversation being conducted here that was entirely different to the words that were being said. Mother continued speaking to Angel but still looked meaningfully at Aunt Charlotte. 'Our understanding is that we are cut off from the outside world at present and we have no ability to call the police or obtain any form of assistance whatsoever. Would I be correct in that assumption, Angel?'

'Yes, Madam. I'm afraid we will have to wait until the weather lifts.' Again, he started for the door, studiously avoiding looking directly at any one of us.

'Angel,' Less called, 'are you not going to ask who the body *is*?'

Angel paused, half-turned to the door. 'Madam?'

'It was your bloody fortune teller!' Aunt Charlotte shouted, pushing Mother's calming hand from her knee. 'Shame she didn't see that coming, eh?'

The tendons on either side of Angel's neck stretched so taut he gave the immediate impression of being a puppet pulled up for its performance. 'If that is all, Madam, I will see to the tea.'

Aunt Charlotte shook her head theatrically.

'Yes, thank you, Angel,' Mother said flatly.

'And don't forget Mr Bojangles's treat,' Bridget called from her snug little chair next to the fire with the dog at her feet. I watched her closely. She looked very content for a woman who'd just been confronted with news of a brutal murder.

* * *

Later, we sat by the fire cradling our warm, steaming tea, staring into the depths of the scorched kindling as if it would somehow heal our eyes and burn away what they'd seen. We studied the amber flames, none of us able to process a thought.

Fear is a great leveller. None of us can know how our neighbour will feel it, but we have all known it. We all *know* it when it crawls in. It has a very distinct flavour. There is no confusing it with any other emotion. Not like love — that can be comfort, passion, lust, the need for companionship. Love can be all of those things or a pick-and-mix bag of emotions. Fear though, that stands alone. It is pure and unmistakable and there was no mistaking that we were all deep within its folds now.

Rule 10: You must set out everything you know. Don't pick out the facts that fit your theory.

THE THINGS WE KNOW

'All we know is that she used to be the lodger and then some-how she's a fortune teller and now she's dead,' Mirabelle said.

'No,' I said quietly.

'I knew we should have stuck to discussing the book.'

'Oh, be quiet, Bridget. Mirabelle is entirely correct,' Mother said, her words sharp with frustration.

'People can change profession, move house,' Less said slowly, as if to emphasize her own stupidity. 'Who are we to say that spiritualist is not a reasonable profession? A person of my gifts has had to consider such options. My guru-mentor tells me regularly, "Less, you should not hide your gifts away."'

'I'll bet he does,' Aunt Charlotte murmured.

'Listen,' I continued, undeterred, 'we know *much* more.'

'Do we?' Aunt Charlotte gave her best impression of someone who was listening.

'She probably didn't mean you, Charlotte,' Mirabelle sighed.

'For a start, we know she's not simply dead.'

'Oh, Ursula, I can very much attest to the fact that she is.' Mother never listens if she can speak. 'We saw her. Trust me, she is not out there stalking the snow-covered forests.'

Less emitted a high-pitched squeak of fear, which, in turn, elicited a similar *yap* from the dog. In many ways, it was amazing how similar Less sounded to an annoying, yappy little dog.

'What I mean to say is, she is not just dead. She has been *murdered*,' I said. The room paused to consider this, and, like that, our view suddenly shifted.

'There is no earthly way she did that to herself,' I continued. 'Someone did it to her and that someone used quite a lot of force. They didn't just kill her, they *meant* to kill her. So now we know two more facts other than that she is simply dead.'

Finally, the congregation began to focus.

'What else do we know?' I continued. I knitted my fingers together tightly, so no one could see them shaking. 'Her name? Possibly. Over ten years ago she went by the name Doreen Dellamer but here she goes by another, Madam Zizi, clearly a made-up name but it lends itself to the possibility that her other name was made up. But that's not important.'

Mother sighed as if she'd been reeled in and then let out too fast. She has a very low concentration level.

'Shouldn't we leave all this *sleuthing* to the police?' Bridget suggested.

'And how exactly are we going to do that?' I was getting impatient. 'We're trapped here, if you hadn't—'

'I just think if we all settle down and discuss the book, it might take our minds off all this nasty business.'

An aggressive silence fell. Nerves were beginning to fray.

I cleared my throat and began in a taut voice, 'What *is* important is that Doreen Dellamer felt the need to hide her identity from us, not just with her name but with her clothes as well. All those swathes of scarves and veils were not necessary to create the impression of being a fortune teller.

There were far too many and, indeed, created a more farcical effect than a simple few would have done. Nor was the wig a necessity. All it achieved was a very hurried change of hair colour. These items were for the sole and intended purpose of *disguise*.'

There was a gasp from Less.

I continued. 'She didn't just want to look like a fortune teller. She didn't want us to know *who* she was.' I paused and looked at my audience. 'So, what next? She could have achieved her aim of hiding her identity from us by not coming here at all. As Angel said, this house is a retreat where people come to escape from the world. No one from the village comes here and, most importantly, no one who visits Ambergris Towers ever goes to the village. There's no need and that's not the purpose of this house. This is a place of solitude. Doreen Dellamer did not need to disguise herself because we would very likely never have seen her — unless, of course, she came here. And she would need a very specific purpose to come here.'

They looked perplexed.

'So now we know two more things about our victim. She needed to come here, to see us or one of us, and she did not want us to know her identity and what connection she had to us. She had a pressing purpose to be here, but she only wanted a certain person or persons to know that purpose. She had to disguise it from the rest of us.'

'This is so complicated, Ursula dear. Are you sure we are on the right track?' said Aunt Charlotte, as if speaking to a child. 'She could just have taken up all this fortune-telling nonsense—'

'It's not nonsense!' Less shouted.

'—and we just happen to be the guests who booked her,' Charlotte finished.

'We really would be better off just discussing the book,' Bridget sighed. Even Mr Bojangles ignored her this time.

'Why the elaborate disguise — wigs, veils?' I pondered. 'Why such an arduous journey for very little recompense?'

Mother sighed and tutted. 'No concept of money, girl.'

'*I* paid the woman!' Mirabelle said.

'Yes, you did go out and see her before she left, didn't you?' Bridget raised her eyes to meet Mirabelle. 'Were you the last person to see her alive, would you say?'

'How the bloody hell would I know?' Mirabelle turned away from her.

'Let's not go blaming anyone yet,' Mother began.

'Oh, and why not, Pandora?' Bridget was as tenacious as her little dog. 'Because she was *your* lodger who you not only fired from her job but then moved out of your home?'

Everyone paused. Bridget may have been annoying but there was no denying she was right.

I watched Mother, her eyes narrowing as if she could kill Bridget quite easily. Perhaps Mother was capable of bludgeoning someone to death. I've witnessed her dealing with enough doctor's receptionists to know that.

'I didn't know it was her,' Mother said, so indignantly it somehow made it sound vaguely unconvincing.

'No,' Bridget strung out the word as she turned back to her dog, 'that is, you didn't *appear* to. Did she, Mr Bojangles?'

Mother stared at Bridget and the dog.

'So why the insistence on seeing us one at a time?' I tried to move us seamlessly on. It seemed like the right time to take the conversation away from Mother. 'Doreen Dellamer would know very well who we were. We'd not changed our names or how we look. And yet she doesn't come to us and announce herself. She doesn't say, "Oh, hello, Pandora. Remember me — the annoying lodger." God knows, she visited us plenty of times after Dad died. She wasn't shy of us then with her insistence on returning for various items she had supposedly left at our house. She knew us and didn't mention it. No, no, this time, she hides away in the library under the cover of candlelight, heavily disguised and using a pseudonym. She does not let any of us know that Doreen Dellamer has returned to our lives.'

We all listened to the wind filter through the curtains and sound a hollow note as it rose up through the chimney.

I leaned in closer and looked at them all. The firelight cast their tired eyes into grave shadows. 'So, now we know much more than the simple fact that she is dead,' I said, softly. 'And somebody knows more than any of us.'

Everyone waited. I felt quite pleased with the amount of anxiety I'd managed to create. After all, that was the only way someone was going to make a mistake.

'But do we know enough?' Bridget sharpened her words now.

Less shook her head, enthralled yet still stupid.

'Well, there are quite possibly people in this room now who know a lot more,' I began.

'Ursula, if this—'

I held up my hand to Mother and closed my eyes. 'What did I say was another strange aspect of Doreen Dellamer's visit?'

They were silent.

'She insisted that she must see each person *individually*.'

I waited for the information to settle in. Their faces were still perfectly clueless.

'But that was to maintain her disguise, you said,' Less piped up.

'What if it had another purpose too?'

'I'm lost,' Aunt Charlotte sighed.

'What if there was a very specific reason she had to see us, or one of us, alone?' I looked from face to face.

But I was met only with blank expressions.

I continued. 'I think Doreen Dellamer did not come here to see all of us. She came here to see one of us. To tell one of us something. Something she didn't want anyone else to know except for one person.'

They continued to sit in stupefied silence.

'Good God, I can assure you I only went to see her under sufferance!' Aunt Charlotte puffed. 'Absolute load of rot. All she kept spouting on about was meeting a tall, dark stranger and how love waits in a mysterious place. Complete nonsense. Nothing would thrill me less than some buffoon of a man. All that touching and . . .'

'But we only have your word for it,' Mother interrupted shrewdly. 'What if she divulged a great secret to you, something she was burning to tell you but couldn't tell any of us? What if she told you something about one of us? You said at the time that she mentioned being your sister's keeper.'

'No, no! That's not what she said,' Aunt Charlotte blustered. 'It was something else, about *who* was my sister's keeper. Look, I can't remember now. It was all hogwash.'

'Hogwash?' Mother looked sceptical. 'Really? We're using that are we?'

'Could one of us be in danger now?' Mirabelle asked.

The possibility was not far from everyone's thoughts.

'Wait,' said Less, 'if you're suggesting Doreen Dellamer knew something and told one of us about it, then she was murdered for what she knew.' She paused, and you could almost see the thoughts writing themselves. 'Whoever she told the information could *also* be in danger.'

A cool silence wove through the room. Another soft wave of air rippled the velvet curtains, passing new shadows across the walls.

Less squeaked and the dog responded again. 'I'm telling whoever it is right here, right now, I know absolutely nothing!'

It was gratifying to hear Less say this. '*I know absolutely nothing!*' It could be her motto or carved on her gravestone. I really should spend less time imagining what might be carved on people's gravestones, though.

'Well, we know nothing either,' Bridget said, feeding a biscuit to the dog.

'Just to be clear, by "we" you mean you and the dog again?'

'Yes, Ursula. *We* spent the evening in our room reading the book and making notes. And can I just add, if you'd all done the same none of this would have happened.'

'Can I see those notes?' I asked.

'No.'

'Why?'

She pursed her mouth. 'I haven't got them anymore.'

'Why not?'

'Mr Bojangles ate them.'

I watched her closely. 'So, you're saying the dog ate your homework?'

'Look,' said Mother, calmly, 'we are assuming the murderer is here, in this house. But it could very easily be a groundsman, someone she met on her journey home, someone she knows. She must have known everyone around here. It's a small village. On the way here, we saw plenty of lone farmhouses out there. The roads weren't blocked then, I bet. She's not that far out. I mean, her body isn't that far from the house.'

These last words had a sobering effect on the room. A life had been extinguished as we slept, maybe even as we readied ourselves for bed or sat reading a book. She'd lain there alone in her icy grave as the life slipped out of her.

'I think we are all in need of some fresh tea,' I said, and rang the infernal bell again.

Angel arrived with his usual expression of nonchalant disdain. It was hard to imagine what exactly he was doing that was so important that it shouldn't be disturbed.

'Miss.'

'Yes, Angel, I think we're going to need some more tea, if that's OK?' I said, tentatively.

'And make it hot this time.' Mother just couldn't help herself.

'Yes, Madam.'

As he left, we all followed his ponderous walk to the door, our heads slightly bobbing with each drawn-out step — every moment raising a new question about our grim butler.

'*He* knew her,' Aunt Charlotte said, so loudly he would definitely have heard. 'He must have known her.'

'And he said he went out and saw the road was impassable at some point,' Mother added slowly. 'Wouldn't he have seen the dead body?'

'And don't forget the biscuits for Mr Bojangles,' Bridget called. 'I can see your shadow outside the door, Angel.'

There was a dead silence.

'Yes, Madam,' his voice was indeed just behind the door. He'd heard everything.

We waited to hear the soft tread of his footsteps move away before we spoke again. Mirabelle poked the fire. It bristled with fresh flames. 'We don't know much about our other two housemates, do we?' she said, her eyes forming into two sharp little slits. She continued stirring the fire distractedly.

I could feel the fear growing sour inside me. My stomach spasmed and I sat with my feet poised on tiptoes, my calf muscles gripping tight. I was scared. That's the thing about being constantly destabilized, when the great gusts of life come at you, they can blow you over easily. I drove my fingers into the palms of my hands and waited for the fluttering inside me to quieten. I closed my eyes and tasted the acrid smoke again, crawling round the dark walls and sinking into my memories. Dad's wave of smoke fell through the room and I held my breath as if bottling it inside me.

'Ursula!'

I opened my eyes. Mother was staring at me as if she was reading my thoughts.

Mother has an uncanny way of knowing how I'm feeling. It's like a telepathy between us. Many mothers and daughters describe this. I've read about it a lot, how some mothers grow so close to their daughters and have such a bond with them that they feel their joy, their pain, their loss. When Dad died, I hoped that Mother was feeling the same desperate grief that I was. It certainly accounted for her actions — sending me away, building a cold shell around herself.

'Perhaps we should question our dutiful butler and housekeeper a little closer,' Mirabelle said, sceptically. 'After all, they did suggest Madam Zizi in the first place.'

'Does this mean that, yet again, we are not going to discuss the book?' We all ignored Bridget.

Rule 11: When there's a murder, everyone starts acting suspiciously, even the innocent. Everyone has something they want to hide.

THE THINGS WE DON'T KNOW

No one spoke as we waited for the Angels to return. The room was solemn. It had a funeral's dark silence to it now. There was a strained atmosphere with so much unsaid, so much held in and all those fears and nerves swilling through us in that deathly quiet. A new figure stalked among us, silent and pensive, a patient spectre who waited. My sour nausea was beginning to subside, but it seemed as if we were just paused before our fates unfolded.

I don't cope well with the unexpected. Someone took that woman's life. They could have fled or they could be in this room — with us right now, watching our every thought. A cold trickle of breath, at the shoulder of the next victim . . . slowly reaching out to touch them.

The sitting-room door slammed like a cell door.

Angel stood in a cold light, a suspicious nature now circling him.

'Madam.' Even his voice seemed to have acquired a slippery edge that I hadn't noticed before.

'Angel, where is your wife?' Aunt Charlotte demanded. 'We asked for you *and* your wife.'

'She is indisposed, Madam.' He didn't meet anyone's gaze. 'If I may be of—'

'Indisposed? Indisposed? There's a bloody body out there, Angel. A dead woman.' Less's voice was now so high-pitched that the dog responded every time she spoke.

Both edges of Angel's mouth slipped down giving him the distinct look of an aged ventriloquist's dummy. Somehow, today he seemed less polished. His hair was not quite combed as smooth as usual, his tie was a little off centre. Something about his general demeanour was out of kilter, as if I was looking at an imitation of the real man. A very good imitation but not quite the same.

He cleared his throat. 'Mrs Angel is unwell, Madam. We were both loathe to intrude as it seemed a matter of some delicacy.'

'Matter of some delicacy?' Less spat. 'The fortune teller's bloody well dead — there's nothing delicate about it at all.' For a woman who spent the majority of her time in a *serene place*, or an *immersive meditative plane*, Less struggled to stay calm. Admittedly, the discovery of a dead body would cause most people alarm but Less had switched from annoying quinoa radiance to raging panic in a matter of mere seconds.

'Right, I'm going to say it if no one else will,' Aunt Charlotte said, firmly. 'Is Mrs Angel dead?'

His face gathered in confusion. 'No, Madam.'

'Look, what the hell is going on here, Angel?' Mirabelle stirred the fire again, as if kindling her thoughts.

I looked around the room. Everyone had a fractious edge to them now, too alert, too jittery.

Great swathes of emotion push people to the outer limits of their personalities. Some become increasingly erratic and unstable, whereas others see it as an opportunity to take control.

'Angel, we need to ask you a few questions,' Mother said carefully, even a little slyly perhaps.

I almost pitied him. Whenever I'm faced with great periods of stress in my life, which I would have to admit I've experienced a few too many times, I always bear in mind my little motto — keep your friends close and your mother even closer. Not that I have any friends.

Angel stood, awkwardly, by the door, as if maintaining a secure escape route. I suppose, from his point of view, if he were not the murderer, one of us, or all of us, could be. Except the dog.

'Angel,' Mother began, 'as I believe we explained quite plainly, there is a dead body some ten minutes' walk from here.'

'Seemed like further than that,' Aunt Charlotte interrupted.

'That's because you're fat,' Less added.

They instantly sat taut like two cats ready to pounce.

Mother took a breath to calm herself and then continued, slowly as if she was setting this out in order for herself, 'As I believe Charlotte mentioned, somewhat indelicately—'

'I was stressed, for God's sake!'

'—yes, Charlotte, we all are. As I was saying, upon closer inspection, we could see that it was the fortune teller you had booked for last night.'

We all watched Angel closely. There was a guardedness about him, an agitation. In fairness to him, we were all staring at him as we disclosed the details of a dead body. He moved slowly from foot to foot, his hands tightly gripped behind his back. Even the way he blinked seemed cautious, pre-judged. I watched him roll his lips between his teeth as if he was sealing in his thoughts.

'That is extremely unfortunate, Madam,' a doubtful shadow crossed his face but was quickly lost. I watched the lump in his thin throat rise and fall as he swallowed deeply. 'Perhaps I should bring the tea, Madam.'

'Tea?' Less shouted incredulously. Her voice was so high-pitched now it was beginning to take on the almost imperceptible sound of a dog whistle. Mr Bojangles looked confused. 'Tea? There is a dead woman out there and you are going to solve that with tea?'

'I think Mr Bojangles could do with some refreshment,' Bridget said. 'He's had a nasty shock.'

'Dear God! Shut up about the bloody dog.' Less was shaking.

'Oh now, what's happened to all your calmness and zen, Less?' Aunt Charlotte goaded. 'Just an excuse to get naked and smoke "wacky baccy", I reckon.'

'Angel, tea would be very welcome, thank you,' said Mother. You can always tell when Mother's stressed because she's polite.

* * *

Angel was gone for an inordinate period of time during which the cold silence was punctured by a single sharp scream that died almost as quickly as it emerged.

'Bloody rooks,' Mirabelle grumbled. 'I'd have them all shot.' She poked the dwindling fire. 'We forgot to ask for logs.'

Aunt Charlotte frowned as if she was trying to remember something and took a swig from her hip flask. She offered it around and there was a noticeably large, stained circle of Revlon Kiss Me Coral around the top. There was something about her lack of secrecy, her blatant showing of the hip flask, that repulsed me. I realize this is hypocritical of me, given my biblical secret, but that's not something I share with anyone else. Secrets are important to people. They make them whole.

No one took Aunt Charlotte up on the offer of her hip flask.

The world beyond the long French doors was now such a ferociously sheer white that it made my eyes ache. It was as if the ice was creating its own light — a light that hovered above the snow in an indigo haze so vivid that vague halos outlined the statues and snow-covered topiary. It was an unreal world that bore no relation to the reality that slept beneath. The unearthly shapes were so completely muffled, the air so frozen still, that the landscape we knew had been suspended. The snow re-drew everything into unfamiliar, enigmatic shapes. The frosty light traced across the snow, glittering in sharp waves.

I couldn't stop imagining the thick stream of Doreen's blood pouring out soundlessly onto this vivid white world — a simple puddle of her life slipping away in a blackening stain.

But it slowly began to occur to me that she had left very little stain though. Her eyes had been open, caught in the moment of her death. Did the film of her eyes reflect the face of her killer in those last seconds? Or maybe the killer crept behind her with such stealth through the frozen darkness that the sudden brutal blow came without warning. How easy it must have been in that dead world of night.

The snow hadn't stopped since our discovery. She would be completely covered now. What would be there when the snow melted and drained away? Would it suck all her thick blood into the soil or would her body still be fringed with the dark crust of it? Would she be beautifully preserved in her violent death as if packed in ice, like meat? A picture began to form in my mind of her fragile form and what exactly we had seen.

Angel returned with the tea tray, visibly more disturbed and nervous, his skin a sickly pallor and gleaming with sweat. He looked ill. Perhaps it had taken some time for our words to worm their way into his understanding. He'd stood, teapot in hand, as they had formed into that picture of the fortune teller out in the woods, her body stowed away beneath the tree, her head caved in. But then it occurred to me that Angel would not be able to form such an image since he hadn't been there and we hadn't mentioned the manner of her death.

'Angel, are you not curious to know how she died?' I asked.

He didn't look up from pouring the tea. 'I thought it unseemly to ask, Madam.'

I wondered if there was a point at which the adherence to strict rules of etiquette became unnatural. Clearly, he did not believe we'd reached that point yet.

'Unseemly?' Less said, a touch of desperation to her voice. 'It was probably *unseemly* for someone to bludgeon the old dear's brains out.'

Brilliant. Less had cut straight through the veil of mystery that we could have used to test Angel. There was to be no 'Ah-ha!' moment or questions as to how exactly Angel knew the manner of the woman's death. Less had leaped upon our upper hand and crushed it. I could quite easily have bludgeoned *her* to death at that moment.

'I see, Madam,' he said measuredly. 'Perhaps we should leave all this to the police.'

'Exactly,' said Bridget, 'and then we can get on with why we came here.'

'And how exactly are we going to contact the police? Send up a flare?' Aunt Charlotte had decided to remain within the persona of a maiden aunt who did not suffer fools gladly. This was fortunate as it was the only persona she had. 'No phones, man. And the roads are clearly blocked, which you already knew, I might add. Should we light up the Bat Signal from the mansion, Mr Old Grey Butler?'

'There are no bats at Ambergris Towers, Madam.' Angel stood motionless in the silent glare of the room. 'Rooks, but not bats.' I could have sworn he gave me a quick glance, but my mind was tiring. He seemed to falter and his eyebrows meshed a little tighter. He no longer had that self-assured gait. It was as if we were being given a glimpse of the real man, which made what we'd seen before all the more like an imitation.

'Mr Angel—' I began, before Mother interrupted, of course.

'Angel will do, darling. There may be a dead body out there but that is no excuse for defying social boundaries.' Mother could be a terrible snob at any time.

'Angel, may I ask why you recommended Dor . . .' Bridget paused, 'why you recommended this *particular* lady as the fortune teller for the evening?'

He cleared his throat, giving himself time to think. 'Because she had performed the duty before, Madam. She approached us some time ago and the owners thought it would gain us some publicity.'

'It certainly will do now,' Aunt Charlotte scoffed.

'The lady has been performing the function for some time and has always been quite a hit with the guests. Nothing like this has ever happened before.'

'Well, I think that's a given!' Mother sneered. 'She could hardly be bludgeoned to death every time she came to read people's tea leaves.'

'She doesn't . . . didn't read tea leaves, Madam.'

Mother attempted to raise her eyebrows but was cosmetically challenged again. 'You seem to know a lot about her *work*. She doesn't do bloody anything anymore. She's dead and buried in the snow.'

Less squeaked again and the dog responded. I felt ever closer to bludgeoning her and the dog.

'What we're attempting to discover,' Mother continued, 'is why you chose Dor . . . *this particular lady* and whether she had any other connection to this place or its owners.'

'Not that I can recall, Madam.'

'Are you attempting to raise our suspicions, Angel?' Mother said in her most acid voice. 'Or are you just naturally evasive?'

'Madam, I do apologize if my answers are not satisfactory, but I am merely here in an employed capacity.' I don't know if everyone sounds suspicious when there's a dead body nearby. I had, up until that day, only ever seen one. But somehow, the whole sound of Angel's voice seemed to shift. It was almost imperceptible, but the vowels were sharper, less deferential and comforting — more condescending. His eye caught mine for a split second, but it was enough. His manner changed again and the congenial old man, dedicated and resigned to service, reappeared. 'Will there be anything else, Madam?' He directed the question towards Mother, whose gaze never broke.

'Yes, Angel. As I said, we will be requiring the presence of your wife.'

The room fell into an uneasy silence.

'As *I* said, Madam, Mrs Angel is—'

'Indisposed. Yes, I know. Perhaps you could redispose her as soon as possible, Angel.'

'That's not a thing is it, Mother?'

'Shut up, Ursula. Just get the woman down here, Angel. This is a murder inquiry.'

We all stared at Mother. That was the beginning of it all. We just needed someone to say it out loud.

'And biscuits for Mr Bojangles,' Bridget added firmly.

Rule 12: Write everything down, even the smallest of things that seem inconsequential at the time might be important. Find a pen. It will be vital.

THE LADY OF THE HOUSE

Mrs Angel looked firmly ahead, purposefully containing her emotions, but I could see her eyelids were swollen and fleshy from crying. She'd not just been crying — this had been a prolonged deluge of emotion. The kind of pain that digs its hands right into your chest. And yet here she was, her face set with an impenetrable casing of powder, the twin set and tweed immaculate. If a model housekeeper was required, she would have been perfect. Every hair, every look, every mannerism was just how you would draw a housekeeper.

'You required my presence.' Her voice was cold and detached. 'How may I be of assistance?'

'There's a body in the woods,' Aunt Charlotte said. 'It's the fortune teller with her head caved in.' I don't know if this was some ploy on Aunt Charlotte's part to shock Mrs Angel into a great revelation but it seemed to have the opposite effect. Mrs Angel's face gathered in on itself, a tight ball of skin forming between her eyebrows.

'How awful,' is all Mrs Angel offered.

We sat in silence and considered what she'd said.

It occurred to me that someone ought to be writing this all down. Still watching Mrs Angel's face, I started riffling through my bag, which was on the floor next to my leg. My hand involuntarily recoiled in horror, as it brushed something long, thin and plastic and I realized it wasn't my bag. I looked down just as Less snatched the bag away. I didn't say anything, but she knew I'd seen it. Mindful living, spiritual hocus-pocus Less had earthly vices. She vaped.

Mother saw this quick exchange and her eyes narrowed. Mother's mantra has always been '*I see everything.*'

Mirabelle broke the silence with another prod of the fire. How she could stand for so long by that fire was baffling. The only reasonable conclusion was that she was as cold-blooded as I'd always suspected. 'Bloody freezing in here,' she moaned. 'Where the hell are those extra logs?'

'Mr Bojangles does need a good blaze, don't you, my baby?' Bridget cooed.

I turned my attention back to Mrs Angel. She was too calm. She held her hands together as if she feared her fingers would fall to the ground if she let go. Thin, broken lines traced beneath the powder on her face, her lips cracked and dry. There was no tilt of the head, no movement of the hair, no casual touch of the forehead. She was captured in that one moment, like a specimen pushed between two slides of glass. I analysed her. Her eyes were so glazed over that it was impossible to think that she could see any of us. She was far away. Perhaps even out there in the snow, staring into the broken skull of Doreen Dellamer — weapon in hand.

Maybe I was being overly dramatic. To be fair, it must have been just as shocking to her as it was to us, the revelation that the fortune teller had met her unforeseen bloody end after a booking made by her.

'Mrs Angel—'

'Shut up, Ursula,' Mother snapped. 'Mrs Angel, did you make the booking for Dor . . . for the fortune teller?' The fact that we knew the lady's name must have been inescapable by now given the number of times we had referred to her as 'Dor . . . the fortune teller'.

Mrs Angel paused as if giving the question great thought. She didn't look at my mother as she responded. 'Yes.'

'Why?'

'I beg your pardon, Madam?'

'Why did you book the fortune teller?' Mother sounded out each word, as if speaking to a fool. It was all too obvious though that Mrs Angel was no fool.

'Because you requested it, Madam.'

All eyes travelled back to Mother. 'At your suggestion.'

Mrs Angel looked at Mother with such intensity that I was surprised Mother didn't spontaneously combust. I have imagined that before.

'No,' was all Mrs Angel said.

Mother is not accustomed to that word. It's like swearing at the Pope.

'You most certainly—'

'*Mr* Angel recommended the activity.'

If 'No' is unpalatable to Mother, then being interrupted is the second deadly sin. One thing I learned from a very young age, is that in Mother's kingdom, there are many sins, some deadlier than others. She is an unforgiving god.

'I think what my mother is attempting to discover is how you knew Dor . . . the fortune teller?'

Mother gave me the withering look she reserves for when I translate what she means in public.

'She has performed the function for the house on previous occasions, Madam.'

'Originally, woman!' Aunt Charlotte blurted out. 'When did you first meet Dor . . . the fortune teller?'

Mrs Angel closed her eyes to give the impression she was considering the question.

'It would be some years ago now, Madam.' I listened to the sound of her voice, broken, almost fragile. Sometimes the sound of the words is more important than the actual words that are said.

'And did she come to you or did you seek her out?' Aunt Charlotte asked impatiently.

'I believe the owners recommended her as a possible source of entertainment for would-be guests. It has always been popular,' she added.

'Is she local, do you know?' Less attempted to sound calm and sympathetic. It sounded insincere as usual.

'I believe so, Madam.'

'Of course she is, you idiot, Less.' Aunt Charlotte didn't concern herself with calm or sympathetic. 'Why else would she walk home?'

'She could have been meeting someone,' Mirabelle offered, and all heads turned to her. Her vast frame was lit by the dwindling fire as she leaned a proprietorial hand on the mantelpiece. 'Perhaps she was meeting the killer.'

'A secret assignation!' Less gasped.

'Why would she choose to do that in the dark and snow?' Aunt Charlotte shook her head.

'Maybe she had no choice,' Mirabelle said.

'Maybe she was in some kind of trouble,' Less added, looking around wide-eyed for affirmation as usual.

'Do I need to be here for this?' Mrs Angel enquired, contemptuously.

'Mrs Angel, I would like to know if you have ever hosted a book club before. Because, to be perfectly honest, there's not really been any opportunity to discuss any books—'

'Do shut up, Bridget,' Mother sighed.

Their bickering fell into the background of my thoughts. I looked around the sitting room with its perfect air of a country house. It had the roaring fire, the oil paintings and tiger skin rug. The leather-topped desk sat in a quiet corner, the sofas were deep, the cushions plumped. But it was not quite right. It was devoid of any human interest.

Mother has tried for many years to strip back our home to a minimalist skeleton but still our own existence bleeds through. Photographs escape her tidying, marks appear on walls where hands regularly search for a light, rugs fray and magazines collect. Papers, plugs, leads, jackets — all the associated minutiae of life builds and accumulates. Life cannot be erased when it regularly touches a house. It is in the air, a fine smattering of existence that filters through all the rooms. Seal up a house or just a room for any period of time, even a holiday, and another force begins to invade. Like a silent creeper it twines through the corridors and sits heavily on the dust-covered chairs, bringing with it a sour, musty taint.

This house had been cleared of all that cold abandonment, but only recently. Every detail had been observed but there was a definite absence of true inhabitation. The overwhelming sense was that it was devoid of real life. I looked around our well-appointed setting. This was a meticulously constructed stage. I looked at us, sitting exactly where we should be: Mother on the sofa by the fire, as if head of the table; Mirabelle next to her, when she wasn't poking at the fire; Less in the last seat of the sofa; Aunt Charlotte opposite in a large, comfy chair, her legs spread wide as always; Bridget in the corner next to the fire with her dog; and me, set furthest back from the fire in my own chair, where I could watch. We were the cast and I could not help thinking how much we looked as if we had been carefully hand selected.

'Mrs Angel,' I began. I paused, waiting for Mother to tell me to shut up but this time she didn't. She had been watching me while I was thinking. She often does this, as if she's searching for the secret of me, the core of me. She could, of course, just ask, but that's not Mother's style of parenting. 'You referred to the owners,' I continued. 'Who are they? Do they live here?'

The room slowed. The shadow of curiosity crossed each face in turn and Mrs Angel seemed momentarily wrong-footed. Perhaps I was flattering my powers of investigation. Perhaps she was just a housekeeper who knew very little beyond her job and keeping the visitors happy.

'The owners, Madam?'

I nodded.

'They don't like to be involved. The place is hired out only intermittently. They are a very private family.'

'Really? Why was I not told any of this?' Mother was moving swiftly to indignation. She clearly did not like the idea of there being a real Lady of the Manor somewhere.

'Well, how the hell did you find out about it, Pandora?' Aunt Charlotte said.

Mother paused, as if trying to remember. 'I . . . I . . . it was a very long time ago when we booked it.' She looked down at her hands and I watched the familiar tremors ripple through them. 'No, that's it, Mirabelle, didn't you get a flyer through the door? Local flyer. Don't you remember?'

Mirabelle looked vague and shot a look at Mother. They were giving a very decent impression that they were hiding something, whether it was from everyone or each other wasn't clear.

'You showed it to me,' Mother insisted, 'or was it in a magazine? Something about book clubs—'

'Even though we never discuss the book!'

'Be quiet, Bridget. *Perfect manor house to host a serene and relaxing get away*, it said. The name seemed to chime with me.' Mother paused, trying to remember. A frown settled. 'That's right, it said, *Ambergris Towers — the ideal location for your literary weekend*—'

'Without any books.'

'Bridget, please! *Complete seclusion to indulge your mind, body and soul*,' Mother continued.

It was as if each word had been crafted to pander to Mother's every need. Almost as if the author had known her very well.

'Well, was that it, Pandora?' Aunt Charlotte said, impatiently.

'No, no. There was a phone number, perhaps . . . and email address.' Mother glanced around. 'It was very sophisticated high-end marketing! There was a picture of the house and everything.'

Eyebrows began to rise.

'I sent an email to a highly proficient secretary who assured me it was exceptionally exclusive with an elite client portfolio only open to select candidates.'

Yes, they knew Mother's type all right. Anything with the words *exclusive*, *quintessential*, *heritage*, *high-end*, *select* and *elite* only drew her in like the fresh scent of mole's breath in a brand-new kitchen. It was catnip to the aspirational and Mother does aspirational as though it's a higher form of art.

'It looked elite!' Mother insisted. 'It was perfect. It was billed as a sort of quintessential manor for the twenty-first-century person who enjoys the finer things. Sort of Downton with Wi-Fi.'

'Only there isn't any Wi-Fi,' Less sniped. 'I don't know how much longer I can go without Instagram.' What exactly she was going to be posting was unclear — dead bodies? Suddenly the image of the photograph sitting on my phone of Doreen Dellamer dead beneath that tree flickered across my thoughts. I'd forgotten I'd even taken it. Things were starting to fall through the gaps again. I had to keep a grip on things.

'We all liked the look of this place,' Mother was beginning to sound desperate.

'Will there be anything else, Madam?'

'Yes, Mrs Angel.' Mother was shouting now. 'Yes, there will! Who are these owners? Who are your employers? Why is there a bloody body out in the snow?'

Mrs Angel didn't respond at first. She had a distinct quality of steel to her, an unshakeable self-assurance. She let the slow crackle of the flames fill the silence. Mirabelle poked the fire yet again.

'Mr Angel and I are contracted by White Chain, an exclusive, members' only group that provides a high-end service to owners of houses such as this and select individuals who may wish to quietly take advantage of that elite service.'

She was word perfect.

'So you don't actually know the owners?' Aunt Charlotte asked.

'No, Madam.'

'You're props.'

'I'm sorry, Madam?'

Aunt Charlotte leaned across the small lacquered table. 'You are not the housekeeper of a great house for a great lord and lady. You pretend to be that for the guests.'

For the first time since our arrival, cracks appeared in Mrs Angel's firm glazed exterior. A rogue curl of hair quivered constantly like a twitch. 'One could see it that way if one was unused to such arrangements, but I can assure you there is no *pretending* to care for this house.'

'You're just the employee of a company that mocks up weekends away. A bit like those medieval banqueting evenings or murder mystery weekends.'

'Only the murder is real here, Aunt Charlotte,' I pointed out.

Nobody spoke. The draught gently dragged the curtains in rhythmic heart beats to and fro from the windows. The snow still flurried against the ashen sky.

'I think what she is attempting to say, if a little clumsily, is that none of this is real, is it?' Mother stared intensely. Mother does not like being misled or having any facts disguised from her. That was the reason she gave me for reading my diary, anyway.

'Quite,' Aunt Charlotte said guardedly. She wasn't used to being backed up by Mother.

Less held up a large vase and scrutinized it as closely as she would a mirror. 'So what you mean is that everything here is a stage set. Nothing is real. If I were to drop this and smash it into a thousand tiny pieces, it wouldn't matter?' Her hands began to twitch.

105

Mrs Angel suddenly lunged forward. 'It's Meissen! For God's sake don't drop that.'

Less panicked and the vase slipped but she fumbled it back into her hands, her face flushed, and she replaced it quickly. 'Sorry. Sorry! None of you are making any sense.'

'How would it not make sense to have expensive ornaments in a house you were intending to market as a luxury retreat?' Mirabelle said viciously. 'How did you get to be so bloody stupid?'

'May I leave now, Madam? There are a number of matters I must attend to, including dinner and might I take this opportunity to assure you there will be nothing *pretend* about it.' The smooth veneer had been disturbed and not just by the news of a dead fortune teller.

'Yes, yes,' Mother sighed. 'You're utterly useless to us. Just go.'

'And don't forget my bath,' Less called, in an attempt to scramble back some authority after her foolish gaffe with the vase. 'Plenty of candles and don't make it lukewarm again. I like it nice and—'

'Mr Bojangles and I will need a bath too, so don't run off all the hot.'

Mrs Angel paused and I saw a distinct stiffening of her shoulders. 'Yes, Madam,' she said, without looking back.

'Well, that was completely pointless,' Mother added, while Mrs Angel was clearly still in earshot.

I waited. 'No, I don't believe so.'

'No,' Less added, still trying to retrieve some credibility after her Meissen incident, 'if you don't tell them you want it hot, they just leave a bath full of filthy tepid water with no oils, no scents, no candles. I don't know where the old bag gets all her airs and graces when she lives in such a cramped little kennel. *It's Meissen*,' she mimicked. She nonchalantly began examining each of her tinkling bracelets.

'Wait, so you've seen the Angels' apartments?' Mirabelle asked.

'Hmmm . . . ?' Less turned her bracelet like a little girl with her birthday present. I wanted to slap those silly hands right there.

'You've seen where they live,' Mirabelle prompted again.

'I like to know all of my environment before I settle. It interferes with my chakras if I feel destabilized by hidden places. I have to be aware of all—'

'Snoop around, more like,' I added.

Less gave me a distinctly non-peaceful look.

'Nick anything?' Aunt Charlotte laughed.

'How dare you!' Less shrieked. 'Pandora, are you going to let your sister talk to me like that?' She began attempting to weep, glancing round the room for sympathy.

Mirabelle grabbed the decanter. 'Oh, for Christ's sake, stop!' She poured herself a shaky brandy and didn't replace the stopper before taking a fat gulp. She shook the remains in the decanter. 'This is not going to see us through tonight. Not a chance.'

Mother reached for the bell.

'Christ, don't bring the bloody woman back. I don't think any of us need any more Mrs Angel for a while.'

'Quite right, Mirabelle,' Mother said.

'Well, I for one don't intend to go through this evening without a large quantity of brandy,' Aunt Charlotte sniffed.

I knew what she meant. I would definitely be paying another visit to the brandy in a Bible as soon as I could sneak away. I'd need to find a way of refilling without being seen, but that didn't worry me. When you are watched so closely all the time you develop new strategies for secrecy.

'I'll go,' Mirabelle said, before quaffing the remains of her glass. 'Be quicker than the corpse couple anyway.' She wobbled out of the room, swinging the decanter like a lantern.

'Listen,' I continued, ignoring Mirabelle's cross reference to corpses, 'we know that Mrs Angel knows enough about this house and its individual ornaments. We also know that she cares what happens to them.'

A room of faces stared with hazy eyes — knowing absolutely nothing.

'Women like that live and breathe the place,' Aunt Charlotte said. 'They care more than the owners usually. She knows all the items because she cleans them every day. To women like her, it matters. All this,' she waved her arm around in a slightly crazed fashion, 'it all matters to women like her. It's not just a job, it's a lifestyle.'

Mother sat up very straight and stared ahead. 'I don't think we know anything about her or Mr Angel. I think we are being lied to and this was all planned very carefully.'

'Don't be ridiculous, Pandora,' Aunt Charlotte said doubtfully.

'I think somebody set all of this up and it's no coincidence that we knew the victim.' Mother's face seemed different in the splashes of firelight. She was troubled and that, in itself, was very troubling.

Rule 13: A death makes people do things they wouldn't usually do. It changes everything. Be careful to look for the uncharacteristic acts.

UNLUCKY FOR SOME

Although I tend to do my drinking privately, Mirabelle had just returned wielding two decanters like a double-barrelled shotgun and the temptation was too much. I indulged in a medicinal sip. It was only after the glasses were emptied that we decided action was necessary. We weren't going to sit around and do nothing while Doreen Dellamer languished in the deep freeze outside: we had to search the house. I found the rallying call much easier after that nip or two of brandy. Bravery is better with booze. That should be on tea-towels. It probably is.

The received wisdom in this kind of situation is that we split up and search the house in semi-darkness. So we waited for it to go slightly darker and set off.

Shadows freely wandered the half-lit rooms like ghosts. They streamed out, thick black ribbons criss-crossing every room and hallway. Every corridor and stairwell was a patchwork of dark shapes and strange silhouettes. I was with Aunt Charlotte, on the basis that Mirabelle could only be with Mother and Less didn't want to play. She'd said she felt drained and had to retire to reanimate her chakras. It sounded painful so no one objected.

'I just need a hot bath to melt away my worries,' she announced. No murder in the woods was going to stop Less's nightly ritual of soaking in all the available hot water. And Mother calls me selfish!

'Well, I for one am going to go up to our room to take advantage of a little peace and quiet to read the book and—'

'No way, Bridget!' Less had suddenly lost all her laid-back vibe. 'I cannot cope with that bloody dog yapping constantly next to me. I need peace!'

'Mr Bojangles has every right to rest in his room with a book.'

'He can't read!'

'Nor can you on the evidence I've seen so far.' Bridget folded her arms, a self-satisfied grin spreading across her lips.

We left them to it and decided to start on the first floor. Mother and Mirabelle would take the west wing, Aunt Charlotte and myself the east.

The house was settling into a disturbing darkness that seemed to consume all the light. We were deep inside that unreal moment when the day unpicks itself from the night and the two slowly split apart. As dusk lingered, the boundaries were becoming increasingly unclear. This had become an entirely different world. Wall lights cast tiny ponds of worthless amber. This was a darkness I had never experienced before — a thick, impenetrable one that absorbed everything — light, sound, us. Our footsteps on the worn scarlet carpet seemed more muffled than before, our breath soundless.

For some reason, we both felt it necessary to whisper. The whole house had taken on the atmosphere of a library after hours.

'What exactly are we looking for?' Aunt Charlotte whispered in crisp words that hissed. She was one of those people whose whisper was louder than her regular speaking voice.

'A murderer,' I offered.

'Right.'

We crept on like extras in a teen horror.

'What exactly does a murderer look like?' she asked.

'It depends.'

'On what?'

'The murder.'

'I see.'

She clearly didn't. 'If it were a gruesome axe murder, we would be looking for a gruesome-looking axe murderer — usually a man, presumably carrying an axe and simply wielding it in a manic fashion.'

She nodded, so I continued.

'If it were a thief caught red-handed, or a burglar, they would be wearing dark colours, usually with their face covered, and they would be sneaking.'

'Sneaking?'

'Yes, sneaking,' and I demonstrated for her by tiptoeing down the corridor a little.

She nodded.

'Here, however, we are dealing with what looks like an opportunistic murder, committed in the moment presumably by a normalish person in a great panic. Although capable of an astoundingly vicious act of brutality, they do however look no different to you or me.'

We stood and looked at one another. This had not been reassuring, so I suggested that we should go and look in the first room.

It was a ridiculous-sized room for a bedroom and looked like it hadn't been used in years. Mother would definitely have converted it into a personal gym.

'*Now* what do we do?' Aunt Charlotte asked. The slow realization was taking root that Aunt Charlotte wasn't going to be particularly helpful in a manhunt situation.

'Look for a murderer,' I offered and began opening the wardrobe.

'Should we ask ourselves whether a murderer would hide in a wardrobe? It's not Narnia you know,' she laughed.

'It's empty,' I said. 'There were no murderers in the wardrobe in *The Lion, The Witch and The Wardrobe*. It was a lion and a witch. The clue is in the title.'

'Well, there must have been something else in there. Would have been a very boring book otherwise.'

I turned to look at her, barely able to disguise my disbelief.

She had the same blank look. Today didn't seem like the day to run through the entire plot of *The Lion, The Witch and the Wardrobe*.

When I was little, I'd been to the stage production with Mother and Mirabelle, and I had managed to get lost again. I remembered watching the two of them from a distance. They didn't look like they were frantically searching for me. In fact, they looked as though they were enjoying interval drinks while giving their best impressions of the Witch.

I decided to continue searching the rest of the room while Aunt Charlotte gazed at the wardrobe. There was nothing on the dressing table. Like every other room there were no photographs, no trinkets, nothing to hint at who lived here. Again, it gave that inescapable impression of this house having been thoroughly cleared of anything personal and being too stripped of life to be real.

'Let's have a look next door,' I said.

It was the same there. A well-proportioned room with large, old furnishings, not well maintained but still heavy with the nostalgic air of past wealth. Nothing on the bedside table — nothing in it either. No clothes in the wardrobe, no dressing gown on the back of the door. It had been diligently swept clean as if a great tragedy or scandal had occurred that necessitated the removal of all trace of previous lives.

We paused only to peek into Aunt Charlotte's room, which had a worrying half-empty bottle of gin we both avoided mentioning. We all have our secrets. Some of us just choose to hide them a little better. I stopped short of insisting on a search of her room as it looked like a rather lonely woman's refuge. Clothes were flung over chairs, shoes discarded where she'd stepped out of them, and the bed remained unmade with a selection of magazines littered around it along with a half-eaten box of Milk Tray and a selection of empty miniatures. The Angels' duties clearly didn't extend to here. But Aunt Charlotte didn't need me poking through her private world of solitude. And I certainly didn't want her going through mine. Her world and the things she carried with her were not intended for others to see. In fact, there'd never been any others to see it. I don't ever remember visiting Aunt Charlotte, even as a child. She was the kind of relative who visited us, never the other way around.

'So, what now?' Aunt Charlotte ventured, clearly a little ashamed of her slightly desperate-looking room.

'Well, perhaps—'

A visceral scream broke through the house before being abruptly cut off, ending suddenly before it had completed the arc of its note.

We stood transfixed, in complete silence as though the noise had sucked up all other sound. There was a pause before noise and movement returned and seemed to radiate out through the house, the ripples spreading through every room.

The familiar surging pulse picked up the beat in my neck, and the anxious, sick feeling swilled round my belly.

Our first movements were slow. My eyes flickered as if I was waking up in thick confusion. Then we fell into a storm of racing limbs and doors being hurled open. There wasn't time to consider whether we should be running towards the sound, whether what we were doing was conducive to our survival. There was something instinctive about our scramble towards catastrophe, as if deep down we embraced it and enjoyed the desperation of chaos.

When we arrived in the corridor of the west wing, it was obvious Mother had already seen the source of our new terror. Her face was drained, a pallid blank expression that made her seem as detached as if she had been sleepwalking.

'She's had a terrible shock,' Mirabelle breathed, and wrapped her arms around Mother's shoulders like a familiar coat.

'Was it you screaming?' Aunt Charlotte breathed.

Mirabelle simply nodded towards the open door. Less's room.

The door next to Less's room clicked open and the dog bolted out.

'Mr Bojangles, no! It isn't safe!' Bridget ran out towards Less's room.

Mother grabbed the dog. 'It can't go in there,' she said, sharply.

'What's happened? What's—'

'Here,' Mother thrust the dog at Bridget. 'Did you not hear the scream?'

'I was reading the book, preparing for—'

'We heard it from the other side of the house,' Aunt Charlotte said. 'How could you not have heard it?'

We stood and looked at Bridget, who made no effort to answer. Aunt Charlotte pushed her out of the way and I followed her inside.

The room smelled different to all the others. There was a lingering acidic scent — a strange hybrid of sharpness and must. We entered like children, aware there was something that we should be afraid of.

Less's room was almost a clean mirror image of Aunt Charlotte's. The bed in the same place but beautifully made, the same walnut dressing table with three large mirrors and yet no detritus or half-drunk bottles and glasses. In one of the triptych mirrors, I saw the mottled colours of flesh hanging limp and naked. I turned and saw Aunt Charlotte, eyes wide at the bathroom door.

'Don't, Ursula,' she said, arms spread wide.

I pushed her aside. I don't like being protected — it makes me feel fragile.

The bathroom was dimly lit by candle flames scattered like stars across the surfaces. Their light rippled on the dark waters of the bath that filled the spaces around Less's body. Smashed, arms hanging heavily and spread as if reconciled to this, her head was thrown back — every feature and limb distorted by the vast black metal spokes of the fallen chandelier. The wrought iron of its framework twisted into her mauled body, as if it had become part of her. The thick rope that had strung it from the ceiling above lay casually across the water and snaked nonchalantly down to the floor. In a single moment, one snap of the rope had taken a life.

I bent to look closely at the end of the rope. The reek of coppery blood was bitter, so pungent I could taste it. I felt myself begin to retch. Even though every part of me was being repelled, I forced myself to keep looking at it. My heart fluttered frantically like trapped wings inside my chest, battering against my rib cage. My head was thick with fear, but I had to keep looking.

Although sturdy, the rope was dirty and old. The break wasn't clean. It hadn't been cut but was instead frayed. It was black and charred-looking. At the back of the room, I saw the remains of the rope's other half hanging from the hook, curling down the wall. I went to examine it, careful not to touch anything. It was visibly scorched. There were candles knocked down all over the floor and still some burning on the small side cupboard next to the rope's hook.

I imagined those last seconds. The rope had burned through, slowly and methodically, as Less lay oblivious to the fate that was slowly kindling. There would have been one final breath as the flame burned through the last bit of rope, and the vast metal chandelier it held fell onto her waiting body below. One final horrified look up. And there she lay, her wild, wide eyes still looking to heaven or wherever she was destined. The colour had drained from her, her skin mushroom-mottled as if she was leeching out into the water.

'Ursula?' Aunt Charlotte said, quietly.

My feet felt heavy. I moved carefully back towards the door, each step a great effort. 'I will not fall,' I whispered. Lights flashed inside my eyes. I couldn't feel the ground. I breathed the blood-rich air slowly and deeply. Dad's face glanced across my thoughts. I felt the walls flooding in and an arm guiding me. Aunt Charlotte. I looked across the bleached-out gardens and the black rook's oily wings splashed up into the sky in one single streak. My legs collapsed from under me.

Rule 14: When you are in a life-threatening situation: survive. Do anything you can to survive. The normal rules we live by have changed.

SURVIVAL

Fear spread like fungus, infecting us all, making each of us act in the most unexpected of ways.

'How do you even know she was murdered?' Mother said. Her words sounded almost angry as if a new inconvenience had been thrown her way. No one had cried. We were numb.

'Mother, two deaths in twenty-four hours are not a coincidence and we categorically know that Doreen Dellamer was murdered. She didn't just accidentally fall on a blunt instrument with the back of her head. So, it makes it all the more likely that *this* murder was planned too.'

Mother shook her head. 'I don't see that logic.'

It is sometimes intensely infuriating that Mother will disagree with literally everything I say even if it is the only possible solution. It does, however, lead me to question even the minutest of details. And that is often where the answer lies.

Mother rang the irritating little bell and Angel appeared.

'There's another dead body. In the house this time. Upstairs. Could you please deal with it?' She didn't look at Angel.

Angel's thin lower lip fell slowly.

'Angel,' Aunt Charlotte began in a conciliatory tone, 'we may have got off on the wrong foot, but it would appear that we are perhaps being picked off one by one. So I suggest for your own sake that you and your wife, if she is not in fact the murderer, throw your lot in with us.'

Angel reacted with the appropriate level of astonishment.

'I think what she is attempting to convey,' Mirabelle added, 'is that some recognition of the gravity of the situation might help.'

'Yes, exactly,' Aunt Charlotte confirmed. 'What she said.'

'I can't believe this. I can't. Mr Bojangles and I just came here to talk about books and . . . and . . . now this.' Bridget held a little handkerchief to her mouth.

My thoughts wouldn't settle. It was like staring at a broken vase with no idea how to put it back together again, even though all the pieces had to be there. There were just so many and they were so randomly scattered.

Mother, however, can always find something to say, even in the darkest, most surreal situations. 'Yes, quite. As my sister said, you need to step up your game here. Just . . . just,' her voice cracked. 'Just go and sort it out for God's sake.'

Angel raised his eyes to meet my mother's. 'You'll excuse me, Madam, I did not realize that you were sisters.' This was not the reaction we had anticipated after telling him there was a dead body, that he must sort it out and that we even suspected that his wife could be the murderer. 'Sisters . . .'

'*Yes*, Angel,' Mother said, bewildered, 'since birth, but really, at the moment, our friend is *dead*!'

She stifled a cry, but I've heard Mother fake tears enough to know when it isn't real. I watched her closely with all her awkward, self-conscious movements.

'I shall speak with Mrs Angel and formulate some ideas as to what we should do, Madam. I will report back to you, of course.'

'Of course.'

I had to concentrate and focus on what was important. I held my jittering leg. I had to try to assemble some sort of pattern to the events. If someone could execute such a brutal and planned murder, they were to be feared far more than the killer I had originally imagined, who had bludgeoned an old woman over the head in what looked like the spur of the moment. I held onto the idea that it must be someone outside our group and we weren't as isolated as we thought. But the inescapable thought gnawed at my brain that the killer was here in this house and could quite easily be one of the people in this room right now. I considered the people in our group and looked from face to face. Each was capable of a brutal act. The panic started to rise again. We had to get out.

So far, we had tried only one escape route — walking through huge snowdrifts in a blizzard. Yet the cars were ridiculous four-wheel drive monsters, which were presumably not just intended for driving around the streets of Fulham.

'If we load up with blankets, shovels and hot drinks we might have a chance of making it through to the village,' I suggested.

'And that is why we never take any notice of you.' Mother sighed. 'Look at the weather! It's freezing. You can barely see through the snow and mist. The cars are totally buried. It would take all night just to dig them out.'

'Did you have something else planned?' I realized it wasn't perhaps the most persuasive argument, but we had to do something. 'Would you prefer that we just sat here in the Overlook Hotel—'

'It's not called the—'

'—waiting for our turn to be killed in ever more mysterious circumstances? We're surrounded by dead bodies, Mother! Can't you see? We're going to die. We're all going to die horrible deaths!'

This was followed by some silence and some staring. I gripped my leg even harder until the pain seemed normal, necessary. I couldn't stop seeing Less's dead, wild eyes, and her pruning skin all puckered and slippery.

'There is another option,' Mirabelle said thoughtfully, which was unusual for her.

'Astound us.'

'We work out who the murderer is.'

We sat in a new silence. And we looked at each other with different eyes. The fire fed on our air, making it dry and sharp with charcoal until it coated the back of our throats. The wind spoke with a soft malice at the window. All our features were the same but somehow the light fell on them differently now. Fearful shadows played at the corners of our eyes. All trust dissolved. No one moved. The fire cracked into the silence.

A vicious thud.

A mess of wings. My breath stopped in my throat. A black shape was caught for a moment, smashed against the glass window. It took slow seconds for my brain to arrange the shape into something that made sense. A bird, the beak up and to the side at an unnatural angle, its wings crooked and held out like the broken hands of a clock. The rook lingered for a moment on the glass, the gloss clouding over on the marbles of its eyes. It fell silently onto the porcelain snow, as if presented on a dish. A grubby red smear was left across the windowpane.

'For God's sake!' Mother's voice broke. 'What next?'

'Oh no! No, no!' Bridget gasped. 'You know what this means — a bird flying into the window? It means someone in the house is about to die!'

'You're kidding, right?' I stared at her.

'Ancient people believed rooks were souls. It's the death of a—'

There was a sharp knock at the door.

Our eyes flickered towards the door in unison.

'Come in,' Mother said firmly.

Angel edged his way into the room with a new look of obsequiousness. My ability to nurture a slow-burning dislike for people is a talent I've developed over many years and it came very easily here. This place was making it clear to me that perhaps I wasn't a nice person all of the time after all.

'I'm so sorry to intrude in these personal moments of grief,' Angel knew very well that there had been no such grieving, 'but Mrs Angel and I were wondering what you would like us to do with the body of your dearly departed friend.'

Angel was goading Mother and she knew it.

Her eyes remained fixed in a needle-sharp stare, as if she were trying to memorize every detail of his features. She answered carefully. 'Do not move anything or any part of the lady. Cover her sufficiently in towels or a sheet so as to protect her modesty.'

'Madam, would that not be a task more suitably performed by one of your party?'

'No, it would not. You are paid to take care of us and see to our every need. There is no mention of whether we should be alive or dead.' Mother had a new steel to her, razor sharp and cold. I watched her smooth, emotionless eyes. If I had any friends, would I feel different if they'd just died? I'd hope so, but then, I am in many ways my mother's daughter.

Angel took a long and difficult breath. 'Very well, Madam.'

'If you are not comfortable with seeing a naked woman, I'm sure Mrs Angel can cover her.' She was trying her very best to make him uncomfortable.

'Yes, Madam.'

'You will leave everything as it is and lock the door. You will then deliver the key to me. Is that clear, Angel?'

'Yes, Madam.'

He waited. There was an awkwardness to him, as if he was anxious to leave, as if something was drawing his attention elsewhere.

'And while you're at it, you can clear up the dead bird.'

He looked at her quizzically. Mother pointed to the fractured remains of feathers scattered across the snow outside. The wizened black feet had drawn in and formed cruel little hands against the clay white snow, as if gripping the last seconds of life.

'That's all, Angel,' Mirabelle added, unnecessarily. That was always Mirabelle's problem, she was *unnecessary* and she was very aware of that.

We waited for Angel to vanish again before we spoke. No one trusted anyone now, least of all the cadaverous butler. He fitted his role so perfectly, but no one can be that much of a butler all of the time.

In my imagination, as soon as he left the room, he allowed his shoulders to slump and loosened the overly starched collar. He had no money, yet was forced to serve those who had. His wife was unhappy and had probably always looked that way — she just got older. Every single day he was forced to ingratiate himself without question or complaint, even when it involved the dead body of a guest. Yes, Angel had every reason in the world to do something desperate. He was, like the rest of us, quite capable of murder.

We were all capable of having committed it. We could only discount people that couldn't have physically done it, because they weren't there or didn't have the strength. So far, no one could be discounted on those grounds.

Mother was quick to seize upon the necessity for an alibi.

'Well, it couldn't have been Mirabelle or me because we were together and not in the room at the time of the murder.' That's one of the rare things I admire about Mother, she doesn't hesitate to protect her own skin, even if it did mean leaving her own daughter and sister in the position of being possible murderers.

'We only have your word for that,' said Aunt Charlotte. 'You could both have murdered her.'

It was in many ways inevitable that we would start hurling our suspicions around. 'Oh, that's typical you, Charlotte, cast doubt on your friends and relatives.'

'Well, that shouldn't cause you any concern then, should it, Mirabelle?' Aunt Charlotte sneered. 'As *you* are neither.'

I watched Mirabelle rest her hand on Mother's arm. Mother patted it reassuringly. Was it reassurance? You could never be sure with Mother.

'What about you, Charlotte?' Mother pronounced slowly. 'You could easily have—'

'I was with your daughter.'

'No one's above suspicion,' Mirabelle cut in.

Mother took Mirabelle's hand away. 'We need to be more practical,' she said.

'We won't be looking at the book tonight either then, I take it?'

'Not now, Bridget!' Mother snapped.

We looked to the heavy sky with clouds sweeping low over the hills. Snow still brushed the air and piled against the long glass doors. Great sandbags of snow stuffed up against our doors and windows, as if we were at war. The thick waves of snow were at least two feet deep now, burying garden furniture, everything under a sombre shroud. All the world had been bleached out.

I thought of Doreen Dellamer in her shallow hollow of snow out there, alone with all her foolish scarves and jewellery — she would be buried deeper with every passing hour. What would she look like when all this was past, when the snow melted away and they found her? But I could not form a picture of all this coming to an end.

'Maybe we should try with the cars,' I offered.

'It's too dark.' Aunt Charlotte peered through the windows. The remains of the bird were gone but the shape of its death was still there, a grey shadow on the snow.

It was a blank world out there now, no movement, soundless. The skeletons of trees were no more than black outlines against a cemetery sky, each one spotted with round rooks' nests. We were in a new unreality, separated and insulated from everything we knew. It had already become impossible to imagine the small village we'd paid so little attention to on our way here, its inhabitants all unaware of the desperate, frightened visitors and the death that surrounded them not twenty minutes' drive away.

'Let's try,' I said, fear breaking in my voice. I had to remind myself when to breathe, as if it no longer came naturally.

We were trapped. We were being picked off like birds flushed out by a beater. Here we sat just waiting for the next death.

'We have to find a way. We have to do something. Anything!' I felt myself slipping. Mother got up. She came over and held my hand, staring intently into my eyes.

'Hold on, Ursula.' Her words, as ever, were plain, emotionless. 'Take a deep breath, hold it. Now, let go. Keep hold of my hand.'

I felt the sweat pool in the curve at the base of my spine. My fingers picked anxiously from one to the next.

My mind swam to its safe harbour. Dad. Sometimes he didn't seem dead at all. I imagined opening the door to him now and breathing a long sigh of relief. 'Thank God you're here. I had the most awful dream. There was a dead body in the bath and one in the grounds dressed up as a fortune teller. And now the birds are dying.' He would swing into action and we would all be safe. That's what he was good at, keeping us safe. He just couldn't keep himself safe.

'The birds are dying,' I whispered.

I felt Mother's hands grip tighter. 'We'll try with the car,' she said softly.

Rule 15: Be prepared for anything and improvise. You never know what small thing might end up saving your life.

HOW TO DIG A CAR OUT OF THE SNOW

We spent at least an hour gathering our equipment. I say 'we' gathered equipment — Bridget said she had to keep Mr Bojangles warm by the fire and the Angels were too busy dealing with the corpse, as I'd now decided to call Less.

We took coal shovels from the understairs cupboard but couldn't find a torch, so we improvised with a standard lamp on an extension lead. We also had the two ornate fireguards to shove under the wheels and give traction, plus a side table Aunt Charlotte had brought out for cups of tea.

By the time we'd assembled everything, there was only a thin remnant of light left over the trees. We had the lights from the house and the small pool from the lamp to work by, but it was growing darker and colder with every passing moment.

We seemed even more isolated when we stood outside. It was a bleak wilderness with nothing to see and only things to imagine — like Doreen Dellamer's mutilated body, buried deep, played at by animals, marbled purple and black from the cold and all the life drained out. The extreme images seemed to surface so quickly now. It was as if something stalked us, circling our small group, watching from the edges.

'Right,' Aunt Charlotte began in her most practical voice, 'let's take a wheel each and get digging.'

'You're kidding me?' Mirabelle said. 'That's it? That's the grand scheme for getting us out of here?'

'And *your* plan would be?'

They took a step closer to one another, like fighting dogs straining on the leash. Mother held out her arms.

'We all have the same plan. Let's stay alive. Agreed?'

Mirabelle and Aunt Charlotte stared at one another. I'm not sure either really cared if the other survived or not.

'Agreed?' Mother said more firmly.

Aunt Charlotte nodded reluctantly. Mirabelle looked away.

Mother let her arms drop slowly. 'Let's get the engine started and see where we are first.'

The violent wind stripped our faces of all expression save for determination. We could barely open our eyes in the brittle cold air. It dug into our chests, bending us in the middle. There we stood, four dark hunched figures in the faded ends of the day with a standard lamp casting only the smallest amber pond on the dark snow. Mother was first to stab her shovel into the hard snow and a flood of crows rose up from the trees, shrieking into the wind. Caught for a moment in the light from the house, their polished wings shone silver against the dead sky.

The Angels had pointed us in the direction of the shovels but there'd been no suggestion that they would step outside and help.

'Probably in there now, plotting our gruesome murders,' Aunt Charlotte offered.

'We need to dig round the door to get in,' Mother said.

Each time we pulled back a great load of snow, it seemed to fall back. But there was a form of distraction in the mundane futility of our task. We just kept digging, however fruitless it seemed.

It soon became clear it was utterly pointless. We couldn't even get the door open.

'What a massive waste of time,' Mirabelle announced. 'We can't bloody drive anywhere if we can't even get *in* the car.'

'You don't need to be so negative all the time, Mirabelle. It's not productive.'

She carefully leaned closer, analysing me closely as if she was peeling me. And then she said in a low voice, 'I see you, *Ursula*, and I've seen you ever since you were that precocious little girl. All that hive of noisy anger like a little wasps' nest.' I could feel her warm, musty breath. 'But one *tap*,' she twitched the shovel at me, 'and that fragile nest will fall apart like paper, won't it, eh?'

Mother and Aunt Charlotte had already abandoned the dig site and stamped woefully towards the house. Mirabelle turned and followed them solemnly without another word.

I looked at where we had dug. Any progress had already been covered over by fresh snow. Mirabelle was right, it had been a massive waste of time. I heard a crack behind me in the small copse of trees near the house. I turned and in the dusk light I thought I saw something move in the dark snow. My eyes scoured the shadows but there was nothing. I know too well how fear can play terrible tricks but as I walked slowly back to the steps, I turned and looked into the darkness.

Angel came to greet us at the door. He smelled sour, like old men who don't go out of the house much. Come to think of it, I'd never seen him out of the house.

'Any luck, Madam?'

'Might have had more luck with an extra pair of hands, Angel.' Aunt Charlotte pushed past, banging snow from her boots with every step.

'Madam, the instructions were to deal with the deceased's body. That was not an undertaking we took lightly and is not a chore we are used to dealing with.' For the first time since our arrival, Angel looked disturbed, almost angry.

'Yes, yes.' Aunt Charlotte remained oblivious to his or anyone else's emotions.

We headed for the sitting room. Bridget was still there, reading *Gone Girl* to Mr Bojangles. 'It's calming us both,' she said, with a sour grin.

Mother and Aunt Charlotte immediately poured fat balloons of brandy for medicinal purposes.

'We'll need food, Angel,' Mirabelle said, stubbornly ignorant of the fact that he had just been dealing with the corpse of her travelling companion.

'Very well, Madam. I will see what Mrs Angel can rustle up.'

Mother stopped, mid-glove removal. '*Rustle up*, Angel? *Rustle up?*'

He jutted his face out towards Mother in a semi-military stance, his hands clenched behind his back, readying himself for inspection.

'When I require you to be informal with me, I will tell you,' Mother said slowly. 'When I require substandard food instead of the glorious bounty we were promised and paid for, I will tell you. Is that understood, Angel?' Mother's words were dry with fury.

'Very well, Madam. When Mrs Angel has finished with the deceased she will commence this evening's supper.'

'I'm glad to hear it, Angel. And don't let standards drop again.'

'No, Madam.'

I absented myself on the pretext of changing my damp clothes, although I hadn't brought a change of clothes with me, which Mother knew full well. I sat on the edge of the bed staring out at the strange, blank land and held the Bible and the brandy. My raw fingers shook as I drank methodically. How many times had I sat with this desecrated Bible? I ran my fingers along the serrated edge of the pages and imagined my father's hands intricately cutting through the text, pulling away each layer of the sacred paper. I drank deeply from the hip flask, just as I'd seen him do, carefully, slowly, and with eyes closed in reverence.

When I'd fortified myself enough to trail back downstairs, we were back at another tawdry meal. My jaw was so tense I could hardly open my mouth to eat.

'We'll need to tell someone,' Aunt Charlotte offered. 'Even *she* must have had relatives.' She spoke so flippantly about Less, even now when she was dead. There was almost a sense of satisfaction in her words.

'Who?' Mother snapped.

'What's her name. Less.' Aunt Charlotte is not well known for her diplomacy. 'I can't eat this swill.' She pushed the plate of stew away. 'I haven't the stomach to eat now. Too many dead bodies.'

Mother spooned up the brown, lumpy liquid and let it flow like effluent from her fork to the plate.

'Less dying cut short our search of the rooms. Perhaps . . .'

'You can hardly blame her for that, Ursula.' Mother pushed her plate away. 'Even in death you cannot stop with the accusations and maligning of her character. Yes, Joy had her faults—'

'Terrible thief,' Aunt Charlotte offered, and again she smiled.

'That's just not helpful, Charlotte.' Mother folded her napkin and placed it slowly and carefully by her plate like a threatening mobster in a Hollywood movie. 'We are all going to have a little more respect for Joy. We are not going to cast unfounded accusations.'

'Well, she was a convicted thief so we can categorically say *that* was founded. She did time.' Aunt Charlotte seemed almost to be enjoying this.

The candles wavered a little under the great weight of the sigh Mother let out.

'Pot head, too,' Aunt Charlotte added, and laughed.

'Just don't say anything at all about Joy!' Mother shouted. She rang the little bell furiously and slammed it into the table.

The dog let out another strangled sound.

'You scared him!' Bridget snapped.

'Boo!'

Bridget did not appreciate my attempt at humour. A heavy silence settled in.

When Angel arrived, he looked even more solemn. He waited at the door with a decidedly morbid expression and a strange gangrenous sheen to his face.

'We need to search your room, Angel.' There was no sugaring of the pill with Mother. 'And your wife's room — if you sleep separately.'

Angel had no chance to look shocked by the first statement before the second was delivered.

'No, Madam, I'm afraid that will not be possible.' His words were measured and flat, each one delivered with a carefully monitored temper.

'Well, Vlad, I'm afraid that's what's happening,' Aunt Charlotte added as she drew back her chair.

'I think we'll stay here by the fire with a book,' Bridget said, smiling serenely at the dog.

Angel looked from face to face before taking a long, purposeful breath. 'Very well, *ladies*. Follow me.' Very little of the gracious butler act remained now. His veneer was slipping as fast as a backstreet dentist's work.

Rule 16: You must search every inch of your surroundings. You never know what dangers could be hiding or who is hiding them.

YOU WILL HAVE TO SEARCH FOR ANSWERS

As our solemn procession passed through the dim corridors it felt very much as if we were descending into the belly of the house. We had only skimmed the surface of the acceptable façade of this vast building. As we journeyed deeper, there was a mildewed air and the house began to wear its age with exhaustion.

The skin of its wallpaper peeled and crumbled and the carpets ran threadbare in places where they had once been busy pathways. This was what aged the house more than anything, not just the lack of life but the memory of so much of it. Reminders of once *vibrant* lives germinated and festered, increasing the sense of silence and passing. This was a house for the ghosts now, and we, the living, were the ones who were out of place. As we journeyed past boot rooms and abandoned laundry areas, sheets of memory suddenly billowed out at us.

Mr and Mrs Angel were all there was now, haunting the old kitchens before retreating into the shade of their little corner. Angel walked on ahead leading us deeper into darkness, past abandoned rooms until we came to a narrow corridor.

'Mrs Angel and I occupy these rooms now,' he said quietly, then knocked on one of the doors and turned the old, black handle.

Inside was a warmer world, still faded but cosier and homely. People lived here in this sanctuary, quiet lives with very few demands but nonetheless an existence. Warm lights glowed in two small bedrooms that were immediately ahead. To the side was a small, heavily furnished sitting room. It was as if they had crammed everything that they needed from the house into these few rooms — packed with all their meaningful treasures like old pharaohs' tombs. It must have been savagely strange to live in such a palace but only inhabit this tiny warren. It seemed such a sad waste, like living in a vast library but only ever reading the same book. Perhaps Mr and Mrs Angel were satisfied but their restricted life didn't seem to bring them any joy. I watched Angel drop his head a little to enter the room. This was not a natural space for him. He was like a vast, aged oak tied and constricted to become a bonsai.

I watched him closely, manoeuvring through the randomly placed chairs and side tables, picking a path like a cat around a table of glasses and plates. Every surface was littered with trinkets and photographs — black-and-white memories choking up any available space with the past, as if there was no thought for the future or even the present.

'Hello?' Mrs Angel seemed to just appear in the living room like a spirit. The bedroom was back the way we had come, and Mirabelle, Mother and Aunt Charlotte were doing a very good job of blocking the entire doorway.

'We have visitors, Mrs Angel.' It's always odd when a married couple refer to each other as Mr or Mrs, almost as if they are reminding each other that they are married. It puts a space between them, a cold barrier that shouldn't be there.

132

'I see,' Mrs Angel said smoothing down her skirt. There was something contrived about their interaction, as if they were both guarding their words.

'We need to search your rooms, Mrs Angel,' Mother announced, without a trace of embarrassment.

'Why?'

We waited and watched Mother run a finger along the length of the old, wooden sideboard. 'Because—' she began.

'Because there is a killer on the loose and we know absolutely nothing,' Aunt Charlotte interrupted.

Mirabelle tutted. 'You make it sound as though a rampant animal is running around.'

'Well, it certainly feels that way!'

'That's you all over, Charlotte. Always melodramatic.'

'Really? Melodramatic? Less has been *impaled* and the fortune teller has told her last fortune.'

'Is this entirely necessary?' Angel suddenly spoke loudly.

Angel stood by his wife and spread an arm across her shoulders. It was the first time I'd seen them have any physical contact.

It was a natural reaction to our invasion, yet nothing about the Angels seemed natural. There was a tension in every interaction.

'I'll begin in here,' Mother said. 'Ursula, you and Aunt Charlotte search the bedrooms.'

There was no point in challenging Mother when she was in this mood.

Their bedroom was small yet somehow failed to be cosy. It had a pathetic feel to it, the two old twin beds with faded pink candlewick bedspreads stranded in the past. The colour had bled out of everything until all the shades merged into one. Painted pictures on the wall were there just to fill space, while their sad bowls of flowers and fruits would have looked more at home in a funeral parlour. The curtains were drawn and didn't look like they were ever opened. It was a stagnant room people just existed in. They woke up each morning and life just carried on the same. There was a deep sadness here, a helpless melancholy.

'What are we looking for, then?' Aunt Charlotte asked.

'Let's not do this again, Aunt Charlotte. We've been through this. A murderer. Or anything linked to a murderer. A weapon perhaps or . . .' I watched her face slip into vacancy. 'Just keep thinking, *We are looking for a murderer.* That should keep you on the right track for a while.'

Aunt Charlotte sat on the bed with a resounding sigh. It was a disrespectful action but I didn't say anything. Her nonchalance was beginning to become quite wearing. It was not only out of place — it was so unlike her.

I began at the small chest of drawers opposite the beds. How they made space for all their clothes in here was beyond me. Mind you, I hadn't noticed them change their clothes since our arrival. They were always in costume.

On the top of the drawers were Mrs Angel's trinket boxes, brush and yet more uninviting photographs of miserable, dissatisfied faces. Whenever anyone takes a photograph now, there is constant shouting of 'Smile, everyone. Smile!', but this wasn't something that seemed to trouble people of previous generations.

Clearly, the Angels held the family in high regard as many of the photographs featured the house and a selection of exceptionally stern-looking aristos. There had been far more staff in previous years too. Nestled among them was a dire wedding photo of the Angels, the kind that makes you wonder what motivated either party. There was also a charming picture of two young girls on the lawn in front of the house playing with a small dog. It was the only sign of happiness on the whole dresser top.

'Come on, girl,' Aunt Charlotte huffed. 'Search the bloody drawers, for God's sake.'

I pulled open the top drawer slowly. Neat rows of socks and underwear stared up at me sullenly.

'Oh, for goodness sake! Stand aside.' Aunt Charlotte had managed to stir herself and shoved her hand in the drawer bringing immediate disorder. It was a very unsettling image watching Aunt Charlotte carelessly invade someone else's private possessions. I wondered what she must look like to an outsider. I watched her carelessness with other people's possessions — how brusque her hands seemed, how stony her face was — and it all seemed like such a terrible violation.

'Aunt Charlotte?'

'Hmmm?' she murmured distractedly.

'Why did you look so shocked when you came back from the fortune teller?'

'What do you mean, dear?' She pointedly didn't look at me.

'When you came back into the sitting room, after you'd been in with Doreen Dellamer, you looked very unsettled — disturbed even.'

'Disturbed?' she said quietly, and turned to face me. 'I'm not sure what you're implying here, darling girl, but I'd warn you not to continue down this line. We've *all* been acting strangely, unsurprisingly given that people are being murdered around us. You are no exception to that, dear.' She leaned closer. 'Don't expect people haven't noticed the stench of booze you bring with you into a room.'

I have always been very aware of the fact that the face my family shows me might not always be the truth, but this unnerved me.

Aunt Charlotte pushed the drawer shut.

'I'm going to check the other room,' I said.

'What other room?' But Aunt Charlotte was too busy raiding the Angels' possessions to look at what anyone else was doing.

A fragile sliver of light was all that hinted at the existence of the other room. It traced round the outline of the door that led off from the bedroom. Inside, there was a much smaller bedroom with only one single bed, a dressing table and a neat array of photographs. The light was on and the bed made. This room had only recently been abandoned. The hairbrush was at an angle where it had been set down, a compact still open and a dark lipstick uncapped. Without thinking, I sat at the dressing table.

I stared into the mirror. 'What have you seen?' I asked it in a whisper. I looked down at the heavy gilt hairbrush, threaded deep with long black hairs. A cold draught passed along my neck and I looked up at the mirror.

A face. Eyes glaring back at mine.

'Can I help you, Miss?' Mrs Angel asked quietly.

'Yes, yes.' I hastily replaced the brush. 'Whose room is this?'

'The room, Miss?' She reached over my shoulder and moved the brush slightly. 'This is my dressing room, Miss.'

'Oh, I see.' I stared at her in the mirror. She seemed unreal, a painting in a frame. I turned to look at her and felt her breath touch my cheek. 'Thank you, Mrs Angel.'

'Is there anything else you'd like to see in here, Miss?'

She was so close I could smell the soap she'd used that morning, the after scent of some lavender or rose water she had diligently dotted on her neck. It mingled with an undertone of aged fabric holding on to its bitter note of mothballs.

I shook my head. 'No, thank you.'

'Then perhaps . . .' She motioned towards the door, just as Aunt Charlotte peered round it, eyebrows raised. I stood up and gravely walked past Mrs Angel, feeling the prickle of her glare with every step. I turned to look at her but as I paused at the door, she was no longer looking at me. She was staring into the deep pool of the mirror.

The search was fruitless. I doubted if the others had bothered to look. Mirabelle and Mother were still rooted to the same places we'd left them in, while Angel stood in silence to the side, a thin film of sweat blistering on his top lip.

Rule 17: Remember, jealousy can be a powerful weapon.

READ ALL THE SIGNS

I insisted to Mother that we hadn't wasted our time by visiting the Angels. 'We need to be patient and read all the signs. Even the minutest detail could be the key to exposing the truth—'

'Read all the signs? You mean like this monstrosity!' Mother shouted and stormed into the sitting room. The cheap brass plaque was slanting and tarnished.

NO SMOKING

Someone had hastily scrawled underneath in black Sharpie *or any form of e-cigarettes*. Clearly there was some awareness of the outside world here.

The fire was dwindling and the sitting room had slipped into a stale coldness. Bridget wasn't there now, presumably doing serious book club work upstairs with Mr Bojangles. When they were left empty, the rooms settled quickly back to their loneliness. A foetid air easily took hold when it went unchecked and a lifeless pallor infected the light, giving it a morgue-like quality.

Although, I've never actually been in a morgue. All the dead people I've seen, three so far, have been in the real world.

Dad, Doreen Dellamer and now Less. Not yet corpses, still dead people. Corpses are empty shells, not people of any description — dead or otherwise. The corpse in the funeral parlour was just an image of the man I knew. But Dad was still Dad when the breath slipped from him and his eyes turned up to the sky.

This room was a corpse. Life had long since departed. I imagined the room teeming with life, a family, children playing on the lawn with the family dog outside this window. The Angels had known it like that.

Mother slumped into the sofa and stared at the dwindling embers of the fire. I wanted to go and sit with her, but I knew what she'd say. She always said it when I was a child and dared to put my arms around her. She'd hold me for a moment, before saying, 'You really must control yourself.' Then she'd let go. Children remember being let go.

'Bridget didn't come and help, I notice.' Mirabelle edged in next to Mother on the sofa, leaving no space for anyone else. 'What else did she have to do? Bloody dog.'

'Fire needs stoking,' Aunt Charlotte announced.

Mirabelle stood. 'I'll do it.'

'I can *manage*, thank you Mirabelle.' Aunt Charlotte pulled aside the vast, slightly bent, fireguard. It had almost survived being wedged under the wheels of a four-by-four but would never really be the same again. Resembling a shot-putter in tweed, Aunt Charlotte grabbed the poker as if it were a weapon.

It was a weapon.

She held it out in silence.

'Diana's arrow,' I said.

There, in Aunt Charlotte's fist, was the large metal arrow that was missing from the stone statue at the front of the house. It had a thick, congealed layer of blood around its tip. Aunt Charlotte stepped towards Mother and Mirabelle and, for a moment, I imagined her slamming it down on them both. Instead, she laid it carefully on the coffee table and we all stared down at it. Without doubt there were small remains of hair and flesh on the arrowhead, caught beneath the sharp angles of metal.

'Definitely the weapon that killed Doreen Dellamer,' I said slowly.

'Very observant,' Mother murmured, without letting her gaze wander from the arrow.

Whoever had taken this weapon to the back of Doreen Dellamer's head had hidden it in plain sight in the poker bucket, smeared with the fortune teller's blood and remnants of her skull.

Words just started to fall out of me. 'This . . . this tells us . . .'

'That the poor cow was killed by a lunatic!' Aunt Charlotte announced.

'More than that, Aunt Charlotte,' I continued undeterred. 'Doreen Dellamer was not killed out in the grounds. She was killed on the steps of this house.' I waited for a gasp that never came. They just stared. 'The killer followed her out of the house and looked around quickly for a weapon. The killer must have seen it, grabbed it and belted the back of her head. Death would have been almost instantaneous, I should imagine.' I mimed the scene, but lowered my hand when I saw the open-mouthed faces staring at me re-enacting Doreen Dellamer's murder with the bloody weapon in front of us.

'We'd worked that out,' Mother said finally.

'But that means the killer most definitely came from inside the house. Don't you see, this is fantastic news. The killer is in the house with us!'

Silence.

I cleared my throat, as if it might somehow clear the stifling air in the room. 'Doreen Dellamer was not murdered where we found her. This was not a local who chanced upon her on her way home or even someone lying in wait for her. This was not thought out. Whoever killed her had been taken by surprise — by Doreen's presence or by something she said or did. They had little time to plan, to think. They just grabbed what they could and did the job quickly.'

My small audience listened with narrowed eyes.

'Doreen's body was then hastily dragged out into the grounds, but the arrow, covered in blood and hair, couldn't be returned. There was no opportunity to hide it carefully, so the killer had to put it somewhere it would not look incongruous. Here. Which means they came back to the house.'

I waited as the penny dropped.

'The discovery would have been much quicker had it not been for the snow fall.' I was on a roll now. 'The blood would have been covered over on the doorstep by the first snow fall. There were no footprints out into the gardens or indeed back to the house. All evidence was softly and silently disguised, so much so that we didn't even know she was dead until well into the next morning.'

'That's all very well and good,' Mirabelle said, her words drawn out, 'but it doesn't explain why anyone would *want* to kill her.'

'No, but look at it this way, Mother fired her and evicted her—'

'You little—'

'Listen, Mother! I'm just hypothesizing.'

'That's because you refuse to eat sugar!'

I paused. 'Hypothesizing, Mother. Not hypoglycaemic. And we've been over this before, I don't have anything like that.' It was best just to continue. 'The Angels knew her, booked her and had been out because they were aware the road was blocked and—'

'Well, at least I'm in the clear,' Aunt Charlotte laughed.

'Really? Didn't you come back pale as a sheet after your session with her? What had she said?'

Aunt Charlotte looked flabbergasted, a stock expression for her. 'I've already told you, dear!'

'And what about you, Mirabelle? You were the last one to see her alive because you went to pay her. Did you *repay* her?'

'Oh my God! What's that? Look away, Mr Bojangles.' It was Bridget at the door, holding her hands over the dog's eyes.

The dog got loose and ran for the arrow. He began eagerly sniffing.

'No! No, Mr Bojangles,' Bridget shouted. 'Oh my God, he can't ingest that . . . that . . .' We watched in horror as the keen dog began licking at the tip of the arrow. 'He's strictly organic!'

'We think it was used to kill the fortune teller,' I said slowly.

'Really, Mr Bojangles,' she hurried over to the dog, 'come on, the poor girl thinks it's evidence.'

'We still have a dead fortune teller and no answers.' Mirabelle kept her eyes on me and leaned in to Mother, much closer than I was ever usually allowed.

'That is because you're not thinking, Mirabelle,' I said.

She watched me with slow, deliberate eyes.

'OK, let's think about how our fortune teller was dressed.'

'Like a fortune teller,' Aunt Charlotte said.

'Yes, like a fortune teller. And who dresses like that, Aunt Charlotte?' I asked carefully, as though guiding a fool.

'A fort—'

'Don't, Charlotte,' Mother shot.

Mother and Mirabelle took a simultaneous deep breath. Their yoga teacher would have been proud. The amount of money my mother has spent on being taught how to breathe, she must have the most expensive lungs in Britain.

'But that's exactly right!' I said with keen excitement. It possibly came across as a little deranged. 'She was here to tell fortunes. That is her job. She dressed the part, told fortunes and left, we assumed, to go home.'

'I don't understand,' Aunt Charlotte added needlessly. Her expression was enough.

'She would have *changed*.'

'Into what? An acrobat?' Mother closed her eyes. She had so many ways of showing her disappointment with me.

'Mother, she would not have walked here and gone home, over dark, inhospitable country roads dressed as a fortune teller. Think what you saw! Vast swathes of material, scarves billowing out like sails, a ridiculous wig. This was not an outfit for the long, dark journey back to the Slaughtered Lamb.'

'Where?'

'When we found her, she didn't even have a coat. It was freezing and beginning to snow. She was wearing ballet pumps. What country woman would start out on a cold, lonely country lane at night looking like the Queen of Sheba's grandmother without a winter coat or boots?'

Aunt Charlotte considered this a moment. 'I once went to a fancy-dress party at the du Summer's country estate in Cornwall dressed as—'

'Aunt Charlotte!'

'Bad affair that, though.'

'Charlotte!' Mother shouted.

'Is it likely that anyone remotely sensible would set off on a winter walk,' I continued, 'particularly in such weather, dressed like that?'

'No, no. Not at all. You would need Dubarry boots, a Wolfskin overcoat—'

'We don't need styling tips for the damned,' Mother cut in.

'I just can't believe all this,' Bridget stammered. 'We only came here to discuss a book and we haven't even done that.'

'Do be quiet, Bridget,' I continued. 'No, no. Doreen Dellamer wasn't dressed for a long winter walk home, because it wasn't long.'

Aunt Charlotte's eyes flickered with the dwindling firelight as if a thought had flashed over them. 'You mean the village, this pub — the Slaughtered Lamb — isn't that what you called it? It is closer than we thought? We might make it?'

'No, Aunt Charlotte,' I said firmly. 'She didn't have far to travel home because she *was* home! Here!'

The room petered into silence. I watched the silver droplets of ice travel down the window and pictured Doreen Dellamer out there, dressed in her farcical costume, bitterly cold, her feet numbing in those silly little shoes, the thin sheer scarves catching on the grim wind.

A sense of falling behind time descended on us. Occasionally, the sky split and the rimed moon watched us. We were in the frayed edges of this day, when clarity fades. This was a world of confusion and as we slipped further from reality, flashes of the real world echoed. Something from years ago, Mother's voice — '*All those airs and graces! All she ever did was ramble on about her privileged life in a glorious mansion.*'

'Yes, Doreen Dellamer had a very short walk home last night,' I said quietly, almost to myself. 'Or so she thought. Don't you remember how she appeared without a trace of her arrival? That's because she was already here. When she had finished with us, she would have just slipped back home round the side of the house as usual. She had no coat, she didn't change her shoes, because she didn't need to. It's unlikely a professional entertainer would wear that sort of elaborate costume to trek home. They would change. Unless they were already home. But she was killed on the doorstep first and then dragged out there.'

'What nonsense. A fortune teller does not live in a house like this,' Aunt Charlotte said dismissively.

'I told you not to get involved in all that heathenism. Fortune telling and nonsense. Look what it's led to,' Bridget added snidely.

I let the air slowly leak out of me and looked past them all. I stared through the French doors. The snow had robbed everything of its shades and form. Everything was slightly misaligned as if put together hurriedly. Hurriedly.

'The disguise was ridiculous because they had to do it in a hurry,' I announced. The sudden, sharp words stood alone. 'They didn't know who we were until *she* saw us. Then she realized and they had to act quickly.'

'Dearest, lame-brain daughter, what are you rambling at?' Mother was intrigued, I could tell.

'Her costume was absurd and hastily put together. The disguise and the nature of the deception naïve. They didn't realize who we were until they saw us.'

'But Doreen Dellamer knew very well what my name was,' Mother tutted.

'Yes, but maybe she had nothing to do with bookings.' I waited and let the words ferment.

'Dear God,' Aunt Charlotte whispered, her eyes wide. 'It's the Angels! I knew it. Sneaky little bastards.'

'Aunt Charlotte, why would the Angels, who also live here, wait until we arrived to murder the only other person who lived here with them? Why would they dress her up to get maximum exposure, then slaughter her on the doorstep? Wouldn't it be easier when there were no guests here?'

Aunt Charlotte looked pained.

My thoughts splintered into so many memories. Words from times I thought I had lost flooded back to me. Meaningless before but not now. *Well, of course it was a marvellous mansion.* I pictured Doreen Dellamer, how she used to tell us all about the rooms, Mother invariably looking on with increasing anger. *Airs and graces!* Mother would always whisper. They were not adopted airs and graces, though. They were genuine. She did indeed live in a mansion with many rooms. Presumably the rest of the tale was not a fantasy either then. She grew up here.

I waited for my thoughts to rearrange.

'Why is your face doing that, Ursula? You look very unattractive.' Mother said.

'She lived here.'

'Yes, you've—'

'She grew up here. She told us she and her family grew up here.'

'Make sense, girl.' Mother was becoming impatient.

'None of it makes any sense to me and Mr Bojangles,' Bridget sighed.

'Now come on, dear,' Aunt Charlotte was beginning to speak to me as if I was having a minor breakdown. I know, because it is exactly how she spoke to me when I *did* have a breakdown — only a minor one, though.

Things felt increasingly like they were hurtling out of control.

Rule 18: Be methodical. Find out what links the deaths.

THE BODY COUNT

I couldn't spin the web together. The murderer had killed more than once but there seemed no connection, no motivation. Where was the revenge, jealousy or simple hatred? Were they protecting something? Thoughts tumbled around in a meaningless storm. Two people had already been murdered. It couldn't possibly be that Doreen Dellamer and Less were coincidentally just hated by the same murderer. No, our killer had needed to silence them.

'They knew something,' I said slowly.

'Who?' Aunt Charlotte was very good at filling in the spaces.

'The victims. They knew something. The killer had to get rid of them both.'

Mother stood up suddenly like someone had put a drawing pin on her chair. I don't do that anymore. 'This is too much, Ursula.'

'It's *conjecture* at this stage of the proceedings, Mother.'

'Please don't shout!' Bridget hissed. 'You'll wake Mr Bojangles.'

'For God's sake, Bridget.' Mother put her head in her hands.

'Whatever it is,' Mirabelle said, as she put a steadying hand on Mother's skirt, 'we need to order our thoughts. Ursula, this is all very good—'

'Thanks.'

'But we need to be more methodical. We've gone round and round in circles and we're getting nowhere.'

'If you go round and round, you won't get anywhere.' Aunt Charlotte sat straight and confidently in her chair, as if she had in some way made a useful contribution.

'Quite. What I meant to say was that at the moment, your random spraying of thoughts is disorientating. We need to be more systematic.' For once, Mirabelle was making perfect sense.

'I think we need to eliminate anyone who isn't in this room.' An unfortunate choice of words by Mother.

'I think, what my mother is suggesting is that we speak to the Angels again and find out if there are any other people hiding or lurking around in the house.'

Mother was standing, prepared and resolute. 'Right, so you're suggesting we go back and see the Angels, again.'

'I think we should remain calm,' Bridget said firmly. 'We could always discuss the book to keep our spirits up.'

'Bridget, forget the book!' Mother had begun speaking to Bridget as if she was the dog. 'Why the hell can't the Angels come here? They're the staff.' She paused for a moment. 'I have paid them to be. Don't look at me like that, young lady. It's my pocket the money's coming out of whether there's murders or not. And I tell you this . . .'

My mind stumbled back to a previous instance of Mother moaning about money and paying for the staff.

'Mother, how many people did you say would be on the staff?'

'What?'

'You said, when we arrived, you paid for *three* members of staff.'

'Yes, I did and I also recall you doubted that too. I can tell you—'

'Well, that settles it! They even charged you for three staff. Doreen Dellamer did live here and the three of them were meant to be working in the house. Right up to the point where we walked through the door. Think. Suddenly, Doreen Dellamer tells the Angels she knows us, she recognized you.'

'Not just me!'

'*We know*, Mother, but somehow, that made them act hurriedly to hide Doreen Dellamer and yet they then went on to reveal her, albeit in a heavy disguise. Why reveal her at all?'

Aunt Charlotte was leaning closer, her mouth dangling open in a pose reminiscent of a dead fish.

'Well, why, girl?' Mirabelle snapped.

I held my knee firmly, so they couldn't see it jittering. The therapist called them 'ticks', like I had some sort of parasite in me. I've learned to control them quite well over the years. However, incarceration in an isolated house with a murderer was really beginning to test my strategies for composure.

'Mirabelle, I do not have all the answers,' I said, in as measured a voice as possible. 'I am presenting a number of scenarios and possible solutions. They may not be true at all. I simply do not know.'

'She would have recognized us all, not *just* me!' Mother seemed to find this point very important.

'Not me,' said Bridget cheerfully. 'I've only ever known you through book club. I had considered socializing with you all outside of it but, on the basis of this experience, I don't think that would be a very good idea for Mr Bojangles and me.'

None of them had ever invited her to any of the drinks or dinners they had.

I looked to the bleak world outside, misted over and fringed with ice. Why hide Doreen Dellamer and then theatrically reveal her, but in disguise? The flakes turned in clouds of silver vapour blooming then fading like breath on a window. She lived here. She had lived with us once. If the Angels took the booking, Doreen Dellamer would not have known who was coming. She knew when she saw us but did not want to reveal herself immediately. Who wants to hide? Who hides from people? Who disguises themselves? Someone who is—

'So,' Mother announced, in her customary manner of slicing straight through my thoughts, 'there are many new matters that we didn't know before. Where they all live, why I've been charged for three staff instead of two, why they hide, wearing bizarre costumes . . .'

'Mother, you do understand these are my conjectures, not gospel truth, don't you? I have no crystal ball.'

'Wait—' Aunt Charlotte appeared to have had a thought, but it was hard to tell — 'so you're now saying *you've* dabbled in this fortune-telling business as well?'

My sigh was long and audible.

'Stop.' Mirabelle stood. 'No more fortune telling. We need some answers, not guesses from some jumped-up Nancy Drew.'

'Who?' We ignored Aunt Charlotte.

'Nancy Drew. Great books.'

'Be quiet, Bridget.' I was beginning to sound like Mother. 'We need to speak to the Angels.'

Mother closed her eyes in frustration. 'Right! Let's get this over with.'

'I'll wait here with Mr—'

'We know, Bridget.' Mother didn't even look at her. If she had, she would have seen the look of contempt.

We set off to revisit the Angels, fuelled on mutual fear and loathing. We formed a bizarre line of bewildered faces. I had so many questions pinballing around my head but not one would settle. Faces drifted around, throwaway lines and cautious looks, all just ghosts of my imagination. It was like bagging steam. I kept coming back to the photograph. Two little girls, here, on the lawn. They played on the edges of my imagination. Happy. Happy times, rich times. Carefree and wealthy. Wealthy. Money.

It always came back to money.

I looked around at the shadowed halls as we went. Bruised furniture that had taken the casual knocks of time, threadbare rugs and little piles of dust that had once been plaster mouldings. The building was falling into history. Even the coat of arms, its glorious wings spread wide, stared down with an ironic echo of past glories.

As night sank its teeth into the fabric of the house, there was barely enough light to see all the details of its decline. A very old darkness settled here. In corners and alcoves, strange shapes hovered. Silhouettes shifted and morphed. Wood splintered and groaned as if an illness infected the walls and the house itself was moaning out in pain. It smelled of neglect, an accepted neglect, just like at school. Musty carpets and damp air filled with disappointment and cold. The portraits had become meaningless faces from another lifetime that had long deserted this house.

And yet the Angels' light glowing at the end of the small, servants' corridor still seemed a welcome sight. As bright as hope, it drew us on with a promise of a more homely air. There was still some life here.

Only there wasn't.

The Angels lay sprawled on the bed in a putrid mess of vomit and blood. Their bodies were wedged together in one last desperate act of pain. Their faces contorted with misery, grizzled and spent. It was as if they wore masks of themselves where the features had slipped. Their skin was the colour of the dirty, stained linen sheets bunched round them. While we had been casually discussing whether they could have been the killers, they had been dying — desperate and unable to muster help. Tissues and buckets lay strewn about them. They had spent their last moments in agonized illness, watching their loved one suffer the same fate. What would be worse, to go first and feel the pain of death as your body

149

resigned itself to this? Or to watch your loved one dissolve, only to face the same fate yourself?

In death, they had sought the solace of each other. Their bodies were twisted, contorted into the unnatural shapes in which they had remained after death. They had convulsed. Their clothes were stained and sticky. I stepped nearer and felt Mother's hand on my arm.

'Don't go any closer,' she whispered. 'We don't know what it was.'

I stared at Mother's hand. We don't touch very often.

'Christ, it stinks!' Aunt Charlotte gagged as she fell back against the door frame, her hand clutched to her face. She was right, but again there was that nagging feeling that she was being unusually insensitive, even for her.

The room was heavy with a blighted scent. There was something unnatural about it, a rich fertilizer smell like freshly spread earth. They had fought death: the covers and clothes ridden up round Mrs Angel's thighs, her feet buried deep in the folds of the soaked covers, told of vile squirming. Angel's hands had gripped hard on the sheets, squeezing them into ragged knots. Everywhere was splashed with a dull, muddied liquid. Mrs Angel's arm was thrown out towards the bedside table among a mess of books and photo frames. A glass of water had been knocked to the ground in despair, not long since, judging by the drips that still fell from its rim to the rug. Clenched in Mrs Angel's other claw-like hand was a photograph, splashed with the brown and bloodied water of her guts. It was the picture I had seen earlier of the two happy little girls. Mrs Angel had chosen this memory to ferry her through the final moments of pain. The little girls' faces shone with oblivious joy, far away in another time that had no knowledge of this foul end.

The door to the other small room was ajar and, for a moment, I imagined I saw a shadow pass through the dim light that spread out from it. Then it was gone. We were being stalked by the phantoms that inhabit imagination and the deepest fear.

What evil had been brought upon them in this small, sad scene? I learned from a young age that death doesn't judge how well we have lived our lives and match the ending to fit that. We should never judge victims by the nature of their deaths — but we do.

They were repulsive. Silenced. Was that the explanation staring blindly back at us — the need to silence them? What had they seen? Did they know what took them down into such pain and death? Perhaps. Did they bring it upon themselves? Unlikely. Such old and tired lives, no one would choose to end their life in such violent horror. Someone did this to them. Someone or something — something in this house.

'Someone murdered them,' I said quietly.

'Oh, Sherlock awakes,' Mirabelle said, with a look of disdain.

'But how?' Aunt Charlotte leaned into the door frame, still looking staggered. 'We were all together. And we're the only people left. Aren't we?'

The words hung in the air like a threat.

'We would know if we weren't alone, surely,' Mirabelle said, but there was no assurance in her voice.

'Listen, that's four dead and five alive.'

'If you don't count the dog.'

'Shut up, Ursula. It's not good statistics.' Mother's voice was sharp. 'If I didn't know better, I'd say we were being picked off.'

I tried to calm my thoughts, but my mind was slipping gear again. Desperately, I cast about for one of the techniques my therapist always suggested. I flicked the elastic band on my wrist exactly six times as I had been told. Useless. As usual, it only stung while my thoughts continued to simmer with so many strange and broken ideas.

'There can't be anyone else,' I said. 'We'd have heard them. Seen them.'

'Why? It's a magnificent house to hide a killer.' As usual, Mother brought no solace.

Aunt Charlotte began coughing theatrically. 'Can we just discuss this somewhere else? I think I'm going to faint if I have to suffer any more of this.' She turned her body round the doorframe and staggered into the hallway.

We all backed out of the room as if from a monarch — or something we should distrust. None of us felt able to turn our backs. I closed the door carefully and we formed a tight cluster in the hallway.

'We need to find out what killed them,' I whispered.

'*Who*!' Aunt Charlotte blurted. 'You mean *who* killed them.'

'I think we will come closer to who when we have worked out how and why.'

'Eh?'

'How and why, Aunt Charlotte. How and why.'

'Can't we just skip to who?'

'No.'

Rule 19: Do not underestimate the dead.

A RECOUNT

We sat for as long as we could bear it in the Angels' living room. The remains of their lives cluttered the surfaces. Photos of people we didn't know, trinkets and souvenirs that only had a purpose while the Angels were alive. Without them, these things became nothing. Only the Angels knew their value, their memories. It had taken moments for it all to become meaningless. A cup and saucer, smart with gold and flowers and Brighton Pavilion inscribed on its side. A painting of a dog, *Beloved Mimi* inscribed on a plaque below. Mimi was nothing now. Her worth had evaporated with their lives. Beloved Mimi. I stared at the dog's portrait. A sweet, small dog — attentive, clear-eyed. Loved. A beloved small dog. Beloved Mimi. The image of the dog circled in my head. Which dog had been beloved? The dog. Beloved.

'The dog!' I announced.

'God, where? Mr Bloody Bo—'

'No, Mother. Beloved Mimi,' I read. No one responded. Aunt Charlotte maintained a look of strained sympathy for me, as if she was indulging another of my 'incidents', as they were referred to in my family.

'The little dog was beloved. The little dog. The dog in the photograph.'

'It's a painting,' Mirabelle corrected.

'No, no. The photograph of the two little girls. I would show you, but it's splattered with the contents of Mrs Angel.'

'Ursula,' Mother snapped, 'please.'

'Mother, the photograph Mrs Angel chose to take to her grave had this little dog in it. Her beloved. Mrs Angel's beloved. The dog in the picture is this dog.' I pointed at the painting. 'The dog Mrs Angel hangs above her mantelpiece, the dog she chose to hold onto as death came — it was her dog. She is the girl in the photograph.'

'So?' An ugly, stupid word, but that would never concern Mother.

'Don't you see? If Mrs Angel is the girl in the photograph, she has lived in this house since she was a girl and she was not a servant in that photograph. This is her house.'

'*Was* her house,' Aunt Charlotte whispered automatically.

They let the thought crystallize.

'You seem to know an awful lot about these people,' Mirabelle said. 'Is there something *you* are not telling *us?*'

'There's no need to start slinging accusations around, Mirabelle. I'm just trying to pull together some thoughts, so we can make sense of all this.'

'Oh, but you've accused all of *us*, Ursula.'

'No, I—'

'Shhh!' Mother hissed. She was thinking. It was always easy to tell when that was happening, as she seemed even more pained than usual. 'So, you are suggesting that this house, this great mansion, was owned by the Angels?' She said it with such disdain that it began to seem questionable.

'Think about it, Mother. Mrs Angel was more than a mere housekeeper. She was very much the lady of this house.'

'Oh, for God's sake, Ursula. What the hell would you know about that? She was just the staff.'

154

'Mother, if you could ever see beyond treating people as if you'd bought them, you would have seen—'

Mirabelle stood. 'Don't speak to your mother like that. I'm tired of watching you grinding away at her with your daily little *needs*. What about her *needs*? A little respect wouldn't go amiss, after all she's done for you.'

Nobody spoke. It was the clock on the mantelpiece that brought us back to the room with its unassuming chiming of the hour, as if time had decided to restart.

'We must work together, or we will die,' I said carefully.

Mirabelle shivered with frustration.

'She's right.' Aunt Charlotte stared at the barren fireplace. 'There are no family photos anywhere in the house. All trace of the real owners has been removed. You wouldn't do that unless you wanted to hide their identity.'

'But why would they do that?' Mother said with rising irritation. 'What possible reason could there be for hiding down here in this stuffy little sink hole, when the entire house was at their disposal?'

'Money.' Somehow, Aunt Charlotte had come alive. Her mind seemed to have been spurred by the last ten minutes. 'Look at the place. Shabby furnishings, unkempt topiary. Two members of staff for all this mansion — to cook, clean and serve. The Angels own—'

'Owned,' Mother interjected.

'*Owned* this place, but they had no money. They opened it up to house parties and pretended to be the staff to avoid difficulties. First, they told us it was a private family, then it was a company. It was them. Nobody wants the impoverished gentry attempting to serve them. They moved out, down here, clearing any hint of themselves from the house, so no one would suspect they were the owners.' Aunt Charlotte whispered the last bit and leaned back with an exceptionally pleased expression on her face.

We sat for a moment in the tiny, damp sitting room packed tight with the memories of a great house, like a junk shop rammed to the rafters.

A long, thin groan came from the other room.

No one moved. We stared.

Another breath-filled noise was followed by a faint scratching.

'Oh Christ, it's haunted!' Aunt Charlotte cried. 'They've come back to haunt their mansion.' She stared rabidly at the rest of us, who could barely believe what she was saying.

'That, or one of them isn't dead,' Mirabelle said.

There was a terrified pause before we ran to the bedroom.

Mr Angel dangled from the edge of the bed and swung a pale arm like a pendulum. His long, yellowing fingers brushed the floorboards rhythmically, the horn-like finger-nails scratching at the worn varnish.

'Dear God, he's alive!' Aunt Charlotte ran forward.

He groaned, a long, guttural noise that rasped with pain. A liquid note bubbled slowly to the surface. 'Angel . . .' He grabbed at the air. 'Destroy . . .' The grey stones of his eyes turned up to the ceiling.

'I'm afraid so, Mr Angel,' Aunt Charlotte said softly.

'*Destroy* . . .' his voice dissolved again.

Aunt Charlotte stepped closer and leaned down.

'. . . *Angel*.'

'I rather think so, Mr A—' Aunt Charlotte had no time to finish her words before a wet plume shot from Mr Angel's mouth and coated the left side of Aunt Charlotte's face. She fell back into the chest of drawers and Mr Angel's head lolled to the side. He was dead and Aunt Charlotte was covered in the remains of his final breath.

There were definitely four dead now. And five of us left.

Rule 20: Do not descend into chaos.

CONFUSION

Aunt Charlotte was gone for a long time. It wasn't just a matter of washing away the blood and vomit. She was trying to erase the image of that moment when the remains of someone's life were being spat into her face.

There was a raw silence to the sitting room. Mirabelle poked at the fire, her eyes reflecting every angry flame. Mother sipped on her brandy, as she watched me with thin eyes, the row of feathery lashes slowly moving up and down as if she had to remind herself to blink. Bridget whispered quietly to her dog.

As far as we knew, the Angels, Doreen Dellamer and Less had no relationship, nothing that bound them in life that would culminate in their joint deaths. Nothing would settle into a pattern. There was no sense here.

We had hastily covered the Angels' bodies in an attempt to restore some dignity to their corpses but, in truth, we just wanted to escape, to get away from the sickly odour of death and the sad end to their lives. We took no time to analyse the surroundings, or forensically examine why they had died in such foul circumstances. The question didn't even seem to raise itself until we were far away from the room.

After the vomiting, Aunt Charlotte could not speak. She had walked the long walk back to the main body of the house as if following a single thread out of the underworld, her eyes unblinking, her mouth sealed, her face covered in the viscid material. I knew she would be fine. Aunt Charlotte was made of stern stuff.

'For God's sake,' Aunt Charlotte's shoulders were hunched with disgust, 'I have never been so insulted in my life!'

'You have,' Mother said.

'Only by you, Pandora.'

I attempted to intervene, which is always a mistake. 'Look, this is not helpful.'

'When has your mother ever been that?' Aunt Charlotte had climbed the stairs to her room, displaying as much dignity as she could muster with the contents of a dead man's stomach on her face.

* * *

We sat in our familiar places staring into the fire, each of us in the tight grip of our thoughts. My head was seizing up again. The possibilities swam around my thoughts, so many avenues to consider that it was crippling. I chewed at the inside of my cheek until the vinegar flavour of my blood pooled behind my teeth. We had to do something. We had to take action. Sitting here, waiting, just thinking, was going to kill us.

'We need to go back to the Angels' rooms and look at them,' I announced.

Aunt Charlotte had just reappeared and begun pouring herself a large brandy. She immediately imitated choking. 'You have got to be kidding me? You must be insane.'

'I can't take Mr Bojangles into a room full of dead people!' Bridget said decidedly. 'That would be cruel.'

'Oh, but it's OK for me—'

'There are so many unanswered questions,' I said.

158

'Such as why someone would choose, with their dying breath, to drown me in their vomit?'

'I realize—'

'No, no, I don't think you can realize anything like that, not until you experience it and I tell you now, young lady, having someone breathe their last breath into your face is . . .' She trailed off.

I didn't speak but the sinking of my eyes was enough.

'I'm sorry, dear,' she said.

'It's OK,' I whispered. I let my eyes close for a moment and breathed in Dad's last breath — his vapour, Mellow Marzipan this time to be precise, another of the strange and wonderful oils he smoked. The sweet remembrance of him trickled away across my cheeks. Such a waste of the breath he couldn't keep, but somehow it felt like a gift. Every time I needed to feel him, to extract that memory and breathe it in again, it was fresh and it smelled of him. The mild, warm scent of him cut through with that usual essence of nicotine. The last breath always remained, never changed by time, as if his soul had drained out in that last moment.

'Ursula.' Mother always made sure I didn't linger too long in the past.

'We need to go back,' I said quietly. 'We need to find out what killed them.'

The walk back to the Angels' apartments seemed longer than before. The corridors stretched out and darkened, as if like a bitter fairy tale, the thorny branches were already starting to grow up around the house. Now that the owners had passed, it was all dying and being sealed up.

'Anyone else got a sense of déjà vu?' Mirabelle stared at me pointedly.

'For once, I agree,' Aunt Charlotte said. Her face was tight and there were sore patches where she'd scrubbed at it. 'This is like some recurring nightmare.'

I didn't respond. There was no sense to it, I knew that. But something itched at the edges of my thoughts. There was something down there, something waiting to be found.

We walked in silent procession, exhausted and with a slow reverence. Even the dog looked grave. We reflexively bowed our heads as we passed beneath the family coat of arms, its great Angel wings spreading out from both edges of the shield. Were they the end of the Angel line? There'd been no talk of children, but then their subterfuge had prevented them from telling us anything real. We had lived with these people, in their home, and we knew nothing about them, even though their crest and their relatives' faces looked down upon us from that first moment. They had watched as these strangers invaded their family seat of centuries and treated them with such easy disdain. They had served us in the rooms of their ancestors. And now they were dead.

The sour distilment of the Angels' bedroom seeped through the hall towards us long before we got anywhere near.

When we looked at the remains of the Angels, we were captivated by the grotesqueness. It wasn't sympathy or sadness we felt, but disgust. There was a savagery to it, a brutality.

'What did this?' Mother said.

'You mean who.' I pinged my elastic band. It was still useless.

'Perhaps.' Her eyes wandered the room. 'Could they have done it to themselves?'

'I can't subject Mr Bojangles to any more of this,' Bridget whispered tearily. 'I'm sorry, I just can't.' And with that, she scurried away as if it was contagious. I began to wonder about Bridget and how many times she'd had to leave, to separate herself from the group.

We stood uselessly, no one daring to enter the sceptic tomb. Their wretched outlines beneath the hastily thrown sheets were unnerving. Slanting shadows from the small wall lights reached out across the stained rug.

'Remember his words, Pandora,' Aunt Charlotte said in a solemn voice, '*destroy Angel*. He wasn't talking about a suicide pact. Someone destroyed them.'

It was a strange choice of words, but who can predict what we will choose to say on our death beds? What will seem important when nothing is important anymore?

'If they'd known their killer, he would surely have named them with his dying breath,' Mirabelle said. 'So we can assume they didn't know their killer — if there was one at all.'

'Well, what killed them?' Aunt Charlotte was rubbing her face instinctively, as if Angel's vomit was still on her skin. 'An overdose of something. Tablets or . . .'

'Something poisoned them, I'd guess,' Mother said, transfixed.

'That's fairly sophisticated for a novice killer,' Aunt Charlotte said.

'Novice?' I said. 'What makes you think this person is a novice? So far, Doreen Dellamer has been murdered on the doorstep with Diana's arrow then dragged into a shallow grave; Less has been impaled by a chandelier in her bathtub; and the Angels have voided their bodies and been reduced to a violent, bloody mess. This person is not scared of killing. I think this person would be ingenious enough to find a vile and miserable end for us all if they could. Who knows, perhaps it's just the joy of killing that's exciting our murderer.'

'Don't be ridiculous, Ursula!' Mother said quickly. 'Are you suggesting some sort of serial killer is getting kicks out of killing us?' The effect of her words lingered. I imagined a face watching us now, hiding, waiting for the moment to sneak out and kill, then retreating back to their hole to watch our horror unfold. There were certainly enough places to hide here and we'd hardly conducted a conclusive search.

'Right, we need to find out what killed them,' Mother said efficiently, returning to the point. 'Let's get going then. Mirabelle and I will search the kitchens and living room. Charlotte and Ursula, you can search here.'

'No way!' Aunt Charlotte blurted. 'Why do we have to search that morgue? It stinks and they're . . . they're . . . still warm.'

161

Mother sighed. 'Very well, Mirabelle and I will search in the bedroom. You two go and see what you can do in the rest of the place.' It was very uncharacteristic of Mother to back down and change her plans because of a complaint from Aunt Charlotte. Perhaps she was sympathetic after the vomiting-in-the-face incident. She had to feel some sort of sisterly love, after all — didn't she? They never really demonstrated much of it. Even Angel had registered his surprise that they were sisters. Yet it was always there as a thread between them.

I glanced at Mother as Aunt Charlotte and I edged slowly towards the open bedroom door. The Angels were contorted into the shapes they left this world in, unnatural and twisted out of all recognition. There was nothing genteel or dignified about them now. All that was left was a dirty knot of limbs.

Mother sighed heavily and gently pulled the sheet over a dangling hand. The dim light caught on Mrs Angel's skin and gave it a slick and greasy sheen, as if life was still coming out of her. Her purple greying fingers gripped the beloved dog photo. Mother looked over at Aunt Charlotte, and the corners of her mouth fell down in dismay. There was a moment of recognition between them and then it passed. They both looked away quickly.

As we slowly walked away from the deathly room, I noticed the slip of light from the small dressing room casting its sad gaze over the bed. Mrs Angel wouldn't visit there anymore. Its mirrors would no longer see her face, powdering and brushing the immaculately groomed reflection. She wouldn't lie on its soft, velvet-covered bed.

As Aunt Charlotte and I left, the sour smell lingered in our throats. The sharp sapor faded slowly and weakened as we headed off towards the kitchens. A coolness spread, watering down the bitter air. The old, grey flagstones shone with a damp gleam. A single straight light guided us down the narrow passage.

At the end, the vast kitchen opened out, a great, sombre room from another era. Tarnished copper pots hung like abandoned soldier's helmets from enormous ceiling racks above the scrubbed trestle table. A whole wall was devoted to a lead black range, mostly unused. One small corner showed a little more wear, with signs of recent use, but the rest remained untouched. A single frying pan sat washed beside the sink.

Everything here was clean and tired. It was an unused clean. The rows of chairs and plates, the pans and utensils all arrayed so uniformly to tell of busier times when this place sang with work and life. The Angels had haunted this place like ghosts lingering through the fading years. Before it had sunk into quiet obsolescence.

'There's nothing here,' Aunt Charlotte said in a surprisingly respectful tone. This was her church voice, cultivated, I assumed, for if she ever visited church. She didn't, but it was useful to have one, just in case. 'Let's go.' There was a bed note of concern, as if something disturbed her.

'I just want to check the stores and the cupboards,' I said.

There was a large, old-fashioned fridge on the far wall. I walked over and noticed a small upturned basket. It wasn't like the Angels to have left something out of place. I bent and picked it up. It was a traditional style, with faded blue-and-white checked material on the inside. It was empty save for a few lumps of black mud and when I held it closer, an unusual earthy smell rose up, musty and rich, like newly turned compost. I put the basket back on the counter and opened the fridge.

There wasn't much there. A large piece of browning beef, presumably for our supper. Some plastic containers of milk and rows of fresh eggs. There wasn't the squash of old jars and pots that accumulates in a busy house.

I closed it and the light was gone. The room fell back to a sickly green gloom.

'Look, I can't see what you'd hope to find among their food. Can't we just—'

'Did they look poisoned to you?' I demanded.

She nodded.

'Well, let's look for poison then.'

She nodded again. I'm not sure what Aunt Charlotte was adding to this process. But then I imagined being in this giant, shadowed kitchen on my own, the morbid green light and rattle of pipes, the sharp little draught, and suddenly I was glad Aunt Charlotte was there.

We searched the untouched cupboards and found stack upon stack of plates, pans, bowls and cups. There were spices and old pickles in an almost empty larder, alongside a few stale loaves. We sniffed and poked at various foodstuffs, but there was nothing that looked like it could do any harm. There were the usual cleaning products in a caddy under the sink, but they had the strong, sharp smell of chemicals. The Angels could not have ingested something like that without being fully aware of what was going in their mouths and it was highly unlikely they would both choose to die by such a vile method, especially with their house full of guests.

None of the meagre supply of bottles and cans, packets and tins showed any signs of having been tampered with. There were no strange solutions or misplaced liquids that screamed foul play. Everything was nestled in the places they had occupied harmlessly for years, just as the Angels themselves had. It's predictability, it's *usualness* was frustrating. We walked back to Mother and Mirabelle in utter confusion. We were not constructing anything. No theories were formulating. The only thing that was building was the body count.

Rule 21: Stick together and don't let anyone pollute the group.

RANDOM THREADS

We went back to the sitting room more disillusioned than the first time we'd seen the remains of the Angels. Bridget was still by the fire whispering to Mr Bojangles, as if she was sharing secrets with him. Somehow, she was still managing to act as if none of this was her concern.

What would happen to this magnificent, faded home? So many lifetimes of memories cut short in such sudden horror. They were desperate deaths, tortured and frightening. Why should such plain, *harmless* people generate such terrible ends? Why end them at all? They had nothing. They lived in the dusk of this great house. They had been reduced to hiding in their own home as a way of preserving it. The glories that had played around them were never going to be resurrected.

I looked at the bare side tables and mantelpiece. The places where the photos had stood were clear now. Gaps in the life of the house. The Angels had systematically removed all trace of their past in this house, so they could masquerade as simple custodians. Perhaps that's how they saw themselves. The keepers of this great home, who must sacrifice everything to keep it in the family. Clearly, it would have sold a thousand times over to some rich property magnate who would have ripped the guts out of it. There could have been shining chrome-and-black tables, media rooms and man caves. There would be oversized fresh flowers on hall tables, a whole palette of grey walls and rooms with TV screens to dwarf real life. These past few days would make this house a challenging purchase for anyone now. What would happen when our ice prison finally melted? What would the world think when they saw all the bodies? What would they think of us?

'It is absolutely imperative that we find the killer,' I announced.

'Good God, Ursula.' Mother slumped into her usual position on the sofa. 'Your knack for stating the obvious is unswerving.' Mother looked ever so slightly worn. Her usual fastidious grooming had a roughness to it that was almost imperceptible to anyone but me. But it was there, the untidy little ends to her, the few wisps of hair that rose and peaked where they shouldn't, the slight crêpey texture to her cheeks where she'd not religiously applied all her usual lotions and unguents. She didn't just look tired, she looked older.

'That girl of yours likes the sound of her voice, I've always said it, haven't I?' Mirabelle jabbed at the fire again.

'Yes, you have,' I said flatly.

We locked eyes.

'Still stoking the fires, Mirabelle?' I said, with a careful smile. I made a quizzical face. 'It's strange isn't it, Mirabelle, that you didn't see the murder weapon right there next to the poker you keep using?'

Her face clouded over with a sour expression of disgust.

Mother, as usual, observed everything. 'Just stop. There's no time for this. Ursula's right. We have to find the killer. We have to get out of this bloody morgue.'

Bridget gave a yelp, or it could have been her dog. 'Please don't use words like that.'

We all stared at the blank window. Snow still glided softly on the bleak air. Soon we would be entirely entombed in this mausoleum, whether we were dead or not. Doreen Dellamer would be buried so deep that she might never be found. Less still reclined in her deathly bath upstairs and the Angels languished in the rotten liquids that had destroyed them. We were surrounded by bodies.

'We have to look for — find — the killer, or . . .' Aunt Charlotte let the thought fester in the air.

'Why?' Bridget said abruptly. 'That's a matter for the police. None of this concerns us. Unless there's something you're not telling us.'

'What?' Aunt Charlotte turned on her. 'I don't know who's more stupid, you or the dog. It'll be a *matter for the police* when they find all our bodies. If we don't find that killer, we'll be next.'

'Look, while we're all awake and here together, we should be safe,' Mirabelle said.

'What makes you so sure of that?' Aunt Charlotte leaned forward in her seat. 'I can't even remember the last time I *slept*.' She was jittering.

'Oh, Charlotte, sleep is the least of our worries.' Mother's tone was the usual cocktail of disappointment and annoyance. 'We are being hunted.'

'Don't be so dramatic, Mother.'

Mother's eyes pinched.

'Don't speak to your mother like that,' Mirabelle warned.

'I'll speak to *my* mother however I see fit, thank you, Mirabelle.'

Mirabelle stood. Her solid frame obscured most of the light instantly. I stood too, since I thought it might make a difference. It didn't. She still filled all the space I could see.

'Listen to me, you pathetic little attention seeker, I'm under threat and I don't like being under threat.' Mirabelle's voice was low and calm. 'Don't cross me, girl. Don't cross me.' Her finger lingered angrily in the air.

'Or what, you'll kill me too?'

I could feel her nerves sharpen.

'I knew it was a mistake coming here,' Bridget said.

'Let's all stay calm.' Mother was agitated. 'We have to think *clearly* to survive this. Come on, Ursula, think!'

'Why me?' I was beginning to sound petulant again.

'Because you're all we've got.' Mother watched me intently.

We returned uneasily to our places: Mother on the sofa, taut with nerves; Mirabelle hovering by the fire, stabbing the flames with her poker every so often in-between staring at me; Aunt Charlotte opposite Mother in a chair that looked too small for her, though she did that to most chairs; Bridget and her dog in the chair closest to the fire; while I still sat slightly back from the group where I could watch more easily, my fingers steepled in thought. We avoided looking at Less's conspicuously empty space, as though it were an ill omen.

The constant patter of the fire played in the background. Ideas and thoughts rattled around my brain, unable to settle or form a pattern. Nothing was clear. We'd fallen down a macabre rabbit hole where nothing made sense and everything could kill us.

'Let's go through what we know,' I said. It was important to remain calm. People were ready to suspect anyone at this point, even me.

'Let's draw together the threads if we can.' My fingers circled one another as if knitting the air together. I gripped them tight to stop the shaking and the raw skin bulged where I'd picked it down on either side of the nails. 'First of all, the Angels lived here. This was their home, and for the sake of appearances and financial constraints, they rented it out, masquerading as the housekeeper and the butler. Are we all agreed on that so far?'

No one spoke, so I assumed they were.

'Secondly, when we arrived, Doreen Dellamer hid her existence. The Angels kept her secret. But rather than simply keep her out of sight, they hastily put together the disguise of the fortune teller, so she could speak to one of us without being identified.'

'Ahh.' Aunt Charlotte made a strange, strangled sound. We all looked at her, instantly expecting another death. 'This is too complicated. It's hurting my brain.'

'It's hardly quantum physics,' Bridget said dismissively.

Aunt Charlotte shuddered. 'I don't see how that would help solve a murder. I found it very dull.'

We paused for a moment to take this in.

'Do continue, dear.' Aunt Charlotte nodded towards me. 'You believe Doreen Dellamer lived here because . . .'

Mother held out her hand and counted off on her fingers. 'We didn't hear or see any approach from her. Her garments were hurriedly put together as if assembled from what she had to hand. She didn't change out of this fortune-telling costume, which included a farcical wig, veils and dainty pumps, to return to the village on a dark, freezing night with the weather closing in. QED, she wasn't going back to the village. She never came from the village. She was here all along.' Mother slumped back into the sofa, exhausted from the effort.

'But,' Mirabelle said carefully, 'why could she not just have been visiting?'

'She's right,' said Mother. 'We've assumed she lived here. But she could just as easily have been visiting.'

'No, Mother . . .'

'Why am I not surprised that that is your response?'

'What I mean is we must gather the threads.'

Mother shook her head. 'Gather the threads. Gather the threads. All such nonsense. While we gather the threads, the killer is—'

'Why would the Angels have visitors when they had a booking for the house? A booking that involved having to pretend they were the housekeeper and the butler. Wouldn't that seem weird to another guest? Why would she come at night, in the dark, and when bad weather was closing in? No, she was living here all right, with the Angels. But why?' I asked.

'Because she liked them?' Aunt Charlotte offered.

'Don't be so ridiculous,' Mother sighed. 'Nobody liked them.'

'Pandora, they are dead!' Aunt Charlotte gasped.

'That doesn't make them any more likeable.'

Bridget cleared her throat, which by now we'd associated with the arrival of another poisonous little comment. 'It is just not acceptable, Pandora, to voice your dislike of the recently deceased, particularly not if they have been murdered.' She smiled like a killer. 'It can so easily cast a person in a bad light and there's nothing worse than being in a bad light when you are suspected of being a murderer, dear.'

'I'm not a suspect!' Mother said astonished.

Silence.

Mother looked from face to face. 'She lodged with us. Perhaps she was just a serial lodger.'

Aunt Charlotte stood up suddenly and began squeezing her hands together. 'Why would you say that? Why?'

'What?'

'You know, *serial lodger.*'

'What's wrong with that?'

'Wrong? Everything.' She started pacing. Pacing assists nothing. 'Well, it sounds a lot like serial *killer.*'

We all stared at Aunt Charlotte. It was quite possible she was beginning to descend into hysteria.

In some respects, it was laudable that no one's sanity had slipped entirely yet. There'd been momentary flirtation with blind panic, but it had quickly subsided. This new outburst seemed to be taking us into a different phase. We couldn't let it pollute the group.

'For God's sake, Charlotte, be quiet! Now!' Mother was excellent at shutting people down immediately.

'Or else what? You'll shut me in a cupboard like you did when we were children?' Aunt Charlotte stood defiantly over Mother. Our family was actually rather used to extreme moments that required locking someone in a cupboard. It had happened a lot in my childhood too.

'Don't be so stupid, Charlotte. I wouldn't have the strength to shift you!'

'How dare you, Pandora! Always bullying me about my weight when you're the one with the neuroses and food issues. *Complete and utter bundle of psychosis*, isn't that what the shrink said? Look at what you've done to your daughter! Look at the way you treated George.'

And it was out there again. His name, spat out in anger, disturbing his memory for a cheap comment in an argument. Dad found himself in the middle of many of these sibling rows, but he never got involved. He would withdraw immediately before the real shots were fired.

Now, his name fell in the room like a grenade, everyone staring at it in silence, before the moment it exploded. When it came, it was with a force no one could have imagined.

'You disgust me,' Mother sharpened her words carefully and rose slowly. Their faces were so close Aunt Charlotte recoiled with every word. 'You leech off my family. You take my money. You come on my holidays. You have nothing. No one. You are nothing. No one. George *hated* you. Did you never notice how he left the room every time you entered it? No. You never notice anything or anyone but yourself. You are a desperate, sorry mess of a woman and I'm ashamed you are my sister. Is there a serial killer on the loose bumping us off one by one? Maybe. I hope they're listening now. If they are, then,' she held her head back and shouted loudly into the air, 'make this one your next victim, for God's sake, and put her out of her misery.' Mother raged out of the room, all bared teeth and anger. We heard her feet stamp into every step of the stairs and fade.

Aunt Charlotte fell back into the chair and stared at the fire.

'Well, this is better than any book,' Bridget smiled. 'Perhaps we all just need a little bit of rest.'

'How very perceptive, Bridget,' I said.

Bridget slowly closed her eyes, as if she was resolutely remaining calm through some saintly duty. 'I was merely suggesting that a few hours' rest in our rooms might freshen our thoughts and bring a sense of perspective to our situation, that's all, Ursula. But if you have a better suggestion . . .'

I watched her closely. 'I think it would be foolhardy to separate at this point. Wouldn't you agree? Why would you want us to split up and be alone, Bridget?' I smiled tightly at her. 'If the killer *is* hiding out somewhere in the house, he or she will be waiting for that exact moment when they can pick one of us off, the moment when we are isolated and at our weakest, when we are alone and easy to despatch without being detected.' I paused. 'Or perhaps that would suit you, Bridget.'

She attempted to look offended.

The room slowed into a frail silence. Two words circled one another — *alone* — *killer* — *alone* — *killer.*

'Mother!' I said automatically. 'Mother's alone.'

'Pandora!' Mirabelle ran for the door. 'Panders!'

Panders? No one had ever called her that. No one. Another manufactured idea of deep friendship from Mirabelle.

'Mummy,' I shouted by way of retaliation.

When we arrived in the doorway of Mother's room, there was a hasty pile of clothes on the bed, steam was coming from the bathroom. The door was open, but she wasn't there.

'Pandora?' Mirabelle ran into the bathroom, clutching one of Mother's shirts. 'She's not here. She's not here.' Her voice was frantic. Her eyes darted all over the room. She gripped the silk shirt until great creases appeared. Mother would not be pleased about that. 'We have to find her. She could be in serious danger!'

'OK, OK, Mirabelle,' Aunt Charlotte tried to calm her. 'I'm sure she's fine. It would take a brave person to attempt to murder my sister.'

'Right, you take the east wing and I'll take the west,' Mirabelle announced. 'Ursula, search the downstairs. She can't have gone far.'

We instantly separated.

'Check the cupboards as well,' Aunt Charlotte added. 'She loves a cupboard.' I don't know if she was trying to be humorous or snide. It's hard to tell in our family.

One thing was certain, Mother was missing and, as we looked around, Bridget and the dog were no longer with us either.

Rule 22: Never ignore the lesser crimes.

THERE MUST BE BLOOD, LOTS OF BLOOD

We'd done a remarkably good job of making sure each one of us was alone. I tried to keep busy and scoured the downstairs, randomly glancing in strange cupboards, pulling out chairs and peering down the backs of sofas. But there was nothing in the dust. No disruption. No footprints or outward signs of disturbance. Mother had just vanished.

There wasn't even any sound of Mother, which *is* unusual for her. Even if you can't see her, you can usually hear her. I checked behind curtains, under tables, in rooms that looked as if they'd never been inhabited by anyone, let alone the Angels.

As I searched, what became inescapable was the image of the Angels living their half-life, surrounded by all the remains of the full life they had once lived here. Such glorious privilege, fabulous summers and glittering Christmases would have been enjoyed in this once merry house. I yanked open a cupboard and a set of croquet mallets fell out. Unused for decades. This was once a hive of activity, visitors and excitement. What must it have been like to have grown up in a busy, lively home? After Dad died, there was a lot of silence. We lost all the sounds of a family.

I thought of the photograph that Mrs Angel had clutched in her last moments. What photograph would I choose? That one slipped in the pages of *Jane Eyre*, of course. Dad.

Mrs Angel clutched her greatest love. But it wasn't Mr Angel. No. The dog and a friend. At this house.

I peered through the door of the sitting room. Empty. I glanced at the piano I so vividly imagined I heard on that first night playing my dad's sweet Clair de Lune.

The lid wasn't dusty now. The Angels had obviously cleaned it. They must have had to be so diligent, working hard to ensure the impression of an absent wealthy owner with staff to perform all the necessary duties. What a burden it must have been to perform the menial cleaning and upkeep on this great house yet never to feel at home, always to be displaced by others.

I glanced down and saw the remains of the dust still feathering the carpet below the piano. It must have been impossible to keep this place spotless with only the pair of them. They would not even have noticed the layer of dust drift to the old carpet and settle. It shone with a strange pale gleam as the lamp's thin light ran over the floor. I bent to look. It was somehow whiter than it should be. I frowned and looked closer. There was some on the pedals too. I wiped my finger through it, sniffed it and, without thinking, licked it. If I'd been thinking rationally, this probably wasn't a great idea in a house harbouring a possible murderer. But no one was thinking rationally anymore. To my surprise, it was sweet. And thankfully not poisonous. It was icing sugar.

I sat back, confused. Nothing made sense here. It was like the time Mother 'lost' me in the house of fun. There is no fun in being disorientated and frantic. My head ran with hectic images.

The room was silent. A cool draught ran down my neck and I turned to look at the door. A loose shadow moved across and then it was gone, dissolved into imagination or fear. I gathered myself into a tight ball, pushing my knees further and further into my chest.

'Help us,' I whispered.

Fear rose up fast like weeds in my imagination, twisting harmless shapes into elaborate faces. For a moment, all I could do was stare at the cold cave outside the window. We had been packed in this ice like carcasses in a larder, ready to be butchered and hung. This was methodical. The lifeless land would soon snuff out all traces of a beating pulse and slow our blood to a stop. But why?

As quick as a thought, the shadow returned and settled across the carpet just beside me. My whisper for help had brought it back. Every muscle gripped my bones tight. I was rigid, as if one push would send me shattering to the floor.

A cool breath of air slipped along my face, a slim, cold finger drawing down my cheek and onto my neck. Just in the edges of my vision I could see a strange dark silhouette, hovering at the side of the room. Although the figure didn't move, it seemed to flicker with life, its outline shifting almost imperceptibly. I felt my heart grip tight in my chest and the sweat pool in the creases of my hand. My breath sounded loud in my ears and yet I couldn't stifle its rough pull.

I didn't dare turn. I closed my eyes, but my mind traced out the dark outline of the figure's shadow on the floor beside me, as if the police had drawn around another body. I was sure a cool breath skimmed my face again, but it was too hard to separate my imagination from reality now. I let my eyes open a little and saw the glimpse of a shimmering outline, flickering in the darkness. It moved again. It no longer seemed to have a simple human shape, its limbs seemed stretched too long. Like a child waiting for the ghosts to come, I sat, scared, clutching my knees to my chest with thoughts of my dad in the darkness. He would have known what to do. He wouldn't have run away and left me.

I rocked myself gently, listening to the rub of my clothes on the floor.

I couldn't look up. I stared at the carpet and the baleful shape shifting across it, a long slip of darkness reaching its way towards me, spreading out on the carpet next to me like a stain. The cold air caught in my chest. The ground held me down. All sound drained from the world and the snow sat still in the air. I tried to look to the window, to focus on the outside world, the real world. Six black crows splattered their wings against the bottomless sky and died away in muted cries.

'Mother.' My voice was muted with desperation. '*Please help me.*'

I screwed my eyes tight shut and held my lips open ready to scream. My breath had stopped. Thoughts rattled in my head so fast I couldn't focus on anything. The room paused.

'Mother,' I whispered. 'Dad?'

I sat for moments, minutes, hours, who knows? Clutching my knees to my chest, trying to ready myself for what none of us can ever be ready for. I rocked myself gently, like a child lulling itself to sleep. If I didn't look, there would be no monsters.

I heard myself whisper, '*Please help.*' It was the last thing I heard.

* * *

I don't know how long I was out for, but when I finally opened my eyes again, motes of light travelled across my white-glazed view. The figure had gone.

I waited in the gloom, desperately attempting to cool my nerves until the frantic pulse in my ears slowed and trickled into a murmur.

I lay on the floor with my body bunched round me and drifted slowly into the haze of memory. I closed my eyes again, listening to the gentle tap of his fingers on the piano keys, the scent of his dry tobacco, a bitter earthy note. The veil of smoke always lingered in a grey pall. My eyes flickered open.

No one here smoked. Yet, on that first night when the closed piano played, there was a distinct flavour of tobacco on the air. *NO SMOKING*, the sign had read, with that crude addition of *or e-cigarettes*.

Yet the night I'd heard the piano music, there was the strong and unmistakable scent of a cigarette — a real cigarette — an analogue, as Dad used to call them, as he chuffed away like a steam engine.

Every time I felt I had opened a new valve, all my thoughts evaporated into nothing more than hot air. Something was just out of reach. Something in the smoke.

Bodies were piling up and there weren't that many of us left. I had to find the link. The death of the fortune teller, the Angels and Less — there had to be a reason. Finally, I crawled on my hands and knees towards the door, the rough braids of the carpet setting their pattern into my hands. I counted each second, slowly pushing myself towards the door. I sat on the cold, tiled floor of the hall and cried until I couldn't find any more tears.

* * *

It took a long time to find the will to gather myself and find someone. I stepped across the hall and at the top of the stairs, it hit me. The iron-rich stench of blood flowed down the dark corridor. This was Less filling up the air until we were choking on the very essence of her remains.

I heard a click. A door. There was an untouched darkness in the hallways. Was that another shadow I saw flit around the corner as I turned to the west wing?

The door to Less's bedroom was open. The reek of blood curdled the air. I could see through to the bathroom and the room was in complete disarray. Less never left her room anything but immaculate just in case she ever got burgled, which seemed to have happened posthumously.

'Hello?' I called tentatively. This was possibly not wise when a killer had returned to ransack the scene of a murder.

I hadn't stepped far into the room when I fell over Mirabelle's great prison-guard feet. I was about to express my frustration at her lying down in the middle of the room when I noticed she wasn't moving and there was blood all over the back of her head.

'Oh Christ, not again,' were probably not the words to use over the body of a murdered woman but fortunately Mirabelle was in no state to complain. I bent down quickly and put my fingers carefully to her throat. There was blood everywhere, soaking her hair in sticky patterns and dribbling onto her face. A viscous pool had formed already beneath her cheek. She must have lost a lot of blood and very quickly.

'What the hell has happened here?' Aunt Charlotte panted at the doorway. She looked very dramatic. To be fair, it was a fairly dramatic scene that had greeted her.

I looked up at her. 'It's Mirabelle. I think she's dead. I think she's been hit over the back of the head.'

'Really?' It did cross my mind that Aunt Charlotte had got to us rather swiftly from the east wing. I kept my eyes firmly on her as she approached.

A groan. It was Mirabelle.

'Mirabelle? Mirabelle?'

There was no response. I had to resort to it. 'Aunt Mirabelle?'

Another groan, this time guttural and with the feeling that more blood might soon erupt.

'She's alive!' Aunt Charlotte ran towards us and a sudden wave of fear passed through me. I'm sure most people seeing Aunt Charlotte running towards them would feel this way.

For some inexplicable reason, I closed my eyes. I felt the blood slippery beneath my hand as I cradled Mirabelle's head. When I dared to peep through my shaking eyelids, I saw Aunt Charlotte was bending over Mirabelle and taking her pulse.

'Pulse seems fine. Let's get her more comfortable. We'll not move her.'

Small feet quickly padded towards us.

'Mr Bojangles, no!' It was Bridget. And her dog had begun nosing at Mirabelle with greedy excitement.

'Are you kidding me?' I stared at Aunt Charlotte and then at the puddle of glistening blood. 'Bridget, get your bloody dog off the blood!'

'Oh, sweetie, is the nasty lady—'

'Now! There's a killer on the loose. They *might* come back to finish the job or finish your dog!'

Mirabelle groaned and her eyes flickered open. She looked up at me with her usual disdain, so I knew she couldn't be dying. Surely not even Mirabelle would allow her parting gesture to be one of contempt.

She lifted her arm.

'Don't move,' Aunt Charlotte cautioned.

'Bugger off, Charlotte.' Mirabelle still had her sting. Her fingers began gingerly probing the back of her head. Parting the matted hair, she winced.

'I really do think—' Aunt Charlotte began.

'I really don't care, Charlotte. I am bleeding. And get that bloody dog off me!'

Bridget scuttled forward. 'Mr Bojangles, come, come, boy.'

'Just pick it up!' Mirabelle stared at her hand all covered in gore. She closed her eyes and for a moment, she could have been fading.

Bridget grabbed the dog and walked away with fast little steps, prim and self-righteous.

We watched closely as Mirabelle sat up, her eyes still closed. She shook her head and small droplets of blood filigreed out across the carpet. Her hand stayed firmly on the back of her head as if she was trying to hold everything in.

'Mirabelle, I really don't think you should move.'

'That's because you're lazy.' The insults still fell easily. 'I, however, am not going to lie in my own blood and wait for that maniac to come back and finish the job or for that idiotic dog to lick me to death.' She was bent double now, as if contemplating the steady drip of blood that fell in a regular beat from a point of her hair. She stared resolutely at the spreading stain on the rug.

'It'll never come out,' Aunt Charlotte observed.

Mirabelle fired her another look.

'Sorry,' Aunt Charlotte muttered. 'Look, you've had a nasty bump to the head—'

Mirabelle swivelled round to face Aunt Charlotte. 'Nasty bump to the head? They've damn near caved my skull in, you stupid—'

I held up my hands. 'Mirabelle, did you see anyone?'

'Through the back of my head? No.'

'OK. Let's just take it easy. That's all Aunt Charlotte was saying.'

Mirabelle watched me. This was rare as she never properly looked at me. It was generally dismissive gestures or eye-rolling but never a complete look.

'There is no time for *taking it easy*. If your mother was here—'

'But she's not, is she?'

Aunt Charlotte and Mirabelle were still. A sour, ammonia air had settled across the room, a rank smell, as if something had curdled and turned rancid. I glanced towards the bathroom where the door stood slightly ajar. Less's spread-eagled body was still in the bathtub, the giant chandelier firmly embedded in her chest. She had been crudely covered by the Angels with towels that had soaked up the water and were beginning to give off a smell of laundry left too long in the machine, a smell I'm very familiar with. The rusty stains of her blood had soaked through the thin material in strange star-like shapes that spread out to form a grubby constellation across the white towels. Her pale marbled arm dangled over the bath side, almost as if she had struck a louche pose, lounging into that final moment of death. But the black red slash, that had oozed down her forearm and puddled below, told a different story.

I went further into the room and the putrid smell had a bitter edge of flowers left too long in a vase. The air was rich with the congealed flavour of blood. I began to feel faint. Waves of nausea flooded through me as the warm flavour of it slipped over my tongue. I could taste the death scent in my mouth, as sickly as overripe fruit. 'Perhaps Mirabelle is right, Aunt Charlotte.' I turned to look at them both, wearily. 'We need to find somewhere safe, get Mirabelle cleaned up and decide what to do.'

Aunt Charlotte nodded and placed a shaky hand on my shoulder. 'Your mother would be proud of you,' she said softly.

'No, she wouldn't,' I said, through a weak smile.

As our beleaguered little group left, I turned and looked at the disarray and blood — such carnage where there had been order. Even the neat little dressing table had been ransacked. And there, in the middle of it, was the Meissen vase from the mantelpiece. I shook my head and took a final look at Less. Even here, she couldn't help her thieving ways.

Rule 23: Watch carefully those who make a habit of disappearing.

BATTLE PLANS

We took Mirabelle to her room with the minimum amount of fuss that we were capable of under such extreme circumstances and made Bridget wait outside the door, to keep the bloodthirsty Mr Bojangles at bay. Although, we told Bridget it was because we needed her and Mr Bojangles to stand guard. We can be sensitive sometimes, especially when it achieves the necessary outcome. They were where we could hear them, which was exceptionally irritating but at least everyone was safe — for the moment. Mirabelle was so agitated by now that we left her to clean herself up in the bathroom, while Aunt Charlotte and I sat in the bedroom and waited. We weren't risking anyone getting picked off again — not even Mirabelle.

'We go down together,' Aunt Charlotte announced. I resisted a response.

My thoughts kept spinning back to Mother. Why did she always have to run off dramatically at every dramatic moment? Why was she never there when I needed her? Why was she not coming back? Perhaps she was hurt like Mirabelle and couldn't move, couldn't call for us. Perhaps she was already—

I wouldn't let my mind settle on that. She had to be all right. Mother was indestructible. Nothing could ever happen to her. I wouldn't let it, not this time. As infuriating and cold as she was, I wasn't going to let her be killed.

When Mirabelle had finally finished in the bathroom, we made our way downstairs. Bridget had disappeared, again. We found her with Mr Bojangles in the sitting room. She had made no effort with the fire. God knows what she'd been up to. She'd done absolutely nothing at all. It was not the first time it occurred to me that Bridget disappeared a lot of the time with the excuse of not doing anything at all.

We took up our usual positions and waited for someone to have an idea. Mirabelle, despite her near lobotomy, insisted on stoking the fire again. It seemed to calm her. The fire had become her territory. I've not stayed in a lot of country houses, Mother doesn't think I *fit in*, but when I have, I've noticed the fire is enemy territory. Someone inevitably wants to control the fire — laying the fire, the lighters, the papers, the stacking of the wood, the dryness of the wood, the blowing. I stay far away from that controversial area, in the darkest corner, unobserved.

'We need a plan of action,' Aunt Charlotte said firmly, a hand on each knee, legs spread open as usual with her tweed skirt stretched taut between them. 'Yes, a battle plan.'

Mirabelle prodded the fire with increasing savagery. 'We need to find Pandora,' she said, eyes fixed on the rising flames. 'There's a lunatic on the loose. We need to find her. She could be in great danger.'

No one spoke. The terrible ideas that lingered, waiting, were quick to take hold and kindle in the nervous silence. Perhaps she had already been in danger. Perhaps she was somewhere in imminent danger. Or perhaps she was the—

'We need to re-group, confirm what we know, find out what we don't know.' Aunt Charlotte was more focused than

I had ever seen her. We stared into the flames, mesmerized and searching for inspiration.

'What do we know?' continued Aunt Charlotte. 'We know about the Angels and the fortune teller. But then there's Less. Where does she come into it?'

'There's always Less,' Mirabelle sighed.

'Not any more,' Bridget said, and smiled.

Again, we paused to stare at Bridget. Increasingly, her smile was disturbingly rabid and self-satisfied.

'Killed in her bath by what would appear to be a rope burned through by a strategically placed candle,' I said. 'What does this tell us?'

I waited. Evidently nothing.

'Well, there was no struggle. It was not a spur-of-the-moment murder. The person set this to go and didn't need Less to die immediately. Undoubtedly, Less did not see her killer. Otherwise she would have leaped up. No, she stayed where she was.'

'And died,' Aunt Charlotte added.

'Yes, thank you, Aunt Charlotte. Then we have the Angels.'

'Or whoever they were,' Mirabelle interrupted.

'Oh, this is getting quite exciting, isn't it?' Bridget grinned. 'Better than the book, eh, Mr Bojangles?'

We watched Bridget.

I thought for a moment. 'No, no.'

'No?'

'Yes. No, Aunt Charlotte.'

'Well, which is it?'

I needed to think. 'The crest.'

Even Mirabelle was looking lost now or perhaps in pain. Dried rivulets of blood were still visible down her temples.

'The crest in the hallway has angel wings rising up. The Angels were the Angels and they owned this place.'

Mirabelle was shaking her head.

'Mirabelle?'

'She is Mrs Angel, her married name, no?'

'Yes, Mirabelle.' I said slowly.

'Oh, God,' Aunt Charlotte buried her head in her hands. 'I don't understand. Will somebody please make sense?'

'Shhh, Mr Bojangles and I cannot hear!' Bridget snapped, as if someone had interrupted her favourite TV show.

'Well,' continued Mirabelle, 'if she is the girl in the photograph at the house, it is *her* family home, not the man she married. Not Mr Angel.'

And, with that, the house of cards I had been elaborately building fell apart.

'Or a whale,' Aunt Charlotte added nonchalantly.

I paused. My mind turned over the words and re-assembled them.

'Why did you say whale?'

'What?'

'No, whale,' I said slowly. 'Why did you say whale?'

Bridget sighed dramatically. 'Why does Charlotte say anything?'

Aunt Charlotte gave her a withering look. 'Because,' said Aunt Charlotte with a long, drawn-out voice, 'because of the crest. The family crest, in the hallway, has angel wings, two tridents and a dirty, great big whale in the middle of it.' She sat back in her chair with her hands knitted over her round, tweed belly. 'And you lot are supposed to be the observant ones.'

We stood in silence for a moment, before racing out to the hallway. And there it was, just as Aunt Charlotte had described, the angel wings that had so pre-occupied me, the two tridents and, as she said, *a dirty, great big whale in the middle of it*.

We stared in unison. We'd been right about them. To think, the Angels, with such a fine, illustrious house and crest, had been serving our eggs and brandies.

'But why the angel wings?' I said quietly.

'It's when families merge — put the symbol of one in the other's crest.' Aunt Charlotte was suddenly very knowledgeable which was disconcerting. 'So, an Angel merged with a whale. Whangel. Sort of like Brangelina, Kimye or. . . Lynbert.

'Lynbert?' I shouldn't have asked but I couldn't stop myself.

'Yes, Lynda and Robert Snell.'

I looked at her blankly.

'*The Archers*,' Bridget explained.

'No, no, no,' Mirabelle said sharply, 'this is nonsense! *Whaling* was their business. Ambergris Towers remember. That's what the Angels said they made their money from — whaling.'

'The sea,' I said.

'Ten out of ten, Ursula,' Bridget said snidely, and grinned rabidly at her dog again.

'The sea,' I repeated. 'There is more than just a whale. Look, a trident, waves. It's all about the sea.'

Mirabelle turned. 'So? Of course it would be. They're whalers. Where do whales live, children?' She continued to walk away. But the crest still held me in its dark folds and strange, cream feathers. It wasn't just the cracked varnish or the faded colours, there was something in this crest that meant more, I could feel it.

'*Maîtres de la mer*,' Aunt Charlotte read from the small inscription below the crest. 'Masters of the sea. I suppose they must have been to make all this.' She too began walking back to the sitting room.

'Say that again,' I asked slowly.

'What, dear?'

'What you just said.'

'I suppose they were. To get this — this place. Don't you think? Must have cost a pretty penny. They weren't always . . .'

'No, no before that.'

She frowned. 'Masters of the sea. What is the matter with you, Ursula? I know this is all quite shocking but it's quite clear and I'm sure you did schoolgirl French at some point. Masters of the sea. *Maîtres de la mer*.' She enunciated each syllable clearly.

'*Maîtres de la mer*,' I repeated.

'Oh, Ursula, anyone would think it was you who'd had a bump to the head.'

'It's not just a bump to the head,' Mirabelle called angrily from the sitting-room door, 'I've nearly had my head caved in.'

'*Maîtres de la mer,*' I mouthed.

'Yes, dear,' Aunt Charlotte put her arm around me. 'Let's get you sat down. It's the shock, you know.'

'*Maîtres de la mer.* De la mer. Dellamer,' I said suddenly and stopped. 'Dellamer. Doreen Dellamer.'

Aunt Charlotte stopped. Mirabelle emerged slowly from the doorway of the sitting room.

'Doreen Dellamer. Doreen Dellamer. She lived here because it was *her* home. She was a Dellamer.' I paused. 'So, if the Dellamers were the family who owned the house, not the Angel line, then Mr Angel married into the family. That would make Mrs Angel a Dellamer too before her marriage to Mr Angel. The women were both Dellamers. They were sisters — Mrs Angel and Doreen Dellamer. That's why they lived here together.'

We all looked at each other and then at the crest. I thought of Mrs Angel and the photograph she clutched to her dying chest. The dog that meant so much and the two girls — two sisters here at Ambergris Towers — Mrs Angel and Doreen Dellamer.

'I can't think of anything worse.' A voice floated down the stairs.

We all turned to look.

'Mother!'

'Who in their right mind would want to live with their sister?' she said.

Rule 24: Exhaustion can make people see things differently and act strangely.

OLD GRUDGES

As we settled back into the sitting room, I watched Mother closely and my thoughts began to stitch together new theories that easily came unravelled.

'Where the hell have you been, Mother?'

Mother gave me *The Look*. 'I was feeling unwell and needed—'

Bridget coughed and pulled her mouth into the shape of a smile. 'Oh dear, I'm afraid that's not going to be good enough. There've been four brutal murders so we're going to need an account of everyone's whereabouts at all times.'

Mother frowned. 'Who died and made you and the dog Barnaby and Sykes?'

'What? Wh—'

'Quiet, Charlotte,' Mother snapped. 'Seems a lot's changed in a short time.'

'Not least of all another murder attempt!' Mirabelle announced.

'I'm sorry?'

'Someone tried to kill me,' Mirabelle stated and folded her arms defiantly.

'What? Who?'

Bridget laughed like a kindly old grandmother — just about to reveal her big, sharp teeth. 'Well, if we knew that, dear, there'd be no more mystery would there?' We all watched Bridget flipping her dog biscuits without a care in the world. She was the very image of a stone-cold killer in her Marks and Spencer's twin set.

'It's so dark,' Aunt Charlotte said quietly.

The nights here scuttled in, spider-black, making it hard to think, colouring everything with fear. Aunt Charlotte flicked on her side lamp, but it cast only a weak pool of light.

'Does it change anything?' I said, changing tack. 'If they were sisters — Doreen Dellamer and Mrs Angel.'

No one answered for a moment. I turned on the lamp next to me. Vague splinters of light escaped from the dark, ornate shade. That's the thing about old country houses, always a lot of candles and lamps but very little light. It would be a nightmare to have to negotiate this room in the dark, particularly if you were being stalked by a killer.

'Of course it does, you stupid girl,' Mirabelle said, with familiar impatience. 'Both sisters and the husband have been murdered, in their own home. This is a grudge against the family that we've somehow managed to stumble into and need to extricate ourselves from immediately. It's got nothing to do with us, this maniac has something against the Angels or Dellamers or whatever they're called, and he's killed them. All of them. In their own home.'

We let the words sink in.

'Doesn't explain Less though, does it?' Aunt Charlotte said.

'I don't know,' Mirabelle said. 'She must have seen something, heard something. It could even have been a mistake. Who knows? All I know is that the whole family has been wiped out in their home. It's clearly a targeted attack on them for some reason and we've just got in the way.'

'She's right,' I said begrudgingly. 'Their whole family has been wiped out and we're the only ones who know.'

'Except the killer,' Aunt Charlotte added helpfully.

'Yes, Charlotte, except the killer.'

We stared at the fire.

'What we don't know,' Aunt Charlotte said, still mesmerized by the flames, 'is *how* the Angels were killed.'

It was the question at the front of everyone's thoughts.

Mirabelle stood up suddenly and poked at the fire again, as if at a raw nerve, causing sparks to stir up as the wood split and fell. The fire had been our constant companion with its biting, sharp scent filling every breath until the texture of the air itself was as dry as a spent match. My eyes smarted and my throat grew tight, making every thought a new pain.

Mirabelle slammed the poker back into the bucket as if she meant to hurt it.

'And I don't think we got to the bottom of where *you* were, Pandora dear,' Bridget said insistently. 'After all, you were the deceased's landlady for a time, I believe.'

'Just shut up, Bridget,' Mirabelle barked.

'All I'm saying, Mirabelle, is that Doreen Dellamer hardly greeted her old landlady with open arms.' Bridget smiled. 'You did sack her, Pandora, and then evict her, didn't you say? And she does seem to have disguised herself to meet you.'

'Doreen Dellamer didn't greet any of us with fondness,' Mother said wearily. 'Why should she? Maybe she didn't even recognize us, and they do this old parlour trick nonsense for everyone — get the staff multitasking, putting on a bit of a show. Hardly new.'

'They were doing all this to make money,' Mirabelle added.

We waited for someone to speak. It had the feel of an aggressive pause, as if each of us had something we were burning to say but were holding back.

I watched Mother closely.

It was Aunt Charlotte who was first to brave the silence. 'Listen, I'm going to die before the killer even gets to me if I don't get some form of sustenance.' She began purposefully walking to the door.

'It'll take a while to starve *you* to death,' Mirabelle muttered.

'Wait, Aunt Charlotte!' I shouted. 'You can't just go out there!'

'I'll be back, dear. I might even bring a little something for you, if you'd like.' She made it sound like she was popping to the corner shop.

Mirabelle sighed. 'What the girl means is you could get yourself killed. And really, the sheer inconvenience of yet another body would be enough to drive us all mad.'

'Not unless the killer is in here.' Bridget smiled.

Aunt Charlotte waited by the door. She picked at her fingers, seeming not to know how to stand or what to do.

'Oh, for God's sake,' exclaimed Mirabelle. 'I'll come with you. Honestly, sometimes I think I could be the only adult left here.' What was admirable about Mirabelle was that she could be irritated so easily, even in the most life-threatening of situations.

Aunt Charlotte paused. She looked suspiciously at Mirabelle. 'But then you and I will be on our own, Mirabelle, and you were the last one to see Doreen Dellamer alive.'

'Oh, and you were the one who came back looking as if you'd seen a ghost when you'd spoken to her, so we're just going to have to put all that aside.'

Aunt Charlotte looked at me. 'Will you be OK?' she said.

'I've got Mother and Bridget.'

Aunt Charlotte looked warily from one to the other.

'We'll be fine!' I insisted. 'I will only open the door to you two. These are heavy oak doors.'

'The killer could have a key,' Aunt Charlotte said, her voice becoming increasingly agitated.

'I will leave the key in the lock and turn it to the side,' I explained. 'I used to do it all the time with Mother.'

'I beg your pardon, Madam?' Mother feigned shock.

'But then we risk having a locked-room mystery on our hands and I simply can't cope with any more.' Mirabelle held the back of her hand to her forehead and mimicked swooning. It didn't suit her cynical face.

Aunt Charlotte held my hands together in hers, as if we were praying together. 'If anything happens, *anything*, I want you to scream at the top of your lungs. Do you understand?' She stared at me with wide, expectant eyes.

'Yes, Aunt Charlotte, I understand.'

'We'll be as quick as we can. We'll just grab anything,' Aunt Charlotte said.

'Bring water, bread, fruit . . .'

'Oh, for Christ's sake,' Mirabelle said infuriated, 'it's not a bloody Ocado shop. We'll get what we see and try to not get killed, OK?' Mirabelle's patience was finite, particularly in a perilous situation.

As they left, I locked the door before scurrying back to my chair like a frightened child running back to their bed in the night. I buried myself in the soft back of the chair. And I watched.

'OK?' Mother asked quietly.

I nodded.

Bridget grinned and stroked the dog slowly.

My chair was half angled towards the French windows. I stared out at the dead, white world. Through the dark mist, the house cast an acid-yellow light across the snow. The snow had settled heavily and was deep now, solid as though it had been moulded from white clay. It seemed to have its own radiance, a strangely mellow magnetic quality that could have been beguiling, almost beautiful if it hadn't been suffocating everything.

Out there seemed so other, silent and desolate, as if preserved in a moment. If I walked through those doors, would it pierce some invisible membrane that separated our worlds?

My eyes began to lose focus. Nothing seemed to have any form anymore. All the edges were disintegrating into the lilac-black light.

My mind wandered and drifted with each new flurry, images as fine as lace gathered in the mist. The Angels crumpled in their death bed; Less splayed in her bath, her room ransacked. Her room. Her dressing table.

The fire let out a single crack and I flinched. My skin stippled with the cold and a sudden, sharp rush of adrenaline flooded through me. I'd fallen asleep. The room was quiet, but the calm had gone. I stood quickly, tense and alert. The unnerving hum of my own thoughts made my eyes dart from corner to corner of the room, my own fear ringing in my ears.

I staggered a little. A cool bead of sweat traced down my skin.

'Ursula?' Mother stood. 'Ursula!'

My fingers twitched with an excited insistence. I looked down at them and realized I had pulled half the nail away on my thumb, the neat crescent moon had torn across to leave bare the livid skin below. A tight fist gripped my stomach and I fell. I sensed the carpet surging up to meet me. The fibres bristled against my cheek as I lay there. The scent of the room changed entirely, as if a sour breath was warming my face. I looked up at the mantelpiece.

I could sense Mother and Bridget standing over me, their gaze crawling over my skin. My mind was overrun with cruel and strange thoughts — a jumbled fear. I was hallucinating. I was falling further into the carpet. Her room. Her dressing table. The vase.

'The vase,' I said. 'The vase.'

I fell into a bleak dream where I was lost. I don't know how long I stayed trapped in the slips of my mind, but it seemed as though everything else would be defined by this one moment.

'I knew we shouldn't have left them! I knew it.'

'Shut up, Charlotte, and get this bloody door open. Use some of that weight of yours.' The unmistakable voice of Mirabelle dragged me back to the surface.

'Ursula? Ursula, are you in there? Ursula?'

'Of course she's bloody in here, Charlotte,' Mother shouted.

'Well, it could be one of your sealed-door mysteries.'

'Locked room, Charlotte. Locked room!'

'Well, whatever it is, get it bloody unlocked.'

Mother opened the door in one swift movement and Aunt Charlotte fell into the room.

I eased myself up, my head sparkling with pain and confusion. I knelt for a second, fearful of being sick or falling again. A small berry of blood dropped from my damaged thumbnail. I imagined the house awakening to the scent of it, finding a new flavour to hunt, setting its sights on me as the next victim. This was a thirsty house. A voice in my head repeated the same thing: *we would not survive, we couldn't*. This house would never let us go. As I swayed towards the door, it seemed to tail away down the side of the wall.

'Ursula? Ursula? Are you all right?'

'Charlotte, stop with the Victorian melodrama! Ursula is fine!' Mother said firmly. 'She needs to eat. If she doesn't eat, the dru—'

'I'm fine, Mother! Don't. I'm fine. I'm fine,' I said in a fractured voice. 'I just need to sit down a second. I'm just a little light-headed. It's the stress. I haven't eaten for a while.'

'She's always been so fragile.' Aunt Charlotte grabbed me firmly by the waist and dragged me to the chair, like she would a carcass. She slammed me down into the back of it. 'You need to rest. It's all been a terrible strain. Look at you. You look like death.'

'Let's hope not,' I said coldly.

We all looked at each other.

'Here, drink this.' Mirabelle held out a glass of brandy. 'Come on, we all know you drink, so let's drop the charade for a moment.'

The familiar smell of warm brandy crept up from the glass.

'It's not poisoned!' She thrust the glass closer to me. We both paused.

I took the glass slowly and drank, draining down the familiar burn.

'What did you say earlier?' Mother was crouching beside my chair.

'I don't know,' I croaked as the brandy scorched my throat.

'"The vase",' Bridget said flatly. '"The vase".'

'What vase?' Aunt Charlotte said, irritated.

'Exactly!' Bridget pointed to the mantelpiece where the Meissen vase had stood before.

'Well,' Mirabelle said. 'Where the hell has that gone?'

'Where do you think?' I took another mouthful of the warm brandy. 'Who was the magpie in our midst?'

'Less!' Aunt Charlotte whispered. 'She stole the vase.'

'We need to go to Less's room,' I said and stood up sharply.

Aunt Charlotte closed her eyes and began slowly shaking her head. 'This obsession with viewing the corpses must stop, dear. They're not coming back. There's nothing we can do now. The best tribute we can pay them is for us to survive. Which is something we won't do if we keep wandering off for you to look at dead bodies.'

'We need to search the room,' I insisted. 'We haven't searched it at all.'

'Presumably because we've spent so much time in the Angels' rooms searching there,' Aunt Charlotte said wearily. 'And I still don't know what we're looking for.'

'A murderer, Aunt Charlotte. A murderer.'

* * *

The door to Less's room, or the room in which Less's corpse now resided, was closed this time. Carefully, soundlessly, I opened it.

'What are you scared of, waking the dead?' Aunt Charlotte barged past. Mirabelle shook her head resignedly. We were all getting tired now.

The air had a metallic flavour, much sharper than the muddied air of the Angels' death bed. There was still the stain

196

of Mirabelle's blood on the pale carpet. It seemed offensive to just leave it without any attempt to clean it up, but if we started trying to clean up the blood in this house we'd never stop. The door to the bathroom was open and we could see Less's crucified form hastily covered with towels that had to engulf all of the giant metal chandelier as well. Spits of browned blood spattered the white tiles. They had slowly rolled down the porcelain like an abattoir's walls before finally drying and setting. I closed my eyes and my head filled with images of that final moment of her looking up and being impaled.

I trod carefully so as not to slip on any blood or in any way disturb the delicate filigree of their patterns. Perhaps it might one day be crucial to someone, maybe even the police, if we ever lived to see them. But that seemed like a very distant idea.

I noticed that the long gash down her arm still leaked the occasional spot into the reddish-brown puddle below — it was strange that no section of the chandelier was embedded there. Perhaps the spike had slashed her arm as she held it up to protect herself in vain. Again, the unwelcome image of her vicious ending played in my head like a film clip. Perhaps the killer had been with her in the room at the time and slashed her to keep her down. No, this had been set as a booby trap, it hadn't required the murderer's presence. It could have been—

'Stop staring at corpses, dear. It won't do you any good.' Aunt Charlotte put her hand on my arm.

She guided me back into the bedroom, where the bed was still covered in a jumble of pulled back sheets. The side table was still set with all manner of bottles and potions that Less had felt were necessary to keep her alive. Unfortunately, evening primrose oil, agnus castus and rosemary water could not save her from a hurtling chandelier. There was a part of me that felt what a terrible waste it was to have denied herself so much, presumably in the pursuit of a long and healthy life, when in fact she might as well have eaten and drunk everything she wanted if she was going to have her life cut so viciously short. Some of the bottles and a book had been knocked to the ground, a bag and some clothes were thrown on the floor. The empty bedside drawer was open.

The wardrobe was slightly open too, filled with clothing that all looked exactly the same, all of it cashmere loungewear and yoga gear. Her bag was overtly expensive and of a size intended to make her look more petite. Her very own wag's swag bag, I always used to say. But she didn't appreciate that.

And there, on the dressing table, stood the Meissen vase, its perfect lustre defiant.

Rule 25: In life-threatening situations, people seek solace and safety with others. Beware of a pack mentality.

DESTROYED

We carried the vase and set it ceremoniously in the middle of the coffee table. Back in the bunker of our sitting room, thoughts spilled around my head until I felt drunk. Mother, Mirabelle and Aunt Charlotte were achieving the same result by drinking a huge amount of brandy. I noticed the level had gone down considerably while we were away but Bridget didn't seem to be drinking at the moment. At least, that's what she said.

While every fibre of me wanted to fly upstairs, and open up my Bible brandy, downing inch after inch of the numbing liquor, I couldn't sit here drinking brandy from crystal glasses with other people. It was not a social activity as far as I was concerned. It was a private feeding of the soul.

The vase itself wasn't big — fifteen inches high at most with blue-painted flowers set in its pearl glaze. Meissen, Mrs Angel had said. It certainly had the mark. That had been enough for Less. She'd stolen far less valuable objects in her time.

'It doesn't look much to me.' Aunt Charlotte sniffed.

'It wouldn't. This is a very special piece.' Bridget looked at it closely as if she knew what she was talking about. 'Worth a fortune, I'd say.'

'Then why wouldn't the Angels have sold it?' Aunt Charlotte said.

'Same reason they were hanging onto this shambolic pile.' I held out my arms. 'It was one of their treasures. A very special piece, as Bridget says.'

'Perhaps in more ways than one.' Mother seemed almost to be talking to herself.

'Mother?'

'Think about where we found it.'

We looked at the vase.

'Oh,' I said slowly.

Aunt Charlotte shrugged. 'Well, we all know she was an inveterate thief. She'd got form.'

Mother sighed. 'Yes, she was a little light-fingered, but—'

'She took the vase, that's for sure.' Aunt Charlotte folded her arms across her chest.

A thief, yes. Less was forever stealing from our home and Dad repeatedly tried to explain this to Mother, but she would hear nothing against Less. Cufflinks, money, ornaments and jewellery, nothing was safe from her magpie ways. I used to hate it as a child, as nothing was sacred from her. I once caught her wearing one of my Hello Kitty hair clips and she swore it was hers.

'Wouldn't be the first time,' Aunt Charlotte slurred at me. 'If it wasn't nailed down, it was fair game. She once stole a gorgeous onyx cigarette lighter I bought your mother. Took it straight from the coffee table and slipped it into that vast swag bag she was always lugging around. Poacher's bag, I'll say. Never owned up to it, but your mother knew where it had gone, all right. Didn't you, Pandora?'

Mother winced a smile and I knew her thoughts exactly.

Less did steal, and repeatedly, but her reputation had been used many times by Mother as a cover to hide the fact that the local charity shop was bulging with items she didn't think were suitable for her beautiful house. The onyx lighter was definitely sitting on the shelf at the local Cancer Research shop, along with a selection of scarves and purses, boxes of photo frames, ornaments and trinkets bought for Mother by various relatives and friends. Not even Mother's wedding dress made the cut. In many ways, it was Mother's life story laid bare on the shelves, each detail that she'd discarded, meaningless by themselves, still less important to Mother but when stitched together they formed a perfect tapestry of what she really was.

Every day, it was as if Mother was clearing out a deceased relative's house, only it was her own home. Nothing could linger, no ephemera could be tolerated. It had to be a clean slate, always. But it wasn't preparing the way for new tales to be written, it just remained blank. When Dad died, I vividly remember falling to my knees on the pavement outside the Cancer Research shop and staring at the model dressed immaculately in Dad's clothes, as if his body had been propped up on display just how it was when he died.

But even taking into account Mother's mania for decluttering, Less had stolen from us on many occasions. Often rubbish. Sometimes more. Perhaps it depended on how desperate she was, perhaps it was simply whatever glittered on the surface of her magpie eyes. We couldn't ask her now. Such secrets don't whisper out of graves, they disappear as if they never existed, so that the living doubt their own recollection.

'She definitely stole this Meissen vase,' Mother said. We all looked at it suspiciously as if it was the culprit.

All these dazzling baubles around her, new and alluring, Less would never have been able to resist. I imagined her furtively lifting the vase, quickly checking the door over her shoulder, smiling to herself. I imagined that sharp little smile sneaking across her lips. Would someone kill simply over this? Had they discovered her crime and confronted her? It had been her last chance so many times in various courts. She couldn't risk it.

Mirabelle sighed. 'Stupid Less. Stupid, stupid Less, with her light fingers. Looks like she signed her own death warrant this time.'

'Wait,' said Bridget, 'her stealing this vase doesn't *necessarily* mean they killed her. And, of course, we still wouldn't have an answer to the question who killed them. So, in fact, it tells us very little.'

'No,' Mother said defiantly, 'it tells us something and if we put it with the other facts we know . . .' She paused as if the thoughts were settling. 'Say you're right and Doreen Dellamer is Mrs Angel's sister.'

'Was,' Bridget added pedantically.

'*Was*,' Mother continued. 'Listen, this is starting to make some sense. Say they live here in poverty, desperately trying to preserve this place. It means everything. They've already lied to us to preserve it and presumably its treasures. Then they discover one of the treasures is lost. They confront Joy. Yes, perhaps Doreen, as the fortune teller, confronted her. She says she's going to tell everyone, unless there is an *arrangement*. There's a row. Joy, in a panic, acts on the spur of the moment and hits Doreen over the back of the head. Realizes she's killed her, so drags her out and shoves her in the tree stump. She quickly stashes the arrow in the poker stand and runs up to bed. Next day, the snow has covered her crime. No one need know. But what Joy doesn't know is that the victim's sister is in this very house. Mrs Angel.' Mother nodded, as if convincing herself.

'Mrs Angel knows who stole the vase,' she continued, 'and therefore she knows who killed her sister. She decides to take revenge. After all, it was Mrs Angel who ran the bath, Mrs Angel who set the candles. Yes,' Mother said confidently, 'Joy killed Doreen Dellamer because she'd confronted her over the theft of this priceless vase. The Angels then killed Joy in revenge.'

'Hmmm,' Bridget said slowly, 'but that doesn't tell us who killed the Angels, now does it? Nor does it explain why Doreen Dellamer hid her identity or why the Angels simply left the vase in her room — a vital piece of evidence linking them directly to the murder. I'm afraid your story is full of holes, Pandora.' She smiled. Bridget was starting to look smarter than anyone had given her credit for.

I stood up to analyse the vase. It was indeed very striking. I imagined Less, the magpie that she was, crawling out of bed in the darkest hours to smuggle this vase into one of her many vast bags. The thrill she would have felt knowing she had a treasure in her hands, but then the sickening realization as the farcical fortune teller revealed so much more to her than she thought she would.

I sat back in my chair. Everyone settled into their thoughts, staring at this frankly quite hideous piece of china. We had gravitated towards all our usual positions around the fire. People like to occupy their own space. The one thing we didn't need any more of was friction so I stayed in my own chair.

I looked over at Aunt Charlotte who had fallen into ferocious snoring. She looked as if she was either drunk or drugged or both. Mirabelle was prodding the fire; Mother and Bridget were bickering over unexplained details of the vase; and I sat back, my face obscured by the wings of the chair. I felt the slow, small rhythm of the blood in my neck.

Nerves were becoming worn. Aunt Charlotte's brow was ploughed deep with worried lines, her eyes twitched with dark unconscious thoughts as she slept. Mirabelle silently fussed around the fire. Mother and Bridget were deep in acrimony about the importance of the vase.

The room was so tight and claustrophobic, with the constant charcoal smoke thick in our lungs and the heavy grind of our own thoughts, that I could barely breathe.

'I need to get out of here!' I blurted.

Mirabelle let out a long, deflated sigh. 'Always the same, somehow she has to be special. We *all* need to get out of here. There's no way out until the snow thaws. So I—'

'I mean this room. It's stifling. I can't breathe. I can't think. I . . . I . . .'

'OK,' Mother said calmly. 'OK, Ursula. Let's—'

'Oh, for God's sake!' Mirabelle shouted. Aunt Charlotte blinked awake at the noise. 'Why do you always pander to her like this?'

Mother stood and walked over to me.

'Where do you want to go?'

Bridget coughed. 'Excuse me, is there something we should know about?'

'No!' Mother barked.

'Well, if *someone* has an issue—'

'No one has—'

'It's OK, Mother. Let Marple nosey around.'

Mother held my hand. 'That's enough. Let's take you to the library. You like it there. You can look at the books and I'll . . . I'll do some more clue-gathering.'

Mirabelle frowned. 'Clue-gathering? What clues?'

'It's where our fateful fortune teller met people, so perhaps we should look there for clues.'

Aunt Charlotte stood up determinedly. 'I'm coming with you. Need a change of scene.'

'What?' Mirabelle snapped. 'Well, I'm not staying here with Barbara Woodhouse.'

'Who?' Aunt Charlotte frowned.

'I'm coming with you.'

So, rather than quiet respite for me in the library, the whole travelling circus was coming with us.

'I'll hold the fort here with Mr Bojangles,' Bridget called merrily. No one answered, but I silently noted another instance of Bridget and Mr Bojangles making sure they were on their own again.

Rule 26: Be methodical. There is no place for panic. It must be a detailed autopsy of the environment and its players.

THE LIBRARY

The subtle darkness that now wove its way through the house blinded us all to the details we desperately needed to see. The years of velvet dust stifled us. The dark pearl light reflecting off the snow was unsettling and all I could focus on was the full, crushing weight of my fear. We were lost in the bleak hours.

The library was stale with a musty air that now permeated the whole house. Everything had teetered on the brink of neglect for so long. But finally, life was abandoning these walls and consigning them to decay. My breath still stuttered in my throat and my chest ached with a constant heavy dread.

Two small, stuffed animals watched me from a side table. Weasels? Stoats? I had no idea. Their vulgar little bead eyes followed me as if I was next. Taxidermy — what was it about the screamingly rich Victorians that inspired them to stuff dead animals full of sawdust and leave them around the house? Perhaps it was a reminder that we could all end up stuffed at any moment.

The books had a settled look as though they were merely part of the décor, not useful or used items, their words forgotten and unread. Nothing had moved since Doreen Dellamer's unfortunate fortune-telling session. I cast my mind back to that innocent evening of entertainment, before all this death. It seemed so long ago. I remember peering into this sombre room with the sulphurous glow of the lamp surrounding the strange figure of the fortune teller. This room had lived so many histories, the canvas staying the same with only the characters changing. The Angels were the last.

Was there someone out there who would mourn? We hadn't known them at all. What sad storytellers we would be, if we even survived.

'Nothing here,' Aunt Charlotte mumbled, as she casually glanced around the room. How she imagined we were going to catch a resourceful and brutal killer by simply casting a quick look around, I don't know. She'd have paid more attention if she was thinking of buying the place, let alone catching a killer.

'Charlotte, we must look for the details,' Mother said, as if speaking to a child.

'What details?' she frowned. 'Books — check; desk — check; chair — check; fireplace — check; gross stuffed rats — check. The end. It's a library. What were you expecting to find, a trapeze?'

When everything in a setting is laid out to perfection, it jars when something is missing.

My eyes greedily scanned the dark walls and wooden shelves. She was right, there was nothing suspicious. The curtains were still open to the barren, dark world outside. The snow still fell in feathers on the air, spinning light across the black. It was a perfect mirror of the star-spiked sky. How could it all look so pure?

I slumped into a cavernous leather chair. I fidgeted around and something sharp wedged into my back. A book. I quickly looked at the others. Mother had found a seat at a small table with Mirabelle and they were deep in whispered conversation. Aunt Charlotte was pretending to look at a book that was upside down.

I pulled out the volume carefully, a rich claret leather like the others lining the room. Its gold-lettered binding read:

FUNGI: A Natural History and Index

I looked up, as if a sly little secret had crawled into my lap. No one had noticed. It can be very useful to have relatives who are so self-absorbed that they pay you no attention.

I flicked the edge of the book with my thumbs and it fell open where a piece of torn newspaper had been left. The page had intricate botanical drawings of mushrooms. It was entitled 'Destroying Angel (*Amanita bisporigera*)'.

I let out an involuntary gasp and Mirabelle glanced round with casual irritation.

I read in short bursts, glancing at the others after every line.

Genus: Amanita
*Toxicity: Among the most toxic mushrooms, the destroying angel (*Amanita bisporigera*) is responsible for most mushroom poisonings. Easily confused with non-deadly mushrooms, such as puffballs, button mushrooms and horse mushrooms, it contains amatoxin, which destroys liver and kidney tissues, leading to death.*
Season: In Britain, August—November.
Found: Woodlands, often at base of fallen and dead trees.

A picture of Doreen Dellamer swiftly took root, her body bent into that lonely, dead tree trunk.

Symptoms: Vomiting, cramps, delirium, convulsions leading to death.

A natural habitat would be a fallen tree or dead stump. The destroying angel is deadly poisonous.

An image came into my mind of Angel standing before us, eulogizing. '*Mrs Angel is partial to an omelette, Madam. We use fresh farm eggs, onions, plenty of wild mushrooms, cheese, a grind of black pepper and a good sprinkle of salt. Every morning. For thirty years.'*

I recalled the soil-covered basket knocked over in the kitchen. The killer only needed to add a few of these mushrooms to their usual selection. *Easily confused with button mushrooms.*

Sharp fingers gripped tight around my stomach. The Angels were poisoned, that much made sense.

I thought of the Angels and those rasping final words — *Destroy . . . angel.* They knew. The bitter illness that convulsed and ruptured their bodies, which tore them into new shapes of pain, they knew exactly what had taken them. In their frantic search for the source, they'd perhaps even knocked the basket to the floor. The poor Angels, to know that their sister had died and that they too would soon follow. Too weak to tell the rest of us, to warn us, Angel had tried to explain his silent killer. *Destroying angel.* We'd just mistaken it for a rather unusual way of telling us that he'd been killed. Mrs Angel didn't have any life left to tell us anything. She had clung to that picture of her sister.

These were not just random, directionless deeds. There was a method here, provoked by something that had only recently awakened. The arrow was opportunistically taken up as a weapon. Mushrooms were gathered and left in the basket. These items were not carefully prepared. They were grabbed quickly in response to something or someone.

'Should we do another sweep of the house?' Aunt Charlotte suggested suddenly.

I quickly pushed the book back under a cushion. Knowledge seemed to be the only thing I had left to protect me.

Mother stood with her hands clenched behind her back — the defiant field marshal rallying the troops. 'We should begin down here.'

'Why do you always have to be in charge?'

'I don't know, Charlotte. I ask myself the same question. Presumably because you still can't even fasten your own shoe laces.'

Our eyes all settled on Aunt Charlotte's Velcro-fastening shoes. The relationship between sisters is strange and shrouded in complication. Some love one another beyond compare, some hate with equal vehemence. But between Mother and Aunt Charlotte is that grey area where sibling mistrust and rivalry flourish, and seething hatred can lead to the worst of crimes.

I thought of Mrs Angel grasping the picture of her sister to her in those final moments. Mr Angel could only think of what had destroyed him, but Mrs Angel craved the comfort of a familiar photograph. Strange that neither one of them tried to point us in the direction of the murderer. Perhaps they didn't know. I thought of their frames gnarled by convulsion and pain — Mr Angel, grey and squalid. His wife grasping the photograph to her with one hand, the other . . . Where was her other hand?

I resurrected them in my imagination. Her hand reaching . . . Reaching towards the bedside table. But what was there? My mind was dull with exhaustion and the image was so dominated by the tortured vision of the couple and their suffering. But there was something, something just out of reach and yet there was nothing but smoke. There were the odd bits of ephemera cluttering the side table, water carafe, ashtray, handkerchiefs, a glass, some face cream but nothing you would reach for in your final minutes. Whatever she'd wanted to alert us to, the killer had presumably already taken but in her hallucinatory death, Mrs Angel had thought it was still there. My mind was running in circles and wouldn't settle.

'Ursula? Ursula?' Aunt Charlotte's large, ham-like hand was on my arm. She had come over and was crouching beside me. She watched me closely, as if my skull was made of glass and she could see straight in to all the shadows of my thoughts. She'd always seemed so straightforward to me, solid, blustering old Aunt Charlotte. But I thought of her face that night after she'd been to see Doreen Dellamer. What had the fortune teller said that rocked her so much?

Aunt Charlotte hadn't always been there for me in a traditional sense. She'd been there every day up to the point where Mother said, 'For God's sake, Charlotte, what makes you think I want you hanging around every minute of the day now my husband's died? Haven't you got a home to go to?'

Even as a thirteen-year-old I could sense the cruelty in denying Aunt Charlotte her grief after Dad's death. Doreen Dellamer and Aunt Charlotte were given their marching orders as soon as Dad died, and I was parcelled off to boarding school. Mother just wanted to be alone with *her* grief. She could never accept that the rest of us were lost too.

'Right, bugger-all use here. Let's move on,' Aunt Charlotte said emphatically. 'It's nearly midnight and I don't want to spend the witching hour in this creepy room.'

Mother and Mirabelle didn't seem keen to move, though.

I looked at my watch. She was right. In fact, it was midnight. I felt a thrill run through me and the old fidgety anxiety welling up. I felt as if I was constantly holding my emotions captive. I held everything inside so tight and close that it could all shatter at any moment.

Again, there was that nagging feeling that something was out of place, in some way dislocated or suspended in a timeless world that didn't relate properly to reality. It *was* timeless this place, as if we were captured in a strange disjointed limbo. No sleep. No meals. No time. It was completely *timeless*. Aunt Charlotte could have said it was any time of the night and I would not have known otherwise. I had no sense of time anymore. It could be midnight. It could be five in the morning. Nothing marked out time anymore. No time. We were timeless. Timeless.

'There's no time!' I announced.

'Oh, God. Here we go again,' Mirabelle sighed.

'Be quiet, Mirabelle. She's fragile and there are bodies piling up. Now, you have a little nip of this and . . .' Aunt Charlotte began pulling something from her handbag.

'Will you listen?' I shouted. 'Just listen.' They pretended to listen by being silent for a moment.

If they ever really listened hard enough, they would hear it. You can hear the sound of people lying. It has a very distinct sound, entirely different to that of the truth. If you pick apart the seams of the noise and separate out each note, then the whole scheme makes much more sense.

If they had tried, they would have heard what was missing but for them the world was simply a sea of noises that occasionally parted for them to speak. Silence was a hole in the air that they were just waiting to fill.

'Can't you hear it?'

They gazed at me stupidly.

'There's nothing.'

They looked at each other with empty faces and gathered closer round me.

'OK, darling.' Aunt Charlotte began approaching me, with a smile that could have been mistaken for malevolent.

'It's midnight,' I hissed. 'What would you hear in a library in an old country house at midnight? Come on.'

The smile wilted on Aunt Charlotte's lips. People don't like being caught looking stupid.

The folds gathered on Mirabelle's forehead, as if some thoughts were forming. 'A murder?'

'The clock chiming!' I said, frustrated.

Aunt Charlotte paused. 'But there is no clock.'

Mother looked around.

'There was,' I said. 'Think back to the tour when we arrived. There was a clock right there in the corner. On a radio, one of those old-style ones. It was a large piece of furniture, heavy and wooden with a clock on the front.' I could see their eyes falling back into memories, as if slowly conjuring the image of this room on that first night.

'Remember I said to Angel I was going to listen to the radio in the library. That was because I knew there was a large radio in here.'

'But Angel told us there wasn't,' Mirabelle said. 'I distinctly remember him saying there was no radio in the library.'

'There wasn't *then*,' I said simply. 'By that point it had been moved.'

They looked incapable of thought.

'Why else would I think there was one? Because it had been there when we first arrived. I suspect if we look over there in that corner, below the pot plant, there will be the clear outline of a large piece of furniture which stood there for many years.'

Aunt Charlotte looked at me dubiously but couldn't resist. She went to the corner and moved aside the large plant.

'She's right!' Aunt Charlotte gasped. 'Look!'

Sure enough, there was a rectangle of darker wood where a large object had sat for many years.

'Where the bloody hell has that gone, then?' Mirabelle said, with shifting annoyance. 'It can't just have vanished into thin air!'

'It's in the dining room,' I said.

'That's a different radio. Isn't it?' Mother looked increasingly confused. 'Isn't it? And why would Angel lie?'

'I'm not sure,' I said. 'But I am sure there is only one clock and it was here when we arrived and is now in the dining room.'

We looked at one another, then moved.

As we walked past the sitting room, I saw Bridget in there whispering to Mr Bojangles. Even that had taken on a deeply conspiratorial air now. We hurried past, avoiding her gaze and carried on to the dining room on the other side.

The old radio with the large clock face stood in the corner. It seemed to have come from a different world entirely, not just another era but part of the history of this house. I imagined all the time it must have marked out, stepping steadily through the years and decades. Time piled upon time like bricks that would eventually wall this place up. It had known the Dellamer girls when they were gleeful, noisy creatures. What voices had they heard through that old speaker? Announcements of dead kings and new queens, wars and births, marking out history in these rooms.

'There is no ticking,' I said quietly. 'There has been no ticking since our arrival. The Angels were definitely fastidious enough to have set the clock each day.'

We all stared at the clock. Its face was defiantly still.

'Ten past twelve,' Aunt Charlotte read for us. 'It's stopped,' she added.

'And what does that tell us?' I asked.

'That it stopped ten minutes after twelve o'clock.'

'Yes, thank you for that, Charlotte. It is important to not overlook the obvious,' Mother sighed. 'But who moves a clock, this size, that doesn't even work?'

We approached it as though it might suddenly swing open and something or somebody leap out at us. It wasn't ornate but the sheer size and age evoked a grandeur.

Mirabelle was frowning. She bent close to the radio. 'It's not real.'

'What do you mean it's not real? Of course it's real. I can see it!' Aunt Charlotte burst out. 'We've got to keep some grip on reality if—'

Mirabelle flicked a small catch on the side of the radio and the whole front of it swung open slowly to reveal a modern integrated clock radio and CD player.

'Good God!' Mother said. 'It's one of those desperate ye olde worlde catalogue buys that you like, Charlotte. It's designed to look like an antique, all "Keep Calm and Carry On", but it's completely modern. Look — DAB, CD . . .'

'A CD player, bit retro,' Aunt Charlotte tutted. 'Personally, I like the green-toothed thing.'

'Blue, Aunt Charlotte. Blue tooth.'

'What, this?'

'It's some old CD alarm clock. Is anything what it seems here?' Mother looked at it closely.

I leaned forward and clicked play. 'Let's see what the Angels liked to listen to.'

Nothing came at first, just crackle.

Then Clair de Lune began. It was played slowly and precisely. The distant notes were clear and defined but with

213

lingering fingers above each piano key as they hung in the air. The notes fell like rain drops. Slowly and steadily at first. Each distinct. Each faded as if the pianist was there with us and his notes, such long breaths, stretched out before they dissolved into nothing.

He was there. In that moment, I felt my father's sigh and his warm soul reached out and touched me. The music swept on a tide into a past I could not properly form into a real image — a patchwork of moments randomly sewn together from glimmers of indistinct memory. But they shone and for that small space in time they were real. A purity of feeling. A glimpse of joy. But as it faded back into the solitary outlines of each note, I felt the string behind my ribs pull tight and I knew it was all falling away, back to an unreliable past I could never relive or capture or even properly remember anymore. And then it was gone. He was gone.

'She's gone again,' I heard Aunt Charlotte calling down some distant tunnel.

'Fetch some water,' Mother shouted. Her form was just an outline above me. My skull was squeezing in on itself, as if it was sealing me in.

'What? Where from? I . . .'

'Just *anywhere*. The carafe. Look. Charlotte, for Christ's sake. Just help.'

I felt Mother's hand under my back and her arm slowly lift me from the floor.

'Here! Here it is,' Aunt Charlotte said. 'Oh, look, I'll just pour it over her.' And she did.

I sat up, soaked. The inoffensive CD player watched me.

'The alarm is set for the CD to go off at midnight for ten minutes,' Mirabelle said. 'At least we know where your piano music was coming from that first night.'

There'd been no spirit of my father playing Debussy to me at midnight. Of course not. How could there be? But there had been a carefully orchestrated hoax.

Rule 27: Try hard to preserve your sanity. It will be tested.

MORE SEARCHING

'We need to go back to the Angels,' I said urgently.

'Oh, really? Again?' Aunt Charlotte groaned. 'Look, there is nothing there except two old dead people. I just don't want to keep visiting them. I can't see why you're so keen to keep seeing them. You didn't really care for them that much when they were alive. You barely knew them.'

People have always been keen to give their opinion on my reaction to death and my relationship with the recently deceased. I've always tried hard to ignore it, for my own sanity. But sometimes it's just too hard not to react.

'In God's name, Aunt Charlotte. That is just too much. I don't want my reaction to death to be analysed anymore. Just let me be.' The words spat out of me as if they tasted rotten. Tears warmed my eyes.

'I'm sorry, OK?' Aunt Charlotte was defensively apologetic. The worst kind.

We perched awkwardly on the arms of the dining chairs. My head still swam with Debussy and I was working hard not to faint again, but the anxiety pooled inside me, sharp nausea gathering in clouds.

'I think what Charlotte was grubbing around at was why you think it's necessary to return to the Angels' apartments given that we've not found anything worthwhile there. Are we looking for something specific?' Mirabelle was increasingly becoming the voice of reason, which definitely didn't cast the rest of us in a good light.

'I think the Angels may not have been quite so innocent,' I said quietly.

Silence.

'Enlighten us,' Mother said, cynically.

I took a deep breath. 'I think the Angels planted that CD and set it to go off at midnight. If that's the case, they knew a lot more about me, about us, than we thought they did.'

'What?' Aunt Charlotte didn't seem to be taking this in.

'I think they purposefully wanted us . . . me . . . one of us at least, to believe that *someone* was playing Clair de Lune on the piano.'

'So?' Mirabelle twisted the word in her mouth until it sounded ugly.

'My dad's favourite piece, not that you'd know.'

There was an awkward pause.

'That night I came down here, I definitely heard Clair de Lune being played on the piano. When I came down, I went into the sitting room. There was no one there and the piano lid was closed. Clearly, it was coming from this CD.'

'So?' Again she screwed the word up into an ugly sound. I could barely stand it.

'Someone wanted us to believe that the piano was being played and the tune was Clair de Lune.'

'But this is the dining room. Surely you wouldn't hear it in the sitting room from here,' Mirabelle said.

'You might if they turned it up loud enough,' Aunt Charlotte answered. 'Where were you, Ursula?'

'Upstairs, to begin with. Then I came down and I was in the hallway. It stopped as I opened the door.'

'There you are,' Aunt Charlotte said decisively.

We all waited for the other to speak.

'So . . .'

'Stop saying that!'

'What?'

'"So"!' I shouted. They watched me cautiously.

'Can you remember anything else?' Mirabelle stepped through the words carefully.

'Not really, only that there was a distinct smell of tobacco smoke. Just like Dad. The piano music and the smell of cigarettes. I could have sworn he was with us.' My voice began to break, and I closed my eyes to lock in the tears. The air filled with the tobacco-scented mist again, one that now had no warmth. 'I felt his presence. His . . .'

'OK,' Mirabelle continued slowly and as gently as she could for someone with the demeanour and grace of an old walrus. I pictured her now with long sabre tusks, grunting and snarling. And then she did it again. 'So . . .'

'Ah, *stop. Stop. Stop.*' I clutched my pounding head.

'OK, sorry. What makes you want to revisit the Angels?'

I frowned and opened my mouth.

Mirabelle held up a finger. 'Please just explain without resorting to extreme drama.'

I took a deep breath. 'If my theory is right, there will be cigarettes there or some evidence of them.'

They all just looked so helpless, like deer resigned to the venison stage of life.

'Wait,' Aunt Charlotte began, 'you think it was the Angels, in there that night, smoking and playing music like a pair of OAP ravers! Good lord.' She laughed, semi-delirious. In some ways, we were all flirting with hysteria now.

I sighed. 'Something like that, Aunt Charlotte.'

We glanced round the door of the sitting room on our way.

'So, Mr Bojangles, you see *that* is why we use the phrase *déjà vu*!'

We decided not to disturb Bridget.

* * *

The Angels' rooms had putrefied. A smell of cold brine had settled. Their bodies still lay semi-covered with stagnant linen.

'I cannot believe we are back here again.' Aunt Charlotte shook her head. 'It really is too much. Can't we just leave these poor people to rest in peace?'

'And how are they supposed to find peace if they are left to wander with no reason for their untimely deaths?' I asked. 'The answer is here, I'm sure of it and we will return as many times as it takes to find it. After all, none of us has any more pressing engagements, do we?'

They watched me closely.

'Just look, will you?'

'For what?' Mirabelle asked frustrated.

'Anything.'

'And we're not going to narrow that down even a little bit?'

'I hate to say it, Ursula, but Mirabelle's got a point,' Aunt Charlotte said quietly. 'We can't just go through all their belongings again, with their corpses watching us.'

'Corpses can't watch anything,' I said matter-of-fact.

They looked at me.

'I don't know about this. Maybe we should leave it for when the police arrive,' Mirabelle sounded unsure.

'If,' I said firmly, '*if* they arrive and if we're still alive when they do. We need to find what killed them,' I looked at Mirabelle, 'unless you want to be next.'

She widened her eyes. 'Was that supposed to sound like a threat?'

Mother sighed and moved between us. 'Let's leave all that until we're safe, OK?' She looked at me and then to Mirabelle. 'OK?' she repeated.

I nodded slowly. Mirabelle looked away.

'Just go and check the living room,' I said. 'I can check here.'

'Well, we will be just next door. Right there. OK,' Aunt Charlotte said hurriedly, as she moved away. 'Literally a few feet from you.'

'I'll come with you, Ursula,' Mother said.

Mirabelle frowned, then turned quickly and walked away.

I looked at Mother and we paused. She leaned a little closer towards me. 'If that's OK with you?'

I nodded.

We entered the Angels' bedroom in silence.

There was an old smell, putrid as if something was living, festering there now. The air was heavy with the febrile smell of something at work. It was not the sterile smell that I had encountered when I saw the shell of my dad in the hospital. This was alive, breathing out a rotten air, like bread forgotten at the bottom of the bread bin, with its bloom of white mould. Whatever killed them had quickly spread its poison through the air. It clung to our clothes, hair, skin and wormed its way into our mouths until we could taste it.

I held my cardigan sleeve over my mouth and let my eyes work their way around the room. My gaze slipped quickly over the two covered mounds on the bed.

The door was still slightly open to the dressing room and my eyes settled on the sliver of bed I could see there. A bed. A dressing room. A dressing table with long black hairs in a hairbrush. Mrs Angel did not have long black hair — hers was a tin-grey.

But Doreen Dellamer didn't have long black hair either. I thought of her now, suspended in cold stasis — her body sharp with ice, beads of blood dangling from her hair and the skin stippled with snow. Would the same decay be taking root there as in this room or would Doreen Dellamer be preserved in that moment of violence, her scarves brutally strewn about her and the waves of her . . .

. . . long, black wig flowing down across the white snow?
I strode quickly towards the small dressing room.

'Ursula?' Mother asked, tentatively.

As I pushed the door further open, it clearly wasn't a dressing room at all. Doreen Dellamer undoubtedly dressed up as the ill-fated fortune teller here. She sat at that mirror and she brushed through the wig. Or her sister did as they went over their plan. Doreen Dellamer slept in that bed. Right by her sister's room. This was Doreen Dellamer's bedroom.

I stood as if looking into a grave, uncertain what this emptiness held. A little piece of her would linger here, perhaps until her death was explained. Until she was free. Perhaps she and her sister might find that little land they had in the photograph again. Perhaps. Dad always said heaven was not a place but a time, the time when you were happiest. I often wondered if he was there now and if a memory of me was with him in his captured moment.

As I turned to leave, I noticed the bin by the side of the bed. Papers and old cosmetic bottles, some used cotton wool. Is this what remained of a life? And there, sprinkled over it all was ash and cigarette butts.

I couldn't remember her ever having smoked. And it seemed unlikely that Mr and Mrs Angel did, with their slightly parsimonious attitude and their signs forbidding it throughout the house. I looked towards the outstretched hand of Mrs Angel, the folds of her sheet gathered round her. She was reaching to her bedside table and there, next to the upset water glass and a box of tissues, was a grimy ashtray.

I went gingerly over, watching her closely with every step as if that limp hand might at any point reach out and grab me.

'Ursula?' Mother said. 'What is it?'

'Look.' I nodded towards the bin.

We both peered down. Again, as with the other bin, there were quite a few partially smoked cigarettes. The ashtray, meanwhile, was empty, except for a coating of grey powder on the surface. It was uncommonly large, especially for a bedside table, even for a good forty-a-day kind of person. For a non-smoker, it was ludicrously out of place. This great marble slab had come from a much grander setting. This had come from the main house, where smoking was forbidden. I followed their shadows through my imagination and began building a picture of them as they carefully brought the filled ashtray back here and tipped it in this bin, rather than the one in the main house.

I remembered the smell, the tobacco-tainted air, as the smoke sifted through the night. That first night, I had been charmed from my room by that scent, as it coiled its way up the stairs accompanied by the melody of Clair de Lune. The Angels had been sending smoke signals. They had attempted to lure someone out. Me? Someone else? Why? There had been a plan and that meant there had to have been a reason. Whatever game they had been playing was a dangerous one. So dangerous that it led to their deaths and that of Doreen Dellamer. All that remained were corpses and a lot of questions. And what of Less? How did she steal into this dark mass? Now there were more questions than answers.

Rule 28: Ignore the people who are purposefully clouding your judgement.

SMOKED

Back in the sitting room, we laid out our haul. Six cigarette stubs lined up carefully on the desk alongside the fine marble ashtray. We'd moved Diana's bloodied arrow to a dark corner, rather than have it on full display.

'Very nice,' said Bridget, wrinkling her nose.

'We think the Angels were attempting to smoke someone out,' Aunt Charlotte began.

'Can I just make an objection from the very beginning?'

'If you must, Bridget. And let's be clear we are nowhere near the beginning,' I answered.

She ignored me and continued. 'Can we jettison the comments about smoke? We know the Angels were up to some sort of game that involved these cigarettes — but can we not resort to cheap nonsense about smoke signals, smoking people out or, indeed, smoke and mirrors? It's just crass.'

We fell into a semi-stunned silence.

'We need to consolidate,' I said.

The sitting room had now taken on the air of base camp and we naturally settled to the seats we'd had since the beginning, still leaving an empty seat for Less.

'Why were there cigarettes in their bin? They weren't using them for their own recreation. They were part of their plan.'

'Plan? Ursula darling. What, are you saying now, that they were evil geniuses with an incredibly cunning *plan*?' Mother shook her head dismissively. 'You need to calm down with the conspiracy theories. They were two lonely old—'

'Three,' I said defiantly. 'I am convinced Doreen Dellamer lived here and was Mrs Angel's sister. She was in on it too.'

'Darling girl . . .' Mother began. It was even more disconcerting when she was kind to me. An insistent throb began in my temple. I wiped the back of my hand across my damp face. I could smell my own sour sweat. None of us had washed, let alone slept. My leg began to twitch again.

'Let the girl speak,' Bridget said sharply.

'She's *my* daughter—'

'And yet you so rarely acknowledge that.' Bridget sat back smugly.

I watched their distorted faces morph into pantomime villains, laughing hyena-like, rocking back and forth with their boiled gammon flesh rippling and black flinty eyes watching. Their smiles were too full of teeth, their tongues slathered around their mouths like they were hungry dogs. Mr Bojangles laughed at me. I felt my knees crumbling and the ground unsteady again. Maybe it was me rocking back and forth.

'Ursula? Ursula?' Mother was at my shoulder. 'Can you hear me, Ursula? Are you all right?' I felt her hand grab my elbow. 'Sit her down,' she insisted, her fingers digging into my skin. 'She needs some water. Something to eat. She's exhausted. This is ridiculous. We need help. Charlotte, get that cushion. Come on!'

I couldn't feel my hands. I was drowning as the room filtered out into a grey blur. It was a comfortable falling. I didn't want to fight any part of it. I wanted to embrace such glorious, unimpeded disconnection. It was a freedom I had never experienced before and I completely surrendered to it. Perhaps, finally, I would find out whether Dad was right and I'd nestle into my happiest memory.

As my eyes closed over and my thoughts turned inwards, all I could hear was panic and strange frantic voices. Yet I was only aware of an overwhelming feeling of calmness. Mirabelle was moving quickly towards the door, leaving behind words about water and bread. Aunt Charlotte had become a strange flightless bird, twittering and dancing at the edges of my consciousness. She grabbed my wrist, I felt her soft, white fingers push into my skin. Mother was holding my head back. She called my name constantly as if she was making a great effort not to forget it.

'Ursula! Ursula! Listen to me . . .'

I could think of nothing less that I wanted to do in that moment than listen to Mother. With all these beautiful, restful thoughts, who would?

A violent urge to be sick suddenly stamped itself into my belly. I couldn't hold it. I felt the acid rise and roll over my tongue. I couldn't even hold my hand to my mouth. I heard Aunt Charlotte shouting, 'Stand back! She's going to—'

'What's happening? What did you do?' I heard Bridget dash across the room and stop in sudden silence with Mr Bojangles.

The sweat poured over me in great rivulets, down my neck and sides. A silty smear had spread across the carpet in front of me. I saw its fingers spreading out, clawing closer to me.

'Drink this,' Mirabelle said quickly, thrusting a beaker into my face. I fell back and she cradled my head as she held the cup closer to my lips. 'Quick, this will help.'

My head filled with a great grinding sound. I couldn't see anything except the beaker. The noise wouldn't let go, gnawing at my brain.

I felt the air slipping out with no thought to replace it with another breath. I'd always thought in my last heartbeat I'd see Dad again. My happiest moments had been with him, surely. But all I saw was Mother's face, her face bent in disapproval.

'It's OK. It's all OK, I've fixed it,' she whispered into my ear.

'Fixed it . . .' I felt the beaker fall and the water bloom out across my lap.

There was a disturbing moment of silence, as if the room held its breath. Through my hooded eyes I could make out Mother's shape. Aunt Charlotte and Mirabelle watched in confusion, while Bridget looked judgemental.

'I'm fine,' I whispered.

Their eyes landed on me like crows on meat scraps. Aunt Charlotte looked from me to Mother; Mother watched me then looked back at Mirabelle; Mirabelle's eyes flitted between Charlotte and Mother. It was like a scene from a western starring middle-aged women who haven't slept.

My mouth still wouldn't move. Their faces tumbled over and over in my mind as if being washed through my thoughts. Now, nothing was clear. The world spun in opposing directions. But I kept coming back to the same thought, the killer wasn't out there somewhere, waiting, watching, picking us off. The killer was here.

Through the rising tide of my thoughts, one thing surfaced time and again. The killer was here. That seemed certain.

'Ursula, listen to me. Listen, girl. Now!' Mother's voice was irresistible. 'Focus! You're feeling sick. It will pass.' Her face slowly grew clearer. Her eyes were set on me. She studied me intensely as if searching for something.

'What's going on?' Aunt Charlotte look disturbed. Soon Mother would feel the need to slap her, she usually did. 'Pandora, what the hell is happening? Explain! Please. Is she going to—'

And there it was, a hearty slap that sent Aunt Charlotte's jowls jabbering and swaying. It had the crisp sound of finality and resonated quite beautifully into the new silence.

'Why must you always slap, Pandora?'

'I do what is necessary,' Mother said staunchly.

Whether it was my hallucinatory state, I couldn't say, but the world seemed so strange and ill-formed, clouding into difficult shapes.

'Is this hell, Mother?'

'Now is not the time for existential explanations.' She leaned closer. '*Just follow my lead.*'

I could see Aunt Charlotte and Mirabelle look at each other. Paranoia raged through my head.

'We need to sit down and be quiet,' Mother had an unnerving ability to sound like Margaret Thatcher in a crisis.

It worked. Mirabelle, Aunt Charlotte and even Bridget lowered themselves into their chairs. Mother remained by me. I wasn't sure if that was reassuring or not.

'I'm fine, Mother. Really, I am. But I think now might be the time for some explanations, if we're going to live any longer.'

Mother watched me closely and squeezed my hand. 'It's all going to be all right,' she said, which made me think it wasn't.

Mr Bojangles barked his disapproval.

No one spoke. We waited, and we listened to the silence. It was amazing just how much silence there was outside of London. Here, in this isolated house deep in the night, there was an ocean of nothing. It wasn't a peaceful quiet, but an edgy, disorientating void that made no sense to my ears. It had confused me from the beginning, now it was unavoidable and unnerving. All I could focus on was the lack of any noise, the reams of bleak silence that seemed to press in from every corner. Although, in fairness to the house, four dead people does produce a very sombre atmosphere.

The cacophony of life in the city had always been a part of my existence. Yet now, there were no birds in the garden, no music, no planes, no vacuum cleaners or lawnmowers, no distant motorbikes, dogs barking, builders' rabble or children's voices. To bleach out all those sounds was disturbing, as if life had been paused for some great disaster to unfold.

Rule 29: Expect nothing when people say they have the answer. Often, they have what they want to be the answer.

MOTHER'S SOLUTION

The stench of my own vomit was resurrecting a taste of bile in my mouth. The nausea began to rise. 'I can't stand the smell anymore,' I announced. 'I need to get some cleaning products.'

Four pairs of eyes watched me closely. Mr Bojangles was asleep.

'I've got some wet wipes,' Aunt Charlotte offered. She scrabbled in her bag and revealed a fist-full of used moist tissues. What she'd used them for wasn't clear.

As I wrestled with my own efforts to stand, I felt Mother's hand on my arm. 'You can't go anywhere until this is done.' There was fresh menace in her voice.

I hovered between standing and sitting, the muddy stain from my stomach staring up at me from the damp floor. My thighs shivered and I fell back into the chair.

'We will make it all clean when this is done,' she said smoothly.

It was an uneasy silence that gave way to the sharp song of the storm. Like a crazed child, it rang round the house in a discordant, high-pitched fury. I saw a flash of the headlines back at home — *Worst storm in living memory, thousands stranded.* The media would be indulging with a dark delight in the destruction wrought on homes and roads. But the rest of the outside world would not fall into focus anymore. We were into our fourth day, but we had drifted so far from reality that imagination had firmly taken root in place of the truth.

We stared at the fireplace as if answers would plume out in great gusts of smoke. My mind swam with the four bodies draped in white: Less in her sheet; the Angels abandoned on their desolate bed; and Doreen Dellamer in a shroud of snow. We were surrounded by a host of spent and wasted lives.

'This vase is the key,' Mother began. She never told me bedtime stories, but I suspect this settled voice is what she would have used if she did. 'Less stole it but the Angels saw it, perhaps smuggled into one of her vast bags, shoved in the bottom of the wardrobe. They could have confronted her, made a scene but they didn't. We'd said enough about Joy's stealing for them to know it was a problem, perhaps a big enough problem that they could fashion an opportunity out of it. We know they were desperate enough for money to masquerade as housekeeper and butler, to hide their true identities.'

'I'm sorry,' Aunt Charlotte interjected, 'I don't follow. How does Less stealing from them give them a financial gain? Surely—'

'Oh, sister, if only you could try to have your brain in gear before you set off with your mouth. *Blackmail,*' she whispered.

I watched Bridget raise her eyes to meet mine. She smiled in a strange way.

'They knew it was risky. Yet they took that risk. Why? Why would impoverished people, who had already gone to fairly extreme lengths to raise money to keep their family home, take such a ridiculous risk? There is only one answer — money. That's what they needed more than anything else and they saw a way, however treacherous, to obtain it.'

Aunt Charlotte leaned forward conspiratorially. 'Blackmail? You think they tried to blackmail Less?' The word hung in the air like smoke.

It was Mother's turn to close her eyes. 'The company,' she said softly.

'What?'

'The name of the company they said owned and ran this place — White Chain. A little clue to—'

'*Blackmail*,' Aunt Charlotte whispered again.

'They even *told* us what they were doing.'

'They told *someone*!' Mother was suddenly becoming very animated. I watched her as she continued excitedly. 'Picture the scene, Doreen Dellamer on that doorstep with Joy — I can just imagine it: Doreen saying, "We know what you've done. You'll go back to prison for this." Doreen knew all about Joy and her chequered past from her time as my lodger. One more time and they'd throw away the key. Doreen confronted her about the theft of the priceless vase and tried to blackmail her. Joy panicked. She couldn't risk going back inside. She grabbed the nearest thing to her and smashed it over Doreen's head. Maybe she wasn't even trying to kill her. Maybe she wasn't thinking of anything except shutting her up.' Mother paused and looked around her. 'Remember this also, when Ursula was testing to see if Angel knew *how* Doreen Dellamer had been killed, her scheme was scuppered by Joy saying "It was probably unseemly for someone to bludgeon the old dear's brains out." That was annoying at the time because it gave away the manner of the woman's death to Angel who could not have known.' Mother paused dramatically. 'But Joy could not have known either.'

We all stared at her.

'At that point, only those who had discovered the body knew.'

'When you came in, when we were in the hallway, you told me she'd been hit over the head,' Mirabelle said, tentatively. 'Less might have overheard as she came down the stairs.'

'All I said was she'd been hit over the head, not that she'd had her brains bludgeoned out. And if she'd been close enough to hear, we'd have seen her on the stairs at that point, I'm sure of it. She ran down those stairs from the top. No, Joy already knew how Doreen had died because she put her there. Because she killed her.'

No one spoke and Mother saw her chance to continue.

'Secondly, consider this. Joy realized what she'd said and, more importantly, who she'd said it in front of. Angel. Angel was no fool. He knew Joy could not have known. She'd not been out with us. The Angels had to be in on it, otherwise why the deception? Joy must have somehow realized, or Doreen told her, that the Angels knew too. She had to silence them as well.'

'But how?' Aunt Charlotte let her mouth hang open.

Mother turned to me. 'I think my daughter can help us there, can't you?'

I stared at her. 'The book?' I asked.

She nodded. Mother felt behind her cushion and pulled out the claret leather-bound volume.

'Finally, we get to discuss a book!' Bridget sighed. 'What is it?'

'Ursula?' Mother leaned forward and handed me the book.

Rule 30: The normal rules involve a denouement delivered by a single person. This is often not the case. Some people will be wrong. Some will lie.

URSULA'S SOLUTION

Mother nodded to me. 'Tell us, Ursula.'

I stared.

'Well, come on girl!' Mirabelle cried.

'It's like pulling teeth,' Bridget sighed. 'I like a much snappier ending. Take *Gone Girl*, for instance—'

'Just hear me out!' I paused. 'It's only one possible solution, but say Less did wait for Doreen Dellamer to leave and then cornered her. Perhaps they'd arranged to meet outside after the fortune telling. Who knows what was said in those moments, what demands were made, what secrets revealed? We will never know. But whatever happened it was clear to Less that the Angels were in on the scheme too. Who knows, perhaps Doreen Dellamer signed the Angels' death warrant with whatever she said just before Less reached for the statue's arrow and slammed it into her skull. Less dragged away the corpse and buried it in a shallow grave, but she knew that wasn't the end of it. The Angels had to know. They could blackmail her or worse. She had to deal with them too. But then she saw the solution to the problem,' I looked around the room. 'It was right there in front of her. She saw the mushrooms growing around Doreen Dellamer's hasty grave.'

'Wait. What?' Aunt Charlotte was the picture of disbelief. 'Mushrooms? Are you serious?'

I took a breath and held out the book for inspection.

Bridget, obligingly, read the title. '*FUNGI: A Natural History and Index*. Not a very catchy title is it? I mean, who would pick that up? The title is so important. It can't be all long and convoluted. It really needs to grab you. Like, say, something like . . .' she paused for a moment, '*Gone*—'

'I think Less remembered Angel's own recipe. The daily omelette he told us of in such pompous detail. It wasn't just Mirabelle who said she foraged. Remember Less was interrupted just as she was telling us about it. "You find the real food when you've foraged for it yourself." She knew these were deadly. It would have been so easy to sneak a few into their basket of mushrooms.'

'Aren't you forgetting something?' Mirabelle said frostily. 'Less is dead.'

'So?' — I hated that they'd driven me to use that word — 'Read your Agatha Christie. You cannot libel the dead: *Death on the Nile*.'

'I don't really like Agatha Christie,' Bridget commented. 'Too many murders.'

Mirabelle cleared her throat and continued. 'Say that this is true, that Less killed Doreen Dellamer. She can't have killed the Angels, she was dead. And we still don't know who killed Less.' Her voice was slipping into anger. She is not a patient woman at the best of times and these times certainly couldn't be described as anyone's best. 'So, as usual, Ursula, you pretend to know everything, but really you know half of nothing.'

I watched her shrewdly. 'Is that right, Mirabelle?'

She shrugged.

'Well, if it's not Less, it has to be someone else — someone perhaps in this room. We could ask ourselves a few more questions. Shall we? Who exactly spoke to Doreen Dellamer? Who spoke to the fortune teller?'

Aunt Charlotte paused before her face folded into indignation. 'Oh, I see where we're going with this! I see all right. Only Less and I went to see the bloody fortune teller. It can't be Less, so it has to be me.' She slammed her hands into the chair arms. 'Well, I'm not going to be bullied by you buggers over this. I've killed absolutely nobody — never have, never will. And that's an end to it.'

'Wait!' I said. 'That's not what I meant. You're missing out a step.'

Mother gathered her lips tightly and watched me with wide eyes, as if willing me towards a solution.

'She had to keep up the pretence of being here as a fortune teller. And what does every fortune teller require?'

'A crystal ball?' Aunt Charlotte offered. 'Because that would certainly have been beneficial to her.'

'They all demand one thing,' I continued. 'That you cross their palm with silver.'

Blank faces looked back at me.

'Payment,' I clarified.

Aunt Charlotte frowned. 'Well, I certainly didn't bother. She was rubbish. Blathered on a lot about *who will be thy sister's keeper now* and *at the opening of hearts all truth will be known*. Struck me that she'd watched a bit too much of that YouTube.'

'I don't want a bloody keeper,' Mother snapped.

I ignored them both. 'No, *you* didn't pay her. But Mirabelle said she went to pay her.'

A cold silence flooded the room. We all watched Mirabelle's motionless face.

'Isn't that right, Mirabelle?' I continued quietly.

Mirabelle smiled. It was a cruelly confident smile.

'You took off into the hallway, determined to intercept Doreen Dellamer before she left. Why? Perhaps I know half of nothing. But then perhaps you know more than you're saying.'

I watched Mirabelle maintain that disturbing smile. She didn't waver. I saw doubt touch Mother's face as she teased through the strands we had unravelled.

And now I slowly began to weave a pattern that had Mirabelle right at the centre. '*You* set the fire every night, every day. You took the pokers from right where the arrow that killed Doreen Dellamer had been stashed. What did you see when you went to pay the fortune teller? Were Less and Doreen Dellamer arguing? Did you see more than that?'

I watched as her jaw clenched tighter and the rigid muscles stood taught on her neck as if wires had been drawn through the flesh and pulled.

'Did you confront Less later? Did you argue, Mirabelle? Did it cross your mind that you might be next unless you took action?'

Mirabelle stepped forward so I could feel the fine spray of her words on my face. 'I promise you, you will regret this.'

I shook my head slowly. 'Like Less? You see, Mirabelle, no one is above suspicion, so let's not start throwing accusations around or criticizing others too readily, eh?'

Everyone paused, waiting for Mirabelle to speak or move. She did neither.

'Aren't you forgetting something, dear?' Bridget said smoothly. 'Mirabelle was with us when Less died.'

'Yes, but she set the candle under the rope earlier. It needed time to burn through. Remember her leaving for more brandy? Returning swinging two decanters in her great display of drunkenness?' I faced Mirabelle. 'You heard her demand that the Angels run her a bath and light candles. It was a gift! You had just enough time to race to her room and set in motion the wheels that would inevitably turn into that frightful accident. *You* set the candle burning under the rope.'

Mirabelle shook her head slowly and began to smirk, a lazy smile that implied no effort or concern.

'You're a fantasist. Pandora, are you going to let this nonsense continue?' There was only the slightest hint of doubt in the back of Mirabelle's voice, but it was there.

'Oh, and there might be another little problem with this scenario you're putting forward,' Bridget smiled. Suddenly, she'd decided to get involved and it was even more annoying than her refusal to do anything. 'Mirabelle was hit over the back of the head by the assassin. She can't very well have hit herself over the head, now can she, dear? Isn't that right, Mr Bojangles?'

I looked at Bridget with new eyes.

Mirabelle laughed. 'Yes, please, tell us, Poirot, how did I cleverly belt myself over the back of the head?

'If you had in fact been hit on the head at all.'

Aunt Charlotte frowned. 'We saw it, Ursula. I can't stand Mirabelle either but really, all this Pierrot nonsense and leading us down a complete blind alley out of sheer dislike, makes you sound like a clown yourself, dear. We have no time for this. We should be looking for the killer.' She threw herself back into her chair.

'Wait. What exactly did we see?' I asked quietly. 'Mirabelle on the floor with blood all over the back of her head. Take yourself back to that room . . .'

'Now?'

'No, Aunt Charlotte,' I sighed. 'I mean in your imagination. Less's blood was already everywhere. Mirabelle had the perfect opportunity to give herself the perfect alibi. She made herself a victim. Mirabelle instantly ran to Less. She smeared Less's blood onto the back of her head and lay there waiting, a fresh victim, disguising a murderer.

The silence drifted across us all. 'Why did you kill Less, Mirabelle?' I said. 'Why did you kill them all?'

Rule 31: Say very little or it will look like you know too much.

ANOTHER SOLUTION

'Oh, but she didn't,' Bridget said, distractedly. She didn't look up. She just carried on thumbing the pages of *Gone Girl*.

'How can you possibly know anything, sitting in your chair all day with your stupid little dog?' I snapped.

She laid down her book. 'Because, dear girl, I listen and I watch.' Suddenly, Bridget seemed to sit in a much more sinister light. Even Mr Bojangles looked a bit suspicious.

'You have ignored a whole section of clues. You cannot cherry-pick clues to fit your solution. Each one has its place, which you would all know if you ever discussed the books rather than seeing book club as a social group.'

Mother tutted loudly.

'You would all know a lot more if you ever read the books! You just skim over the pages and you never properly take in what is there on the page.' She held up the mushrooms book. 'The answer was right here, staring you in the face, if you'd just taken the trouble to read it carefully.'

We leaned closer, our faces a mix of confusion and fascination.

236

'So, are you ready to talk about books now?' she said slowly, insufferably. 'The answer is clearly there—'

'Oh, for God's sake, just say it, woman! If it wasn't Mirabelle, then which of us killed Less?' I couldn't hold back anymore.

Bridget gave me her most patronizing smile. 'The Angels did, of course.'

'The Angels?' Mirabelle's voice was cracking. 'So, who killed the Angels then?'

'Joy,' Bridget said simply.

She could see the disbelief spreading across our faces. 'Let me offer a scenario. As you said, that's all we can do. That's all any of us can do until we escape this tomb. But it really is the only scenario that is plausible.' She nodded at Mr Bojangles who settled himself in. 'You were quite right. Joy did indeed kill Doreen Dellamer with Diana's arrow. A hurried, unplanned affair that indicates a sudden need to act. Joy also realized the need to kill again. But from the other side of the mirror, the Angels had set this all up, they'd known the secret and would know who killed Doreen Dellamer — or Mrs Angel's sister, as you so rightly identified her. They too saw the need to kill, but in revenge.'

She looked around for acknowledgment but saw only bemused faces. 'May I read to you from a book?'

'Not *Gone Girl*,' Aunt Charlotte sighed.

'No, no. This is more . . . more appropriate.'

Aunt Charlotte couldn't have looked any more confused.

Bridget began reading in a flat, emotionless voice. '"Among the most toxic mushrooms, the destroying angel (*Amanita bisporigera*) is responsible for most mushroom poisonings. Easily confused with non-deadly mushrooms, such as puffballs, button mushrooms and horse mushrooms, it contains amatoxin, which destroys liver and kidney tissues, leading to death.

'"Symptoms: Vomiting, cramps, delirium, convulsions leading to death.

'"Season: In Britain, August to November.

237

'"Found: Woodlands, often at the base of fallen and dead trees."'

She paused, looked up, then turned the page. '"First symptoms appear six to twenty-four hours after consumption. Often symptoms subside and then reappear with a vengeance at which point kidney and liver damage is well underway and death is almost inevitable."' She left the words to settle on us.

'Joy put the mushrooms in among their basket of normal mushrooms and they added them to their omelette. From the moment the Angels ate those mushrooms, they were dead men walking. However, dead men walking are still very capable of killing. Unaware of the clock ticking on their own lives, the Angels set the chandelier trap to kill their sister's killer. It had the desired effect and Joy did indeed die. But then the mushrooms began to take effect. All the murderers and blackmailers killed each other. All this time, you have been chasing phantoms. There are no murderers left.'

We watched her in stunned silence. She was enjoying herself.

I cleared my throat. 'You . . . you say the Angels killed Less because she had killed Mrs Angel's sister, Doreen Dellamer. What makes you so sure they knew *who* had killed her?'

She shook her head in an exaggerated fashion. 'Oh, Mr Bojangles, shall we explain it to them?'

The dog yawned obligingly.

'When we discovered Doreen Dellamer was dead, the Angels knew. They knew Joy had killed her. Doreen Dellamer had spoken with the Angels before she left that night. She'd had ample opportunity to tell them their scheme had in fact worked and she'd nailed their target and was ready to plunge in and begin negotiating the terms of their silence. Remember Angel attempting to cancel the rest of the fortune telling after Joy had finished? Remember how loudly he had to shout outside the door that there was another guest, Charlotte, who wished to have their fortune told and how long it took for Madam Zizi to be ready for you? She'd already packed up, finished. They'd got what they wanted.

'When you discovered Doreen Dellamer's sad body, the Angels knew full well who had perpetrated the crime. They may have even known before us. Remember, the next day Angel told us he'd been out to find the road impassable. Why had he been out? To look for Doreen Dellamer. Joy had already slipped the mushrooms into their basket the night before, however. They'd already had their morning omelette. They were already dying. It would just take time.

'Time, however, was not Joy's friend. That window of digestion was enough for the Angels to enact their gruesome revenge for the murder of their sister. They drew the bath. They set the candles to burn through the rope. They killed Joy. And then the effects of the mushrooms they'd eaten earlier that morning came in thick, fast waves that sent them to their deaths. Joy killed the Angels. They just died after her.'

We sat in hollow silence, not daring to breathe too deeply in case we broke the spell.

Mother smiled a baleful smile. 'So, what you're saying is we have been in fear of a killer and hunting for one. But the murderers were already dead.'

Bridget gave a self-satisfied smile. 'Yes, Mr Bojangles and I have been amused watching you all running around, haven't we, Mr Bojangles?'

'And all for this stupid vase?' Aunt Charlotte said in disbelief.

'Well, it is priceless,' Mother sighed.

Bridget laughed. 'Oh, Mr Bojangles, aren't they silly? Of course it wasn't about a vase. Was it, Pandora?'

Rule 32: People will usually only kill when they see no other option.

MURDERER

Mother leaped from her chair as if her cage had suddenly been unlocked. 'How bloody dare you?' She was shouting.

Bridget continued to smile in a manner so infuriating that I suspected another murder might be about to occur.

Mother's face was livid with rage.

Mirabelle stood up next to her, as loyal as a stalker. 'Don't you try and hang this on Pandora. You have no place here. None.'

'Let the dog woman speak.' Aunt Charlotte was quiet and calm. We looked at her.

Mirabelle snorted. 'Oh, trust you to twist the knife.'

'No knives were used,' Bridget said. She let the smile drift away. 'But these deaths certainly weren't about a vase, priceless or not.'

'You've got nothing,' Mother spat. It seemed a strange selection of words.

'I told you earlier, you cannot cherry-pick clues. *All* the clues are necessary, aren't they, Mr Bojangles?'

'For God's sake, stop bloody addressing the dog.'

'Why? Are you somehow more intelligent or fun to be around?' Bridget shook her head. 'You have all ignored the entire first night we spent here. You have ignored moving furniture, smoke, phantom pianists and disguises.'

'We don't need your Maigret act,' Mother sniped.

'Who?'

'Shut up, Charlotte,' Mirabelle snapped. 'Look, it's brutally cold in here again. Let's get a good fire—'

'Stop,' Bridget said quietly. 'You don't need to keep lighting the fire, Mirabelle. Now, we need to look at *all* the clues. I am going to show you all something.' Bridget walked towards the fire. 'Watch very carefully.' She raised her hand to the mantelpiece and pushed a small, round button, which appeared to be some sort of servants' bell. A grinding sound began. She stood to the side and, slowly, the back of the fireplace swung open to reveal a dark hole at the end of which we could clearly see through to the library.

'You see,' she continued, 'I thought it was odd in a house such as this, that we had to resort to using that ridiculous, irritating little bell every time we needed the staff. It took me a long time to notice the bell up here, since someone had placed this large Meissen vase in front of it. Thankfully, *someone* moved it. But only after Joy died. Habits are easily formed and none of us sought to change what we were doing or question it. We had settled easily into a pattern, in the same way we settled into specific chairs. But what we need to do now is question all the things that have become normal, that we have made assumptions about or simply accepted.

'It was the sudden announcement of there being no time at breakfast that alerted me to this.'

We all looked adrift now.

This didn't seem to break Bridget's stride. 'There was a clock on the large radio but it had stopped. Ursula was sure there'd been a radio in the library. Ursula is profoundly useless and annoying in many ways—'

I took a sharp breath and she paused to enjoy my reaction.

'But when it comes to noting irrelevant details, she's useful.' She gave me a toxic smile. 'We have an enormous piece of hideous furniture, which is in fact a vulgar customized CD alarm that anyone can buy at one of those cheap, nasty shops you like, Charlotte. But this one doesn't even tell the correct time. The clock has stopped. Not strange, in itself. Most things here are grotesque or don't work. But why move it from the library where it was before to the dining room if it didn't even work? No one played the CDs and it didn't tell the time. Add the music coming from a closed piano and the cigarette smoke — music and time now become very important characters in our story.'

'It's ghosts,' Aunt Charlotte said, open-mouthed.

'No, foolish Charlotte. This was a very real person. People, in fact. Our first night here, Ursula hears piano music and smells tobacco smoke. She comes downstairs to find a *closed* door. When she opens it, no one is there, the music stops and the lid is closed. There is no way out other than the door.'

'Except the fireplace!' I exclaimed. 'Whoever it was, ran through the fireplace.'

Bridget shook her head at Mr Bojangles. 'Aren't they silly people? No, no, no, stupid girl, there was no time for someone to get up, put the lid down and get through the fireplace before closing it. The piano still had dust on it.'

'Icing sugar.'

'I'm sorry?'

'It was icing sugar,' I said. 'I found some and I tasted it.'

Mother tutted loudly. 'No wonder you get sick.'

'Yes,' Bridget continued thoughtfully, 'that makes sense. The back of the fireplace was left slightly open. You would not have seen it over there at the other side of the room in the dark. The music came from another room, the dining room where the alarm clock went off at midnight, playing the music you heard for ten minutes. It didn't need anyone's presence. It had already been set.' She nodded as if confirming her own theory, as if she was just making all this up as she spoke. 'Hence, it is always ten past twelve. Some time before, someone smoked cigarettes outside this room, leaving the smoke to travel upstairs. You found the cigarettes in the Angels' bin. When you opened the door to the sitting room, you would not have been able to see the fire back was open. You would simply see an empty room with a dusty, closed piano that looked like it hadn't been played in years and the music had stopped suddenly.'

I shook my head. 'But this fireplace opens to the library and they moved the CD player to the dining room.'

Bridget pointed triumphantly to the other side of the room. 'Who said it was *this* fireplace?' Her finger hovered in the air.

We all turned and looked at the opposite wall. Another fireplace. Bridget walked proudly through the room, with Mr Bojangles, as if they were about to be knighted.

Another button behind a vase and instantly the scheme began to open out. There, through the back of the fireplace, was the dining room. The clock was visible in the corner. 'From where you were standing, Ursula, *this* fireplace would have been entirely obscured by the open door.'

'But why go to all that trouble of moving the clock? They'd carefully set the alarm to play the music at midnight. The fireplace to the library would have achieved exactly the same effect, a closed piano being played by a ghostly presence,' Mirabelle said, bewildered.

'Because you, Mirabelle, kept setting fires in this fireplace. It would have sprayed coal and embers everywhere if they'd opened it and immediately given the game away. They wanted to give the impression of a ghostly pianist, not burn their house down.' Bridget stood with her arms crossed over her chest and winked at Mr Bojangles.

'But I still don't understand why?' Aunt Charlotte said quietly.

'Bait,' Bridget said. 'Smoke signals to lure someone out.'

'What on earth are you talking about? Smoke signals? Bait? You're making it sound like a kipper factory.'

'What I don't understand is why would they need to do all this, if they already knew who stole the vase and intended to confront Less,' I said slowly, thinking it through with every word. 'We arrive and Doreen Dellamer hastily hides herself away, without saying a cheery "hello, remember me". She didn't need to do that at that time. The vase hadn't been stolen.' I wasn't really speaking to any of them now, I was piecing it together for myself. 'That night, the clock is moved — again, no need. A signal is sent — piano music, with no pianist. Cigarette smoke.' I screwed up my face. 'None of this is necessary! The Angels then suggest the fortune teller, who is Doreen Dellamer in disguise. They were attempting to lure someone out. Someone whose identity they *didn't* know.'

'But if they already knew Joy stole the vase—' Mirabelle started.

'Forget the vase.' Bridget stamped her foot. 'It's a complete red herring,' she said. 'All these clues point very clearly to the fact that it is not about the vase. Doreen Dellamer hid herself away before the vase was even stolen — remember Less nearly dropping it? Which leads us to the inescapable truth that someone planted the vase to make us *think* that was why Joy was killed.' She paused, and then looked up smiling. 'Didn't they, Pandora?'

Rule 33: Remember, people lie for many reasons — for money, for reputation — to protect themselves or others.

LIES

'You stupid, interfering cow, Bridget.' Mother's words were rich with malice.

'Not stupid enough though, eh, Pandora?' Bridget smiled. 'Now, open your bag.'

'Mother?' I whispered.

Aunt Charlotte stood up. 'What's going on? Pandora, you don't have to do anything this vicious little woman says. She's just a book club member!'

'Better to do it now, wouldn't you say, rather than after we have left here.' Bridget was enjoying this.

I looked at Mother.

'Mum?'

She closed her eyes and slumped back into the sofa.

'Mum, please say something. What have you done?' I gripped my leg hard, driving my nails into the jeans.

She looked at me. 'Oh, Ursula,' she sighed.

'Don't say anything,' Mirabelle interrupted.

Mother shook her head and carried on staring at me. 'It's too late for secrets.'

'The bag, if you please, Pandora,' Bridget insisted. '*Open it!*'

Mother paused, then leaned down to her small, brown bag. Such a normal, innocuous little bag. She opened it and reached inside. Gently, she held out her hands and there it lay.

Less's vaping pen.

'I don't . . .' Aunt Charlotte's voice trailed away.

'Would you like to explain, Pandora, or should I?' Bridget said primly.

'I planted the vase in Joy's room and . . .' Mother paused for a moment before continuing in a dream-like voice, as if the words had no more impact than the air. 'It wasn't just you, Ursula, who saw the vaping pen in Joy's bag. I saw it too.'

'What?' Aunt Charlotte still felt the need to contribute.

Mother continued quietly, 'I knew what it was, so I had to hit Mirabelle on the back of the head and take it.'

We looked on in horrified wonder.

'You hit me?' Mirabelle whispered slowly.

Mother nodded once.

'For this?' Aunt Charlotte asked.

Mother nodded again. And I watched her. I watched how she sat so still, so tight within her frame as if she was holding everything in.

'Mother?'

'I saw it in Joy's bag. I saw you try to take it from her bag, Ursula, then drop it.'

'Try to take it? I didn't—'

'You hit me over the head. You could have killed me.' Mirabelle stared resolutely at Mother.

'I had to. I had to try and hide this away.' She gripped the thin, black vape pen in her hands.

'I don't understand, Pandora.'

'I know,' Mother said softly to Mirabelle. 'I had to protect my daughter.'

246

They all now stared at me, the jury suddenly swayed.

'Mother? How could you suspect—'

'At first, I thought you might have done it and I had to hide the evidence, but then I realized I had to protect you from the truth.'

'Done what? What truth? Mother, you're scaring me.'

'This was your father's,' her voice cracked. 'And it is . . . it is what killed him.'

I watched silently as if I was on that point of waking, trying to sieve out the pieces of the dream from reality.

'His strange *experiments* down in the shed? They weren't experiments at all.'

My thoughts flittered to the light of the past like moths drawn in before their wings are burned.

'He was simply mixing.' She held out the vaping pen. 'For this. "E-juice", they called it. It was in its infancy then. He'd spent so much energy on trying to give up smoking that it became his new habit. He bought patches and when they didn't work, e-cigarettes and finally this. A vaporizer pen. Cartomizers, clearomizers and e-juice became a new addiction. He became fascinated by the mixtures, their taste and effect.

'He found new tastes, a new taste for life. There were all manner of farcical names and ridiculous flavours. It *thrilled* him. Lemon Tart; Purple Haze; Devil Teeth — they were all there. They had garlic flavoured for Vamporizers; Viagra-flavoured VapoRise; Smoke on the Water for the old rockers; rhubarb and custard or salted caramel for the sweet-toothed; almond-scented Marzipan Delight for Christmas. Like a twisted Willy Wonka, he tried them all. Little phials would appear, glass bottles, endless hours in the shed, the tell-tale vapour creeping out. I even had nightmares that some Hyde-like creature would slink out of that shed one evening.'

I watched her knuckles whiten as her grip tightened.

'I knew, you see,' A tear escaped and travelled down her face. She looked directly into my eyes. 'Yes, his heart was weak and gave up. But I think we will find he died from *what* he smoked, not *being* a smoker. He knew exactly what he was doing to get the effect he needed without harm to himself. He wanted to live to see you grow up more than anything in the world.'

Another tear fell.

'You're scaring me, Mother.'

'At first, when I saw the vape pen in Joy's bag and saw you grab for it, I thought you knew or worse. Perhaps you were more guilty than that.' She let that linger there in the air. 'And that is why I tried to protect you from all this.' She stopped to take a deep breath. 'And for that, you must forgive me, Mirabelle. You walked in at the wrong time. I couldn't let you catch me in there taking it. I just wanted to hide the truth, Ursula. The truth that your father was poisoned, not accidentally, but purposefully, coldly and exactly.'

No one moved.

'It was you, Charlotte—'

'No! No, I—'

' . . . you, Charlotte, who fired a memory that meant nothing to me until I saw that vape pen in Joy's bag. It was when you said she worked on the farm producing cannabis that I remembered why Joy stopped working there.'

Aunt Charlotte gasped. 'Because she'd killed someone?'

'Don't be so ridiculous, Charlotte. Because they were using some pesticide and she didn't think it was *environmental*. There were *concerns* about it. I thought nothing of it at the time.' Mother paused for a moment as if deciding whether to continue. 'Your father was up for trying anything in this damn stupid stick. When she came back from her America trip, I was surprised to see Joy speaking to George so frequently, going down to his shed. I believe she gave him cannabis oil — *hemp* oil she called it, CBD — for this vape pen. And I believe she poisoned it. Spiked, I think we'll find, with something that killed him almost instantly. You see, she couldn't have the truth coming out about the vast sums of money she'd stolen and George just wouldn't stop. He wouldn't let it go. Constantly saying we had to do something. That she had to pay it back. Joy knew she'd be straight back in prison if she was caught stealing again. When George mentioned perhaps "taking it further", I suspect that was it.

'All this time I think I must have known, deep down. I must have known he didn't just die. But the only evidence would have been the vape pen, which I could never find after he died. All I had was a vague feeling. But when I saw his vaping pen in Joy's handbag, I knew. I believe your father was murdered by Joy and your father's own vaping pen was the murder weapon, which he then administered to himself.'

I felt the seat of the chair drifting away from me. I felt myself lifting up to the ceiling, floating there. Just watching. Listening not hearing.

'Ursula?' Mother was by my side. I think her hand was on my arm. I couldn't feel it.

'Are you satisfied now, Bridget?' I could feel the heat of Mother's anger. 'Ursula? Do you understand me? Ursula.' Her hair brushed my hand as her head fell.

I turned to face her, but she was just a space that looked different to the rest of the air around her. She was completely out of focus now.

'Joy murdered George?' Aunt Charlotte's voice drifted around me like the slow snow. 'With that?'

Mother paused. Then nodded.

Rule 34: Never blackmail a killer. They've already passed over the moral barrier of taking a life.

MURDERERS

Mother's words had opened a wound that would never close.

'No! No!' I heard my own voice, shrill and brutal. I let the long stream of my tears branch out across my face, before I fell back in exhaustion.

Mother's face was slack. She began to speak, her voice as flat as stone. 'George had found Joy stealing again when she came back from America. This time large sums of money. He confronted her.' She paused, her face sallow and weary. 'She waited, biding her time. They'd been very clear that last occasion she was in court, it would be a sizeable prison sentence next time. She told me more than once she couldn't face that again.' She wiped a smear of tears down her cheek.

'After George's death,' and she held out the small vape pen again, 'this disappeared. It didn't trouble me immediately. Why would it? It's only a vape pen. And the way he died — a lifelong smoker with a weak heart dying from a heart attack? No one could argue with that. But . . . but something always troubled me, a lurking little doubt.

'I had my suspicions over the years. I'd wonder if I was sending myself mad and that he'd just died of a heart attack and that was that. But then, after all these years, I saw this in *Joy's* bag and I knew then.' She glanced at the vape pen on her lap. Her head dropped. 'I could have killed her myself. But they got there first. The Angels, for the pain Joy had wrought in their lives, for the death of *their* loved one, as if Doreen Dellamer was more important than my—'

'Mother,' I whispered, and held her hand. She didn't pull it away this time.

'Wait.' Aunt Charlotte's voice was riddled with confusion. 'Why would Less bring such a thing with her years later? I don't—'

'Understand? Of course you don't, dear. Of course she doesn't, does she, Mr Bojangles?' Bridget sighed deeply as if a new burden had fallen to her. I could see she was relishing every moment. 'Joy didn't bring it with her. Doreen Dellamer lodged with Pandora at the time of George's death. I suspect she saw things she did not understand. You were forever moaning about her nosing around, sitting in her little window watching. But then she really did see something and she didn't quite know what to do. This.' She pointed at the vaping pen. Mr Bojangles yapped appreciatively. 'The naïve little chancer took what she thought might one day be useful. And that's where the story ended — until now.

'When she left and came back home here to her funny big, ruinous mansion she forgot all about the unusual goings-on and whatever she'd seen. That is, until we chanced to walk back through her door. All the characters she had seen twelve years ago stood ranged before her and she told her much cleverer, more desperate sister and brother-in-law. She told them what she'd seen. And what had she seen? George smoke this and instantly collapse. Perhaps he even tried to indicate what had killed him. He knew she watched from her window every day. Perhaps she even saw *someone* pass George the phial? But crucially not *who* it was. And if we accept all of my deductions so far, then we can clearly see that this is what drove everything from that point onwards. It is the only deduction that explains all of the clues, not just some of them.' She sat replete with smug satisfaction.

'But . . .' The blood was swarming in my head. I fell into the words. 'But when I held him, I heard his last br—'

Bridget had no time for this interlude. 'Doreen Dellamer may well have been there just before you, Ursula. He may have been alive when she took it. Or she took it in the chaos after. We can't know that.' Her voice was careless, callous.

The excitement glimmered in Bridget's eyes. 'But imagine it! As she saw us walk through the door years later, she told the Angels everything, of her suspicions and what she'd seen. At first, perhaps just a little gossip to titillate? *'Oh, I remember these people! I know them. A strange thing happened . . .'* Doreen Dellamer never took it seriously or even understood what she'd seen before, but her sister did when she told her. Whatever Doreen Dellamer told her sister of what she'd seen, it made a lot more sense to Mrs Angel than it ever had to Doreen. The Angels realized she had a potential murder weapon and that the murderer could well be here. But who? That was the question they were trying to flush out the answer to. Oh, there was potential here. It was worth a chance to make some money.

'The only problem they had was, I believe, that whatever Doreen had seen didn't identify the culprit. If we accept that they were trying to find out *who* killed George, then it all falls into place. They hatched a plan swiftly and somewhat clumsily. It was worth it. They had nothing to lose. Or so they thought.

'Doreen Dellamer's existence would be hidden from us, since obviously we would recognize her. They couldn't risk that. We didn't know she was here. We had landed with coincidence's dark light guiding us. The first night they tried to smoke out which one of us was the killer — cigarette smoke, George's piano music, the ghostly call of a dead man. They even graffitied their own no-smoking sign with reference to e-cigarettes but still no sign of the killer.

'So they turned to less subtle means on the second night. The rather dramatic fortune teller, Doreen Dellamer in disguise, who would drop hints in turn to each guest and maybe even let them see the offending article. Joy took the bait. The Angels had their killer and even attempted to end the fortune-telling session, although Charlotte trampled all over that.'

Aunt Charlotte looked confused.

'Later, Joy met Doreen Dellamer as agreed on the step to discuss terms. Joy, however, had other ideas, panicked and smashed her over the head with the arrow.' It was disconcerting to watch Bridget mime this with a sharp grin on her face.

'Joy dragged the body into the woods and shoved her under the tree. She knew the Angels were in on it, of course. They'd organized the whole charade. Who knows, perhaps Doreen herself had even told her — "*We know what you did.*"'

Bridget continued, revelling in every moment, 'Joy, who you correctly noted, had mentioned her foraging, picked the mushrooms and left them in the Angel's basket. They ate them the next morning, sending them on their way to a grisly death. But before the mushrooms could take effect, the Angels killed Joy with some carefully placed lighting. Revenge for killing Doreen Dellamer. Job done.' She sat back and smiled. 'Then the Angels began their slow disintegration into death.'

Bridget's gaze landed on Mother. 'But you'd already worked most of that out, hadn't you? You decided to muddy the waters and take the vaping pen to protect your daughter. You initially suspected she could have been the murderer, didn't you?'

I looked at Mother.

'You were in the perfect spot on the sofa to see Ursula find the vape pen in Less's bag. But when you realized Ursula had nothing to do with it, you certainly didn't want her to discover her father had been murdered. You hatched the alternative vase scenario, a rather fetching red herring—'

'Fish again?' Aunt Charlotte sighed.

'You realized, Pandora, that you could still have the cross-over murder solution — the dying Angels killing Joy. It would just be over the theft of a priceless vase and blackmail over that rather than this vaping pen.' She laughed extravagantly and shook her head at Mr Bojangles. 'But you *stupidly* didn't account for any of the first two nights of activities. The vase would have given them no reason to act in the many strange ways they did with fortune tellers, smoke and phantom pianists. It also provided no one to have hit Mirabelle over the head and no reason for doing so. Well, except for everyone's obvious dislike for her. You overlooked all of that because you are not as clever as me!'

We all looked at Bridget and, in that moment, I believe that every single person in that room was considering murdering her.

Rule 35: In the midst of death and danger, there is only one real rule: survive.

THE TIES THAT BIND

We survived. There had been no danger to us whatsoever once Less and the Angels died. Bridget, irritatingly, had been quite right: the murderers had all killed each other. In fact, she'd been right about everything, so she was never asked back to book club again. It was fear that stalked us through that house.

We had no option but to stay there one more night, barricaded in by the snow, but the fear had gone.

We stayed in our chairs, the ones we had appointed for ourselves from that very first naïve moment. We stayed in that room together, waiting until the world outside the house began to thaw. The window ledges rained with melting snow. Beyond, the trees surfaced from the ice, black and bare against the sky, as if they had been burned.

When we finally managed to get the cars out, and we escaped, it was in bewildered silence. As we peeled away one by one, I looked back at Less's car standing on the drive alone and thought of her lying there. Did she watch us leaving her behind? When she'd arrived, she could not have imagined what the next few days would have held. Had she faced justice for what she'd done? There was no justice in any of this. I had no idea what that meant any more.

I turned from the house and stared out the car window. The world seemed strange, too bright. Overwhelming. I was burdened by answers I'd never asked for and didn't want. I knew I wasn't leaving any of the pain inside that house, as we drove away. I wasn't escaping anything. I was taking it with me.

It would take a long time to unfurl all that it meant. There are layers to an aftermath, some more challenging than others, but none of them can be lost or ignored.

We didn't speak. We drove mutely along small country lanes and through villages unchanged by our horrors. It was as if nothing had happened. No one we passed would have suspected that our convoy had escaped a murder house.

Mother drove and I sat beside her. She had one hand on the steering wheel, the other held mine. We stayed like that until we found a phone signal, then she carefully removed her hand. The mobile phone synced to hands-free and rang through the car. She looked over at me once and took a breath. Then slowly, and in her very best voice, she asked for the police.

'I'd like to report a murder.'

How do you deal with people who have been locked away with death? When we were met on the road by the chaos of lights and sirens, compassion and suspicion seemed to be the two emotions the police had to offer. And that didn't change much in the days and weeks that followed.

The house was sealed, every inch photographed, every word we uttered recorded. It was as if it was all being logged for posterity. We couldn't breathe without it being analysed. We were wrapped in blankets and given too much tea. The bodies were removed. We were removed, at first taken to a small village police station that wasn't prepared for our story. Then to somewhere else. We were treated like victims. Which came as a surprise. I hadn't realized I was. It just hadn't occurred to us that we were until we began to explain it to those who hadn't been there.

The barrage of questions didn't stop.

We were repeatedly interviewed. Asked for our opinions and theories. I'm not sure whether they really wanted them or whether they were just fascinated by us. I suppose none of them could accept so many crimes could be committed without anyone being alive to blame.

Police, newspapers, friends and enemies all continued to take their fill of us in the months that followed. So many would sit in judgement on the events of the Slaughter House. Speculation was rife.

The horrors were routinely unearthed in new rounds of revelations. The destroying angel mushrooms were indeed later found growing on the estate and in the Angels' decaying bellies. It had taken only one last omelette to kill them. All the bodies gave up their secrets.

In the end, they exhumed Dad's body. That's when the fresh madness infected us all, in different ways. Dad's vaping pen was analysed and immediately transformed into the murder weapon when some strange, mysterious pesticide, Eagle 20, was discovered in large quantities in the remaining CBD liquid. The press loved that part. There'd been safety concerns at the cannabis farm Less had worked on in America. The pesticide was safe enough when people used cannabis in the old way, but they'd been made aware that when heated up in a vape pen the pesticide instantly turned into hydrogen cyanide. In enough quantities, it would kill immediately. There'd been a little press around it before but not much until then. After Dad's murder was made public, the pesticide was exposed as a possible killer even in much smaller quantities if it was used in products for vaping. It got the ball rolling. There were even some repercussions for the manufacture of CBD liquid for vaping especially when a number of other cases started to come to light.

But what did I care? The quantities of the pesticide found in Dad's vape pen were, sadly and incontrovertibly, deliberately put there. Less's trip to some Colorado weed farm was confirmed, as was the reason for her leaving their employment. Theft, of course, of cannabis oil and the pesticide. They thought it might have been going on for some time, but they only needed to catch Less once. Just as it took only once for Dad to inhale the huge amount of the pesticide she gave him. It was not marzipan I smelled on his last breath, but almonds — the scent of his killer, cyanide.

My old familiar, the night terrors, came thundering back. But the bird in my nightmare no longer pecked at my father's eyes. Dad was still dead, but the bird only looked at me one last time before it flew away. As it turned and sailed into the dream's sky, I saw the flash of white in its wings. It wasn't a rook at all but a magpie.

I never lost that image. It was a sign. A warning. We'd survived — this time. But we needed to be careful if we were going to do more than just make it out alive. We needed to be prepared. I came around to the idea that perhaps we could all do with learning how to survive. Persuading Mother, however, was going to take a lot more thought.

THE END

Thank you for reading this book.

If you enjoyed it please leave feedback on Amazon or Goodreads, and if there is anything we missed or you have a question about, then please get in touch. We appreciate you choosing our book.

Founded in 2014 in Shoreditch, London, we at Joffe Books pride ourselves on our history of innovative publishing. We were thrilled to be shortlisted for Independent Publisher of the Year at the British Book Awards.

www.joffebooks.com

We're very grateful to eagle-eyed readers who take the time to contact us. Please send any errors you find to corrections@joffebooks.com. We'll get them fixed ASAP.

Milton Keynes UK
Ingram Content Group UK Ltd.
UKHW011326200923
429050UK00004B/195

9 781804 052044

DOG WALKS
SOUTH DEVON & DARTMOOR

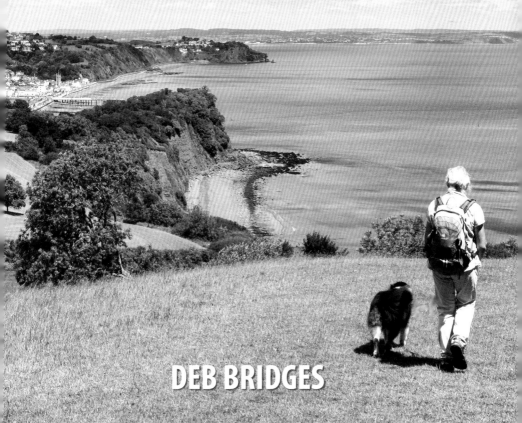

DEB BRIDGES

ACKNOWLEDGEMENTS

The directions for each of these walks have been tested by volunteer walkers and I'd like to thank everyone who's bravely sallied forth, armed only with written instructions and no map, in order to assess their clarity. Particular thanks go to Linda, friend and frequent walking companion, who's got cheerfully lost with me on more than one occasion, to Nean and her Golden Retriever, Bess, who are regular partners in crime and to Karen and her spaniel, Daisy, random strangers who became friends and the book's most prolific walk testers. Thanks also to Carla, for technical back-up and to Mole for everything.

Most of all, thanks to Ula and all the wonderful dogs who've shared my life and my travels.
Without you, it just wouldn't be the same.

Deb x.

Published 2021
© Deb Bridges 2021

DogFriendly Ltd
Unit 4 Bramley Road
St Ives, Cambridgeshire
PE27 3WS

Go to www.dogfriendly.co.uk to discover the best places to visit, stay and play with your dog in the UK

ISBN 978-1-3999-0207-6

All photographs by author Deb Bridges, except where indicated

Design by William Dawes
Printed by Cambrian Press Ltd, Pontllanfraith

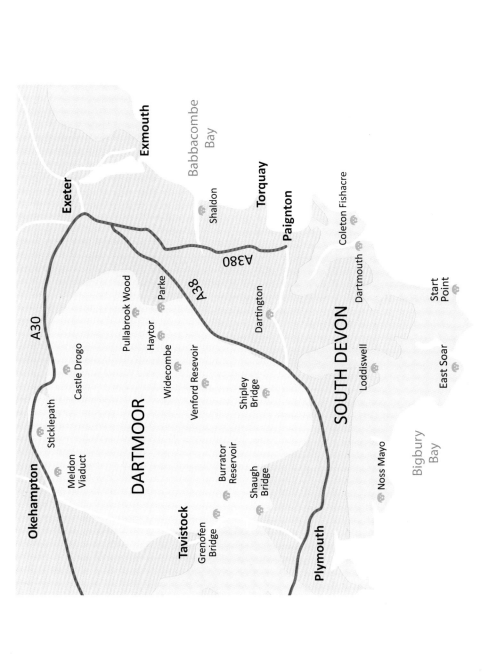

Hello from Deb and Ula

Sharing your life with dogs gives you the only excuse you'll ever need to take time out of your day, rain or shine, to simply have fun in the great outdoors. And what could be more pleasurable than spending time with your best friend, whether you're heading out for a quick stroll or a more adventurous hiking expedition?

Walking the dog has always been pretty well numero uno on my list of favourite pastimes and moving to Devon, some years ago, nudged the enjoyment levels up a notch or two even further. Devon has a great deal to offer the enthusiastic dog-walker and my current canine companion, Ula, and I have spent many happy hours, and sometimes days, exploring the beautiful county we're lucky enough to call home.

The moors, in all their wild and untamed glory, are steeped in both history and legend. Setting foot on this vast, and sometimes hostile, landscape can be a daunting prospect and, if Ula could talk, she'd no doubt tell you we've had our fair share of harum-scarum moments out there. But in this book, you'll find details of several moorland walks which are designed to give you a good taste of Dartmoor, safe in the comforting knowledge that you're never too far from a road or a village.

For some dogs, a walk just isn't a walk without a chance to get good and wet and many of the walks described in these pages tick that particular box. There are rivers aplenty, as well as reservoirs, estuaries and, of course, the sea - you might want to throw a few extra towels in the boot of the car, if your dog is a water-baby!

And when all the excitement's over, what could be better than relaxing over a frothy coffee, or maybe a long, cold beer, with your dog snoozing contentedly by your chair. Once again, Devon comes up trumps and there are few cafes or pubs that don't welcome our four-legged friends. Many's the time I've waited patiently, tongue hanging out, while Ula has been plied with biscuits from the jar which seems to be a fixture on the counter of so many eateries here. At one regular haunt in Dartmouth, I'm frequently asked if my dog would like a warm sausage, which is a bit like that well-known question about what bears do in the woods ....

Much is made of the simple act of having fun together being a way of strengthening the bond between people and their dogs and there's no doubt in my mind this is true. But watching Ula as she's blossomed from anxious rescue dog into a confident and stalwart walking companion, I'm convinced there's even more to be gained from pushing the boundaries with new experiences and I believe a good part of Ula's transformation can be attributed to the adventures we've shared.

This book contains just some of the walks we've enjoyed together and it gives me a glow of satisfaction to imagine other people and their dogs following in our footsteps (hopefully!) with equal delight.

Happy walking, everyone!

Deb & Ula

CONTENTS

Paw Rating:
🐾 : Easy   🐾 🐾 🐾 🐾 : Challenging

The Walks

These twenty walks are dotted around quite a large area, across Dartmoor and all the way down to the south coast. Consequently, they offer a good deal of variety, as different parts of the moor or sections of the coastline have a character all of their own. Whether it's stunning views, an historic bridge, a quiet cove or a beautiful stretch of river, each of these walks offers interest along the way. The length and level of difficulty varies, from an easy stroll to the foot of a dam at Shipley Bridge, suitable for the very young or less mobile, to a particularly rigorous stretch of the South West Coast Path at Shaldon. This selection ensures there's something for everyone!

Post Codes

Nearest post codes are given in the directions to the start of each walk and, in rural areas, they can be misleading. Keep an eye on the written directions and be prepared to ignore the sat nav!

Maps

The Ordnance Survey 1:25,000 map or maps that cover each of the walks is mentioned in the general information. It is highly recommended that you take the relevant map with you on your walk and familiarise yourself with the route before setting out.

Stiles

Stiles have been avoided, as far as possible. However, there are a limited number on some of the walks and these have all been tested for accessibility to dogs. At the time of writing, all stiles have either a purpose-built means of access, such as a sliding dog door, or were found to be manageable by other means.

Livestock

Cattle, sheep and horses are a fact of life in Devon and cannot be entirely avoided. Although some of the walks are livestock-free, this is not always possible and, where animals are likely to be encountered, this is mentioned in the walk directions. However, changes can occur and it's always a good idea to check for livestock before letting dogs off-lead.

The Countryside Code

Advice for visitors to the countryside is available on the Government website (www.gov.uk/government/publications/the-countryside-code/the-countryside-code-advice-for-countryside-visitors) and the specific section relating to dogs reads as follows:

Always keep dogs under control and in sight.

The countryside, parks and the coast are great places to exercise your dog but you need to consider other users and wildlife.

Keep your dog under effective control to make sure it stays away from wildlife, livestock, horses and other people unless invited. You should:

- always keep your dog on a lead or in sight

- be confident your dog will return on command

- make sure your dog does not stray from the path or area where you have right of access

Always check local signs as there are situations when you must keep your dog on a lead for all or part of the year. Local areas may also ban dogs completely, except for assistance dogs. Signs will tell

you about these local restrictions.
It is good practice wherever you are to keep your dog on a lead around livestock.

On Open Access land and at the coast, you must put your dog on a lead around livestock. Between 1 March and 31 July, you must have your dog on a lead on Open Access land, even if there is no livestock on the land. These are legal requirements.

A farmer can shoot a dog that is attacking or chasing livestock. They may not be liable to compensate the dog's owner.

Walking on Dartmoor

Dartmoor is a place of great beauty, studded with relics such as stone circles and crosses which offer glimpses of its ancient history, stretching back through millennia. It is wild, rugged and given to sudden changes in the weather and it can be dangerous when low cloud causes poor visibility. Always check weather forecasts before venturing onto the moor but probably the best advice is to expect the unexpected! Be prepared by carrying extra clothing when out on the moor, including waterproofs and take plenty of water. Stout footwear is also recommended, as some spots remain boggy, even in the driest of spells.

Animals graze the moor and, as advised in the Countryside Code, you are required to put dogs on their leads in the vicinity of livestock. Dartmoor ponies and foals look very appealing but, for their safety, the Dartmoor Rangers ask you not to approach them and, most importantly, not to feed them.

Dartmoor has been used for army training purposes since the early 1800s and some parts remain designated Army Firing Ranges. The walks in this book do not venture into these areas but, should you decide to do so, more information and advice, including scheduled firing times, can be found on the website www.gov.uk/government/publications/dartmoor-firing-programme.

Walking on the Coast

Where walks include a section along the coast, you will be walking on part of the South West Coast Path, which is England's longest waymarked long-distance footpath and a National Trail. Stretching for no less than 630 miles between Minehead in Somerset and Poole in Dorset, it draws visitors from all over the world and, from your short forays along its length, you will find it is completely breathtaking - usually in both senses of the word!

As on the moor, be prepared for changes in the weather and make sure you have enough water. The path can be rugged in places and footwear should be sturdy and offer a degree of grip.

The specific danger of walking on the Coast Path is the proximity of the cliff edge at times. It is generally unfenced and safer to put dogs on their leads where necessary, especially if they're fond of chasing seagulls!

Nasties To Look Out For

- *Ticks* - Ticks may be lurking wherever sheep or deer graze and it is advisable, in these areas, to keep exposed flesh to the minimum. Long trousers can be tucked into socks if you have to walk through rough vegetation which, although not a great look, could be worthwhile if it means avoiding one of these horrible critters! Check yourself and your dogs for ticks and remove any you find as soon as possible, preferably with a tick hook.

- *Adders* - Adder bites are fairly rare and only occur when the creatures feel threatened. During the summer months, it is best to avoid undergrowth and the possibility of inadvertently stepping on one. If the worst happens, seek medical attention as soon as possible. In the event of your dog being bitten, it is best to carry them (if this is possible) and seek veterinary help at the earliest opportunity.

Dog Fouling

Piles of poo or, worse still, mouldering bags of the stuff, can mar an otherwise delightful walk. Responsible dog-owners pick it up and a Dicky Bag, or similar, solves the problem of what to do with full bags, allowing you to carry them discreetly and odour-free until you reach a suitable place for their disposal. Branded *Love Moor Life* Dicky Bags are available in Dartmoor Visitor Centres or you can purchase one online at www.dickybag.com.

Extra Kit

A basic First Aid kit, including tick hook and tweezers (useful for removing thorns from paws), is a good idea.

If your dog is susceptible to the heat, a cool coat can be an invaluable addition to the rucksack. There are many on the market and Ula (possibly the hairiest hound on the planet) wears Ruffwear, ruffwear.co.uk.

Distance	4.5 miles
Suggested time	2¼ hours
Level of difficulty	

This is a walk of contrasts, starting on paths high up on the side of the Teign Gorge below Castle Drogo, which is an early 20th century country house, built in the style of a castle. After dropping steeply down through woodland, the route follows the River Teign to a picturesque suspension bridge, before climbing back up for a dramatic end, with far-reaching views across surrounding moorland and a glimpse of Castle Drogo. At about the halfway point, the dog-friendly Fingle Bridge Inn occupies an idyllic spot on the riverbank, offering an irresistible photo opportunity, as well as refreshment. Here you have the option of taking a more challenging diversion off the main route. For most of the way, you will be walking on well-made, although occasionally uneven paths. There is one short section on a quiet road and where the route goes over a stone wall, there are large, granite steps which are quite easy to negotiate.

How to get there - Turn off the A382 between Chagford and the A30, opposite The Sandy Park Inn, signposted Drewsteignton, Castle Drogo and Fingle Bridge Inn. Follow the road for approximately one mile and turn right into the Castle Drogo entrance, following the long driveway to the car park at the end.

Map:
OS Explorer Map OL28

Grid Ref:
SX 7225 9016

Nearest Post Code:
EX6 6PB

Parking:
National Trust pay and display car park

Facilities:
Toilets and cafe at start and dog-friendly pub halfway round

You will need:
Leads, dog bags, water for dogs

Return to the car park entrance, turn left onto the driveway **1** and then right after a short distance onto a track where a sign points to Estate Walks. Walk downhill and turn left onto a grassy track where there is a sign for Sharp Tor Viewpoint.

Follow this track and symbols on posts for the viewpoint until you reach a gate. Go through the gate, down steps to a stony path and, with the viewpoint directly ahead, turn left **2** signposted Hunters Path and Fingle Bridge. As you follow this path, the River Teign is to your right and far below. Where the path forks, a short distance after a gate, take the righthand fork **3** signposted Fingle Bridge.

Follow this path for some way downhill and where the track becomes noticeably more stony as it bends left, be aware you will soon be emerging onto a road, which you will see below and to your right. At the road, turn right **4** and you will soon see The Fingle Bridge Inn on your left.

You now have two options, depending on energy levels and fondness for rugged terrain! For a more challenging walk, go through the gate on the right just before the stone bridge and follow the path for

some distance, with the river on your left, to a suspension bridge, where you will rejoin the main walk at point **7** . For a more leisurely option, cross the river by the stone bridge and turn immediately right **5** onto a wide, grassy track alongside the river.

Follow the path with the river on your right. Shortly after passing a wooden bench on your left, you will see a wooden bridge, also on the left. Cross the bridge to join a stony track and turn right **6** . Continue on this path for some way, ignoring any tracks to the left, until you

Go up the steps ahead, turn left and then almost immediately right onto a track leading uphill. Continue uphill on this path, past two entrances to Gibhouse and eventually onto a tarmac driveway, where you may see the occasional car. After passing a cattle grid, keep an eye out for a turning to the right, signposted Hunters Path and Castle Drogo. Turn right here **8** and go through a gate.

At a sign which points left to Hunters Path/Castle Drogo and right to Hunters Tor Viewpoint, turn left in the direction of Castle Drogo. Follow this path as it winds its way back up to the top of the gorge, where the river will be to your right and far below, once more, and you will have a glimpse of Castle Drogo, above and to your left.

reach a fork, where you can take either track (left for the more energetic, as it adds an extra hill!) since they will soon converge, at a large gate.

Pass through the gate and follow the path straight ahead with an old stone wall on your right. This is the muddiest section of the walk when the weather is wet but it is short-lived! Where you see granite steps and a sign indicating 1 mile to the Castle, turn right, using the steps to go over the wall. Follow the path downhill and cross the river by the suspension bridge **7** . This is where the more challenging path rejoins the main route.

After some distance, you will see a sign for Castle Drogo, Shop and Cafe, pointing up steps to your left. Turn left **9** here, go up the steep steps and through a gate, continuing up another set of steep steps which end in a path, leading uphill to the main driveway. Turn left at the driveway and retrace your steps to the car park.

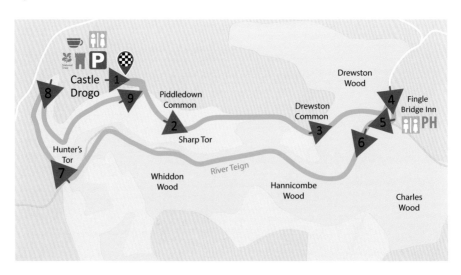

Distance   2 miles

Suggested time   1 hour

Level of difficulty 🐾🐾

This walk through an area managed by the Woodland Trust is an excellent choice for a hot day, being under the trees for a good part of the way, with many sections of the river easily accessible for dogs to enjoy a cooling dip and a drink. It is generally level, although the track is uneven in places and can be muddy. There may be sheep grazing in one field towards the end and there is a short section on quiet lanes leading back to the car park.

How to get there - From Bovey Tracey, take the B3387 towards Haytor and Widecombe, bearing right where the B3387 forks left. Follow the road for about 1¼ miles, turning right where there is a sign for Lustleigh 1½ miles. Follow this narrow lane and, after almost a mile, the car park is on the left, immediately before a narrow, stone bridge, which is Drakeford Bridge.

Map:
OS Explorer Map OL28

Grid Ref:
SX 7894 8009

Nearest Post Code:
TQ13 9SR

Parking:
Free but spaces limited

Facilities:
There are no facilities on this walk

You will need:
Leads and dog bags

Go through the gate at the far end of the car park onto a bridleway **1**. After a short distance, you will see a path to your right, just before a logging working area. If you take this path, you will spend more time alongside the river but at a cost, as there's a steep climb to rejoin the main track! For a less strenuous route, continue straight ahead, taking care if machinery is in operation as you pass through the working area.

As you continue gently uphill on a well-made track, you can see and hear the river below and to your right. Nearing the top, you will see a path going steeply downhill to your right **2** which is where the riverside option rejoins the main walk. Continue straight ahead, through a gate and, at a junction of paths, turn right **3** onto a stony track which leads downhill, levelling out where a leat crosses the track.

After some distance, turn right again **4** where you see a huge, rounded granite boulder (known as the Pudding Stone) on your right. Pass through a gate and you will see Hisley Bridge ahead, which is a medieval, stone packhorse bridge. Here, you may decide to pause and take advantage of one of the benches at this idyllic spot, which also provides the perfect place for dogs to enjoy a splash about in the river.

To continue, cross the bridge and turn right **5** passing through another gate after a short distance and, keeping the river on your right, follow the main path, ignoring several smaller tracks heading off to the left. Take care, as this is where the

The Pudding Stone

track is a little rougher, with exposed tree roots waiting to trip the unwary walker. You may also see Dartmoor Ponies, as they sometimes graze this section of the walk during the summer months.

After approximately a third of a mile, you will reach a gate into a field **6** and this is where you may come across sheep. Pass through the gate and follow the wide, grassy track, with the river still close by on your right. Before the end of the field is reached, the path curves left, away from the river and following the line of trees on your left. Leave the field through the gate and turn right **7** onto a quiet lane.

Continue to a T junction and turn right **8** passing a gateway on your left with a sign for Ivy Cottage, before crossing the narrow, stone bridge and turning immediately right into the car park.

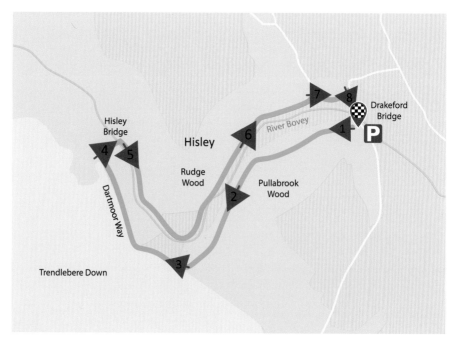

PARKE

Distance 2.5 miles

Suggested time 1¼ hours

Level of difficulty 🐾

This is a flat, easy walk on a National Trust estate, suitable for more elderly and arthritic dogs (and owners!). Being close to the town, it is well-used by local dog-walkers, so sociable canines can enjoy meeting new friends and there are plenty of spots for water-loving dogs to enjoy a dip in the River Bovey. The route follows a riverside path, which can be muddy when wet and is uneven in places, before returning along a disused railway line, which is excellent underfoot in all weathers. Although cattle and sheep are used for conservation grazing in some areas of the estate, there are none on this walk. And it's worth making time for a visit to the award-winning, dog-friendly Home Farm Cafe!

How to get there - Leave Bovey Tracey on the B3387 towards Haytor and Widecombe. The entrance to Parke is a short distance along this road, on the right. Head up the driveway, following the signs to the Visitors' car park.

Map:
OS Explorer Map 110

Grid Ref:
SX 8052 7848

Nearest Post Code:
TQ13 9JQ

Parking:
National Trust pay and display car park

Facilities:
Toilets and dog-friendly cafe

You will need:
Leads and dog bags

becomes wooded, look out for a boardwalk on your left. Turn left here ❸ and, at the end of the boardwalk, bear right onto the riverside path. Stay on this track as it meanders through the trees, keeping the river close by on your left, for almost a mile, ignoring any paths leading away to the right and continuing until it bears right, away from the river, where there is no longer a path straight ahead.

From the car park, walk back onto the driveway and turn right ❶ heading downhill, past a walled garden on your left and Home Farm Cafe on the right. Ignoring paths to left and right, keep going straight on and downhill. The path levels out and you will cross two small, stone bridges.

After crossing the second bridge, turn left ❷ onto a path through a wide, grassy area, with the river on your left.

Shortly after the path narrows and

On the way, you will pass a field on the right and, after crossing a small wooden bridge, you will see the weir, which is believed to be medieval. Further on, you will pass rough, stone steps leading up to a small bridge over the river and then a large log where people can sit beside the water. This is where the path bears right, taking you uphill onto a wide, well-made track. Turn right ❹ here onto the remains of the old railway line which ran between Newton Abbot and Moretonhampstead from 1866 until 1964. It is a shared-use path, so keep a wary eye out for bikes and horses.

The track continues in a straight line with trees on either side. You will pass under an old bridge and where the embankments alongside the track rise up in places, it is easy to imagine steam trains puffing their way along these cuttings in days gone by. Continue on this track, ignoring all turnings to the left and right, until you see a sign for the Car Park, Cafe, Toilets and Rangers' Office. Turn right here **5**, walk downhill and you will see the small, stone bridge you crossed earlier straight ahead. Cross back over the bridge and retrace your steps to the car park.

Distance   3.5 miles

Suggested time   1½ hours

Level of difficulty   🐾 🐾

This walk is great on a clear day when the panoramic views across Dartmoor, all the way to the South Devon coast, can be appreciated. The ascents are fairly gentle and the iconic granite rocks of Haytor remain reassuringly in sight along the way. Descending from Haytor Rocks, the route takes in a disused quarry, a tranquil spot where dogs can enjoy a swim in the lake, before returning along the remains of a granite tramway which conveyed granite from Haytor to the Stover Canal from 1820 to 1858. Sheep, cattle and Dartmoor Ponies may be grazing anywhere on the moor, except in the enclosed area around the disused quarry.

How to get there - From Bovey Tracey, take the B3387 towards Haytor and Widecombe, bearing left at a fork in the road and continuing on the B3387 which climbs uphill and crosses a cattle grid onto the moor. After approximately one mile, look out for Haytor Barns on the left and take the sharp right turn opposite, following a narrow road with moorland on either side for approximately a quarter of a mile to car parks on both sides of the road. The Visitor Centre and dog-friendly cafe at the Moorland Hotel are a short distance past this turning, on the left.

Photo Credit: Karin Brooks

Map:
Ordnance Survey Explorer Map OL28

Grid Ref:
SX 7702 7781

Nearest Post Code:
TQ13 9XS

Parking:
Free parking

Facilities:
No facilities on the walk but cafe nearby and toilets at Visitor Centre

You will need:
Leads, dog bags, water for dogs

1 Head for the far end of the lefthand car park, on the upper side of the moor, and take the wide, grassy track directly ahead and leading uphill away from the road. The path soon levels out a bit and opens up on the right. After a short distance, there are two places where a narrower path forks left off the main track and you are looking for the second of these, taking the left fork where you pass a lump of granite in the grass on your left as you do so. The path goes straight ahead, with gorse on

either side, and you will be able to see the distinctive twin peaks of Haytor in the distance to your left. You will pass a line of granite boulders on your left and, after a while, the rocky outcrop of Smallacombe Rocks will appear directly ahead. Just before the rocks, the path widens out. Head for the rocks, where you will find their wide, flat surfaces make a good viewing platform.

To continue, turn to face the way you've just come and look to your right, where you will see a wide, grassy path leading directly towards Haytor Rocks. Take any of the small paths through the gorse, heather and rocks to join this path **2** and walk towards Haytor.

After following the path gently uphill for a while, you will arrive at the remains of a granite tramway, visible as two parallel lines of granite in the grass. If you wish to take a shorter walk, turn left here and follow the granite tramway to point **10** where the main route turns right to join your section of tramway. From here, continue straight ahead on the tramway, following the directions back to the car park.

To continue on the main route, turn right onto the granite tramway **3** and, ignoring a spur to the right, continue straight ahead, with Haytor above you to the left. The tramway travels slightly uphill for some distance, becoming less distinct where it forks to the right. At this point, turn left **4** and follow a grass track with a mound of earth and rocks on your right - this is the spoil from the quarries.

Once again, you are walking directly towards Haytor on a path that leads to a narrow and overgrown entrance into a disused quarry. Do not take the path into the quarry but follow a grass track which skirts around it to the right, still heading uphill towards Haytor. Be aware there is a considerable drop into the quarry on your left, which is hidden from view by vegetation, so you may wish to keep dogs and small children close by until you are safely past this area.

Reaching the top end of the quarry, take any of the small paths that lead uphill to Haytor **5** and pass between the two Haytor rocks. Climbing the rocks for a better view is a popular pastime, although not for the faint-hearted!

After walking over the wide, grassy area in the gap between the rocks, turn left and, keeping the rock on your left, continue until you are level with its highest point. Turn right **6** here onto a grassy path which is punctuated by large rocks and heads downhill. Follow this path downhill with Haytor behind you and the road running parallel, at a distance, on your right.

After a while, the track becomes less rocky and then widens out. Looking to your left, you will see a large pile of rocks and, beyond them, a wire fence. Bear left here and walk towards the rocks and when you reach them, you will be able to see a wooden gate to their right. Pass through the gate into the disused quarry and turn left **7** taking care as there is a steep drop to your right for a very short distance. Follow the path around the edge of the lake. If you've brought a picnic, this is the perfect spot for a break and a dip for the dogs.

To continue, exit by a gate on the far side **8** and, at the end of the narrow path, head downhill with a mound of earth and rocks on your right, following the path as it bears

right at the bottom of the mound. Ahead you will see another mound of earth and rocks and beyond this, a section of granite tramway. Turn left ❾ onto the tramway and follow it as it curves round to the right, where it becomes a causeway for a short distance, before meeting a junction with another section of tramway. Here you will see a stone to your left, indicating the start of the Templer Way.

Turn right onto this next section of tramway ❿ . After some distance, you will see a small group of trees on your right as the track bears right and, about fifty yards further on, there are two tracks to the left which converge to become one wide, grassy path, forming a triangle around a patch of gorse. Turn left ⓫ here and follow the path back to the car park. Alternatively, a short diversion will take you to the Moorland Hotel where there is an excellent dog-friendly cafe - you will

find it to the right of the telephone box in the group of buildings you can see directly ahead at this point, on the other side of the road.

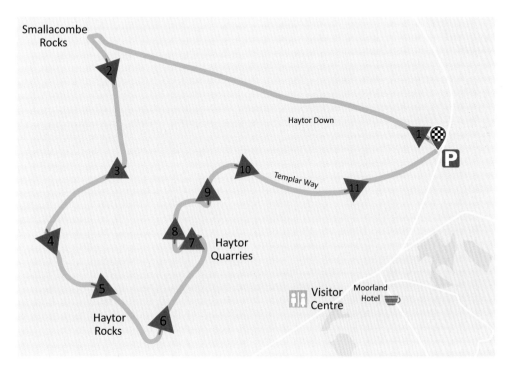

Distance   7.3 miles

Suggested time   3½ hours

Level of difficulty   🐾 🐾 🐾 🐾

Nestled in a valley, or 'combe', with the moors rising majestically on either side, this picture-perfect Dartmoor village is definitely worth a visit. Starting opposite the 14th century church - known as the cathedral of the moors - this walk starts with a long and fairly arduous climb onto Hameldown. For some way, it follows the clearly defined route of the Two Moors Way, before descending over open moorland and returning by paths and quiet lanes to Widecombe, where a visit to the dog-friendly Cafe on the Green is another must!

How to get there - From Bovey Tracey, take the B3387 towards Haytor and Widecombe, bearing left at a fork in the road and remaining on the B3387 as it goes uphill. After crossing a cattle grid, continue following this road for approximately 4½ miles. You will drive downhill into Widecombe and as the road goes uphill again, you will see the Cafe on the Green ahead on the right, opposite the church. The entrance to the car park is on the right, immediately before the Cafe on the Green.

Map:
OS Explorer Map OL28

Grid Ref:
SX 7196 7682

Nearest Post Code:
TQ13 7TA

Parking:
Pay and display car park

Facilities:
Dog-friendly cafe, pub, shop and public toilets at start

You will need:
Leads, dog bags, water for dogs

Facing the church at the car park entrance, turn immediately right ❶ to walk along the path between the village green and the Cafe on the Green. Follow the path to a narrow lane and turn right, passing the entrance to another car park on your right and then The Old Inn car park on your left.

Almost immediately after passing a small bridge which leads to a children's play area on your right, turn left ❷ to walk uphill on a narrow lane. From this point, you will be walking uphill for quite some time - so you might want to pace yourself! After passing Bowden Farm on the left, the lane turns into a rocky track, which continues uphill to a gate.

Once through the gate, you are on the open moor where livestock may be grazing. Taking the track directly ahead, you will soon be walking with a wall on your right. After a while, the wall bears away to the right and you will see the track initially follows this curve and then goes slightly left, leading you away from the wall.

Continuing uphill, you will see another wall ahead of you. Follow the path with the wall on your right and where there is a fork in the track, take the righthand fork and stay on the path which is closest to the wall. At the end of the wall, take the path which goes straight ahead and uphill.

You may notice a wall away to your left which, as you continue walking uphill, is getting gradually closer. At the point where the path meets the wall, you will see Hameldown Beacon ❸ at the top of a mound to your left. From here, follow the grassy track with the wall close by on your left and, at the end of the wall, continue straight ahead. Dotted around you will see some tall wooden posts which are clearly from days gone by. These were erected during WW2 to prevent enemy aircraft from landing and few now remain. You will pass close by two of these posts on your left and you will then see a low grassy mound ahead. Ignoring a path which forks left and goes straight over the mound, follow the path to the right ❹ as it skirts around it.

Stay on this grassy track as it bears round to the right and starts heading downhill. After walking downhill for some time, you will see a stone monument to your right, commemorating the crew of an RAF bomber which crashed at the site in poor

Photo Credit: Karen Howell

visibility in 1941. At this point, the track bears left for a short way and then right, continuing downhill on a wide, grassy track. Looking ahead, you will see an enclosed plantation of trees to your left and may be able to spot the point where the track you're on meets the plantation wall. When you reach this point, keep walking with the wall beside you on the left and continue alongside another wall with mature trees overhanging. Eventually, you will cross a small stream and see a gate in front of you which takes you off the moor and onto a road. Turn right **5** on this quiet lane and walk downhill.

Follow this lane for approximately a mile until you come to a cattle grid. After the cattle grid, turn immediately left **6** and head uphill on a wide, rocky track which leads to a gate. Go through the gate and

continue straight ahead on the stony track which passes below Honeybag Tor, Chinkwell Tor and Bell Tor. You are now back on the moor and there may be livestock.

After walking along this track for some way, you will be able to see the grand spire of Widecombe Church in the distance to your right and, as you near the end, you will see Bonehill Rocks ahead of you, on the other side of a narrow road. When you reach this road, turn right **7** and you will now be freewheeling downhill on this quiet lane all the way back to Widecombe.

Reaching a T junction at the end of the lane, turn right and, after a short trudge uphill, you will see the car park and the Cafe on the Green on your right.

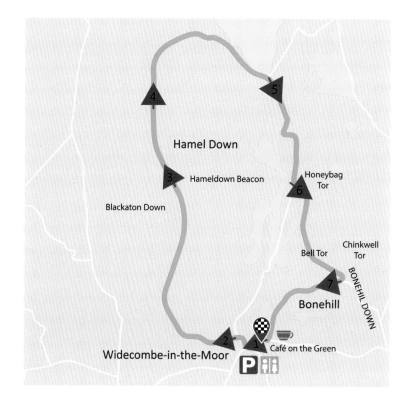

Distance   3.5 miles

Suggested time   1½ hours

Level of difficulty

This walk starts with a gentle stroll around the reservoir, before striking out onto the moor and ascending the rocky outcrops of Bench Tor. Although the climb might be considered a little arduous, it is largely shaded, with the moss-covered boulders of White Wood lending a timeless and almost magical quality to this section of the walk. Take your time and enjoy the accompanying sounds of birdsong and the river below. There are views across the Dart Valley to be enjoyed as you emerge from the woods and a panoramic view at the top, which makes the effort it takes to get there worthwhile!

How to get there - From Ashburton, take the B3352 in the direction of Princetown. The winding and sometimes narrow road will eventually cross a stone bridge and bear sharply right. Follow the road uphill and bear left where you see a sign for Holne 1¼ miles. Stay on this road, initially following the signs for Holne and then Hexworthy and Venford Reservoir. After crossing a cattle grid, continue until you see the dam ahead. Follow the road over the dam to the car park which is on the right.

Map:
Ordnance Survey Explorer Map OL28

Grid Ref:
SX 6852 7124

Nearest Post Code:
PL20 6SE

Parking:
Free parking, honesty box for donations

Facilities:
Seasonal toilets in the car park, shop, tea room and pub in nearby Holne

You will need:
Leads, dog bags, water for dogs

Exit the car park by the path at the lower end, with the toilets and a noticeboard on your left. Cross the road, to walk on the grass with the railings enclosing the reservoir close by on your left until you reach a gate in the railings. Go through the gate to join the path ❶ which bears right and takes you all the way round to the far end of the dam, on a pleasantly shaded track with the reservoir on your left. Take care as the many exposed roots are a bit of a trip hazard.

Eventually, the path will lead you slightly uphill to a gate onto the road by the dam. Go through the gate, turn left and then right ❷ onto the moor immediately before the dam and the entrance to the Venford Water Treatment Works. You are now on the open moor, where livestock may be grazing.

Keeping the Water Treatment Works on your left, walk straight ahead and turn left ❸ at the end of the fence, following the path as it winds downhill to Venford Brook, which offers a last chance for dogs to have a dip and a drink.

With the brook on your left, continue on this path which is initially open but soon leads into White Wood, with the River Dart coming into view below and to your left. The path is easy and flat to start with but, do not be deceived, after some distance it will become rocky and climb steeply uphill, before levelling out again and leading to a gate. Turn right ❹ in front of the gate and, leaving the woods behind, head uphill on a grassy track with a wall on your left.

Pausing for breath, turn around to enjoy views across the Dart Valley, with Dr Blackall's Drive visible high up on the other side. Now popular with walkers, horse riders and cyclists, Dr Blackall's Drive was constructed in the 1880s at the behest of one Dr Thomas Blackall, in order to allow the splendours of Dartmoor to be enjoyed from the relative comfort of a small, horse-drawn carriage.

To continue, carry on walking uphill and, where the wall bears left, continue straight ahead and uphill. You are almost at the end of your climb and about to be rewarded with spectacular views, including Venford Reservoir, which you will be able to see sparkling way below and ahead of you. Turn right here **5** to explore the rocks and take in the vista of the surrounding moorland.

From here, it is easy to find your way down as you have the reservoir as a reference point. Turning away from the rocks and looking towards the reservoir, you will see several paths leading downhill to join

a more obvious track. Head for this and then take any track towards the Water Treatment Works, arriving at the road where you started, by the dam and the entrance to the Water Treatment Works. Turn right **6** here to walk over the dam and back to the car park, which you will see on your right after crossing the dam.

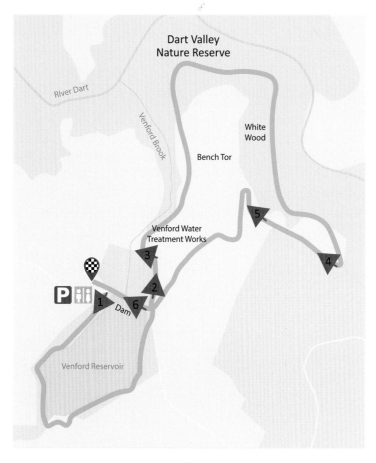

Distance   2.7 miles

Suggested time   1¼ hours

Level of difficulty

Dartington is a 14th century estate which underwent substantial renovation in the 1920s to become the centre for education and the arts it remains today. This gentle stroll through the estate follows the River Dart for some distance, through meadows where cattle sometimes graze although, as the route is a popular one, they are well accustomed to the sight of walkers, dogs, picnickers and wild swimmers. During the summer months, steam trains may be glimpsed on the opposite bank as they make their stately progress along the line between Buckfastleigh and Totnes and, if time allows, a scenic trip on the dog-friendly South Devon Railway is highly recommended. The paths are generally good but there are one or two sections along by the river where a good pair of waterproof boots would be advisable if the weather has been particularly wet. The short road sections are on quiet, private roads.

How to get there - Dartington is approximately 2 miles from Totnes, on the A385 between the A38 Devon Expressway and Totnes. Turn off this road where you see a sign for the Dartington Estate and a church on the corner. This will be on your left if travelling from the A38 direction and on the right if coming from Totnes. Follow the driveway all the way to the car parks at the top of the hill.

Map:
Ordnance Survey Explorer Map 110

Grid Ref:
SX 7980 6280

Nearest Post Code:
TQ9 6EL

Parking:
Pay and display car park

Facilities:
Toilets and dog-friendly cafe

You will need:
Leads and dog bags

Starting from the main entrance to Dartington Hall, cross the road and take the road which runs between the Green Table Cafe on the left and a car park on the right. At the end of the car park wall, turn immediately right **1** and walk downhill towards a field.

You will pass the car park exit on your right and see a kissing gate ahead on your left. Go through the kissing gate, bear right and walk downhill. Staying in the middle of the field, keep the distant buildings on your left in sight and a large thicket of trees on your right as you head for the far end, where you will find a gate in the bottom righthand corner. Pass through two gates into another field and follow the path, a little to the right and then straight ahead towards a gate. Go through the gate and continue downhill to a junction with another path. Go through a gate and turn left **2** onto a riverside track.

You will be following this clearly defined path, with the river on your right, for 1¼ miles, passing through gates, over boardwalks and ignoring any paths leading away to the left. Listen out for the whistle of a steam locomotive on this section of the walk which will alert you to the possibility of the train coming into view on the opposite bank.

This riverside stretch is mainly through open meadowland but you will also pass through a wooded area, after which the path continues through a meadow, where trees obscure your view of the river to the right but you may see deer in a field to your left. Eventually, you will reach a

gate into a wooded area ahead of you and, after passing through the gate ❸ you will be walking uphill and away from the river on a well-made, stony track through the trees.

At the end of this path, you will see a gap in an old stone wall. Go through the gap and turn left ❹ to head uphill on a wide, stony track, with the old stone wall on your left. This is the wall to the former deer park and dates from the 18th century. Further along, you will see lower sections in the wall and there is a plaque which explains this was to allow deer to jump in but not out, as the ground is lower on the inside.

As you near the end of the wall, you will see two large, timber blocks nestled against its base. These are viewing platforms for anyone who'd like to look over the wall at the deer in the field on the other side. Ahead, you will see a gate. Go through the gate onto a road ❺ and continue straight ahead. You may be interested in the houses on your right, which are a striking example of 1930s architecture.

Arriving at a junction with another road, continue straight ahead and you will soon see the car parks on both sides of the road.

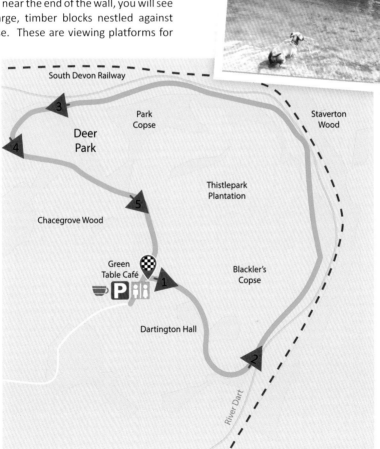

SHALDON

Distance	6 miles
Suggested time	3½ hours

Level of difficulty 🐾 🐾 🐾 🐾

The pretty fishing village of Shaldon occupies an idyllic spot, sheltered by towering red sandstone cliffs at the mouth of the Teign estuary. After completing this substantial walk, you might want to spend time relaxing on Ness Cove Beach, which is dog-friendly all year round and popular for swimming, with the added excitement of being accessed by the Smugglers' Tunnel. You may also like to take a trip on the historic Shaldon to Teignmouth ferry, which is reputed to be the oldest passenger ferry service in England and dogs travel free of charge! The walk is hard going in places, with some seriously steep climbs, particularly on the Coast Path section towards the end. There is some road walking at the start and it is recommended you check the tide times (bbc.co.uk/weather/coast-and-sea/tide-tables/10/26a) and set out around low tide, when you will be able to take the tidal path along the edge of the estuary,

rather than the high tide road alternative.

How to get there:
Turn off the A379 Teignmouth to Torquay road onto Ness Drive, south of Shaldon Bridge and Teignmouth. Turn left into the car park immediately after Cafe ODE.

Map:
Ordnance Survey Explorer Map 110

Grid Ref:
SX 9378 7192

Nearest Post Code:
TQ14 0HP

Parking:
The Ness pay and display car park

Facilities:
Toilets near car park and in Shaldon, dog-friendly cafes and pubs in Shaldon, dog-friendly pub in Stokeinteignhead halfway round

You will need:
Leads, dog bags, water for dogs

Leave the car park by the exit to the right of the Tourist Information hut, cross the road and take the tarmac track between the telephone box and the wishing well. When you reach a junction with another path, turn left ① to walk down the steps. At a small road, turn right, signposted Ferry to Teignmouth, and walk downhill with the estuary on your right.

After a short while, you will be walking on a pavement with the beach (with seasonal dog restrictions) on your right. You will pass a sign for the ferry to Teignmouth, where a flag in the sand marks the place to stand if you want to catch the ferry. Continue along this road, passing the Ferry Boat Inn on your left and immediately after the Clipper Cafe on your right, turn right onto Riverside where you will have glimpses of the estuary between houses on your right. You will leave the estuary briefly as the road bears left and, turning right past the Riverside Surgery, you will be back alongside it again. After passing the Methodist Church on your left, you will come to Shaldon Bridge on your right. Cross the road and continue straight ahead

on the pedestrian tarmac path ②.

Shortly after a sign for The Shipwrights Arms, follow the path as it bears left and turn right at the road. After passing Brook Road on the left, the wall to your right makes a righthand turn and you will see signs for The Strand and Ringmore at the end of a narrow roadway which leads to the estuary. At this point, the route splits into the low tide and high tide options.

If the tide is out, turn right ③ here. At the estuary, turn left where a sign indicates the Templer Way Tidal Route and Combe Cellars 1½ miles, to walk on a mixture of stones and shingle, with the estuary on your right. Take care along this path - it tends to be strewn with seaweed which is more slippery than any banana skin! After a bend to the left, you will be walking alongside a wall at the edge of a static caravan holiday homes site. After a concrete slipway and a children's play area, you will pass a large, red brick building, after which the wall makes a left turn. Turn left here and climb the narrow, uneven steps leading steeply uphill.

Continue uphill to a road at the end of the path and cross over onto the stony track which is almost directly opposite. This is where the high tide option rejoins the main route **4**.

If the tide is in, continue straight ahead on the road, following it as it bears right, past Higher Ringmore Road and then Long Lane on the left. After a while, the road ceases to be residential and turns into a country lane. Very shortly after passing the Devon Valley Holidays entrance on your right, you will see a narrow track to the right. Take the stony track on the other side of the road, almost directly opposite. This is where the high tide option rejoins the main route **4**.

Head uphill for some way on this stony track. When you see a path leading away to the left, carry straight on and you will shortly come to a road. At the road, turn right **5** and walk downhill into the village of Stokeinteignhead. At a crossroads, where the church is directly ahead, turn left and walk towards the War Memorial, passing The Church House Inn on the right and the village shop on the left. Continue on this road, passing the War Memorial on your left, followed by the Parish Church and Primary School on the right. Immediately before the Village Hall, turn

left **6** onto a public footpath.

Walk uphill on this stony track and where you see a path to the right, bear left and continue uphill. Shortly after this, bear right and uphill once more where a public footpath sign points left. Continue on this track which will eventually become less steep. After passing a sign on a gate for Higher Commons Farm on the right, you will arrive at a junction with another path. Turn left here **7** and head downhill to the main road.

At the road, turn left and walk the short distance along the lay-by and across the verge to the end of a lane, signposted Stokeinteignhead. Cross the road carefully here and go through the small wooden gate to the right of the metal field gate. Turn right **8** and follow the path around the edge of the field with a hedgerow on your right. Shortly after it bears left at the top of the field, go through a gap in the hedge, turning immediately left to follow the path to a gate.

Once through the gate, take the footpath straight ahead, walking downhill on a grassy track with the sea ahead. After going through a wooden kissing gate, turn left. You are now on the Coast Path which crosses fields where livestock may be grazing and comes close to the cliff edge in places.

You will be following the Coast Path for about 1½ miles, all the way back to Shaldon and, whilst the route is clear, there are several points to look out for. Firstly, where you find yourself walking up steep steps on a narrow path, with a chainlink fence to your right and then a wooden handrail on the left, you are approaching a busy road, which you will be walking alongside very briefly **9**. Secondly, where you see a wooden bench after exiting a field, the signage can be confusing - go straight ahead here, with the wooden bench on your left. Lastly,

after passing along the edge of the golf course, you will go down steep steps to a junction with another path. Turn right here, walking downhill on the stony track.

When you see a car park and the Sea Scouts hut behind railings on the left, look out for a Coast Path sign pointing to the right. Leave the Coast Path here, walking straight ahead and downhill on the narrow track, past an entrance to the car park. At the entrance to Shaldon Zoo (Wildlife Centre), turn left onto a tarmac track. You will see Cafe ODE directly ahead and, after crossing the road, you will be back in the car park.

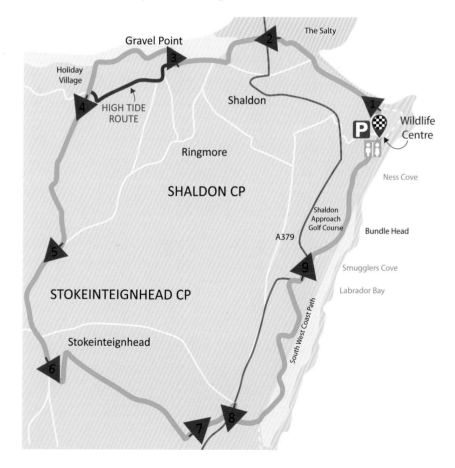

COLETON FISHACRE

Distance   4.5 miles

Suggested time   2¾ hours

Level of difficulty 🐾 🐾 🐾 🐾

This walk takes in a glorious stretch of the Coast Path between Scabbacombe Head and Froward Point, with no shortage of the ups and downs often associated with coastal walking. There are a number of well-placed benches along the way, so take your time and enjoy the view! You may wish to combine your walk with a visit to the gardens at Coleton Fishacre, built by the wealthy D'Oyly Carte family and described by the National Trust as a 1920s country retreat. Dogs on leads are welcome in the gardens, cafe and shop. There is some road-walking at the end of the route, first on a rough road where you are unlikely to see cars, followed by a short distance on the lane back to Coleton Fishacre.

How to get there - Turn off the B3022 between Paignton and Brixham onto the A379 where there is a sign for Dartmouth and Kingswear and a brown sign indicating 4 miles to Coleton Fishacre. At a mini roundabout, turn right and almost immediately bear left, following the Coleton Fishacre sign. Just after passing a bus stop on the right, turn left where there is another sign for Coleton Fishacre. Turn left at a T junction and follow the road as it bears right. Immediately before the entrance to Coleton Fishacre House and Gardens, turn left, following the Coleton Camp sign to a car park.

Map:
Ordnance Survey Explorer Map OL20

Grid Ref:
SX 9096 5123

Nearest Post Code:
TQ6 0EQ

Parking:
Coleton Camp National Trust Car Park, honesty box for donations

Facilities:
There are no facilities on this walk

You will need:
Leads, dog bags, water for dogs

Photo Credit: Wayne Howell

Take the path opposite the entrance to the car park, to the left of the information board. After a short distance, go through a gate and turn left ❶ onto a stony track, signposted Scabbacombe Head and Link to Coast Path. Follow this track as it heads downhill, with the sea ahead of you. When you come to a metal gate across the path, go through the small gate to the left and continue on this grassy path between fields, towards the sea.

The path ends at a gate, where there is a wooden bench and a sign pointing right to Pudcombe Cove. Go through the gate and turn right ❷ . You are now on the Coast Path, which comes close to the cliff edge in places. It is a dramatic stretch, resembling a rollercoaster with its steep inclines, plunging descents and occasional zigzags.

Walking with the sea on your left, you will pass a sign, pointing to a left turn to Scabbacombe Sands. The truly energetic (or masochistic!) may be tempted to investigate the lovely, unspoilt beach here, which is dog-friendly all year round and a good place for seal-spotting but the inevitable stiff climb back up to the Coast Path should be factored into this decision! To continue, follow the Coast Path sign in the direction of Pudcombe Cove and Kingswear, looking out for posts bearing the Coast Path acorn symbol along the

way, which will help to keep you on track.

As views open up of the coastline stretching away into the distance, you will also see the Daymark to your right and may like to know you will be passing close to this historic navigational aid on your return journey. After passing through a wooden gate, you will be skirting the lower end of the gardens at Coleton Fishacre and, on a hot day, this section of the walk is pleasantly shaded. There is a viewing platform at either end of a small bay and this is Pudcombe Cove, which once provided a tidal bathing pool for the D'Oyly Carte family, although the steep path that led down to the cove has now been eroded. From here, you will be following the Coast Path signs in the direction of Froward Point, ignoring smaller paths leading into the woods and walking uphill as you leave the garden behind.

Along the way, you may have noticed a group of rocks out to sea ahead of you (the largest of these is Mew Stone) and these make a useful point of reference, as you will be heading steeply uphill and inland **3** after passing these rocks. As you walk uphill, follow the Coast Path sign for Kingswear.

You will pass a wooden bench on your right and go through a gate. Continuing on the track through the trees, you will come to a post, indicating the Coast Path going to the left and downhill. This is where you leave the Coast Path, taking the path to the right **4** instead.

Arriving at a small road, **5** turn right signposted Brownstone Car Park and, if you look behind you as you go through a gate, you will see a National Trust sign for Froward Point. Follow this road, which is no more than a rough track in places, as it heads uphill. After some distance, you will see the Daymark on your right, looking strangely incongruous as it rises some 25 metres from the arable field in which it is situated. The hollow tower, which was built in 1864, is hexagonal and made of limestone.

Continue following the small road as it bears right, where the sign points to a car park **6** and when you reach the Brownstone Car Park, go through the gate and walk to the far end, taking a grass track which runs parallel to the lane until you reach a gate, where a footpath would take you to the Coast Path. Bear left here, leaving the grass track and walking straight ahead **7** on the lane.

After passing a turning to your right, you will see the entrance to Coleton Fishacre House and Gardens on your right. Go straight ahead here and follow the lane back to the car park.

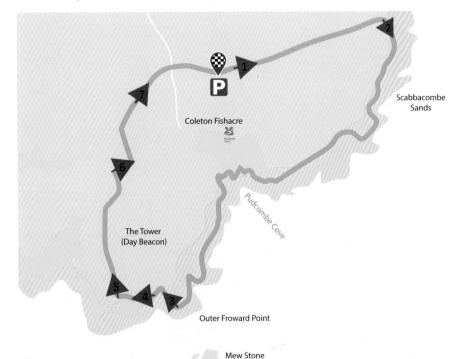

Distance   6 miles

Suggested time   3 hours

Level of difficulty 🐾 🐾 🐾

This walk has a lot to offer in the way of variety. Starting with a stroll along quiet paths and lanes, the route takes in the historic and very dog-friendly town of Dartmouth and you may wish to allow extra time for a look in the shops or for taking advantage of one of the many benches along the quayside, from which you can enjoy watching all the comings and goings in this busy estuary. The route then climbs steeply out of the town and returns along a stunning stretch of the Coast Path on a good path which can be muddy in places. There is one short section on a busy road near the start, but it is only for a few yards. Other roads, as you approach and leave Dartmouth, are quiet.

How to get there - Leave Dartmouth on the A379. Coming out of the town, turn left at a mini roundabout and continue following the A379 in the direction of Stoke Fleming for approximately 1¾ miles. The turning you want has no signpost and can be tricky to spot. After passing a sign

to Venn and Bowden on the right, the sea will come into view ahead of you. Slow down here and be prepared for a small turning on the left. After turning left onto this narrow lane, continue to a crossroads and go straight across. You will pass a postbox on your left and where the road bears left, you will see car parks on both sides of the road.

Map:
Ordnance Survey Explorer Map OL20

Grid Ref:
SX 8745 4920

Nearest Post Code:
TQ6 0JR

Parking:
Little Dartmouth National Trust pay and display - payment by phone only

Facilities:
Toilets and dog-friendly cafes and pubs in Dartmouth, toilets and refreshments at Dartmouth Castle

You will need:
Leads, dog bags, water for dogs

Follow this lane to a house at a road junction and bear right just before the house and right again onto the main road. Take care here, as you will be on a busy road for approximately 25 yards, before turning right **4** once more, onto Jawbone Hill.

Continuing along this quiet lane, you will see a water tower on the left ahead of you. Just before reaching the water tower and a car park ahead, turn right **5** onto a rough track and walk downhill. You will start to catch glimpses of the Dart estuary ahead and, after some distance, the vista opens up in front of you. At this point, you will part company with the Diamond Jubilee Way, which takes a turn to the right as you bear left to follow the main track, passing allotments on your right. Shortly afterwards, the track becomes a road and you will see an imposing red brick building in the distance ahead - this is the Britannia Royal Naval College.

Walking steeply downhill on the road, you will come to a junction, where you bear

Leave the car park along the narrow tarmac lane, which is signposted as a bridleway, the Diamond Jubilee Way and Dartmouth Castle **1** . Walk past a farm and turn left, following the sign for the Diamond Jubilee Way and Weeke Cottage. Go through a gate and continue straight ahead on a path between fields. The path soon goes steeply downhill, bending as it levels out. You will go through two gates, passing Weeke Cottage on your right, and come to a road.

Turn left at the road and, after about 50 yards, turn right **2** at a footpath sign for Higher Weeke. The driveway goes uphill towards farm buildings and another sign directs you to the left of a shed and a house. Continue uphill on a grass track to a gate and turn left **3** onto the lane.

right onto a narrower road with houses on either side. Stay on this road as it winds downhill to arrive at a busy main street. If you're not planning to hit the shops or cafes, cross over and walk down a small alleyway between buildings. On reaching the quayside, cross over and turn right to ❻ walk along the wide pavement.

At the end of the quay, the road turns sharply right and then left, passing the slip road to the Lower Ferry, which is the last remaining tug and float ferry in England. Continuing straight ahead, you will pass the 14th century Bayard's Cove Inn on your right and find yourself walking along the cobbled wharf of Bayard's Cove and there are records of ships being unloaded here which date back to 1368. Reaching the 16th century Bayard's Cove Fort, go under the archway and head for the exit on the far side, turning right to go up the steep stone steps. At the road, turn left ❼ and walk uphill.

Continue on this road for some way, turning left onto Castle Road at a sign for Dartmouth Castle. With the estuary on your left, continue following the road as it bears left and then goes uphill. At the sign for Castle Road, take the footpath straight ahead between two roads and running parallel to the lower road and where it meets the road, turn sharply left and then almost immediately right towards Dartmouth Castle.

Follow this pleasantly shady, tarmac road, taking the left fork where you see a sign which points right to the Castle entrance. You will pass St Petrox Church and, at the end of the churchyard, shallow steps will take you uphill to Dartmouth Castle, where you will pass the tearooms and see a track leading uphill, signposted Coast Path and Stoke Fleming. Go up the steep steps, turn left onto the road and, shortly after, take the righthand fork towards Compass Cove

Cottages and the Coastguard Station. Take a deep breath - this is the most strenuous section of the walk!

Follow this road all the way to the top of the hill, passing Compass Cottage on your right and a sign to the Coast Path on your left. After walking steeply uphill for some time, you will pass Compass Cove Cottages and the Coast Guard Station on your left. Go through the kissing gate into a large field. There may be livestock from this point. Walk straight ahead on a wide track until you see a small bench below you and to your left. Turn left here, walk down the

steep slope and turn right **8** at the bench onto a narrow track.

You are now on the Coast Path. Keep following this undulating path for almost a mile, with the sea on your left, as it takes you out onto the headland. The wide, grassy track eventually bears right and uphill, where the village of Stoke Fleming is visible ahead. At a gate, the path makes another right turn **9** onto a well-made path which leads uphill all the way back to the car parks.

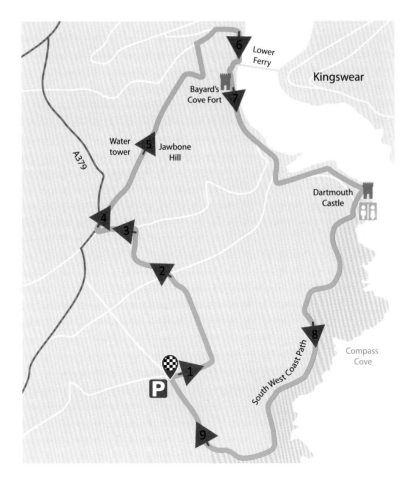

Distance	3.7 miles	1.6 miles
Suggested time	2 hours	1 hour
Level of difficulty	🐾🐾	🐾🐾

Here are two options for a walk around this beautiful stretch of coastline. The longer route starts with a bit of a yomp along the roads but the lanes are scenic and generally quiet (beginning with almost a mile along the lane leading to the car park, which may be busier at weekends or during the holiday season). However, the moment you reach the coast, your dogs will be rewarded with the run of Lannacombe Beach, which is tucked away in a sheltered cove and dog-friendly year-round. Returning along the Coast Path, there is another opportunity for a romp on the beach at Great Mattiscombe, where dogs are also welcome throughout the year, after which there is a choice of route for the final ascent back to the car park. For those who'd prefer a shorter walk and perhaps more time on the beach, the second option involves no road-walking and takes in the beach at Great Mattiscombe, before returning along the Coast Path. This is an historic section of the coast and you might want to factor in time to visit the ruins of the lost village of Hallsands, which is a little further along the Coast Path and you can also follow a tarmac path from the car park to Start Point Lighthouse which dates back to 1836.

How to get there - From Kingsbridge, follow the A379 in the direction of Dartmouth for approximately 6 miles. Turn right at the mini roundabout at Stokenham and follow the brown tourist signs for Start Point.

Map:
Ordnance Survey Explorer Map OL20

Grid Ref:
SX 8205 3748

Nearest Post Code:
TQ7 2ET

Parking:
Parking at Start Point car park, flat rate per visit, payable on arrival

Facilities:
Portaloo in car park and possibility of seasonal refreshments van

You will need:
Leads, dog bags, water for dogs

3.7 mile walk

Walk back past the payment kiosk and exit the car park the way you drove in, walking straight ahead on the small lane **1**.

After almost a mile, you will pass an unmarked turning on your left and arrive at Hollowcombe Head crossroads. Turn left **2** at the crossroads, signposted to Lannacombe and head downhill along the narrow lane.

After approximately half a mile and just before the lane levels out, you will see a turning on your left, and a sign indicating this is a single track No Through Road. Turn left **3** here. At first, you will have glimpses of gardens through the high hedges to your right and, after a short distance, you may notice a little brook running alongside the road on the right.

The lane eventually turns into a rough track and you will see a sign for Lannacombe Beach. Follow this track, with the sea directly ahead, until you reach a small car park. This is where you will make

a left turn onto the Coast Path but not before the dogs have let off steam on the beach. Quieter than many of the larger beaches along the coast, Lannacombe is an unspoilt spot, nestled in a sheltered bay and flanked by craggy outcrops of rock.

To continue, head back to the little car park at the back of the beach and, facing the sea, turn left **4** and go through a gate onto the Coast Path, which is signposted Start Point. The path will take you close to the cliff edge in places. Continue with the sea on your right and, after some distance, you will see another sheltered bay below. This is Great Mattiscombe, where there is another chance for dogs to enjoy some fun on the beach.

On the path above the beach, there is a wooden post **5** indicating the Coast Path going to the right and another footpath to the left, which is a grassy track heading uphill to pass between two stone pillars. At this point, you have the choice of returning by the slightly longer, more strenuous Coast Path route (about a mile) or the grassy path which heads inland, ascending gently for half a mile.

To take the inland route, head uphill, pass between the stone pillars and follow the path as it bears left **5** . Go through a gate and continue walking uphill with the sea now behind you, pausing occasionally to turn round and admire the view. After two more small wooden gates on the path, you will see a gate on your left **6** which leads directly into the car park.

To return via the Coast Path, bear right, as indicated on the wooden post and follow the directions and map for the 1.6 mile walk from Point **3** below.

1.6 mile walk
Facing the sea, leave the car park by the exit in the far righthand corner, go through a gate and turn right immediately to go through another gate **1** signposted Great Mattiscombe Sands.

Follow this path downhill for approximately half a mile, passing through two gates on the way and with the sea directly ahead. At the end of the path, you will pass through a final gate and see a gap in a stone wall to your right. Turn right **2** here to pass through the gap and walk downhill to a wooden post. Turn left after the post and follow the steep, winding path down to the beach, taking care over

the rocks between the end of the path and the sand.

When you're ready to return, head back over the rocks and uphill, bearing right instead of following the path straight ahead, by which you descended. You will arrive at the Coast Path **3** which you will be following for approximately a mile, with the sea on your right and Start Point Lighthouse ahead. This section of the path comes precipitously close to the cliff edge in places!

As you draw near to the lighthouse, you will see a yellow arrow on a wooden post, pointing to the left and uphill. Follow the arrow **4** walking away from the sea and over a ridge to a small, tarmac roadway. Turn right here to visit the lighthouse, or left **5** to return to the car park. You might notice the Coast Path sign which tells you it's 168 miles to Poole - maybe save that for another day!

Long 3.7 Mile Walk

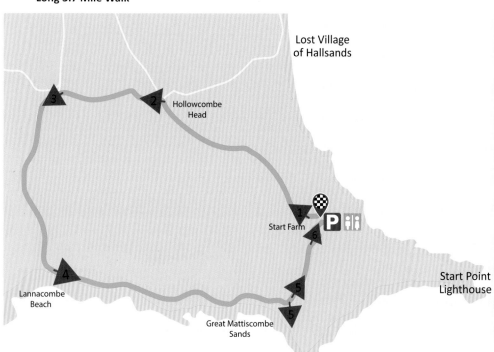

Short 1.6 Mile Walk

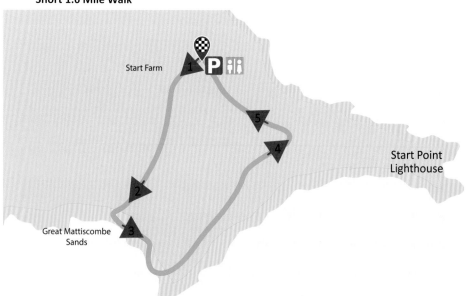

Distance	7.5 miles
Suggested time	4 hours

Level of difficulty 🐾 🐾 🐾

How to get there - Turn off the A381 Kingsbridge to Salcombe road on a sharp bend at Malborough, where there is a sign to Village Centre and a petrol station almost opposite. Follow this narrow road as it bears left in front of the church, passing the village shop and public toilets on the right. Bear left at a fork in the road, signposted Bolberry, Soar and Rew. Stay on this road for approximately 1¾ miles, until you see a brown sign for East Soar and turn left here. Continue until you see a windsock in an airfield to your left. Turn left after the windsock into the car park.

Map:
Ordnance Survey Explorer Map OL20

Grid Ref:
SX 7129 3749

Nearest Post Code:
TQ7 3DR

Parking:
National Trust pay and display car park - payment by phone only

Facilities:
Walkers' honesty cafe and toilets near start, seasonal refreshments kiosk at Overbeck's

You will need:
Leads, dog bags, water for dogs

With the windsock on your left, leave the car park on the well-made path opposite the entrance, signposted Overbecks and East Soar Outdoor Experience .

Follow this track with fields on either side and, where you see a footpath heading across a field to your left, continue straight ahead ❷ signposted Sharp Tor, Starehole and Bolt Head.

The path leads through a farm, where facilities include a walkers' honesty cafe,

toilets and a children's play area. With the buildings on your right, walk straight through and exit by a kissing gate at the far end, signposted Bolt Head, Salcombe and Link to Coast Path. Follow the path around the edge of a field, with the hedgerow on your right, and then through a gateway. Continue straight ahead on a well-used grassy track. The sea will come into view and, walking towards a rocky outcrop with the sea beyond, you will come to a gate. Go through the gate and turn left **3** signposted Sharp Tor, Overbecks and South Sands. You will be walking with the sea on your right for a time, on a path which comes close to the cliff edge in places.

Continue on this very obvious, easy path and when you see a wooden bench to your right and a granite block marking a viewing point, you can look ahead to Salcombe and the open countryside stretching away for miles beyond.

The path narrows and you will pass a memorial to the Salcombe Lifeboat Disaster of 1916 on your right. Care is needed as you descend uneven stone steps, which can be slippery when wet. At the bottom of the steps, turn right **4** signposted Overbeck's and Salcombe, walking downhill on a stony track. The gardens at Overbeck's are on the the the other side of a stone wall which will appear on your right and you can stand on the large slab of stone to have a look. There is another chance to glimpse the gardens at an ornate gate, after which the path continues downhill along an avenue of palms to the road.

Follow this narrow and winding road downhill, past the entrance to Overbeck's on the right (note - dogs aren't allowed in the gardens here), the seasonal refreshments kiosk on the left and then a car park on the left, continuing until you see a footpath sign for the Coast Path and Starehole on your right. Turn right **5** here. You will now be following this glorious stretch of the Coast Path, with the sea on your left, for over 3 miles. There are places where it may take you close to the cliff edge and there are sections where you might come across livestock. Follow signs to Bolt Head, Bolberry and Soar Mill Cove on this well-marked path and where signs indicate two options for Soar Mill Cove, take the path to the left, keeping you closest to the sea.

You will know you are approaching Soar

Mill Cove when, after walking downhill over an open, grassy area, you cross two small wooden bridges, one after the other, and see a gate in a stone wall ahead. After the gate, the path narrows, becoming rocky and uneven and, as it goes downhill, Soar Mill Cove will come into view.

Keep walking downhill as the path opens out, go through a gate and cross a small, wooden bridge. If you're visiting Soar Mill Cove, turn left here and follow the track down to the beach.

To continue, turn right **6** after the gate and go through another gate into a field, signposted Malborough. Follow the path uphill, through a small boggy area and carry on straight ahead when you come to a stony track, still going uphill. After the track opens out again, you will arrive at a gate with Soar Mill Cove Hotel directly opposite. Go through the gate, turn left onto a small lane and continue walking uphill.

At the end of a stone wall on your right, turn right **7** at a Link to Coast Path sign and follow the narrow track past houses on the right and over a tiny stone slab bridge to a gate. Go through the gate and continue straight ahead, between

hedgerows. After another gate, the path heads uphill, initially through an open, grassy area and then through the bracken, to a further gate which takes you into a field. Keep straight ahead, with the hedgerow on your right and, after some distance, you will pass a stone structure nestled in the arable crop to your left. This is the West Soar Admiralty Signal Station, built in 1794. For a full description, see the nearby information board.

Photo Credit: Nean Newell

Shortly after the Signal Station, you will arrive at another gate. Go through the gate, turn left ❽ and continue with the fence close by on your left and the sea at a distance on your right, taking care as there may be sheep in this area and in the fields further along.

After passing a distant house on the other side of a wall to your left, turn left ❾ and go through a gate, signposted Malborough. Follow the path along the edge of the field and through two metal gates into another field. Continue on this path, past the house on your left and through a gap in a stone wall. Walking straight ahead, you will pass a post with a yellow footpath arrow at the end of the garden fence, eventually leaving the field through a gate beside a cattle grid and passing between two stone pillars onto a small road. Turn left ❿ and, after a very short distance, you will see the car park on your right.

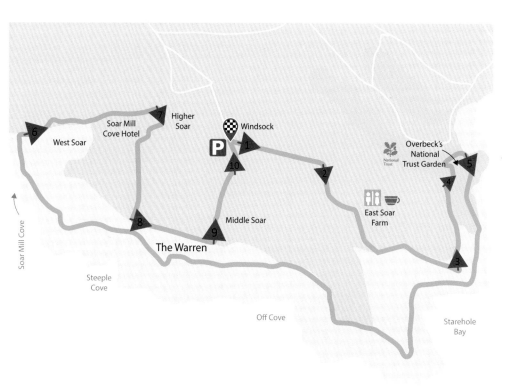

Distance	4.5 miles
Suggested time	2 hours

Level of difficulty 🐾 🐾

Although largely on level ground and fairly easy, this walk features some tricky riverside sections where the path is uneven, as well as a steep climb uphill towards the end. There is a little road-walking on quiet lanes, both at the start and on the way back. This is a very pretty walk, mainly through woodland and following the river in one direction before returning along the opposite side. There are signs of the old railway line which ran between Kingsbridge and South Brent from 1893 to 1963, including a picturesque stone bridge. Sections of the route follow the disused line and eventually pass the now privately-owned station buildings. The excellent dog-friendly cafe at Avon Mill Garden Centre is handily situated just before that last push uphill!

How to get there - Loddiswell is located on the B3196 between Kingsbridge and the A38 Devon Expressway and the car park is signposted off the main road through the village.

Map:
Ordnance Survey Explorer Map OL20

Grid Ref:
SX 7195 4861

Nearest Post Code:
TQ7 4RJ

Parking:
Parking is free but spaces limited

Facilities:
Public toilets in car park, pub in village, cafe towards end of walk

You will need:
Leads and dog bags

Turn right out of the car park, then left onto a one-way road and left again onto the main road through the village passing a postbox on your left as you walk downhill towards the village green, where you will see a war memorial as you head towards the church.

Walk to the left of the church along a narrow lane between the church and the cemetery, staying on the tarmac as it bears left and then right, before joining a

right. Pass through a gate onto a narrow, wooded track ③ .

Follow this track for some distance, as it wanders away from the river and back again, over little wooden bridges and fallen logs. Take care on the uneven steps and where exposed rocks make the path tricky to negotiate. Shortly after passing two Public Footpath signs, pointing back the way you've come, you will see an old railway bridge. Climb the steps to the bridge but do not cross, instead turning left ④ onto the disused railway line.

road. You will see a triangle of grass with a stone bench on your left and a signpost indicating this is Ham Butts. Go straight ahead on a No Through Road towards Reads Farm ② .

Follow the lane downhill and just before the farm, turn right where you see a Public Footpath sign and pass through a gate. Keeping close to the fence on your left, continue to a metal kissing gate, after which you will be walking along a narrow path with a stream on your left.

At the end of the path, cross the stream by the small wooden bridge and pass through a gate into a large field. There may be sheep here but it's only a short section. Turn right and, skirting the hill in front of you, follow the grass track as it bears left, where the river appears on your

This well-made path takes you away from the river and, after following it for some time, you will see a Woodland Trust sign for Avon Valley Woods and Aveton Wood on your left. After crossing a stone bridge, turn immediately right, go over a small wooden bridge and turn right again ⑤ onto a path through the woods with the river on your right.

The path on this side of the river is generally easier, although it can be muddy after heavy rain and there are several short boardwalks to help you over the worst. Eventually, the path forks and, taking the righthand fork, you will find yourself at the opposite end of the railway bridge where you turned left a short while ago. Don't go back onto the bridge, but take the path straight ahead.

After a short distance, you will be on the disused railway line again, with steep embankments on either side and where the embankments disappear, you will see the river once more on your right and a little way below you. The railway line path ends at a gate, beyond which is a garden belonging to the private house which was once the station. There is a stile to your left onto a narrower path which passes close by the now privately-owned railway buildings. The fence either side of the stile is only a few strands of loose wire and generally easy for dogs to manage but, if you're having trouble, you need only retrace your steps for a very short distance to a Welcome to Avon Valley Woods sign, where the fence ends.

As you follow this path, be aware you are approaching a road which appears rather suddenly. At the road, turn right **6** passing the remainder of the re-

purposed railway buildings. After going under a bridge, go through a gate on your right at a Public Footpath sign and follow the path through a field, with the river on your right, exiting at the far end onto a road and turning right **7** over a bridge. You will pass Avon Mill Garden Centre on your right (where a visit to the dog-friendly cafe is highly recommended) before the road climbs steeply uphill.

Turn right onto a concrete driveway at a sign for Cloverwell Farm and just before the entrance to the farm, turn left at an Unmetalled Road sign. This rough track continues uphill for some time and, shortly after it levels out, you will see a road ahead. This is the Ham Butts crossroads, seen at the start of the walk.

Turn left **8** at the crossroads and retrace your steps, past the church and village green, back to the car park.

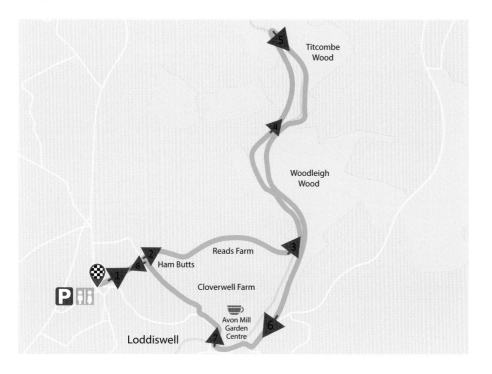

Distance	4.2 miles
Suggested time	2 hours
Level of difficulty	

This is a popular walk, affording great views of a beautiful stretch of coastline without the effort required on many sections of the Coast Path. A pleasant stroll into Noss Mayo and alongside the estuary is followed by a gentle ascent through woodland and over a mile of easy and uncharacteristically flat Coast Path walking on a well-made track. There are short sections on quiet lanes and a dog-friendly pub in Noss Mayo, where you can sit on the terrace and, if the tide is in, watch the activity on the estuary below.

How to get there - Turn off the A379 at Yealmpton, between Plymouth and Modbury, onto the B3186, following the signs for Newton Ferrers and Noss Mayo. In Newton Ferrers, turn left at the Green onto Bridgend Hill, signposted Bridgend, Noss Mayo and Stoke Beach. At a junction at the end of the road, keep the estuary on your right as you turn sharply right onto

Stoke Road. Keep following the road as it goes uphill and bear left after passing the church on your right. Continue on this narrow lane and turn right immediately after the Old Rectory Cross signpost and Revelstoke House on the right. Follow this narrow lane to a T junction and turn right onto a No Through Road. The Warren car park is on the left after almost ¾ mile.

Map:
Ordnance Survey Explorer Map OL20

Grid Ref:
SX 5409 4659

Nearest Post Code:
PL8 1HB

Parking:
The Warren National Trust Car Park, payment by phone only

Facilities:
Public toilets and dog-friendly pub in Noss Mayo, not far from start

You will need:
Leads, dog bags, water for dogs

Photo Credit: Wayne Howell

At the car park entrance, turn left onto a narrow lane and, after a very short distance, turn right ❶ at a Public Footpath to Noss Mayo sign. Follow this rough track downhill for some way, being ready to put your dogs on their leads where it becomes a tarmac road.

After passing tennis courts and a car park on the right, turn left and follow Foundry Lane as it bears right, passing between houses and downhill to a junction, where you will see another car park (where the public toilets are located) at the end of the estuary directly ahead and the village hall on your right. Turn left here ❷ onto Passage Road which goes uphill, passing houses on both sides and the dog-friendly Ship Inn on the right.

Continue following this small road for some distance, with the estuary on your right and, as you leave the houses behind, woodland on your left. Shortly after passing a sign for Kilpatrick Steps and several benches on the right, you will arrive at a forked junction of two footpaths. Take the righthand, lower path ❸ signposted

Ferryman's Cottage and the Coast Path, which becomes quite narrow as it passes several houses. Just after passing Ferryman's Cottage on your right, you will see a wooden gate in front of you. Go through the gate and, as you follow the woodland path uphill, you can still glimpse the estuary through the trees, below and to your right. Take care here as the path is uneven in places.

At the end of the path, go up the steps onto a small road and turn right ❹ where you will see an information board on your right and a sign for the South West Coast Path. Follow the rough track past cottages on your left to a gate, where the path becomes wooded again. It's worth pausing here to take in the fine view over a field gate on the right. Continuing along this well-made track, you will go through another gate and emerge onto the headland, where you will see the mouth of the estuary on your right and, as the path bears left **5**, the sea directly ahead. Sheep and cattle may be grazing on this section of the walk.

Photo Credit: Nean Newell

You will be following this path for approximately 1¼ miles, passing through several gates along the way and staying on the well-made track, with glorious views of the coastline and out to sea to your right. Eventually, you will see a curved stone wall on your right as the path bears left and away from the sea. Stay on the gravel path, ignoring a grass track which branches off to the right and heads downhill to a gate. This is where you part company with the Coast Path, continuing on the main track to a gate. Go through the gate **6** and follow the short path which takes you to another gate on the left, leading back into the car park.

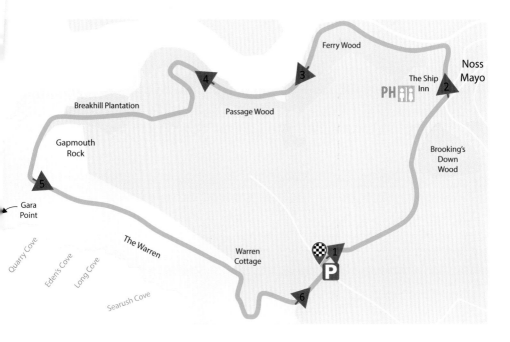

Distance	4.5 miles	3.5 miles
Suggested time	2 hours	1½ hours
Level of difficulty	🐾 🐾	🐾

Shipley Bridge is a small stone bridge which spans the River Avon in a picturesque spot towards the southern edge of Dartmoor. The two walks described are very different in character. The longer option follows tranquil woodland paths as far as South Brent, before returning along quiet lanes which take in the ancient Lydia Bridge, views across the river valley and a pretty stretch alongside the river. The shorter option is a there-and-back walk, leading to Avon Dam, on a tarmac access track, suitable for wheelchair users and pushchairs, which offers a stark contrast as it emerges onto the moor after a shady, riverside start. You can choose to stay on tarmac as far as the foot of the dam or follow a stony track uphill for a spectacular view of the reservoir and remote moorland which surrounds it. Why not take a picnic and do both?

How to get there - Turn off the A38 Devon Expressway at South Brent. If travelling from Exeter direction, take the first exit at the roundabout towards South Brent and Avonwick. At the next roundabout, take the second exit, signposted Harbourneford, Didworthy and Avon Dam. At a crossroads, go straight ahead, signposted Didworthy and Avon Dam. Follow the road where it bears left and continue straight ahead, following a sign to Shipley Bridge, where you pass a turning to the left. After a cattle grid, you will cross Shipley Bridge and the car park is on the right. If travelling from Plymouth direction, take the third exit at the roundabout, signposted Harbourneford, Didworthy and Avon Dam and follow the directions above.

Map:
Ordnance Survey Explorer Map OL28

Grid Ref:
SX 6801 6290

Nearest Post Code:
TQ10 9EL

Parking:
Free parking, honesty box for donations

Facilities:
Toilets in car park and seasonal snack van (you can check Taylor Made Coffee Van at Avon Dam on Facebook the evening before your visit, to make sure the van will be there)

You will need:
Leads, dog bags, water for dogs

4.5 mile walk

Woodland and quiet lanes. Exit the car park onto the road and turn left. Walk over Shipley Bridge and continue along the road to a cattle grid. Turn right **1** after the cattle grid at a Public Footpath sign and go through a gate.

Follow the path straight ahead and over a stile. Ignoring smaller paths to the right and passing through gates along the way, continue for approximately half a mile. After passing a wooden bench on your left, the path goes downhill and turns into a concrete driveway between a house and outbuildings. Once past the buildings, go through the gate, cross a small road and continue straight ahead **2** following a Public Bridleway sign for Lutton, on a tarmac driveway leading to several large properties. When you see a parking area on the right and a driveway ahead, take the track to the left of the driveway. Passing through a series of gates, you will be walking through woodland with an old stone wall to your right. After passing a newly built section of the wall and going through a gate, you will emerge to pleasant views across the river valley to your right.

After a metal field gate on the left, the path goes steeply downhill and the stones on the track are quite loose, so do take care. As the path levels out, you will come to a gate. Go through the gate and cross a ford, using the small stone bridge to the right if you don't want to get your feet wet! Follow the stony track uphill to a lane and continue straight ahead to a T junction. Turn right **3** here onto a quiet lane and walk downhill for some distance.

At the bottom of the lane, turn right **4** signposted Aish, Zeal and Didworthy and continue walking downhill to a small stone bridge. This is the historic Lydia Bridge, which was once a packhorse bridge and, as you cross, you will see the water cascades spectacularly over the rocks to the right. After the bridge, continue uphill for some way, passing a turning to the left as the road bears right **5** at a sign for Didworthy, Zeal and Shipley.

You will be following the lane for a little over a mile from this point, towards the end of which you will cross a small, weak (according to the sign) bridge, to walk with the river on your right. As the road starts to leave the river, you will pass a turning to the left and, shortly after, you will see a turning to the right, directly in front of Bridge House, signposted Didworthy and No Through Road. Turn right ⑥ here and follow the lane as it crosses the river.

Continue uphill on this lane, passing Didworthy Cottages on the right. At the sign for Didworthy Bungalows, turn left ⑦ where there is a Public Footpath sign for Shipley Bridge. Go through the gate and retrace your steps through the woods, back to the car park.

3.5 mile walk
To Avon Dam. There may be livestock at any point on this walk. Exit the car park onto the road and turn left and then left again ① before the bridge, past wooden gates and onto the tarmac access road, signposted Public Bridlepath, Brockhill Ford (Abbots Way).

Walking under the trees, with the river on your right, continue on the tarmac path, passing a turning to the left at a South West Water sign and bearing right ② where a bridge takes you over the river and onto the moor. The river reappears on your left after a short distance.

Continue following the tarmac path until you see a stony track, leading uphill to your right ③ . Carry on straight ahead here to visit the foot of the dam or, for a more dramatic view, turn right and follow the stony track uphill. You will soon glimpse the dam ahead and the path will lead you alongside the reservoir. To return, simply retrace your steps.

**Long 4.5
Mile Walk**

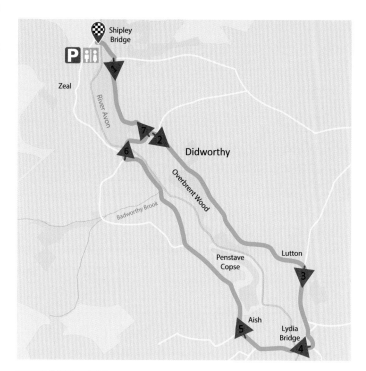

**Short 3.5
Mile Walk**

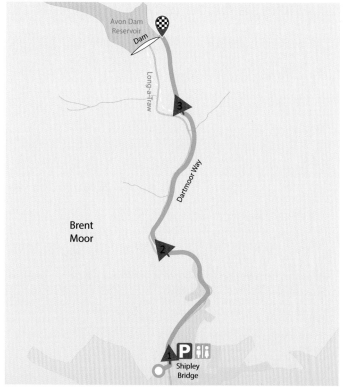

Distance	5 miles	7 miles
Suggested time	2¼ hours	3¼ hours
Level of difficulty	🐾🐾🐾	🐾🐾🐾

The beauty of Shaugh Bridge can be appreciated from the moment you step out of the car to dappled shade and the sound of the river. This is an area steeped in history, with ancient stone circles and crosses out on the moor and remnants of the china clay works, redolent of a bygone era, gathering moss here and there in the woodland. The pillars of Shaugh Bridge date back to the 17th century, although the bridge itself was washed away by a flood and rebuilt in 1825. The walks follow the same route to a point where the longer version makes an extra loop, so a decision can be made here, depending on energy levels! Both routes are only strenuous at the start and feature woodland and riverside walking, quiet lanes and open moorland, but some paths are rocky and uneven, so care is needed.

How to get there - In the village of Roborough, turn left off the A386 onto New Road, signposted Bickleigh and Shaugh Prior, passing Roborough Village Hall on the right. Roborough is approximately halfway between Yelverton and the A38 Devon Expressway and the turning will be on the left if coming from Yelverton and on the right if coming from the A38. Turn left after the Royal Marines barracks at Bickleigh, signposted Shaugh Prior, Wotter and Lee Moor. Follow this road for approximately 1¾ miles and, after passing a turning to the left to Goodameavy and a small car park, you will cross Shaugh Bridge and the car park is on the left, opposite a bus stop. In the car park, you can see the remains of the drying kilns which once served the china clay works.

Map:
Ordnance Survey Explorer Map OL28

Grid Ref:
SX 5332 6361

Nearest Post Code:
PL7 5HD

Parking:
Free in National Trust car park but spaces limited

Facilities:
Dog-friendly pub on longer option, otherwise no facilities on this walk

You will need:
Leads, dog bags, water for dogs

Facing the road at the car park entrance, turn left and walk up the steep steps into the woods, signposted Cadover Bridge and Dartmoor Way. At the top of the steps, go straight ahead, with the road on your right, and turn left **1** onto a Public Footpath which also indicates the Dartmoor Way.

Walk uphill, go through a kissing gate and continue following the rocky track for some way. After passing a house and then a gate on your right, take the main track straight ahead, indicated by a Dartmoor Way sign, not the path to the right. The gradient becomes a bit kinder here!

Continue on this path for some distance. Gradually it will level out and you will hear and then see the river below you, to your left. Ignore any paths to the left, keeping to the main track, with the river in view. Eventually, as the path takes you a little away from the river, you will see Cadover Bridge ahead. Go through a kissing gate into the car park, head for the road and turn left **2** . You are now on the open moor where livestock may be grazing.

Cross over Cadover Bridge and turn left **3** at a National Trust sign for Lower

Cadworthy Farm. The stony track ends at a gate with a No Access sign. Turn right here, to head uphill on a grassy track with a wall and fence on your left.

After passing a stone cross, continue straight ahead. As the wall on your left curves away to the left, keep going on your path in the same direction - straight ahead and uphill, ignoring any paths to the left and right. You will soon see the vista opening up ahead of you. Reaching a fork in the path, take the left fork which leads gently downhill, heading in the

direction of a small group of dwellings in the distance on the road ahead. The path will arrive at the road, to the left of these dwellings.

Turn left **4** onto the narrow moorland road which passes another stone cross and a cattle grid, before becoming pleasantly shady as it heads downhill.

Just before a small stone bridge, you will see a stile and a National Trust Goodameavy sign on your left. Turn left here if you are taking the shorter route and follow the directions from point **9** to the end of the walk.

If you are following the longer route, cross over the bridge and turn right **5** where there are signs for the West Devon Way and Dartmoor Way, passing over a stile into a narrow field with the river on your

right. Where the path forks, take the left fork away from the river and follow the main path straight ahead, continuing over a stile and along a wooded path.

At the end of the trees, go over a stile and follow the path alongside the river through two fields where horses graze. At the far end of the second field, go through the gate beside a ladder stile onto the road and turn left **6** , following the road as it bears left, passing houses as it goes uphill.

You will pass under an old railway bridge and go past a cattle grid as you continue uphill and a small detour will take you to the dog-friendly Skylark Inn, which soon comes into view ahead. If you're not visiting the pub, turn left with the village hall on your right, signposted Drake's Trail. A short distance along this tarmac track, the cycle path bears right and goes through a gap beside a gate. Go through this gap but leave the cycle track and turn right onto a path, leading uphill.

Follow this path on the edge of the moor for some distance, until you see a small wooden bridge to your left. Go over the bridge and bear right, heading for the road. Turn left **7** at the road and walk downhill. Continue past a cattle grid and where the road levels out, you will see a turning to the left to Goodameavy. Turn left here **8** , go under the old railway bridge and over the small stone bridge you

crossed earlier in the opposite direction.

Once over the bridge, turn right immediately ❾ at a National Trust Goodameavy sign and follow the well-made stony path, with the river on your right. From this point, both versions of the walk join, to return by the same route.

Continuing on this track, you will come to a gate, after which you will pass a stone building on your left. Immediately after this building, bear right to follow a Dartmoor Way sign, heading downhill, with the river to your right. Take care here, as the track is quite rocky and wet in places. Follow this path all the way to a gate onto a wooden bridge and, after crossing the bridge, you will be back in the car park.

Photo Credit: Nean Newell

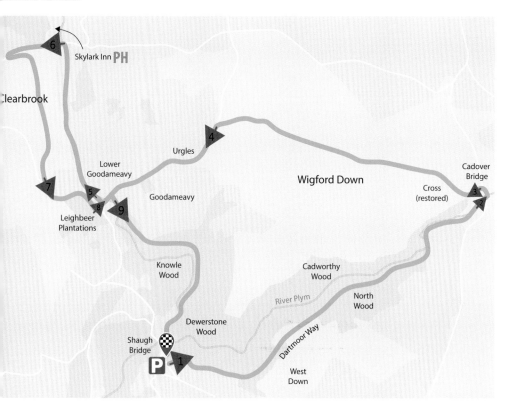

Distance	5.5 miles
Suggested time	2½ hours

Level of difficulty 🐾 🐾

This walk has it all, starting with a peaceful stroll beside the River Walkham and passing an idyllic spot where it joins the River Tavy. After an uphill trudge, which is lengthy rather than steep, you are rewarded with far-reaching views across the valley as you skirt the edge of the moor on wide, grassy paths, which are popular with dog-walkers and Dartmoor Ponies alike. There is easy walking along a section of the Drake's Trail national cycleway which takes you over a viaduct, before returning on a quiet woodland track to the start.

How to get there - Turn off the A386 at the village of Grenofen, between Tavistock and Horrabridge, onto a small lane opposite Drake's Cafe, passing Grenofen Manor on your left. After a short distance, you will pass two houses on your right. Turn left almost immediately and drive downhill for nearly half a mile to the end of the lane, where you will find the car park directly ahead, after crossing a very narrow bridge and a cattle grid.

Maps:
OS Explorer Maps OL28 and 108

Grid Ref:
SX 4903 7102

Nearest Post Code:
PL19 9ES

Parking:
Free parking

Facilities:
There are no facilities on this walk but nearby Drake's Cafe is dog-friendly

You will need:
Leads, dog bags, water for dogs

Exit the car park by walking back past the cattle grid, over the narrow bridge and uphill on the lane for a short distance. Turn left onto a driveway, where there is a Public Bridleway sign and Dartmoor Way symbol.

Bear right as the driveway reaches a group of buildings at another Public Bridleway and Dartmoor Way sign. Continue on this stony track and, after a gate, you will be walking with the river on your left, on a well-defined and easy to follow path, which is uneven and rocky in places.

At a wooden post marked Public Bridleway and Dartmoor Way, take the right fork, staying on the main track. You will pass a tall chimney on your right, which is a relic of the mining industry once prevalent in the area. The path eventually bears right **2** leaving the river and heading uphill.

The track levels out as it passes a house and then it's uphill again to a junction with another path. Turn left **3** here, signposted Public Bridleway and Watersmeet Cottage (on a sign behind you).

The track winds downhill, passing a house on the left. At the bottom of the hill, bear right to walk through a wide, grassy area with the river on your left. Ahead, you will see a wooden bridge. Keep to the right and walk steeply uphill onto a rocky outcrop, passing between the rocks, before following the path downhill and bearing left to the bridge. This is where the River Walkham meets the Tavy. Cross the bridge, bearing right for a few paces and then left, crossing a stream and walking uphill to join a well-made track. Turn left **4** here.

Continue on this stony track which, after passing a property on the left, becomes tarmac for a long, slow trudge uphill. You are now on the edge of the moor and likely to see livestock. Eventually, the tarmac will become a stony track once more. When you see a cattle grid ahead and a small parking area, turn left **5** before the parking area, to walk along a wide, grassy track, with far-reaching views across open moorland and beyond to your left. Eyes down here as navigation can be tricky, with a myriad of paths criss-crossing this section of the moor!

At a junction of several paths, where you see a bench ahead and to the left, take the path furthest to the right, beside the corner of a fence. Continue on this grassy track as it bears away from the fence for a short way. After passing a water trough on your right, turn left before the path takes you between two gateposts and then right onto a much wider track, passing a bench on the right.

At a second bench on your right, which has two small commemorative plaques, continue walking straight ahead for approximately 60 paces, before making a 90 degree left turn ⑥ onto a narrower path, leading downhill through the bracken. After a short distance, the path crosses a wider track and approximately 50 paces further on, arrives at a junction of five paths. Of the two paths ahead of you, take the one to the left and continue downhill, ignoring any further paths to the left and right.

At the bottom of the hill, follow the path as it bears left ⑦ and becomes stony, taking you under the trees and continuing less steeply downhill, with a small stream

on your right. Walk towards the stone viaduct ahead and cross the stream, to walk under the viaduct with the stream close by on your right, then bearing right to stay on the path alongside the stream.

Where the stream crosses your path in a clearing, bear left to follow a track uphill into the trees and, after a short distance, turn right onto a path running parallel to the stream. At the next junction, turn left ⑧ onto a well-made track through the trees. Reaching a wooden post at a fork in the path, take the left fork, heading uphill.

Continue uphill until you see a stone bridge ahead. Turn right immediately before the bridge and, after walking downhill for a short way, you will arrive at another junction. Turn left here and then right ⑨ onto a tarmac track. You are now on the Drake's Trail national cycleway, which follows the route of a disused railway line between Tavistock and Plymouth. Watch out for bikes!

After a gate beside a cattle grid, you will step onto Gem Bridge, a modern-day replacement for the original Brunel-

designed viaduct which was built in 1859 for the South Devon Railway and demolished in 1965 when the railway closed. Spanning the Walkham valley at a height of 24 metres, the bridge we see today was completed in 2012. You may want to pause here to enjoy the view from the viewing platforms.

Once over Gem Bridge, follow the tarmac path as it bears left, going gently uphill and over a small bridge. You will then see two wooden gates on your left. Go through the second gate ❿ , marked Dartmoor Way, and head downhill on a track through the woods. Pass through another gate and, as the path levels out, you will be walking with a fence close by on your left.

Continue to a gate onto a small lane. Turn left onto the lane and, crossing the narrow bridge once more, you will see the car park ahead.

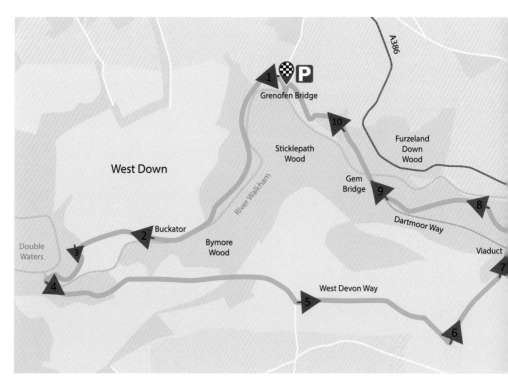

BURRATOR RESERVOIR

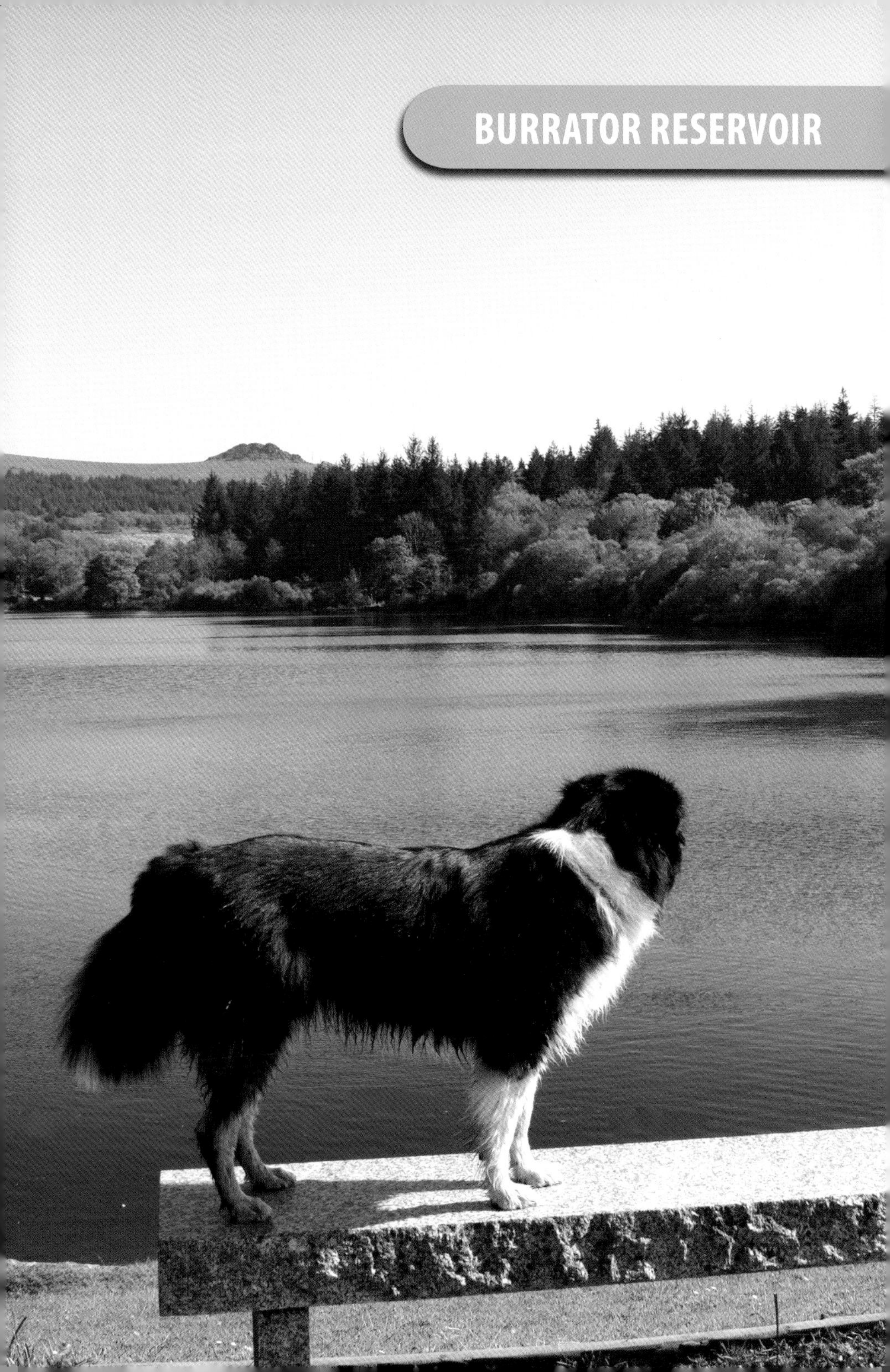

Distance   4.5 miles

Suggested time   2 hours

Level of difficulty

Nestled towards the south western edge of the moor, Burrator Reservoir has been described as the jewel of Dartmoor. It is a tranquil spot with excellent paths through the surrounding mixed woodland and there are dramatic views of the rugged tors and open moorland beyond. Circling the reservoir, this flat route is easy to follow on tracks and quiet roads, accessed by gates or stiles with dog openings, although the paths are uneven in places and can be muddy in wet weather. There is a specified dog exercise area, where high fences prevent livestock from wandering in.

How to get there - Turn off the B3212 onto Burrator Road, adjacent to The Burrator Inn, in the village of Dousland, between Princetown and Yelverton, where you will see signs for Burrator Reservoir, Sheepstor and Meavy. Follow this residential road beyond the houses and turn left at a sign for Burrator Reservoir and Sheepstor. Continue on this road, passing the Quarry car park on the left and then the dam on your right, followed by the Burrator Discovery Centre on the right. Stay on this road, following signs for the Norsworthy Arboretum, for nearly 1½ miles. After crossing a small bridge, you will see the car park on the left, opposite an information board.

Map:
Ordnance Survey Explorer Map OL28

Grid Ref:
SX 5690 6927

Nearest Post Code:
PL20 6PG

Parking:
Norsworthy Bridge car park, free parking

Facilities:
Toilets are available at the main dam, nearby Burrator Inn is dog-friendly

You will need:
Leads, dog bags, water for dogs

Leave the car park and turn left ① onto the road. Shortly after passing another car park on your left, you will see a stile on your right. Go over the stile and turn immediately left onto a path. Following this path, the reservoir comes gradually into view on your right and you are soon walking close beside it. After a while, this path peters out where there is a wooden barrier. Turn left here, pass over the stile and turn right to walk along the road for a short way, before going over the next stile and turning left to rejoin the reservoir path.

An information board and the stone remains of Longstone Manor will appear on your right and, at this point, you can see a dam at the far end of the reservoir. Continue with the reservoir on your right and where you cross a small, wooden bridge, you may find yourself picking your way through a boggy area but, take heart, the path soon firms up and becomes stony and you will see it bears right ② to cross the dam ahead. This is a good spot for admiring the view to the far end of the reservoir and the rugged moorland beyond. As there are a number of well-placed benches, you can take your time and admire it in comfort.

Follow the path as it passes to the right of a gate onto the road and continue until you reach a sign that tells you the track ahead leads to a dead end. Turn left here, pass through a kissing gate and turn right onto the road which soon bears right ③ to take you over a second dam.

At the end of the dam, remain on the road and turn right ④. Walking along the road for a way, you will pass a small waterfall on your left and, a little further on, the Burrator Discovery Centre on your right. Almost immediately after the Discovery Centre, you will see a gate on your right, marked Permissive Path. Take this path ⑤ which leads down some steps, before winding downhill towards the reservoir. Once again, you will be walking with the reservoir on your right. Shortly after passing through a small clearing, where the grass slopes gently down to the edge of the water, you will arrive at a junction in the path. Take the righthand path towards the reservoir.

Photo Credit: Susan Peace

After a while, you will go through a tall gate where a sign indicates you are entering the Dog Exercise Area. This is an excellent place to allow dogs off-lead, as the high fences are designed to keep livestock out - so there should be no danger of coming face to face with a sheep! As you continue

on this path, a high fence will be close by on your right.

You will pass through another tall gate to leave the Dog Exercise Area. Turn right here and continue on the same path, with the tall fence still on your right. Where the fence ends, you will find you are walking along with a river on your right and, after a short way, a weir comes into view. Take extra care after passing the weir, as the path becomes very uneven here.

As the track improves, you will see Norsworthy Bridge ahead and the path bears away from the river, leading to a kissing gate onto the road. Turn right **6** onto the road and cross the bridge. The car park is on the left, a few yards further on.

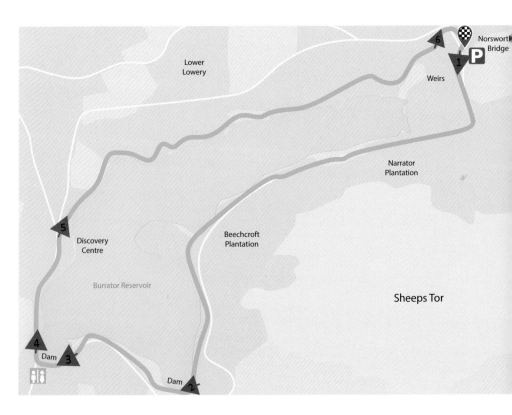

Distance	5.5 miles
Suggested time	2½ hours
Level of difficulty	

This walk is pleasantly varied, with far-reaching views at many points along the way. After a tranquil woodland stroll, it crosses Meldon Viaduct, which rises majestically above a deep valley to a height of 46 metres. Constructed in 1874 to carry the London and South Western Railway across the West Okement River, the viaduct closed in 1990 and now forms part of the Granite Way, a popular cycle track which runs for 11 miles between Okehampton and Lydford. Leaving the Granite Way, the route returns by moorland paths and a gentle descent on a shady bridleway, ending with a short section along quiet lanes.

How to get there - From Okehampton, head south on the B3260 Tavistock Road for approximately 3 miles. Stay on this road when it turns into a No Through Road that leads into Meldon, bearing left after passing under an old railway bridge, where there is a sign for the Reservoir Car Park.

Map:
Ordnance Survey Explorer Map OL28

Grid Ref:
SX 5615 9180

Nearest Post Code:
EX20 4LU

Parking:
Meldon Reservoir pay and display car park

Facilities:
Toilets in car park, cafes and pub adjacent to the Granite Way cycle track

You will need:
Leads, dog bags, water for dogs

Walk between the information board beside the parking payment machine and the toilet block, go up the steps and through a gate. Turn left onto a wide track where you will see Meldon Reservoir ahead of you. Turn left again almost immediately ❶ to pass through a gate onto a bridleway along the edge of a field (where there may be livestock) signposted Meldon Viaduct. Walk downhill on this stony track and pass through a gap in an old stone wall.

After the path levels out, you will pass a wooden bridge on your right, then a lake to your left and you will see the viaduct ahead. After passing through a gate, walk under the viaduct and approximately 200 yards further on, where you can see the track bearing left ahead, there is a narrow path to the right, leading downhill to a gate. Turn right ❷ here and go through the gate onto a woodland path, with the river below and to your right. Follow the track all the way to a wooden bridge and cross the river.

Once over the bridge, go straight ahead and uphill. Cross a small lane and continue uphill on the footpath directly

opposite. Meeting another path, where there is a sign for the Meldon Reservoir pointing back the way you've come, turn right ❸ and follow this track through the woods, going straight on where a Public Footpath sign points to the Viaduct and Moor.

After a while, an old stone wall will appear on your left and you will see steps going uphill ahead. Go up the steps and follow the path as it zig-zags beneath the viaduct. After a final flight of steps, you will emerge into a large open area with an old train yard on your right and Meldon Viaduct to your left. Turn left ❹ here onto the viaduct, where it's worth pausing to admire the view.

You are now on the Granite Way cycle track, so keep an eye out for bikes! You will be walking on this well-maintained tarmac surface for almost two miles, with plenty of opportunities for a sit-down along the way. Refreshments are available towards the end of this section and you will see signs first for the Pump and Pedal and, shortly after, a path to the right leads to Devon Cycle Hire (whose services include the hire of bike trailers for dogs), where doggy ice creams are available in the cafe - opening times are seasonal and can be checked on the website devoncyclehire. co.uk.

Back on the Granite Way, you will pass a large boulder in the middle of the track, a little beyond the Devon Cycle Hire turning, after which there is a gate onto a narrow road. This is where you leave the Granite Way, going through a gate to the left of the continuation of the cycle track and onto a bridleway across the open moor, ❺ where livestock may be grazing. Do not go straight ahead, but turn slightly to your left and follow a grassy track which passes to the right of a telegraph pole and heads uphill, with a distant tor on your right and the small road you just crossed some way off to your left.

After walking uphill for a while, you will see a stone wall ahead. When you reach

the wall, turn left ❻ and continue walking with the wall close by on your right until you see a gate, bearing signs for the West Devon Way and the Dartmoor Way. Pass through the gate and go straight on, following the grassy path, with old stone walls on either side.

After another gate, the path continues with a fence close by on the left, until a gate takes you off the moor and onto a stony track between hedgerows. Follow this track as it heads gently downhill. Eventually, it joins a small lane where stone posts on the right mark the entrance to two houses - Moors Edge and Higher Bowden House. Continue straight ahead on this quiet lane and turn right ❼ just before the old railway bridge and the sign for the Reservoir Car Park.

Follow this lane for a little over a quarter of a mile, back to the car park.

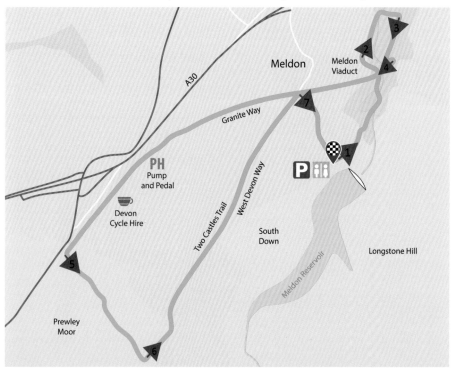

STICKLEPATH

Distance	3.5 miles
Suggested time	1½ hours
Level of difficulty	

This peaceful walk starts at the historic Finch Foundry, a 19th century water-powered forge which ceased operations in 1960 and is now maintained by the National Trust. It follows the River Taw on woodland paths and over little bridges as far as the small village of Belstone, where refreshment is available at the dog-friendly Tors Inn. The path on this side of the river is quite rugged in places, requiring stout footwear and a spirit of adventure! The route then doubles back to Sticklepath on the opposite side of the river via much easier paths and a quiet lane. Although not a lengthy walk, it may take longer than anticipated as it can be slow-going on the trickier bits of the riverside paths.

How to get there - From the A30, take the Okehampton Whitehouse Services exit onto the B3260 in the direction of Exeter. The village of Sticklepath is approximately 1½ miles from the A30 and Finch Foundry is about halfway along the main road through the village on the right, where you will see a brown Finch Foundry sign on the opposite side of the road. Beware - the entrance is very narrow and there is a height restriction. Drivers of larger vehicles might find it easier to park on the street outside.

Map:
Ordnance Survey Explorer Map OL28

Grid Ref:
SX 6415 9406

Nearest Post Code:
EX20 2NW

Parking:
Free at Finch Foundry

Facilities:
Toilets (in National Trust shop), cafes and dog-friendly pub at start, dog-friendly pub at Belstone

You will need:
Leads and dog bags

Standing in the car park with Finch Foundry behind you, exit at the far end by a gate in the lefthand corner into a wooded area. Follow the path as it bears round to the right and, with the river on your left, continue to a bridge. Cross the bridge and turn right **1** onto a stony path.

Continue to a gate across the path and, once through the gate, turn right **2** again joining a stony track where the Dartmoor Way is indicated on a Public Footpath sign.

Follow this stony track through the trees and, after a short while, you will be walking with the river on your right and you will pass a number of houses and gardens on the opposite side. Go through a small wooden gate and keep straight ahead, following the Dartmoor Way sign and ignoring a smaller path leading downhill to the right. The path will soon become quite rocky and can be slippery in wet weather, so take care here.

After a while, the path will take you up steps to a gate onto a small wooden bridge. As you cross the bridge, you may notice an inscription on the handrail from 'Tarka the Otter', as this is part of the Tarka Trail. After crossing the bridge, follow the path as it bears right and you will soon meet a junction with another path. Turn left **3** here.

Follow this stony track, keeping a sharp eye out for a bridge to your left - it's easily missed! Turn left here and walk downhill to cross back over the river. Once over the bridge, turn immediately right **4** to follow the path, with the river on your right once more. You are now on the edge of moorland, where you may encounter livestock.

From here, the path can be a bit wet and there are occasional little streams to cross, some of which have well-placed stepping stones for the purpose. Continue until you see two large boulders ahead of you, where the path splits, with one track going left and uphill and the other straight on between the boulders. Take either of these paths, as they will eventually converge, although it's worth noting the lower option, which takes you alongside the river, is the more rugged of the two. After passing the point where the paths meet, you will see a wire fence above you and a little way off to the left. The path goes downhill here. At the bottom of the

from the river, winding its way up to an open, grassy area (where sheep are likely to be grazing). As you pass a wooden bench on your left, you will see Belstone ahead and you may like to know the dog-friendly Tors Inn is straight ahead and to the left of the small road.

To continue, turn right before you reach the end of the grassy area, passing a metal bench on your left as you walk downhill. Keep following the path as it bears right **6** taking you in and out of the trees. Entering one of the more open areas, where there is a large oak tree directly ahead, look to your right and take the narrow track **7** which you will see heading steeply downhill.

As the path levels out, you will hear, and then see, the river below and to your right. Continue following this woodland path, with the river on your right, for some way. The track will eventually become wider and, a short distance after a small stream crosses the path, you will arrive at an open area where cars may be parked, beyond which is a narrow lane. Walk through the parking area and take a track to the right of the lane, which leads through the trees towards the river. Bearing left at the river, you will be walking parallel to the narrow lane. Continue until the path

hill, follow the path as it bears right and then left in a clearing, passing a wide and very inviting section of the river.

A short distance further on, you will see a wooden bridge on your right. Cross the bridge, bear right **5** and then follow the track as it goes steeply uphill and away

Photo Credit: Carla at www.pawsnshoot.co.uk

brings you back to the lane and turn right. After passing a cattle grid, you are back in Sticklepath.

Walk straight ahead until you see a tarmac footpath behind a wall on the right. Follow this footpath to the main road and turn right **8** to walk along the pavement. You will pass St Mary's Church and, shortly after, an old methodist chapel fronting directly onto the pavement.

You may notice a stone plaque set into the wall relating to the introduction of drinking water to the village of Sticklepath in Queen Victoria's Jubilee year, 1887. Immediately after passing the garden adjacent to the chapel, turn right **9** onto a tarmac path which will lead you back to the car park.

Photo Credit: Carla at www.pawsnshoot.co.uk

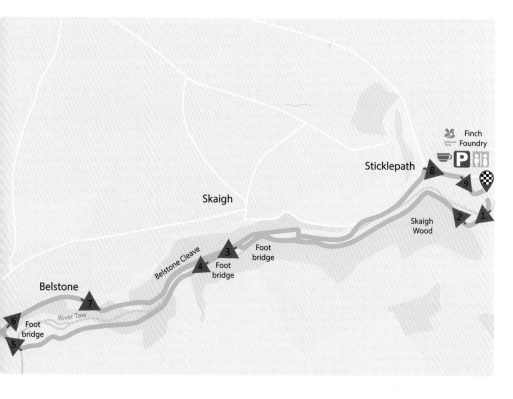

ABOUT DOGFRIENDLY...

DogFriendly was set up in 2003 to provide dog owners with a resource of website information to find places where they would be welcomed with their dog. The website is more popular than ever and holds information on over 50,000 dog friendly cottages, hotels, pubs, restaurants, cafes, days out and many other places. Our DogFriendly Magazine also provides its readers with comprehensive reviews of places where dogs are welcomed.

Over the years we have had lots of interest in dog walking books from our members. But we couldn't find one dedicated to Devon. So we were delighted when Debbie approached us with the idea to publish a Devon Dog Walks book and have worked with her to produce this very clear and beautifully illustrated book covering South Devon and Dartmoor. We do hope you enjoy exploring the walks, which have all been tried and tested by her dog walking friends and family. And don't forget to visit our website (www.dogfriendly.co.uk) to search for dog friendly places to drop in on your travels while you discover this wonderful county.

All our very best

Steve and Lin Bennett

Discover the best dog friendly places